# A WARNING ... AND A KISS

"I'll say this only once," Alex said, her back to him. "Then I will forever hold my peace."

She spun around, and Jackson was awed by the picture she made, the smoky light smudging the contours of her face. He imprinted the vision on his mind, knowing this was how he would paint her someday. "Tell me," he said.

"I think you'll regret marrying Megan. I know that's a harsh thing to say, but I feel it as strongly as my love for you both."

He looked away.

"I know you love her," she went on, "but neither of you is willing to step out of the fog for a moment to see reality, to see what life is going to be like for you together." She looked at him intently. "You don't know her, Jackson."

He got up abruptly and walked over to Alex. When he lowered his face to hers, she didn't turn away. He kissed her as she remembered being kissed when she was younger, their tongues circling quickly, desperately. But the passion died as they woke up to the day, the moment, the thought of a woman standing in a church dressing room in Sausalito, thrilled to be getting married that day.

"At least," Jackson said, "I won't regret never doing that."

# PRIVATE
# SCANDALS

## CHRISTY COHEN

FANFARE ™

BANTAM BOOKS
NEW YORK • TORONTO • LONDON • SYDNEY • AUCKLAND

PRIVATE SCANDALS

*A Bantam Fanfare Book/January 1993*

*FANFARE and the portrayal of a boxed "ff" are trademarks of Bantam Books,
a division of Bantam Doubleday Dell Publishing Group, Inc.*

ISBN 0-533-56053-0

*Published simultaneously in the United States and Canada*

*Bantam Books are published by Bantam Books, a division of Bantam Doubleday Dell Pub-
lishing Group, Inc. Its trademark, consisting of the words "Bantam Books" and the portrayal of a rooster, is Registered in U.S. Patent and Trademark Office and in other
countries. Marca Registrada. Bantam Books, 666 Fifth Avenue, New York, New York
10103.*

PRINTED IN THE UNITED STATES OF AMERICA

RAD     0  9  8  7  6  5  4  3  2  1

*F*or Robert,
who always believed

# PRIVATE
# SCANDALS

# PROLOGUE

SHE STOOD RIGID AS STEEL, HER EYES CAST downward, and Jackson felt a familiar sickly dread gnaw at his gut. She must have changed her mind, and this time there would be no second chances for him.

When the minister asked her to repeat her vows, she raised her head. Her gaze met his, and a warm flood of relief washed over Jackson. Her eyes, so clear and beautiful, were sure and strong and loving. She spoke her promises firmly, confidently, with the smooth voice he'd come to love as he loved no other. And when they sealed their marriage with a kiss, her lips were soft and trusting, and he could sense the smile that tugged at their corners.

In the receiving line she stood beside him, his wife, with the satin sleeve of her dress brushing against his arm. Her expression was bright and happy as she greeted their guests. He put his arm around her waist and marveled again at the way her body conformed to his so perfectly, filling in every crevice.

The guests filtered past, a blur of puckered lips and embracing arms. Jackson paid little attention. How could he when he had the woman of his dreams beside him? She brought him so much happiness, blanketed every aspect of his life with the gauze of perfection, that he often found the past forgotten, left behind like a child's blanket no longer needed for comfort. This woman gave him everything.

He was thinking of that, of the laughter that grew more frequent between them every day, of the house in New Hampshire that awaited them, when he felt her squeeze his hand. Turning quickly, he saw the color drain from her face. He followed her desperate gaze and held himself steady against a wave of dizziness when he saw what she was looking at.

"She's here," his wife said needlessly, her silky voice marred by an uncharacteristic tremor. "I can't believe she's here."

He pulled her close to him and pressed his lips to her ear. "I love you."

She stood motionless for a moment, then he watched her transform. She pulled her scared, hunched body up straight again and smiled the smile that haunted men the world over. Her eyes met his, and he saw the tears filling them.

"And I you," she said, running her fingers along his cheek.

He returned his attention to the guests and watched, out of the corner of his eye, as she approached. He couldn't help being surprised by her beauty. It had been more than three years since he'd seen her, and she seemed to have grown softer, more feminine, more fragile. She was next in line to greet them, and the guilty pangs, long banished to the unnoticed, unwanted recesses of his mind, returned with violent intensity.

Finally, she stood before them, her chin up, her fists clenched. The woman he'd left behind. The woman once cherished as his wife's best friend. The woman who had loved him so much he couldn't breathe. She stood before them after years of bitter silence and, following a deep, drawn-out sigh, began to speak.

# CHAPTER 1

*AFTER A HEAVY RAIN, THE PICKET FENCES* that ran along the twisted sidewalks of Sausalito were slippery as Popsicles. No one knew this except for two twelve-year-old girls with sandpaper shoe soles and an aptitude for balance that only children and highly tuned athletes possess.

The girls hoisted themselves up onto the three-inch-wide wood planks and stretched their book-laden arms out to either side. The brunt of the storm had passed, but the sky remained a trench-coat gray, draping a continual soggy mist over the city.

"Do you think we'll have gym?" Megan asked, brushing a few stray blond curls off her forehead. She stopped walking for a moment to glance at the sky, but felt her balance slipping and concentrated again on her body.

Alex stuck her tongue out to catch the beady water droplets. "No. The field must be soaked after last night. I'll bet we won't even have to dress."

They continued along the fence until it gave way to an open field of waist-high weeds that lay between them and the school. They hopped off the planks and smiled at the delightful array of dirt mounds and shallow, muddy pools stretched out before them. Without hesitation, they took off through the field laughing, stomping their bright red rain boots in puddles of chocolaty water, mindless of the splatters on their coats. They kicked the water at each other, giggling when the splashes stuck to their faces like freckles.

At last, though, they reached the end of the field, with the entrance to the brick school just across the street, and they stopped their play. They smoothed down their coats and hair, trying to brush away the mud that was already caking dry. They were in junior high school now, after all. It wouldn't do to be seen acting like children. Even if they had seen at least a dozen of the other seventh graders having as much fun in the mud as they had.

• • •

"Alexandra Holmes."

"Here."

Mrs. Carmichael, better known as Mrs. Fartmichael to most of her English classes, squinted and searched the room.

"Where, Alexandra?"

Alex pulled her head away from the whispered conference with her best friend, Megan, and raised her hand.

"Here, Mrs. Carmichael."

"I suggest that in the future you remember the rules, Alexandra. When I call your name, you raise your hand and say 'Here.' Understood?"

"Yes, ma'am."

Alex waited until the teacher had continued with roll call before she scrunched up her face and stuck out her tongue, eliciting a chorus of chuckles from the back corner of the classroom. Mrs. Carmichael immediately stopped talking and walked down the aisle to Alex's chair.

"Would you like to tell me what's so funny, Miss Holmes?"

Alex squeezed her hands together beneath her desk and forced herself not to laugh, even though Johnny Piedmont was laughing so hard in the seat in front of her, she was just waiting for him to pee in his pants.

"Well?"

"No, ma'am. Nothing's funny."

Mrs. Carmichael put her hands on her hips, a pair of misplaced camel humps as far as Alex was concerned. "I think not."

She started to walk to the front of the class, but then decided on a different tack.

"Megan?"

Megan Sanders, seated beside Alex, glanced anxiously at her friend before pulling herself up straight in her chair.

"Yes, Mrs. Carmichael?"

"Can you tell me what your friend Alexandra thinks is so much more interesting than roll call?"

Megan looked to Alex out of the corner of her eye, but saw that no help was coming from that quarter. Alex had become the model student, her wild dark hair pushed behind her ears, her back straight, chin up, chest out, hands folded. Megan swallowed hard.

"No, ma'am."

Mrs. Carmichael sighed loudly, a sigh that Alex had learned to mimic to perfection, then returned to the front of the room. She finished calling the roll without incident and then faced the class.

"Well, children," she said, smacking her hands together and moving to the chalkboard, "I have an important announcement. We have a new student in our class today, and I'd like all of you to make her feel welcome."

Mrs. Carmichael took the hand of a girl who had been sitting in the corner seat of the front row, where nobody with any brains at all ever sat in Mrs. Carmichael's class. Death Row, they called it. Mrs. Carmichael pulled the girl to the front and stood her before the class as if she were a skeleton exhibit like the one in the science lab.

"Class, this is Clementine Montgomery. Her family just moved here from Denver. Please say hello to her."

For the first time all year, the students were speechless. The girls glared at the newest addition to their class, all hopes of being chosen the prettiest seventh grader squelched with one look at her. The boys, however, were mesmerized. Their gazes fixed on the new girl's face, as if she were a deluxe model pinball machine, complete with flashing lights and bells and bonus points. Clementine looked like Barbie come to life—tall and skinny, with long light brown hair and translucent blue-green eyes. Alex was just waiting for the drool to start sliding down the boys' chins. Even Johnny, Mr. I-Don't-Care-About-Any-Girl Piedmont, had his mouth hanging open. Alex gritted her teeth when their squeaky, pubescent voices for once resounded deep and rich.

"Hello, Clementine."

Alex leaned over to Megan and whispered, "What a snob she is. Look at the way she sticks her nose in the air. If she thinks she's gonna be my friend, she can just forget it."

"We'll just ignore her, that's all," Megan said. "After a while, after the newness wears off, the boys won't think she's that great, and then she'll be sorry she wasn't nicer to us."

Alex nodded in agreement. She saw Mrs. Carmichael heading in her direction and quickly opened her notebook and took out a pen to make herself look busy. Unfortunately, she was too late. Mrs. Carmichael and Little Miss Perfect appeared beside her.

"Alexandra," the teacher said, "I think that you and Megan are the perfect choice to show Clementine around. Don't you agree? You've lived in Sausalito all your lives and know this school like the back of your hand. Why don't you two take her with you at lunch and show her the ropes?"

Alex stared up at Mrs. Carmichael in horror, but managed to cover the look before she turned to Clementine. The girl was gazing straight at her, unflinching, unblinking. It was the same look Alex turned on the little kids still in elementary school when she wanted to scare them by pretending she was dead. A chill ran through her. "Of course, Mrs. Carmichael," she said as sweetly as she could.

"Wonderful."

Clementine returned to her seat without even a nod or a thank you or anything. Alex waited until Mrs. Carmichael had turned her back, then leaned over to Megan.

"She can tag along if she wants to, but that doesn't mean I have to talk to her."

Megan looked over the students' heads and watched the new girl take out a piece of paper. Maybe if Clementine were a little less sure of herself, Megan thought, she would be easier to like. The girls might even have become friends if Clementine hadn't stood so straight and tall in front of the class, like she was a queen or something. It was almost as if the new girl had expected the boys to respond to her the way they did. Megan wondered how she would feel if it were her first day in a new school, a new state, where she didn't know anyone. She decided she would be scared to death.

"You're right," she whispered back to Alex. "Mrs. Fartmichael just asked us to show her around. She didn't say one word about being nice."

• • •

Alex stuck her arm out limply and pointed to the largest building in the school. "Gym," she said.

The girls had suffered through a silent lunch. There was no way Alex was going to be nice, especially when Clementine didn't even say "Hello" or "Glad to meet you" or any of the things she was supposed to say. Instead, she just sat there on the cafeteria bench and ate her stupid lunch of half a tuna fish sandwich and an apple and hardly seemed to notice that Alex and Megan were there at all.

Since then, they'd pointed out the administration building and the shop and the science room, and still Clementine hadn't said a word. She simply walked two paces behind them, and every once in a while, Alex turned around just to make sure she was still there.

"Maybe she can't talk," Megan whispered to Alex as they headed toward the auditorium.

"I can talk," Clementine said, her voice startling the girls. They stopped walking and turned around.

"Well, then, why didn't you say anything before?" Alex asked.

"I didn't have anything to say."

Alex glared at her, ready now to challenge her to a staring duel, but Clementine paid little attention. She was watching the other students walk by, especially the boys, many of whom slowed their pace to watch her or even smile. Alex ground her teeth.

"Why did you move here from Denver?" Megan asked.

Slowly, as if it were one of the world's greatest efforts, Clementine answered.

"My stepfather got a job with a law firm in San Francisco. I forget the name of it. And, as usual, no one bothered to ask me if I wanted to move or not. So here I am."

"You mean your parents are divorced? I'm really sorry," Megan said.

"Are you from the Dark Ages or what?" Clementine tossed her hair back. "This is 1967, you know. Divorce happens all the time. Besides, my father was never around much. I haven't seen him for the last two years. Good riddance, I say."

Before Megan could continue, Alex pivoted and pointed to the auditorium. "Well, that's the end of the tour. The auditorium. I'm sure you can find your way around from now on." She took Megan's arm and was steering her toward their next class when Clementine spoke.

"Alexandra," she said.

Alex's back shot up straight at the sound of the name she hated, the name only Mrs. Carmichael dared to call her. She refused to turn around and instead only tilted her head to the side to show that she was listening.

"Thanks for the tour."

Megan and Alex whirled around, but Clementine was gone.

•   •   •

Clementine Montgomery was the talk of Grover Junior High School and knew it. She'd planned all along to make an impact, of course. Being the most sought after seventh grader at Napoli School in Denver was one thing, but carrying that image to California was another. Everyone knew that California was the capital of pretty girls. Ordinary good looks and a nice personality wouldn't cut it there. So Clementine had decided on a plan of mystery—she'd keep quiet, reveal little of herself, and modify what she did reveal to suit the image she wanted to project. It was a tack she had learned from one of the sexy novels she'd stolen from her mother's nightstand. But even Clementine was surprised by the success of her California debut.

She'd been there only three days when one of the eighth-grade boys asked her out. She would have laughed in his face if he hadn't looked so earnest and nervous. He was sure he could get his mom to drive them to the movies and then come back to pick them up. Clementine had tried to make her smile sympathetic while she told some story about not being able to date yet.

After that came a swarm of offers. Sometimes only one a week, sometimes as many as three in one day. Did she want to go to the school dance, to the movies, to his house for dinner, to the park, out on a boat, anywhere at all? It was what she had wanted—attention, and boys waiting in line just to talk to her. But the more the boys came after her, the more Clementine realized she wanted no part of them. Sure, their attention was flattering at times, but more often than not it made her want to scream with frustration. Time was passing by so slowly. Sometimes it seemed as if a whole week had passed when, in fact, it had been only an hour in a boring math class where three or four boys passed her lustful notes.

Couldn't they see that kiddie dates were not in her game plan? Not ever? She was going straight to the top with no detours. Some afternoons, she would lock herself in her bedroom and pound her fists into the pillow, overwhelmed by the thought of suffering through five more years of childish dances and awkward, pimply faced teenage boys pawing at her before she was finally free and able to begin her life.

Still, she knew she had much to learn. English class for grammar and clear enunciation, art to spur her creativity, history and science to develop her intellect, and gym to keep her slender and athletic. By the time she graduated from high school she would be in tip-top condition both mentally and physically. And then, world, look out. Clementine Montgomery, future superstar model and actress, will knock your socks off.

•   •   •

It was the best kind of day in the Bay area. Early spring and the sky gloriously blue, as if it had awakened with unaccustomed joy and wanted to shout its happiness to the world. A breeze was up, but only slightly. Just enough to jiggle the docked boats and slosh an occasional wave against the restaurants' and souvenir shops' walls to delight their customers.

Megan pulled the white lace curtain back from her window and watched a sailboat glide toward the Golden Gate Bridge. Her parents had chosen this house for its bay view. It was magnificent, particularly on a day like this. Megan had known her parents to spend hours on their balcony, sipping tea or wine, eating scones or cheese, and staring at the bridge in silent awe and appreciation. After looking out her window for two or three minutes, Megan was hopelessly bored.

She figured her parents didn't have any better way to spend their time. Her mother and father didn't particularly like doing things together, or even talking to each other. And running a nationwide chain of large men's clothing stores seemed to Megan the easiest job in the world. Her father spent three hours on the phone in the morning, played tennis or golf in the afternoon, and hardly ever went to the office. Once a week, he and Megan's mother flew off to some city to check something or other, to see the sights for a couple of days, then they came home and sat on the balcony again.

Megan walked back to her bed and picked up the United States history book she'd left there. She had nothing else to do this weekend, so she might as well study. Alex was out again with her friends from the girls' volleyball team. For the last three weekends, the team had spent Saturday and Sunday together at Grossman's Park, swimming in the heated pool, buying ice-cream sandwiches from the food stand, practicing strokes and serves and saves at the volleyball court. Before the first couple of meetings, Alex had askcd Megan to come along, but after she made up two ridiculous excuses, Alex stopped suggesting it.

Megan tried to read the section on the Civil War, but couldn't concentrate on anything except the pain in her chest and stomach. Last Sunday, she had ridden her bike past Grossman's Park and seen Alex in the midst of her friends, laughing. They hadn't been swimming or playing. They'd been sitting on a large blanket beneath the trees whispering. What were they talking about? she'd wondered. And why was she so certain that Alex was talking about her? Alex was probably telling the girls she was tired of Megan and their baby games in the mud and balancing acts on the fences. She was telling them that she was a woman now and Megan was still just a girl.

Megan had pedaled home as fast as she could and cried until she couldn't breathe. Since then, day and night, no matter what else was going on, a dull ache swam through her chest and stomach. It was like a mixture of the flu and the feeling she'd had when Donald Alskers had stuck chili peppers in her sandwich, and they had burned her throat and chest for hours, no matter how much water she drank.

Alex had always had friends other than Megan. The volleyball team, the math club students, the kids on her block. Girls liked her because she was smart and funny. Boys liked her because she was the star goalie in soccer, threw like a boy, and, from what Megan overheard, kissed better than anyone else in the whole school. It always hurt a little to see Alex laughing, playing, comfortable wherever she was, whether Megan was nearby or not. But these particular friendships, with the pretty, popular, cool-crowd girls, pricked Megan's heart deeper. This time, she couldn't just walk up to Alex and ask her to play with her instead. This time, Alex might say no.

Megan had other friends, too, but no groups formed around her on the playground. No one asked her for the answers to homework assignments, even though Megan did almost as well on exams and essays as Alex did. And, anyway, Megan would have given up the friends she did have in a second to be with Alex.

She knew she was being silly. Alex acted the same as

she always had when they were together, friendly and fun. She still called her every night. They were still best friends. But none of that mattered. Megan knew Alex felt differently and was just trying to cover it up. She was growing up, and Megan wasn't. And Megan had never felt so miserable in all her life.

She tossed her book on the floor and returned to the window. A few clouds had appeared. She could make out a fish in one and a strange-looking dinosaur in the other. She closed her eyes and, prying her mind away from Alex, imagined Clementine. They'd rarely spoken since that first day when she arrived at school. Just an occasional "Hello" and "How are you." But Megan hadn't forgotten about her. In fact, many times, she found herself watching Clementine, studying her. Clementine was the complete opposite of Alex—dignified where Alex was outrageous, calm when Alex was wild. Yet they both had that specialness, that added something that drew people to them, made people stop in the hallway and turn around to take a second look. That extra magic that Megan lacked.

With Clementine, it wasn't anything specific or obvious. It was little things, like the straightness of her back. The quiet steadiness of her voice. Her understated, yet always stylish clothes. The way she sat reading by herself at lunchtime and recess, not glancing up even once to see if anyone was making fun of her for sitting alone. All in all, Clementine was everything Megan wanted to be. Beautiful, refined, self-assured. Megan was certain that no matter what the situation, Clementine would never be jealous over a friend's volleyball team. She would never ride her bicycle past the park to see what they were doing. She would never cry.

Megan opened her eyes and watched her dinosaur take the shape of a warped old witch. Maybe if she made an effort to be closer to Clementine, she could learn something from her. Maybe Clementine could teach her how to be sophisticated and popular, then Alex would quit the volleyball team and everything would go back to normal again. It was worth a try. Megan would have tried anything to get Alex back.

• • •

Alex was the volleyball, baseball, soccer, and tennis champ of her gym class. That left only gymnastics, and in that event, Clementine had managed to sneak in and steal her thunder.

Alex sat with her back against the girls' gym wall and watched, eyes hooded, while Clementine meticulously performed her balance beam routine. Alex couldn't say exactly what it was about Clementine that she so vehemently disliked. At first, she thought it was her picture-perfect looks, but now Alex knew that wasn't the case. Megan had been right. After her newness wore off, the boys got tired of her constant refusals, and their hormones cooled down. Alex's average brown eyes may have been no match for Clementine's unique, almost clear ones, and her kinky dark hair was too ordinary when compared with Clementine's shiny light brown locks that always hung straight and perfect. But Alex was funny and almost always said yes to the movies or roller-skating. Eventually she became, once again, the most popular girl in the school.

The best Alex could figure, what bothered her about Clementine was her arrogance and her newfound friendship with Megan. Alex had no idea how or when that friendship had started, but for the last few weeks, it had been going full swing. At first, she hadn't minded. After all, she was spending more time with the volleyball team, and she knew Megan felt left out. But they were still best friends. They still walked to and from school together and had sleep-overs every other Friday night.

Megan was changing things, though. Alex turned her gaze on her friend, sitting on the floor directly in front of the beam. It had started with phone calls between her and Clementine and occasional meetings after school, and now Megan and Clementine walked together between classes. Clementine even had the nerve to sit with them at lunch. Alex couldn't believe it. The worst part was her act—and not a very good act, at that, Alex thought—of being nice. She included Alex in the conversation as if she were some poor, friendless girl who needed pity. It was enough to make Alex want to kick that swishing little butt of hers so hard, she'd never be able to sit down again.

Alex stood up and walked toward Megan. Clementine had finished her routine and was now showing the other girls how to do beam rolls and pirouettes. Alex pushed down her desire to spit. She reached Megan and sat beside her.

"Your friend sure knows how to be a show-off, doesn't she?" she said.

Megan turned to her quickly. "She's not showing off, Alex. She's just good at it. Just the way you're good at all the other sports and math and most everything else."

"Humph." Alex glanced up at Clementine and gritted her teeth. "Well, I suppose you should know. Since you spend so much time with her."

Megan picked at the dirt beneath her fingernail and wished that some of Clementine's poise would rub off on her already. She had approached Clementine two months ago, nervously asking her if she wanted to come over after school. Once Clementine said yes and they spent the afternoon giving each other facials and makeovers, their friendship progressed easily. But still, Megan was the same as she'd always been. Boring, average, plain old Megan who bit her nails and hated it when someone was mad at her, as Alex was now.

"I just spend time with her when you're with the volleyball team."

Alex drummed her fingers on the floor of the gym. Her stomach was rumbling, and pressure was building behind her eyes. She knew the feeling well. She experienced it every time she was about to get in trouble, either with the teachers, for punching out some wimpy boy who got in her way, or with her parents, when her younger brother, Joey, got on her nerves and she put spiders in his bed.

"That's not true, and you know it, Megan Sanders," she said. "I'm only with the team on Saturday and sometimes Sunday, and lately, because of the rain, we haven't gotten together at all. You're just trying to make me jealous, and I just want you to know that I don't care anymore. You can do whatever you want with Miss Snobby. See her as much as you like. Just see if I care."

She stood up and stormed to the locker room. She'd get a bad write-up for leaving class early, but she didn't care. At her locker, she quickly changed out of her shorts and T-shirt and into her regular clothes. She'd be damned if she'd let those two get the better of her. She didn't need Megan. Megan was just a baby, anyway. She still liked running through the mud and playing baby games, and they were almost eighth graders now. Besides, Alex was the most popular girl in the school. And the smartest. She got the highest grade on most every test, despite goofing off much of the time. The boys always asked her out, and she had a dozen friends on the volleyball team. Who needed Megan, anyway?

Alex nodded in agreement with her thoughts and slammed her locker shut. Walking outside, she stood in the single beam of sunlight that broke through the clouds. When the bell rang ten minutes later and Megan and Clementine walked out of the gym together, Alex began to cry.

# CHAPTER 2

*MEGAN AND ALEX DID NOT MAKE UP UNTIL* their eighth-grade year was half over. After eight years of friendship, they had their fights down to a science. During the first few weeks of warfare, when they were both confident of their positions and viewpoints, they avoided each other completely, sitting at opposite ends of the cafeteria, self-righteous smirks on their faces. The second stage began when their certainties about who said what and what they meant when they said it and who started the whole thing in the first place began to wobble, like unsteady toddlers. At this point, each girl spent countless nights alone, staring at the ceiling, thinking of calling the other and pretending that nothing had happened at all until, at the last minute, she reaffirmed her commitment to a duel to the death and turned away from the phone.

Finally, as time passed and the reasons why they started the fight in the first place were forgotten or, at least, no longer important, the real war of wills began. It was a battle of honor and stamina, of each one's not giving in before the other did, of showing that losing her best friend didn't bother her in the slightest.

For this fight, letters were their weapons, folded expertly into sixteenths and stuffed through locker slats. They'd received and written hundreds of letters during the many battles they'd fought since they met in elementary school. The years of training had turned them into professional fight writers.

Alex, armed with her dog-eared thesaurus, had honed her name-calling to cutting perfection. She practiced enough with the boys on the playground when they beaned her with the soccer ball. For six straight years, she'd held on to the prestigious honor of possessing the worst female mouth in the school. But when it came to Megan, she needed more than a few filthy words to get her point across. Formulating the meanest, most demeaning phrase took hours and the ability to remember Megan's most recent weaknesses and insecurities. This time, Alex began her letter with:

"Dear Megan (alias the world's most conniving, double-crossing, despicable, ugly, fat, worst grade in the class on the science pop quiz, frizz-head if she doesn't blow-dry her hair, never cared about anyone but herself monster)."

After that, there hardly seemed anything left to say. Alex finished with "I hate you," and scribbled her name at the bottom.

Megan, on the other hand, with what she perceived during their fights as a lifetime's worth of torturous suffering at the hands of Alex, pleaded her case with guilt. She sat up late at night, writing quickly on her best stationery, making sure her tears wrinkled the paper. Before she knew it, the brief note was seven pages long, filled with every thought that had come into her head—how Alex never really cared for her, how she had cast her aside each time she found a new friend, how Megan had been hurt so deeply by Alex's sadistic cruelty that she didn't think she would ever recover from the emotionally devastating pain, and so on.

Added to all this were the reinforcements called in on either side. Alex had her volleyball friends and the math club, who joined her in glaring at Megan and walking far around her when they passed in the school hallways, as if she had some frightening communicable disease. Megan had Clementine, who said over and over that she didn't want to get involved, but who disliked Alex for disliking her and avoided her anyway. A few of the girls in Megan's classes, who saw this as a chance to get back at Alex for her popularity and ease with the boys, allied themselves with Megan and practiced shooting death stares and occasional paper airplane bombers from the back of the class. Johnny Piedmont, who, along with all the boys, found it beneath him to get involved with any of the girls' stupid quarrels, nonetheless told Alex he thought it was "one hell of a damn good fight."

But as had always happened between them, the letters became tedious, the glares brought on eyestrain, and their stoic shoulders began to fall limp. As the strength behind their six-month-long standoff withered and their Friday nights, void of giggling and sleep-overs and popcorn, became something to dread rather than to look forward to, they started thinking of making up. Not obviously, of course, but in some covert, clever way that wouldn't admit they were wrong—because they weren't—but would get them back together.

In the end, ironically, Clementine provided the answer.

"Megan, look," she said as they walked home together after school, something they'd started doing since Alex chose a different route to reach her house. The wind in their faces was strong and cold, with Christmas just around the corner. "I don't want to push you or anything, but I think this fight you have going with Alex has gone on long enough. I mean, you don't want to look childish, do you?"

Megan turned her head away. Of course she didn't want to look childish. That was her worst fear. It was the reason Alex had turned to the volleyball team, to find girls more mature to talk to. And "childish" was the way she felt every time the girls in gym class giggled about French kissing and she longed to ask them what it was. It was the way she felt around Clementine, who never raised her voice or laughed too loud or wore clothes that were outdated. Clementine even walked like an adult, with her head high and her arms close to her body, never flailing or pointing or dropping books the way Megan did.

"I mean, you two have been best friends forever," Clementine continued, "and it's stupid to let that go just because of one argument."

Megan stopped walking. The wind strained against her, almost knocking her down. She had to push hard just to stand straight.

"Why are you saying all this?" she asked. Clementine stopped a few paces ahead of her and turned around. "You don't even like Alex. Why would you want me to be friends with her again?"

Clementine looked down at her nails, gleaming with chipfree rose polish. Megan wondered why the wind didn't even seem to brush her. Her hair fluttered like dandelions in a gentle breeze while Megan's whipped violently against her face, slapping her.

"To be honest," Clementine said, "it's because of Mr. Handleman's science project. You know how much I want to do well in school, and, let's face it, science just isn't my subject. But I know we could get the best grade if we had Alex in our group. She's a whiz at that stuff. And besides," she went on, pushing her hair behind her ear and staring at a group of boys pushing their bicycles up the hill, "I don't dislike Alex. Actually, I don't really know her at all."

Megan stuck her icy hands in her coat pockets and started walking again. "What do you want me to do?" she asked when they reached the break point between their houses. From there, Clementine continued to the top of the hill and Megan turned the corner, heading to the more expensive end of the neighborhood. "Just ask her to be in our group? She'd probably say something awful to me."

"Jeez, Meg, you're such a baby sometimes," Clementine said, transferring her books from one hand to the other. "Just tell her you're sorry and want to make up, and oh, by the way, how about being in our science group? She's probably as sorry about this fight as you are."

· · ·

Megan took a deep breath as she stood in front of the bright red front door to Alex's house. How many times had she stood there before? One hundred, two hundred, maybe even a thousand times? She'd always loved this house, the cheeriness of it, but today its red-trimmed windows and overgrown garden made it look like a bleary-eyed monster just waiting to swallow her up.

Finally, she knocked. Joey, Alex's younger brother, opened the door almost immediately.

"Oh, hi, Megan. Alex is up in her room. Come on in."

She followed Joey inside, noticing how his sandy blond hair toyed with the collar of his sweatshirt. She'd always been fascinated by Joey, by the amazing differences between him and Alex. It was as if he'd been plucked out of some other world, another time, and dropped unceremoniously into a loud, social, fast-paced family where he'd never belong.

Joey was the one piece of the Holmes's family puzzle that didn't fit. He was normal. The others were extraordinary characters who could fill a thousand-page novel with life and vitality. Alex's mother, Jo, was an art museum curator who never stopped moving or laughing or talking, and had more silk scarfs and bottles of perfume than anyone else Megan had ever known. Her father, Paul, was a liberal math professor at Berkeley with a ferocious attachment to causes who invited his students to his house for barbecues. He'd even been on television once, when he'd thrown himself in front of a fisherman's harpoon meant for a whale.

And then there was Alex. Each time Megan walked into the house, she was struck by the way every object, every piece of furniture, every knickknack and work of art, even every color perfectly reflected Alex's personality. In the living room, a traditional-style couch was covered in a chintz patterned fabric of red and gold. Black-and-white striped pillows were thrown on top of it, and a slender black lacquer floor lamp stood at the side. In front of the couch, at a right angle, was an oxidized bronze triangular table, and behind it stood a mahogany desk. A mixture of abstract and French Impressionist paintings dotted the walls. The staircase beyond the entry was circular, with a red rug running down the middle of the hardwood steps and a railing carved out of copper. Everything in the house seemed to be taken from a different time and place, and yet, when it was all tossed together, it somehow meshed. Like Alex. A crazy concoction of dark frizzy hair, bushy eyebrows, full lips, a ready smile and laugh, bright clothes, and outrageous behavior. Yet no one had ever looked as put together or right as Alex.

Megan watched Joey walk to the grand piano in the corner of the living room. If only he were four years older, she thought. He sat down, breathed deeply, laid his fingers reverently on the keys, and began a classical piece she distantly recognized. He'd begun piano lessons only a year earlier, and already he'd progressed far beyond most. In the world of his music, everything else was forgotten. His fingers were small and awkward, unable to expand an octave yet and reach many of the chords, but still the music was chillingly beautiful. She stood spellbound in the entry, listening, her anxiety about meeting with Alex dispelled for the moment.

He was staring intently at the sheet music, and she studied his face. It was softly handsome, so different from Alex's regal angles. He was like a marble statue, perfectly carved to have no hard edges. Most of the time when she saw him, he was playing the piano or reading mystery novels, his wavy hair hanging over his forehead and cheeks. He was shy, quiet, always thinking before he spoke and looking before he walked, as if he wasn't sure of his surroundings and had to constantly check his path for obstacles. But he was only nine years old and Megan was thirteen, and the gap could have been a hundred years, it seemed that unbridgeable.

"I'll just go on up," she said, although she knew that once sealed in his musical, worldproof box, Joey heard nothing else.

She kept her eyes focused upward while she climbed the staircase, which curved around itself three times. She always did, so she wouldn't get dizzy. Finally, she reached the upstairs landing and was met head-on by the blare of Alex's record player. She'd forgotten how loud Alex liked her music. Alex had once told Megan it wasn't loud enough until the hairs on her neck stood on end and her bones vibrated.

Megan took one more deep breath, then walked to Alex's door. After unsuccessfully trying to make her knocks heard, she walked in.

Alex was wearing her favorite outfit, a long white T-shirt over a bright yellow knit skirt. It was a strange combination, but on Alex it looked fitting. She had added more posters to her walls since Megan had been there last. A picture of baby seals hung beside one of James Dean, and a San Francisco Giants pennant dangled beside her Oakland Raiders helmet. Alex was sitting on her window seat, staring out at the magnolia tree that hovered just outside, but when Megan walked in, she turned her head.

Megan was sure they stared at each other for hours. Alex didn't seem surprised to see her. She just looked straight into her eyes until, as usual, Megan had to turn away.

Alex stood up and walked to the far wall, which held her stereo, three shelves full of albums, and an array of math and science books her father had brought her from the university. She turned off the record player and returned to the window seat.

"So?" she asked.

"So, I ..." The words Megan had planned and rehearsed two dozen times on the way over stalled just below her throat. Her eyes filled with tears, and despite all of her self-made promises to the contrary, she started crying. She put her hands up to her face and sobbed until Alex was at her side, her hand on her arm, leading her to the bed. They sat down together.

Finally, Megan's tears subsided and she looked at Alex. She was surprised to find her eyes were red too.

"I'm sorry," Megan said.

Quickly, without speaking, Alex stood up and walked into the adjoining bathroom. She returned with a pair of manicure scissors.

"Give me your finger," she said.

Megan lifted her index finger and squeezed her eyes

shut as Alex stuck the tip of the scissor's blade through her skin. Alex did the same thing to her own, then pressed their fingers together.

"There," she said. "Now we're blood sisters. This means we'll be best friends forever and ever, no matter what."

"Are you sure?" Megan asked.

"Of course, I am. And, Megan, let's don't ever fight again, okay?"

Megan nodded as they walked arm in arm to the bathroom to wash their hands. "It's a deal."

•   •   •

Three months later, Clementine waved good-bye to Megan and Alex and continued up the steep hill that led to her house. Occasionally, she stared down at the certificate in her hand and smiled.

When she reached the final house on the road, her house, she stopped. She stood behind the wide, gnarled trunk of the oak tree at the edge of their yard, a place where she knew her mother couldn't see her. Leaning her cheek against the rough bark, she stared at her house.

Why her mother and stepfather had chosen it, she'd never know. It was by far the ugliest house in Sausalito. The clapboard walls were so badly weathered, they could never be fixed. The paint, what was left of it, was a dark gray, similar to the sky on one of its usual foggy days, so that the house seemed to melt into the background and disappear. The ground was hard and rocky, unyielding to any vegetation other than weeds.

But Clementine's stepfather, John, had liked it. "It's got character," he'd said. "It'll be great, the three of us working side by side fixing it up."

Clementine shuddered. If she'd thought he was serious, she would have told him right then and there that she wanted no part of side-by-side work with him. But she'd known he wasn't. If he had his way, he'd hunt down Clementine's father, Duke, and shuttle her off with him. He didn't have the time or patience for a teenager. Clementine could tell by the way the wrinkles at the edge of his mouth multiplied whenever she talked to him, and how his voice got louder and meaner whenever her mother stepped out of the room. Saying nice, normal things and smiling too widely were just some of the ways John tried to trick her into doing what he wanted, like he tricked defendants into confessing to crimes by claiming he had evidence he didn't have. He laughed off her shouts of ethics, claiming he did it all for justice. But Clementine knew that everything John did, he did for himself, for some benefit to him and only him. She walked inside the house.

"Clemmie, is that you?" her mother said. "I'm in the library."

Clementine held back her retort. Since when did a room holding three unread Hemingway novels and a 1958 dictionary qualify as a library? She set down her purse and walked in the room.

"Hi, Mom. How was your day?"

Angel Montgomery was avidly dusting the coffee table. Every day when Clementine arrived home from school, her mother was dusting something. Clementine had yet to see a speck of dust settle on anything in their house.

"Fine, dear," her mother answered. "I went to the store and bought a leg of lamb. You remember John's mentioning the other day that he'd had it at one of those conventions and how much he liked it. I found a recipe in *Good Housekeeping* and decided to try it tonight. I'm quite nervous about it actually. I . . ."

Clementine walked to the window that overlooked the houses below. Dark swirls of smoke billowed from a few chimneys, further clouding the chilly March afternoon. Her mother's voice droned on behind her about lemon sauce and which vegetable would go best. Clementine waited for a pause for breath and then jumped in.

"Mom, guess what. Megan and Alex and I won first prize on our science project today. Look at the certificate I got."

Angel had been kneeling to get to the wood feet of the table. Slowly, with a deep sigh along the way, she set down her rag and stood up. Clementine handed her the certificate.

"Well, isn't that nice."

"See, it says that our rat maze won because of its originality and usefulness. Some of the boys in class made radios and stuff, but they do that every year. This was the first time anyone ever did a rat maze."

"I'm proud of you, dear. Really I am. And I wish I had more time to talk about it, but I really do have to start on that lamb. And I want to get the bedroom spotless before John gets home. You know how he loves a clean house. Congratulations again, dear."

Angel kissed Clementine's forehead and left for the kitchen, taking her rag and furniture polish. The first prize certificate felt heavy in Clementine's hand, as if she'd been holding it up for hours, waiting for someone to notice. She was tempted to tear it into a hundred pieces. The impulse passed, though, and she straightened her back and stuck out her chin. She'd tack the certificate to the bulletin board in her room, next to the graduation slip she'd received from her ballet class in Denver. Who knows what other competitions she might enter and win? She'd have to leave room on the bulletin board just in case.

She sat down on the couch and stared at her reflection in the newly polished coffee table. The rat maze had been Alex's idea. Once she'd agreed to be in their group—after days of pleading by Megan—she had been full of ideas. Since Clementine had known she and Megan needed her to win, it hadn't been that hard to put her personal feelings aside. She'd just swallowed her pride and let Alex's brain do the work. Alex really wasn't all that bad, and besides, winning was what counted.

Clementine thought back to a year earlier, when she'd first moved to Sausalito. The instant she'd seen Alex, joking with the kids in the back of Mrs. Carmichael's class, she'd known she had some stiff competition. She saw the way the girls looked at Alex, with awe and admiration. And when she watched Alex running like mad on the soccer field, or with her head bent down over a math test, her pencil quickly writing in answers, she saw the boys' eyes widen in respect. Those first few days, despite her own impact, despite the dates she was offered, Clementine had been furiously jealous.

She'd never felt jealous before. What was worse, she'd known the jealousy was unfounded. Everything had gone the way she had planned it. And Alex wasn't even as pretty as she. In fact, when Clementine looked really hard at her, she'd have to say Alex wasn't pretty at all. Her nose was too big, her lips too full, her eyebrows too bushy, her almost black hair too kinky. Still, when Alex was in a group of people, as she usually was, and holding center court, as she usually was, Clementine found herself absolutely dumbstruck. With her eyes sparkling and her hands flailing about the way they did when she spoke, Alex's features pulled together into the most distinctive and striking beauty Clementine had ever seen. In fact, at those times, she was certain she'd never seen anyone quite so attractive. That was the problem with Alex. She was always changing, as a chameleon changes from one color to the next. Alex was so alive and vibrant and energetic, she left Clementine exhausted.

Clementine had known she could put the jealousy aside for the sake of the science project. Surprisingly, once they'd started working on it, pulling together with the same desire to win, the jealousy tapered off until one day, she laughed aloud at one of Alex's jokes and realized it was gone completely. Oh, they'd definitely been wary of each other at first, and each had wanted to do things her way. In fact, if it hadn't been for Megan in the middle holding them together, Clementine was sure they would never have made it.

They'd been working together only a few days when Clementine realized just how intense Alex was. Alex put everything she had into everything she did. Clementine had thought her good grades came from incredible luck, but once she saw Alex in action, she changed her mind. Alex was fun-loving and often blunt and outrageous, but when work needed to be done, she focused herself entirely and didn't stop until every last detail was perfect. Watching her work and think and move and laugh, without a moment's hesitation or doubt, Clementine finally understood the reason for her jealousy. Alex had no fear. Though many would say the same of her, Clementine knew it wasn't true. She feared much. She just refused to show it.

A week into the science project, the three of them started walking home together. It had started as a casual request by Megan to get to know each other better and to save her the impossible task of choosing which friend to walk with. Because neither Clementine nor Alex wanted to admit her trepidations or awkwardness, they agreed. Initially, they walked far apart, with some imaginary but impassable wall between them. They came together slowly, and now they actually bumped into each other and laughed.

Clementine had felt at first that she and Alex were mismatched beads strung on either side of Megan, but they were beginning to come together on their own. Alex and her intensity, Clementine and her ambition, and Megan, who only wanted peace and good times. It was amazing that the three of them got along at all, so different were they. But somehow, like complementary colors on the spectrum, they accented the best in each other. Most surprising of all, Clementine's feelings for both of them were growing. For the first time in her life, she knew what it was like to have friends.

She thought back to the science project award ceremony earlier that day. The whole school had come to the auditorium for the presentation, and afterward, the three of them had hurried outside and hugged one another so hard, their arms hurt.

"We did it," Alex had said. "I knew it. Of course, it was my idea."

Megan and Clementine had laughed.

"All right, Miss Wonderful," Megan had said. "But Clementine ran most of the tests, and seeing if the rats remembered where the food was was my idea. We all did an equal amount of work."

"I know. You guys did great."

Clementine had suddenly wanted to tell them how grateful she was. She'd never had anyone before. In fact, she'd prided herself on her ability to be alone. But there they were, hugging her, trusting her with their confidences, inviting her to walk home with them. It felt so good, as if someone had wrapped her in a warm, fuzzy blanket that kept out the cold.

She was thinking of all that as they walked home. Alex and Megan laughed and talked most of the way, while she racked her brain to find the words to express what was in her heart, without sounding silly. It had never been necessary to express her feelings before. No one cared. Her father never bothered to let her know where he was living, her mother wasn't concerned with what she felt as long as it didn't interfere with her life with John, and any feelings that Clementine had for John were better left unsaid.

They reached the point where Megan and Alex turned toward their homes and she continued up the hill. She tried one more time to think of something to say, then gave up in frustration.

"Well, I'll see you Monday," she said.

She was already continuing up the hill when Alex spoke. "Hey, Clementine." She turned around. "Thanks for being in our group. I hate to admit it, but we probably couldn't have done it without you."

She smiled, Alex and Megan smiled back, and it was obvious that they knew what she felt. Words were unnecessary. Clementine warmed inside with the memory. She stood up and headed for her bedroom upstairs. It wouldn't take that much rearranging to add friends to her plans for the future. She was sure she could squeeze them in somewhere between international fame and amassing an incredible fortune.

•   •   •

No one doubted that Alex would finish ninth grade, her final year of junior high school, at the top of the class. The only question was how close Clementine could make the race.

Megan liked to think she helped them both. After all, there were times, albeit few, when Alex stayed out too late at the movies or the skating rink to finish her homework and Megan let her copy hers. And even though Clementine acted as though she'd never need anybody her whole life, she sometimes asked Megan's opinion on what type of essay a particular teacher would like best.

In the end, Alex got the report card filled with A's, Clementine settled for mostly A's sprinkled with a few B's, and Megan worked her tail off for B's and C's. She was average. Her teachers knew it. They filled the comments section of her report card with phrases like "middle of the class" and "unextraordinary but good." Her parents knew it and never pressured her. More than anyone else, Megan knew it herself.

That June afternoon, the last day of junior high, Megan walked out onto her parents' balcony and sat down in a cushioned lounge chair. She and Alex and Clementine had talked so much about this day and the coming September when they would begin at Lincoln High School, it had turned into a faraway, wonderful dream that didn't seem likely to ever come true. But today, finally, the dream was reality, and Alex and Clementine had hardly been able to control themselves. They'd kept pinching each other's arms and laughing when they thought of all that lay ahead. When they had turned to her, she'd made sure she had the same silly smile on her face. If there was one thing she'd learned through her long friendship with Alex and her newer one with Clementine, it was that the two of them did not understand fear or nerves or anxiety about the future. It was beyond their comprehension that a rosy-hued fantasy about growing up and gorgeous high school boys and interesting classes could turn into a nightmare, for all that Megan could envision was an unknown building with unknown teachers and hundreds of students she'd never met. In their minds, the road ahead was filled with beauty and excitement and challenges. Just thinking about the future filled them with determination to conquer it. Megan drew her sweater closer around her and stared out at the sea.

Her parents were down at her grandmother's home in Monterey for the weekend, leaving her alone with the fifth housekeeper they'd hired in the last three years. They'd apologized for missing her junior high school graduation that night, but, of course, it was only *junior* high school, and Megan must understand that her grandmother was old and the pains in her head she'd been complaining about might be a sign of a stroke. They couldn't, in good conscience, attend her graduation and leave Grandma all alone, could they?

Of course not, Megan had said. She understood. She always understood. That was what everyone loved about her. They could say anything they wanted, and she'd smile and say it was okay. Her parents missed her dance class recital, her fifth-grade play, and now her graduation, and she understood. At the school dances, the boys quickly passed by her on their way to Alex or some other pretty cheerleader type, and she understood. In fact, Megan was sure a person could tell her he was a psychotic killer and she'd smile and say, "Isn't that nice?" She was too damn afraid of saying anything wrong or bad or mean to even think of telling anyone what she really felt. Sometimes she wondered if she had any feelings of her own at all.

She stood up and walked to the railing. It was foggy again. If you lived in Sausalito, or anywhere in the Bay area, you came to expect the dense, ghostly clouds that pocketed the shore most of the year. But Megan still hated it. She wanted to live in sunshine. Bright, warm, yellow sunshine 365 days a year. She wanted to turn golden brown instead of lobster red and splotched with ugly freckles the way she did. She wanted to wear shorts and tank tops all year long.

She lived in foggy Sausalito, though. And her best friends were beautiful Clementine and exciting Alex. And she was certain they would rise to the occasion of high school with dignity and determination, while she hung on to their coattails with white knuckles the way she always did, just along for the ride. Timid, boring, average Megan. In the end, she'd be left wondering why they bothered with her at all.

# CHAPTER 3

*H*IGH SCHOOL CHANGES EVERYTHING FOR girls. Snoopy lunch pails and plastic red-and-blue rain slickers are discarded for the latest fashions. Wide-eyed puppy posters are exchanged for eight-by-ten glossies of rock stars and boyfriends that are taped to the inside of gray lockers—lockers in which hand mirrors, hair-brushes, and mascara are stacked on top of thick books. Boys evolve from the gawky, runny-nosed brats who used to cry like babies when tomboys socked them in the stomach, into alien, unapproachable, incomprehensible creatures covered in leather, cologne, and blue jeans. Life itself, once structured and warmly familiar, filled with the scents of cookies, lemonade, and Mom, takes a detour on a high-speed train, jetting through uncharted territory where love and hate and everyday problems are magnified twenty times normal.

The air in high school is different. It is thicker, oxygen-depleted and laced with perfumes, cigarette smoke, and sweat. Decisions that seemed so simple only a year or two earlier, like what to wear, whom to see, what to do, and where to go, are now rife with anxiety and complications. Suddenly, the world is no longer cast in pink hues and filled with candy and sunshine.

For high school girls, once easy friendships are replaced by an intricate system of competition. A girl needs good grades for college, cheerleader status for popularity, and club presidency for respect. Some girls strive to be the most beautiful, some the most stylish, and others the friendliest. A few vow they don't care about any of these high school quests, and the competition for apathy is perhaps the fiercest battle of all. And lastly, there is the contest that makes the most headlines, arouses the most emotion, and ruins the most friendships: the competition for boys.

Despite the large number of boys actually enrolled in high school, every girl knows there is only a small pool of eligible boy*friends* to choose from. They come from the football and baseball teams and a few shop classes. They sometimes even emerge from an academic class, as long as it's nothing like Shakespearean classics or advanced calculus. Too many pimples and they're out. An IQ of over eighty, out. Still stuck in that awkward time between youth and adulthood when arms and legs dangle like Slinkies, forget it. And they can't be too nice. Girls get suspicious of that.

Never mind that the nice, pimply, smart boys will grow into the doctors and lawyers and businessmen the girls will later wish they could meet and marry. In high school, they're class-A nerds and not even under boyfriend consideration.

Clementine, Alex, and Megan sat up late in Clementine's bedroom one night during their second month of tenth grade discussing this.

"You can't possibly like that oaf from biology class, can you, Meg?" Clementine asked. "God, he's such a geek."

Clementine picked up a pack of cigarettes and pulled one out. She opened the window beside the vanity where she was sitting and lit the cigarette, aiming the smoke outside. Megan watched her closely, trying to remember how she breathed, without coughing, a professional smoker after only one week of practice. She might need the pointers if she ever took up the habit.

"No, of course I don't like him," she replied, lying.

She smoothed out the creamy satin comforter before sitting down on the bed. Actually, Billy Weinstein had been talking to her a lot lately, and she'd thought she might have a chance with him. Okay, so maybe he wasn't the coolest boy in the school, and he did wear thick tortoise-shell glasses and his pants were too short. But he was nice. And he talked to her. No other boys seemed even the slightest bit interested.

"That's good," Alex said, sitting cross-legged on the bed. Alex drew attention wherever she went, but in Clementine's bedroom, she stood out like a light suddenly turned on after hours of darkness. Clementine's room was a palette of creams—off-white walls, ivory carpet and bedspread, cream curtains and marble vanity. Then along came Alex in pink and purple shirts and scarfs, her hair wild against the pillow, a gust of ice-cold air blowing away the stuffiness.

"What you need," Alex went on, "is some huge, god-like football player to crush you in his arms and give you hundreds of wet, hot, passionate kisses."

Megan fell back on the bed and laughed. Only Alex seemed to know about wet, hot, passionate kisses. Within two weeks, she had become, once again, the most popular girl in school, and almost every boy was interested in her. Megan found it incredible the way Alex could walk into a situation, any situation, and take over.

Sometimes a gorgeous blond hunk would walk up to Megan, and instantly a lump formed in her throat. This was it, she would think. He'd seen her in the hallway, and it had been love at first sight. He had to have her. But, of course, the truth was that he'd seen her with Alex and he wanted to know if Alex was dating anyone seriously and what her phone number was and, gee, thanks for helping him out.

Clementine inhaled deeply on her cigarette. When the exhaled smoke momentarily shielded her face, she relaxed her tight smile. She loved it when the three of them got together, but why did they always have to talk about boys. You'd think they didn't have any other interests.

And what did it matter, anyway? Let Alex date every

moronic football player in the school. Eventually, the gawky boys in Megan's biology and math classes would outgrow their awkwardness, and Megan would then find someone to live happily ever after with. As for herself . . . Clementine inhaled the smoke off the butt of her cigarette, then ground it out. Boys weren't in her game plan. Never had been. She would find some way to become a model and then an acclaimed actress, and every boy who had ever passed her by on his way to Alex would kick himself for letting her go.

Irritated at the silence that had fallen over them, Alex grabbed a copy of *Seventeen* from Clementine's nightstand and pretended to read it. Since high school had started, she'd felt a distance settle between the three of them. It was like a layer of dust so light it wasn't noticeable, until you turned around the next day and saw everything was covered with a thin, suffocating film of dirt. The uneasiness had developed so suddenly and unexpectedly, she hadn't been able to stop it. Now she wasn't sure how to handle the situation. Once they'd entered this school, all they had known had changed. Here, everyone was fighting like mad for the top, for good grades, student council seats, the best boyfriend. No matter how hard they tried, she and Megan and Clementine got swallowed up in the battle.

Could she help it if the boys liked her? If Megan would open up a little, they'd like her too. Megan was far prettier than she was. In fact, she was exactly the type most of the high school boys liked. Small, blond, and cute. And if Clementine would only come down from her high horse, they'd be all over her in a second.

It wasn't fair. Alex knew they were mad at her. Not openly mad, but she saw the way they stopped listening when she talked about Jerry or Bob or Tim. She'd have to be blind not to notice how they tapped their feet or folded their arms over their chests when she bowed out of going to the movies with them so she could go on a date instead. Boys had never come between them before. She'd dated just as much in junior high, and they had understood and accepted it then. Was she supposed to stop being popular just to make them happy?

Well, she thought, at least when they did show an interest in dating, it was with totally different boys than she would choose. Megan concentrated on the brains, and Clementine, when she admitted it, leaned toward the loners. If either of them ever did decide to get a boyfriend, they wouldn't be competing for the same ones.

"How about some ice cream?" she asked suddenly, slamming the magazine shut and standing up.

Clementine and Megan smiled. "Great," they said together. They headed downstairs for the kitchen, and for a little while, the magic of vanilla ice cream, chocolate syrup, whipped cream, and sweet red cherries weaved its sugary spell and all thoughts of boys were forgotten.

•   •   •

Tony kissed her hard on the mouth, so hard that Alex was sure her lips would be black and blue in the morning. But she didn't stop him. With one arm around her back, he slid her down on the squeaky vinyl front seat of his parents' car. His other hand massaged her side down to her hip. Alex closed her eyes and knew this was what heaven was like. Hard lips and warm hands. Mmmm.

She let him work his hand beneath her sweater and up to her bra. But when he started for the clasp in the back, she pushed him off.

"That's enough, Tony," she said, sitting up. She pulled her sweater back down and fixed her hair. "Why do we have to go through this every time we go out? I told you before that I wouldn't take off any clothes, and I meant it."

Tony Maclivio, his wild dark hair falling over his forehead and into his eyes, breathed heavily. He slouched against the door, his face hidden in the shadows.

"Goddammit, Alex. This is our sixth date. It's not fair. You're such a tease."

She laughed and took her lipstick out of her purse. Craning her neck to see in the rearview mirror, she put it on expertly. "I am not. I told you what I'd let you do, and I let you do it. It's your own fault if you got yourself all worked up over nothing."

Tony turned on the engine and pulled out of the vacant lot on the highest hill in Sausalito. Below them, the house lights glowed yellow and white. He drove slowly toward her house. Alex kept her head turned away from him, looking out her side window.

"You know," he said when they were almost there, "you're not the only girl at Lincoln. I could have any girl I want. I can make them beg me to be with them. I don't know why I even bothered with you in the first place."

She was used to Tony's whines at the end of the evening, but something hard-edged in his voice caught her attention. She straightened her back and turned toward him.

"Listen, Tony, it's no big deal. We went to the movies, we kissed a little, and now I'm going home. Why do you have to act like such a baby?"

He slammed on the brakes, letting the car skid to a halt by the curb. He shut off the engine and grabbed her arm.

"Listen, you little bitch, nobody messes with me. You got that? You hear me?"

She stared at his eyes, normally brown but now totally swallowed up by blackness. When she'd first noticed him a couple of months earlier in the midst of the tough crowd, the drug crowd, that hung out by the school parking lot wall rather than in the classroom where they belonged, she'd been intrigued by his panther eyes. She'd approached him one afternoon, with the excuse of asking him for a ride home, and they had quickly gone from there.

Tony had no hang-ups about getting straight to the punchline, discarding the games teenagers were supposed to play when they date. He kissed her hard the moment they were in his car, not more than ten minutes after they'd met officially, and she hadn't made any moves to stop him. She'd been impressed by his honesty, his bluntness, his unwillingness to waste time. He'd made her feel sexier, more wanted, than anyone she'd ever met. Since then, he'd taken her to the movies a couple of times and out to dinner, but she knew he wished those moments away so they could get on to the making-out section of the evening. At first, she'd been flattered. But tonight, as his fingers pinched the skin on her arm and she bit her lip to keep from crying out, she was beginning to feel different.

"I hear you, Tony," she said evenly, hoping he didn't notice the thumping of her heart. "Now take me home."

He stared at her a minute longer, letting the fire in his eyes soak into her brain like oil. Then he released her and started the car. He reached her house five minutes later.

Alex had her hand on the door handle, ready to jump out before the car had stopped completely, but he grabbed her hair and yanked her head toward him. Despite her efforts, a painful moan escaped from her mouth.

"You just remember what I said, bitch," he whispered. "I can have anyone I want. Anyone at all. You'll see."

He pushed her away from him, and she stumbled out of the car. She slammed the door behind her and kept her walk steady until his car was out of sight. Then she ran inside the house and up to her room.

• • •

One week later, Megan burst into Alex's bedroom an hour after school, her chest heaving from an all-out run up the hill.

"You're never going to believe what just happened to me," she said.

Alex set down her paper and math book and walked over to the bed where Megan was sitting, trying to catch her breath.

"Tell me."

"Well, I was leaving my sixth-period class today when someone touched me on the shoulder. You'll never guess who it was."

She paused expectantly, and Alex laughed.

"Engelbert Humperdinck."

"No."

"Elvis Presley."

"Alex."

"Okay. I give up. Who?"

Megan smiled, drawing the moment out as long as possible. "Tony Maclivio." She sighed deeply. "Can you believe it? He said he's been wanting to talk to me for a long time but didn't have the nerve. God, I was stunned. He's in my Spanish class—when he shows up, that is— but I didn't think he even knew I was alive. I thought I was gonna die . . ."

Alex felt the blood drain from her face. Megan was continuing, but Alex hardly heard her. Instead, Tony's words rang loud in her ears. "I can make them beg me to be with them," he'd said. "I can have any girl I want." Getting Megan would certainly prove that. She remembered his fingers on her arm, the bruises she'd found there the next day. The crushing hardness of his lips. She looked at Megan, never even kissed before, and turned away when she imagined she saw a dark shadow cross her friend's face.

"Megan, there's something I need to tell you," she interrupted.

"Wait, let me finish first."

Alex nodded and scooted back to the headboard. Leaning against it, she pulled a pillow to her chest and clutched it tightly.

"So, anyway," Megan went on, "Tony asked if he could walk me home. That's why I didn't show up with you and Clementine. He walked me the whole way. Even held my books for me, can you believe it? It's like he's so old-fashioned. He asked me about my classes and my family, and when he saw my house, he was amazed. I've never even been glad that my parents had money before, but I am now. I invited him in, but he said no. And then, guess what he did."

Alex looked out the window. "I don't know, Megan. What did he do?"

"He kissed my hand. Can you believe it? I almost died again. It sent shivers down my spine. And then he asked me out for Friday night, and of course I said yes. As soon as he left, I ran over here, and here I am. Aren't you thrilled for me?"

Alex turned her gaze back toward Megan and was stunned by what she saw. Megan was transformed. Her eyes were bright, alive, not darting nervously like a scared rabbit's the way they usually were. She was sitting straight, not hunched, and Alex had never seen her smile as wide or look as purely happy before.

It had been a week since Tony had brought her home from their date. Maybe he'd forgotten. Maybe he'd just been kidding. His words had seemed rehearsed, as if he'd heard them in an old James Dean picture and practiced saying them in front of a mirror. Maybe he really did like Megan. It wasn't as if Alex and he had been anything special to each other. Just a few dates, a few kisses, a few fights at the end of the night. She tried to imagine Megan and Tony together. Tony, with his leather jacket, dangerous eyes, and steel arms. And Megan, with her romance novels and high ideals. Alex stood up.

"Listen Megan, I—"

Clementine burst into the room.

"I saw you walking with Tony Maclivio!" she said. "I can't believe it. You snared the toughest guy in the school. You better tell me every gory detail. Don't leave anything out."

Megan laughed and pulled her to the bed. Once again, she recounted the story and, urged on by Clementine's enthusiasm, talked about what she would wear on Friday and what she should do or say. In the end, when Megan remembered Alex wanted to tell her something and asked her what it was, Alex kept her fears to herself. She was being melodramatic, she decided. Tony had simply seen Megan, liked what he saw, and had only good intentions. He'd never be rough with Megan the way he'd been with her. He was intelligent enough to see that Megan couldn't take it. And if he wasn't, well then, Alex would simply break every bone in his body.

• • •

Megan and Tony went out every Friday night. She would have been with him every Saturday night as well, but her parents forbade it. "Once a week is plenty," her father said. Megan was amazed that he was paying attention to her life at all. It was the first time her parents had ever imposed a rule on her, and although Tony chided her for being a baby and not disobeying them once in a while, Megan never broke it. It made her feel almost normal.

Tony was perfect. When she was with him, the rest of the world went away. He would knock at her front door and walk her to the car, then once inside, it was as if the doors and windows walled them into another dimension where only the two of them existed. There was only Tony, his hand wrapped around hers, his voice deep and rich and full of laughter just for her, his wavy hair falling carelessly around his forehead, crying out for her to touch it.

At first, they went to the movies and occasionally out for hamburgers, and Megan was more impressed than ever by Tony's old-fashioned ideas. He held her hand, opened doors for her, and kissed her on the cheek when he said good night. It was just like every romance novel she'd ever read. Tony respected her and didn't want to rush her.

After a few weeks, though, she began to long for his lips to touch hers. He had the most sensual mouth she'd ever seen. His lips were full and curved, and when he once leaned toward her to whisper something in her ear, she almost turned her head and pulled him to her.

"It's only a matter of time," Clementine told her. "He's just trying to go slow. Not to scare you. You should be thrilled." Just the same, Megan wished he'd get on with it already.

Finally, after a month, when he was saying good night, he put his hand behind her neck. His fingers were cool, and a shiver tingled along her spine. He seemed to stay like that for hours, frozen like an ice statue, until she looked up. Her stomach was churning so loud, she was sure he could hear it.

"I've wanted to kiss you for so long," he said huskily. "Really kiss you."

"Oh, Tony."

His lips met hers, and Megan felt her last hold on reality slipping away. He opened his mouth, and she followed his lead. Soon, his tongue was touching hers, playfully and then forcefully, and she put her arms around his neck and held on with all her might.

From then on, when Tony asked her to sneak out after her parents thought she was asleep on Saturday night, she did so without a second thought. On weeknights, she told her parents she was at Clementine's or Alex's house, then instead flew into Tony's arms. Forfeiting their trust was a small price to pay to be with Tony.

She lost interest in studying, in eating and sleeping, in everything except what she should wear when she saw Tony next, what they would do, where they planned to go. She found it hard to concentrate on any conversation other than one about Tony. Clementine and Alex were relegated to the distant corners of her life, brought in only during the brief gusts of free time she had in between dates and trips to the store for new outfits and phone calls with Tony, when she fell asleep with the receiver still clutched in her hand. Clementine warned her about becoming too dependent. Alex flat out told her to pull away from Tony, give herself some breathing room. Even her mother mentioned once that she thought Megan was a little too serious with "that boy." Megan barely listened and tossed away all of their advice.

She knew she was losing her grip on every part of her life that didn't directly relate to Tony. But she didn't want to hold on to those sections, anyway. She had never realized how miserable she was until Tony made her happy. She would have lied and stolen and cheated to be with him. He had strode into her life, picked her up, and turned her whole world upside down. And frankly, she had no desire to put it right side up again.

"I have a problem," Alex told Clementine one night when Megan was out again with Tony.

"You? I don't believe it." Clementine laughed and walked over to the vanity mirror in her bedroom. She had just read an article in *Vogue* that said a bedroom was a direct reflection of the person who lived in it. Looking around hers, she knew that was true. All three of their bedrooms had a theme. Megan's was lace and romance. Alex's was loud music and sports. And Clementine's was understated elegance. Thank God she was the one with the style. She sat down on the stool and brushed her hair.

"I'm serious," Alex said. "It's about Megan and Tony."

Clementine stopped brushing and turned to face her. "Go on."

"I think he's just using her."

Clementine slammed her brush down and stood up. "I can't believe this," she said, walking to within inches of Alex. "You can have any guy you want, but when Megan finally finds one, and he just happens to be one of the best-looking guys in the school, you don't even have the decency to be happy for her. What kind of friend are you?"

Alex stood, too, and paced the floor. "You don't understand. I was out with him before. He—"

"Oh, I get it. You can't stand to see him like someone other than you. I can't believe this, Alex. You—"

"Would you just be quiet and let me finish!" Alex shouted.

Clementine crossed her arms and sat down on the bed. "Fine."

"Thank you." Alex related the entire story of her last evening with Tony, watching Clementine's reaction closely. When she was through, Clementine returned to the vanity and picked up her brush again.

"Okay, I misjudged you. I'm sorry. But I think you're all wrong. If Tony was trying to get back at you, he would have done it already. Megan has been out of her head in love with him for weeks. He would have dumped her already, shown you he can hurt someone just like you can. Stop worrying and be happy for them. Tony has been reformed by the power of love."

"God, I hope you're right." Alex walked to the window and stared out, although she saw no farther than the images in her mind. She imagined Tony's fingers twisted into Megan's flesh, and she shivered. "You better be right."

• • •

Tony spread the blanket on the rocky ground and pulled another one over them when they sat down. Megan had always wondered about this place, a quarter-mile hike from the road. "Lover's Rock," Alex called it. She should know, Megan had thought. She'd been there often enough. Tony had apologized to Megan for bringing her there, explaining that he didn't think of her *that* way, but they had nowhere else to go where they could be alone. Megan couldn't believe how good he was.

It was two o'clock in the morning, the fog was in, and a light drizzle fell around them. The trees shrouding the clearing were like cloaked villains in black masks. They chuckled with the wind, and Megan trembled. Even Tony's arm around her could not ward off the chill.

"Relax." His voice was husky and soothing, and she buried her face in his chest. Smelling him, a mixture of perspiration, cigarettes, and cologne, she felt the villains retreat. She had no doubt that Tony could protect her from anything.

"I love you, Tony," she said, still practicing the words, saying them just for the sake of hearing the remarkable sound of it.

"I love you, too, babe." He lay back on the blanket, bringing her with him. She balanced her elbows on either side of him, silently counting off the hours they had left before she had to sneak back into her bedroom. Three hours—180 minutes and counting. She wondered if married people realized how lucky they were, together always, forever, with no limits to their time, no moments stolen.

Tony ran his fingers through her hair. "You're so pretty, you know that? Like a model or something. Have you ever thought of being a model?"

She blushed and kissed him. How had she gotten so lucky? Why didn't he love Alex or Clementine? Why her?

"You're the kind of girl I never thought would like me. So smart, you know. And pretty. Your hair is like sunshine. And you're softer than anything, Meg."

He ran his fingers down her arm, and she stretched out in response to the hundreds of pleasurable needles prickling her skin.

"I thought you'd like some brain or something," he said.

"Oh, no, Tony. I like you. I love you. I could never love anyone but you."

"Are you sure?"

"Of course I am."

He kissed her, and she was so entranced by his hands

roaming over her back that she hardly noticed the hardness of his lips against hers. He rolled over and pinned her beneath him.

"I want you so bad, Meg."

She felt only an instant of fear, remembering the sex education class warnings of diseases and pregnancy. Then the fears were lost beyond Tony's eyes, begging her to be with him. How could she deny him? Of course they should be together. They loved each other. No one could expect them to wait.

"I want you too," she said, sliding her sweater up over her head.

In the darkness, Tony smiled.

•   •   •

Alex had all but forgotten her worries about Tony by the end of their tenth-grade year. He and Megan were still together, happy as ever. Alex had even double-dated with them once. She'd picked a boy from her woodworking class—she couldn't even remember his name—and the four of them had gone miniature golfing. She'd seen no signs of the Tony she remembered. He'd been pleasant and charming and didn't say one word of the last evening he and Alex had spent together. He'd hovered over Megan as though she were an expensive china doll that might shatter at any second. It had been obvious that he loved her, and Alex had breathed a grateful sigh of relief.

Two weeks into summer vacation, she and Clementine and Megan planned a day of sailing. They'd hardly spent any time together, all three of them, with Megan so busy fluttering around in gaga land. Surprisingly, the sailing was Megan's suggestion. She wanted to share her joy with them, so to speak, and although Alex wasn't thrilled about listening to a full day's worth of Tony this and Tony that, she wasn't about to pass up a day on Megan's parents' twenty-five-foot sailboat.

Alex and Clementine packed a picnic lunch and waited at the dock for Megan to arrive. She was almost always on time, so when the appointed meeting time came and went, then another half an hour passed and she still hadn't shown up, they began to worry. Finally, forty-five minutes later, Megan arrived, her hair messed and her eyes red. Panic knotted in Alex's stomach. She could almost feel Tony's bones cracking beneath her hands.

"Are you all right?" she asked.

Megan shook her head, a few tears spilling from the corners of her eyes. "Let's get out on the water first. I need to get away from here."

They headed for the Golden Gate Bridge. There was only a slight wind up, and they sailed slowly. While manning the sails, Alex kept looking over her shoulder at Megan, sitting with her head in her hands, her body heaving up and down like a buoy. Clementine warned her not to say anything.

When they reached the bridge, they took down the sail and sat in the open stern of the boat. Megan wiped her eyes and looked up.

"I'm pregnant."

Clementine grabbed Alex's hand and squeezed it tightly. Then she reached out her other arm and put it around Megan's shoulders.

"When did you find out?"

"This afternoon. Just before I got here."

"Does Tony know?"

Megan opened her eyes wide, and the tears came again, easily, as from a leaky faucet that refuses to be fixed. "No. Oh, God, I don't know what to do."

Alex opened her mouth, but Clementine jumped in before she could speak.

"I'll tell you exactly what to do. We'll turn this boat around, and then you are going straight to Tony's. You will tell him you're pregnant, and if he loves you at all, he'll help you through this. If not, then I will. Either way, I promise you, everything will be fine. Do you understand?"

Megan bit her lip and nodded.

They steered the boat back toward the dock. Alex waited until just before they had reached the shore before sitting down next to Megan.

"Clementine can be such a rock sometimes," she said. "I wonder if anything ever fazes her."

"I doubt it," Megan mumbled, clutching her stomach as if the pressure would make the baby inside go away.

"You know I'll always be here for you, don't you?"

Megan leaned her head against Alex's. "Of course. It's my own fault, Alex. I know that. It's just that when I'm with him, I don't think. At all. Especially not about birth control and unromantic things like that. I just feel. I know it sounds horrible, but actually it's wonderful. It's the most wonderful feeling in the world. And you know what's even crazier?"

"What?"

Megan laughed, a bittersweet sound that made Alex hold her tighter. "When the doctor told me I was pregnant, all I could think of was how happy that made me. Can you imagine anything more ridiculous? Fifteen years old, pregnant, and happy about it. But, you know, I just keep thinking that this isn't just any baby. It's Tony's. This will bind us together forever. I know it will change my whole life, but I don't care. Tony and I will get married, and we'll have this baby."

Alex swallowed the lump in her throat and helped Clementine guide the boat back to the dock.

•   •   •

Tony was in the garage when Megan reached his house, his dark head bent over the motorcycle he'd been fixing for weeks. She watched him for a moment, still awed by the fact that he loved her, months after he'd told her for the first time. She took a deep breath, walked up behind him, and kissed his neck.

"What the hell?" He whirled around, and she jumped back, startled.

"Oh, Megan, it's you. God, you scared me."

"Sorry."

He set down his tools and walked toward her. "Hell, it's okay. I just didn't expect to see you again today."

"I know. But we need to talk."

He looked at her closely, then took her hand. "Come on. Let's go inside. Nobody's here."

They walked in the house and sat down on the living room couch. Megan had only been inside his home twice, and both times his parents had been away. Taking a quick look around, she guessed Tony was embarrassed by the shabbiness of the furnishings; the outdated orange-and-brown carpeting, the rips in the brown vinyl sofa, the newspapers littering the floor as if the trash can in the kitchen five steps away was five steps too many to walk. By now, she thought, he should know she didn't care about any of that. He could live in the streets and she wouldn't care.

"So, what's up?"

She took his hand and held it firmly. She'd practiced it a hundred times on the way over. It would be easy. Just say it. He'd be surprised, maybe even a little upset, but eventually happy. He'd want to marry her.

"Tony, I'm pregnant."

She couldn't look at him at first. She focused on a crumpled newspaper on the floor, trying to read it through the wrinkles. As time passed and the silence grew heavier, until she could feel it actually weighing her down, she could no longer stand the suspense. She raised her head.

Tony was looking directly at her and smiling. But it wasn't the smile she had expected. It was fixed and strange, like the painted-on ones on department store mannequins. His full lips looked thinner and whiter than usual, strained and bloodless. And his eyes didn't fit the smile. The pupils were so dilated, his eyes looked entirely black.

"I'm pregnant," she said again.

Finally, like a curtain coming down on a scene, the smile faded. His face became tender and considerate again, the face she knew.

"What do you think we should do?" he asked.

She breathed deeply. It had only been shock that had transformed him, and now he was Tony again, the man who loved her. She lifted a finger to his cheek. "Well, I don't think we have a choice. If we get married this summer, it won't look too bad. You've graduated, so you can get a job. I'll finish high school after the baby's a little older."

He leaned closer to her, so close that she could feel his hot breath on her cheeks. She waited for his proposal. She knew he'd want to do it right, romantically, maybe even on bended knee.

"How bad do you want to be with me, Meg?" he whispered.

She shook her head, wondering if she'd heard him right. His voice was strange, excited, harder than she'd ever heard it. She tried to pull away, to see his eyes more clearly, but his hand was behind her head, holding her close.

"You know," she said, her own voice unsteady.

"Tell me."

A sickness gnawed at her stomach. It rose up in her throat, the taste of bile hiding just beyond her mouth.

"More than anything. You know that," she said.

"You're gonna have to beg me to be with you. You should know that I don't come to anyone easily. Beg me to marry you, Meg, and then we'll see."

She turned her head and squirmed without success to get out of his arm lock. "Why are you acting like this? I don't understand. I . . ."

"It's plain and simple. If you want me, you'll have to beg." His fingers twisted into her hair, pulling her head back.

Megan stared into his black eyes. She knew what she should do, what Alex or Clementine would do. Clementine would think of some memorable, scalding exit line; Alex would spit in his face. But Megan loved him. And she'd always believed that love came first. Before pride and honor. Before everything.

"Please marry me, Tony," she said, a tear slipping down either cheek. "I beg you."

He held on to her hair a moment longer, then released her. She fell back against the couch, and he stood up. He grabbed her chin and forced her head up until she looked at him.

"Your friend Alex will be interested to know you said that."

His hand dropped, and he walked to the front door, throwing it open. "Now get the hell out of my house."

# CHAPTER 4

*C*LEMENTINE HELD THE SMOKE IN HER LUNGS until she couldn't breathe and the heat scorched her throat. Alex warned her about lung disease, cancer, dying a young death. As if Clementine would want to grow old and wrinkled and flabby, anyway. Her mother and stepfather complained that she smelled up the house and dirtied the ashtrays. Besides, they said, she was too young to smoke. They didn't think it looked right, a cigarette dangling from her lips. As if she cared what they thought.

Smoking was part of her image. She looked glamorous, more Hollywoodish, with the long, thin cigarette resting between her fingers. Added to that, the steadiness of smoking, breathing in and out, watching the silver ashes burn continuously upward, relaxed her. And if ever there was a time when she needed something to calm her down, it was now.

She turned away from the rain-splattered window. Megan was finally asleep, her chest rising and falling evenly. Her face was pale, and the dark circles beneath her eyes were pronounced, but they would leave with time. That was the only consolation Clementine could give her. Eventually, time dulled even the most devastating pain.

She ground out her cigarette and walked to the bedside. Megan shivered once, and Clementine tucked the blanket beneath her chin. A strange feeling passed through her. For the first time in her life, she wished she could take on someone else's pain. She knew what she'd do. She'd jump out of that bed, show up on Tony's doorstep with a shotgun, and blow that smug smile off his disgusting face. Instead, Megan, whose only fault was loving the wrong man too much, was trapped in her own misery, and there was not a damn thing Clementine could do about it. Quietly, she left the room and made her way downstairs. Alex was sitting on the edge of the couch in the living room.

"If you sit up any farther, you'll fall off."

Alex looked up and unsuccessfully attempted to smile. "How is she?"

"Asleep. I really don't think she should go home tonight. Her parents will know something is wrong. We'd better make up some excuse."

"I've already thought about it. I'll tell them I'm planning a surprise slumber party for her birthday tonight and forgot to tell them before. They already think I'm a scatterbrain, so that should be right in character. Her birthday isn't until next month, but that'll have to do. The odds are they won't even give a damn. They rarely do where Megan is concerned."

Clementine nodded and sat down. She wondered where her mother was. She must have been there recently. Even heaven couldn't compete with the shine in the newly polished end tables. Angel was probably out shopping or running errands for John again. Could it be that one of his shirts was already three months old? Angel never let a shirt pass the three-month mark. Clementine's father had complained about that. He hated old clothes. And old food. And the same old people, for that matter.

Clementine shuddered and stood up again. It was only when something bad happened that she thought of him, her father. When someone was hurt, or had died, or her mother was too busy with John to pay much attention to her, the image of Duke's face, almost a mirror of her own, with only a few harder edges and brown stubble on the chin to differentiate it, appeared on the inside of her eyes, burning them until tears formed. Not that it bothered her anymore. She could live without him. She'd done it for years. And she'd long ago learned to live with her mother's devotion to her stepfather. Angel was not going to lose John, too. No, sir. When she was dusting, Clementine often heard her mumbling, "I won't lose John. I won't lose John," over and over like a scratched record.

"How are you doing?" Alex asked, shattering Duke's image.

Clementine turned around and smiled. "Okay. Tired, I guess. Megan seemed so weak for a while. I wasn't sure if she'd ... Well, it just looked like something went wrong. But she's past the worst of it now."

Alex rubbed her forehead. "I want to kill him. I don't think I could even stand to look at him without trying to claw his eyes out. I'll—"

"Alex, don't." Clementine sat down beside her. "I know how you feel. Believe me. But if there's one thing I've learned, it's that you can't stoop to someone else's level. Tony will get his some day. Wait and see. The worst thing we could do to him would be to ignore him completely. Act as if what he did to Megan doesn't even matter. That'll hurt him most of all."

"I don't know."

"I do. Think about it. Everyone wants a reaction. That's why Tony carried it so far. He wanted you to react to his cruelty. It'll drive him crazy if you don't. And in the meantime, Megan needs us."

"Oh, God, Megan."

Clementine leaned her head against Alex's.

"She wanted the baby, you know," Alex said. "God only knows why, but she wanted it."

"I know. She almost didn't go through with it. And I almost wish she hadn't. It's my fault what happened. I'm the one who chose that doctor, if you can even call him that."

"You didn't have much of a choice. She needed to have it done quickly, and you did the best you could."

"I know that. But I feel so responsible. I could have taken an extra day, at least. Checked the guy out thoroughly. I'd sue him if Megan was willing to go out in the open. The man was a butcher. She lost a lot of blood."

They leaned back against the couch, listening to the ticking of the clock, steady and unmoved no matter what events transpired around it. Suddenly, the room was pierced by an agonized scream. Alex and Clementine jumped up and ran for the stairs.

"Tony!" Megan shouted. "Tonyyyyyyyyyyyyyyyyy."

*          *          *

Clementine told no one about the Saks Fifth Avenue young model search taking place in San Francisco. If she won, it would be a different story. But if she lost, nobody could know. No one knew about her dreams. Not even Alex or Megan. Sometimes the three of them talked about what colleges they wanted to go to and what they wanted to major in, but Clementine always managed to talk in generalities and possibilities, never definite answers.

They wouldn't understand. She knew that. Oh, maybe Alex would a little. She had ambition. She wanted to go to Berkeley and become a financial genius, or some such boring thing. Still, that wasn't the same as wanting to be a star. She couldn't bear to hear Alex laugh at her for putting her pride and entire future on the line by entering such a risky, unforgiving field.

Alex's taunts, though, would be nothing compared with what Megan would say about her plans. Last she heard, Megan wanted to be a teacher. Or was it a nurse? Clementine wasn't sure. Something helping people. Good God. She'd tried to make Megan realize there was no money in helping people, but Megan didn't care. That wasn't the point, she'd said. Like hell it wasn't. Money meant power and respect. Money meant you didn't need anyone. Once she made enough of it, she could kiss her stepfather, the memories of her father, and even her mother's well-intentioned advice good-bye. It would be her life then, completely and totally. If she wanted to smoke, live in New York City, travel the world alone, she'd damn well do it. Clementine smiled just at the thought of it.

To enter the model search competition, she'd had to fill out a two-page application form, write an essay about why she wanted to be a model, and send in two eight-by-ten glossy photographs, one of just her face and one full-length. Luckily, she'd saved most of her allowance for the past year and had had enough to cover the costs of a professional photographer for one session. Her appointment was that afternoon at one o'clock. She'd leave school early with a stomachache and finally be on her way. First, Saks Fifth Avenue, and then, who knows? By this time next year, she could be on the cover of *Vogue*.

• • •

Though neither Alex nor Megan would admit it openly, a strained tenseness had grown between them over the last few months. Always there, it was like the stench of something dead that invades a room and lingers, hovering over everything, though the source of the odor is long gone.

If Megan had had only the abortion to deal with, she could have faced it, grieved for her loss, and moved on. But every night, the moment her eyes closed, the movie began. Tony's last words, his cruelty, played over in her mind, rewound and replayed, until she opened her eyes in a panic and turned the light on, hoping that would chase the picture away. She knew there was more to what had happened between her and Tony than just Tony's losing interest, or hating her for getting pregnant, or falling out of love. She'd caught a glimpse of something sinister behind his eyes. Something he'd hidden from her all along, while he made her believe that he loved her. Something that had to do with Alex.

More than anything else, his last words about Alex haunted her. What did Alex have to do with it at all? Megan knew Alex had dated Tony a few times, but surely that was over and forgotten. Alex was her friend. Her best friend. She'd known how much Megan loved Tony. For once in her life, Megan had had someone totally to herself, someone who wanted *her*. At least, that was what she'd thought. She'd felt beautiful and smart and good enough for the first time in her life. But when she thought of his words, the knife sharp pangs of insecurity cut her, opened the old wounds, and thrust a wedge of unanswered questions between her and Alex.

Alex felt like she was on a country fair wild ride, darting left and right and missing by inches every conceivable danger. She desperately wanted to be the friend Megan needed her to be. It had been six months since she and Clementine had brought Megan home from the doctor's office, and still Megan wasn't back to normal. She had a look of tiredness all the time, even when she was running the track in gym class. Her shoulders hunched, her chest and stomach dropped. It even seemed to be an effort for her to hold her head up. She rarely spoke unless spoken to, and even then it was in short, monosyllabic replies without an inkling of emotion. She never laughed. But what scared Alex more than anything was that she never cried, either.

When Megan was lying in Clementine's bed after the abortion, Alex had squeezed her hand as tight as she could and sworn that she would be there for her. Whatever she needed, Alex would get it. But Alex knew she wasn't keeping her promise. Megan held back from her, and in response, without thinking, Alex held back too. She kept her feelings to herself, and her words, afraid of saying the wrong thing, bringing up a bad memory, or perhaps even making it worse by letting Megan know how badly Tony had deceived her all along. Or did she know? Had Tony told her about his last date with Alex? Did Megan blame her?

It would have been easier if they were fighting. Then they could have said what they felt, yelled, shouted, cried, written a few nasty letters, called in the reinforcements, then made up. The phony friendliness was much worse. They still walked home together. They ate lunch together. They got together after school just like before. But their posture was rigid, their sentences curt, as if they were political diplomats who could shake hands and smile at the cameras after an hourlong screaming tirade in private.

Alex longed for Clementine. If she were around more, she could break the ice, pull them back together. But Clementine was becoming more and more mysterious— leaving school early and acting evasive about where she spent her afternoons and weekends. So the distance between Alex and Megan grew, as if they were in separate cars, trying to see each other through the glare of the midday sun on the windows and keep an eye on the road at the same time.

• • •

The finals of the model search were to be held during the last week of May. It was between Clementine and nine other girls. Clementine was where she wanted to be. She'd made it this far, which was more than the other hundred or so girls who'd entered the contest eight months earlier could say. Yet nothing had been as she expected.

You were supposed to be pretty (she was), take a few pictures (she did), get discovered (not yet), and then get rich (ha!). To date, Clementine had spent every penny of her savings account on clothes and makeup; had had eleven excruciating photo sessions with belligerent photographers who wanted to either sleep with her or create an image of her on film that she would never be comfortable with; and had lived on the brink of exhaustion through quarterfinal and semifinal matches. They lasted for hours while she and the other girls sweated beneath hot lights and walked up and down the runway to give the judges just one more look.

Yet here she was. The finals were two weeks away, and Clementine felt more confident than ever before. A few months earlier, with her clothes bill running much higher than she could afford on her five-dollar-a-week allowance, she'd had to tell her mother what she was doing. She'd expected to hear anger and reason after reason why modeling was a horrible profession and how she was too young and inexperienced and needed to concentrate on high school.

Instead, her mother had taken her hand and led her to the living room couch.

"It's a difficult life, you know," she'd said.

"I know, Mom. But it's all I've ever wanted to do."

Angel looked away, but Clementine saw the melancholy smile that lingered on her mouth.

"I modeled for a few years before I met your father. Runway fashion shows, mostly. A few catalogues too."

"You?"

"Don't look so shocked, Clemmie. I was young once. And quite pretty. At least, your father thought so."

Clementine looked at Angel and, layer by layer, peeled away the wrinkles and prematurely gray hair. Beneath, she could almost see a young, vibrant woman with blond hair, bright blue eyes, and a dazzling smile. It was strange how, until that moment, she'd never thought of her mother as anything but old and married. Never in her wildest dreams would she have thought of her having her own career, her own life.

"I'm just surprised, Mom, that's all. I didn't know you worked."

Angel stood up and walked over to the end table. A dust rag lay on the floor, and she knelt down to polish the table legs.

"I was actually quite independent when I was your age, just like you. I wanted a lot of things back then. But then I met Duke, and, well . . ."

"Well what?" Clementine asked, sitting forward. Just the sound of his name brought him back full and strong. She could almost feel his arms around her, lifting her high in the air, throwing her up toward the top of the trees. There was a moment of fear at being alone in the sky and falling too quickly, but then Duke's arms were around her again, and he pulled her to his chest, where his smell was strongest. Sweat and tangy cologne and the lingering odor of beer spilled on his collar.

Angel stopped rubbing the table legs and sat back on her heels. "I don't know what happened. Duke was just so powerful, so overwhelming. All he had to do was touch me, and suddenly everything but being with him seemed pointless."

Angel's voice was even, but Clementine wondered if it bothered her now, just a little, that she'd let everything that belonged solely to her, to Angel, slip away. And for what? Duke had left a few years later, when Clementine was four years old. He needed someone more independent, with more to contribute, he'd said. Clementine stood up and walked over to her mother. Bending down, she kissed her head.

"Well, I'm not going to let anyone come in and take over my life. Long ago, I decided that I was going to be a star, and I won't stop until I get there. If I don't win this contest, I'll enter another one and then another one until I finally hit the big time. No one is going to stand in my way."

Angel stood up and stared into her daughter's determined face.

"And there'd be no place in your life for a man, even if you loved him?"

"Oh, Mom, I don't think I'll ever be in love. Not really, anyway. I'm just not romantic enough. Love is full of sunsets and butterflies and dew-covered flowers. What do I need with those things?"

Angel sighed and put her arm around her. "All right, Clemmie. I understand. And I'll help you with this contest. But try to remember that life can be full of many things. Maybe I've gone too far in one direction with your father and now John, but perhaps you're going too far the other way. Balance, my dear. Balance is the key."

•   •   •   •

"Well, look who's here," Alex said, glancing up from the table in the corner of Megan's bedroom where she was filing Megan's nails. "Miss Montgomery. Eleventh-grade Lincoln High School student who cuts class about once a week and vanishes into thin air without any explanation at all to her friends."

Clementine sat down on Megan's bed, still covered with the lavender ruffled bedspread that she'd told Megan countless times was much too juvenile for her. She'd been afraid to come there, knowing she hadn't been as good a friend as she could have been lately. Megan was still hurting, Alex was angry, and she could see the distance between the two of them as clearly as if a wall had been erected to keep them apart. Yet she had her own life to lead. She was growing up, and now was the time to act if she wanted to be a success. Models had to start young. She didn't have time to let other people's problems interfere with her goals, even if those problems belonged to her best friends.

Clementine agreed with all of her rationalizations intellectually, but as she watched the two of them ignore her, she wondered how to rid herself of the gnawing guilt pangs in her gut.

"I'm sorry," she said softly. She lay back and ran her hand over the antique lace lining the edges of the bedspread.

The room was quiet except for the sawing of Megan's fingernails. Clementine closed her eyes.

"I've entered the Saks Fifth Avenue model search," she said. "The finals are next week. I was hoping you guys would come."

Alex slammed down the nail file and stood up. She marched over to the bed and stared at Clementine until she opened her eyes.

"You listen to me, Clemmie. I've had it with you. I should have stuck with the first instinct I had when we met. You're nothing but a selfish, egotistical snob, you know that? All you care about is you. You've ignored us for practically the entire school year, and for what? A modeling contest? Is that more important than friendship? Is that more important than what happened to Megan? She needed you. She had an abortion, for God's sake. Where were you?"

"*I* was the one who took her to the doctor," Clementine yelled back, standing up. They stood face-to-face, jaws tight and fists clenched. Clementine was more than a full head taller than Alex, but Alex made up for it in intensity. She leaned forward until Clementine had to pull away just to see her straight.

"*I* held her hand," Clementine went on, still shouting. "You were too goddamn guilty to even look at her. *I* didn't lead Tony on, you did. It wasn't *my* fault he did what he did. Maybe if you had been up front with Megan from the start about what happened between you and Tony, none of this would have happened. So don't you dare give me your high and mighty speech."

"You just wait one minute . . ."

Megan opened the door and hurried out into the hall. Her parents were downstairs in the dining room, thank God. There was no way they could have heard. She firmly gripped the oak banister as she made her way down the stairs, pausing when she felt dizzy and hanging on to the railing to hold herself up. Only ten more feet, and then she'd be outside. She'd be able to breathe again. Three. Two. One.

The night was warm and sultry. There was no breeze. Not a leaf moved. She breathed deeply, filling her lungs until she thought they would burst. Again and again, she gulped at the air, feeling like a rubber raft inflating until it's full and strong again.

She waited until she was steady and sure on her feet before heading around the side of the house to the gazebo on the edge of the hill. Reaching it, she leaned against the railing. From here she could see the bay, colorless now beneath the black, moonless sky, except for the sparkling lights from the yachts and sailboats that dotted the edges.

Megan inhaled again. The pressure felt good in her lungs. It had been so long since she'd really breathed. Almost a year. She didn't remember much of that time. Somehow, she'd gone on with her life, like a robot who could perform certain duties but was turned off and put away at the end of the evening. She hadn't felt alive at all. She rarely knew the date or the day of the week or the hour.

Only once had she let life in. It was soon after it happened and she'd been at the docks with Alex. A young couple had been coaxing their baby to walk from one parent to the other. Alex had tried to steer her away, but Megan had been captivated by the child's smile, pulled to it. She'd wanted to run over and snatch the child out of their arms. Her baby would have looked like that. It had Tony's dark hair and her light eyes. She had walked toward it, in a spell, until Alex grabbed her and shook her.

"It's not yours," she said. "It's not yours." Megan had run home and locked herself in her room until the next morning. And then, in self-defense, she learned to shut out everything.

Megan knelt down on the cherrywood floor of the gazebo and rested her chin on the railing. She thought of Alex, her best friend, and how much she loved her, no matter what had happened between her and Tony. For a while, it had seemed terribly important to shut her out, to hurt her with her indifference. A few times, she had thought of asking Alex what the real story was with Tony, but at first, she'd been afraid to know the truth, and then, as the hollow emptiness inside her grew, it ceased to matter. She knew now that Tony had only used her to get back at Alex. Learning all the details couldn't possibly hurt her more than the pain of losing her baby and knowing that Tony had never loved her.

She thought of Clementine too. Strong, brave, and calm Clementine. She had been there for her. She'd held her hand while the doctor stuck the cold metal contraption inside of her. The anesthesia hadn't worked completely, so she'd felt him prodding her, pulling the life out of her in a gush of blood. After that, every time she had looked at Clementine, no matter how hard she tried not to, she remembered.

She thought of her parents, who were so captivated by the riches around them, they hardly noticed she was there. Not once did they ask what was wrong with her, why she wasn't eating or talking or laughing anymore. She wondered what would have happened if she had died on the doctor's table.

And then Tony, who'd taught her how to love, how to fear love, and how to hate. Finally, Megan wrapped her arms around her stomach and thought of her baby. The doctor had said it was a boy.

Footsteps fell on the ground behind her, and she turned around. Alex and Clementine stood together holding hands. They approached her cautiously until she held out her arms. All she wanted now was her best friends back. They knelt down in front of her and held her tightly until, at last, Megan cried.

$$\bullet \quad \bullet \quad \bullet$$

Clementine stood third in line on the stage. Head up, shoulders back, chest out, stomach in, right leg out, left leg back, eyes wide, smile bright, hands at her sides. She had rehearsed it so many times, her mannerisms had become her second skin. She never relaxed them, whether onstage or in school or at the dinner table.

Her gaze darted to her mother and stepfather sitting beside Megan and Alex in the fourth row. On a foolish whim, she'd sent a letter to her father asking him to come. He moved so much, from Denver to Seattle to Cleveland to Miami to Atlanta last she heard, she wasn't sure if he'd even received it. Most likely, he had and had simply decided to ignore her request. The way he ignored her. Why did she even try? She blinked her eyes and looked away. Better not to think of him or anyone at all. It would only distract her.

The girl in front of her was called, and she walked up and back the runway. Unsteady, Clementine thought. Her legs were wobbling slightly. She looked awkward in four-inch heels. No model had a chance unless she looked like she took a shower in heels. Clementine had done that once and found it really wasn't that hard once you got a good footing. She wore heels constantly. She had a pair in every color.

"Clementine Montgomery. Sausalito, California."

Clementine raised her chin and smiled broadly. For a moment, before stepping forward, she mentally checked every aspect of her looks. Her light brown hair was swept up, leaving only a few wisps around her forehead and cheeks. Her clear blue eyes had been worked on to perfection by the makeup artist, who had been so entranced by them, he'd spent twice as much time on her as anyone else. Her royal blue silk dress with silver sequins lining the V neckline fell all the way to the floor, showing only a glimpse of royal blue pumps when she walked. Her smile widened. She looked perfect.

Through weeks of visualization techniques, Clementine had prepared herself for the terror of facing hundreds of unknown, critical faces. She had accustomed herself to the feel of the lights on her neck, the microphones jammed into her face, the butterflies dancing sporadically in her stomach. But with her first step, she realized her intense training regimen had been for nothing.

She looked out at the audience and felt a rush of unbelievable power. Every eye was on her. Every smile was for her, because of her. She walked down the runway, the swish of her hips born of newfound confidence. She felt no awkwardness. This was where she belonged. She had *it*. Chemistry. The undefinable star quality agents and producers and modeling scouts were always talking about. She was in control, beautiful, powerful, and safe. The audience saw her facade and no more.

She returned up the runway and pirouetted to a round of thunderous applause. She could hardly keep from laughing out loud at the pleasure of it all. She walked back to her place in the corner of the stage, but the audience kept right on clapping. To their delight, Clementine curtseyed. The judges chuckled.

The remaining first half of the competition passed in a haze. The following seven girls were called. Some were pretty, some confident, but none received the response that Clementine had. She chanced a glance at her friends and saw them smiling at her. They sensed her victory too.

The second half of the contest was an interview. The host asked each of the girls what she wanted to do with her life. Most answered with the usual responses. A nurse, a veterinarian. I want to help the poor, feed the hungry, push for world peace, and so on and so on. Clementine had thought long and hard about what to say. Sure, she could lie. Say she wanted to join the Peace Corps or become a teacher. But that wasn't good enough. Clementine Montgomery was different. And if she was going to be the star she wanted to be, they needed to know that from the start.

Ken Strickland, the head coordinator of the contest and host, called her name and, with a bored smile, asked her what her plans for the future were. Clementine looked at him only once, then turned her gaze to the audience. They leaned forward expectantly.

"Well, Mr. Strickland, I want to be perfectly honest.

The other girls here have so many wonderful, good-hearted goals that I feel almost ashamed. You see, I've always had ambition. I can't and won't settle for an ordinary life. I have a dream of success."

She closely watched the judges' faces for their reactions and saw that most had set their pencils down. She had their complete attention.

"I'll tell you why," she went on. "So often, women give up their dreams. Sure, we have them when we're young and single, but soon enough we meet a man, get married, and then spend the rest of our lives helping our husbands get ahead, helping our children grow, helping everyone but ourselves. Well, I want to change that."

Applause trickled through the auditorium, and Clementine smiled. "What is so wrong with a woman wanting her own life, her own success for herself and no one else? Are we less intelligent, less qualified, less able to contribute to society? I think not. For centuries, half the world's population has been denied a major role in running the world. Just think of the genius, insight, and fresh ideas that have been lost because of that."

She glanced around at the audience. Confident no one was turning on her, she continued.

"If I become a well-known model, I would help other women learn to stand up for themselves. To be on their own, independent of a boyfriend or husband or family. I would tour the country and make speeches about self-confidence and doing what you want to do in life instead of what society dictates women should do. We have choices. Many more than just becoming a nurse or teacher, although those are very admirable professions. But should we rule out becoming scientists and politicians just because we are female? Of course not."

Ken Strickland had taken a step back, giving her center stage. She took advantage of it and gazed down at the judges, pausing to look each one in the eye.

"My point is that the whole world is open to women. We don't have to give up our opportunities when we fall in love. Life is so much more worthwhile and fulfilling when we choose to live it completely and independently, using all our talents and capacities. If I become a famous model, Mr. Strickland, I would help to change the world."

The room was pin-drop quiet for an instant, and Clementine could feel her back curving forward, hunching. She had gone too far. But then she saw Megan and Alex jump to their feet and clap, followed quickly by Clementine's parents and the rest of the audience. The applause was deafening. Clementine pulled herself up straight and bowed her head in acknowledgment. She saw the women smiling their approval. She saw the men laughing, impressed with her gusto. But most of all, she saw the judges bent over their scorecards, writing furiously.

After the applause quieted, the last two girls reverted to being nurses, somewhat more shakily than before, but with the same wholesome phoniness Clementine found tiring. At last, the interviews were finished and Mr. Strickland took the scorecards from the judges. He stood before the audience and waited until they quieted.

Clementine pressed her hands hard against her sides and smiled until her cheeks hurt. Strickland started with the third runner up, and she said a silent prayer that it wouldn't be her. She'd be first or nothing.

Tracy Benito. Thank God. Followed by Louise Shumaker and Linda Ellsley. All that was left was the winner.

"And now, ladies and gentlemen, we have the winner of the Saks Fifth Avenue young model search. The winner is . . . Clementine Montgomery."

She had a moment of doubt as she wondered if she had passed a border with a no-return entry. It was only a moment, though, then she was caught up in the applause and fulfillment of her dreams. The doubt was gone forever. Clementine Montgomery took her place center stage as the newest face to hit the modeling world. And she knew deep inside that life would never be the same again.

# CHAPTER 5

*A*LEX SAT IN THE DEAN'S OFFICE WAITING room with her hands folded on her lap. The dress she was wearing was only two days old, and already she wanted to rip it to shreds. The elastic was tight around her waist, and the tag on the back collar scratched her neck whenever she moved. The last time she'd worn a dress was at her junior high school graduation, and she'd hated every second of foo-fooing around in lace and ruffles. After that, she'd used her distaste for frills to fight for women's rights. Surely, women should be able to wear pants as often as men did, no matter what the occasion. She'd even convinced Clementine to join the battle, and in the last year, the two of them had worn nothing but blue jeans—torn at the knees for casual wear and stiff and tight for evenings out.

Today was different, though. Clementine, with her flair for style, had helped Alex pick out the white cotton dress. She'd stared at herself in the mirror for forty-five minutes that morning, and although she hated to admit it, the dress suited her. The white fabric contrasted nicely with her olive skin and dark hair. She looked feminine but strong, what she assumed the dean would be looking for.

What was taking him so long? Probably having an affair with his secretary right on the desk at that very moment. She giggled, then stopped herself, recrossing her legs and smoothing her dress. She'd been only five minutes early, exactly as the book on how to have a successful interview had told her. She must have been waiting for half an hour by now. She tapped her feet, scrunched so tightly into the white pumps Clementine had insisted she buy that she was sure her toes had lost all circulation and would never recover. She glanced at her watch. Impossibly, it read one o'clock. Exactly five minutes since she'd arrived.

The office door opened and a surprisingly young-looking man walked out. His hair was light brown, with only a tinge of gray over each ear, and he wore his clothes the way they were supposed to be worn, with seams hanging in all the right places, the navy wool fitting his skin like hot fudge on ice cream. Alex swallowed hard, wished she'd taken a double dose of mouthwash, and stood up.

"Miss Holmes, I presume?" he said, with the deep voice only men who graduated at the top of their class and were sitting pretty in a tenured job possessed.

"Yes, sir."

"It's nice to meet you. I'm Wendell Thornby."

He held out his hand, and Alex silently cursed her sweaty palms. His grip was firm and strong. He released her hand and smiled, and she followed him inside the office.

The room looked just as she had expected. The University of California at Berkeley might have been the most liberal university in the country, but the administration still leaned toward traditional, intellectual offices. Dark paneled walls, mahogany bookcases jammed with books found only in secondhand bookstores and college stockrooms, and oversize desks littered with papers. Organized clutter. It was what Alex imagined for herself some day. She could smell the success, the respect, and the power that hung in the air.

Mr. Thornby sat down and searched the desk for her application. Finally locating it, he took a pair of bifocals from his coat pocket, leaned back, and studied it closely. Alex clenched and unclenched her hands methodically, getting a strange kind of pleasure from the sting of her fingernails digging into her flesh. Why wasn't all of that relaxation, mental imagery crap Clementine had shoved down her throat working?

"Holmes," Mr. Thornby said. "You wouldn't by any chance be related to Paul Holmes, a math professor here, would you?"

"He's my father."

Mr. Thornby set the application down and studied her anew. His eyes seemed to see right through her, to the door behind her, creating an uncomfortable heat that brought beads of sweat to her forehead. Alex forced herself not to slide down in her seat.

"Yes, I can see the resemblance now. Funny, he didn't mention to me that you had an interview."

"I asked him not to, sir."

Mr. Thornby watched her a moment longer, then smiled. He returned to her application.

"Quite impressive, Alexandra. You've done well over the years. Obviously, we'll have no problem with your grades. But what I'd like to know is why the school of business interests you. What you plan to do with your degree should you get it here. What your goals are, say, five or ten years down the line."

Alex scanned her brain like a speed reader, searching for a few key words, the rehearsed answers she'd drilled countless times the past few weeks. In a panic, she realized the files were empty, her mind blank. Why was she so nervous? Good God, she'd never been nervous for anything in her life, and yet now, when it meant so much, she couldn't even function. She was going to blow everything if she didn't speak soon. He was looking at her intently. Watching, studying. He had to know she couldn't think. She was acting like an idiotic high school kid. Think, Alex. Think.

"Miss Holmes," he said, interrupting her thoughts. "I realize you're nervous. It's quite understandable. But please don't be. Your grades and extracurricular activities certainly stand on their own. I just want to know your motivations. We here at Berkeley are a little idealistic, as I'm certain you know from your father. We're not happy with simply handing out diplomas like some kind of factory. We want students who share our love for knowledge, our determination to make a difference. I simply want to know if that's you."

Alex leaned back and thought of all the nights she'd sat up in bed, unable to sleep while her thoughts of the future caromed like out-of-control rockets in her brain. The dreams had started when she was young, in junior high. They were different then, brought on by nights of kissing, warm hands, and passionate words whispered as if the world were about to end. After each date, she'd stay up imagining her future: some dashing, wealthy man would burst into her life, sweep her off her feet, and carry her away to a remote tropical island that he just happened to own.

When she entered high school, the picture changed quickly. It became glaringly obvious that the boys were all the same. Some were funny, some handsome, some strong, but all only human, with less brains than she, less determination and drive, and certainly less ability to sweep her off her feet than she'd have to sweep them off theirs. She kept trying to find someone special, someone good enough to match her fantasies, but not one boy came even close to meeting the standards she set for herself. With that realization, the idea of a man having control over her life lost its appeal. She could think better than any of them, work better than any of them, tell jokes and dream and plan her future better than all of them combined.

So the dream and late-night thoughts changed their focus, first to a broad image of success and money, then she narrowed them down to the field she'd always loved. Business. It fascinated her. Numbers, calculations, making money with money, stocks, bonds, and power.

She had one image that she loved in particular. She was dressed in a black business suit, her hair pulled back so tight, it stretched her brain muscles. She was standing in her office, the penthouse suite overlooking the bay. A few modern paintings adorned the walls, a gold paperweight held down the summary of the latest corporate takeover she'd pulled off—the coup of the business world. She was looking over her kingdom, San Francisco at her beck and call, knowing full well that she'd made it. President of a major financial corporation, her name mentioned often in all the right circles. She was both respected and feared. Her expertise had helped shape the world's economy.

Alex smiled and smoothed down her skirt. Damn right she was determined to make a difference. She was going to make the biggest damn difference this school had ever seen.

"As a matter of fact, Mr. Thornby," she said at last, her nerves calm, her palms dry, "I believe I am exactly the type of student Berkeley is looking for."

She stood and poured herself a cup of coffee. Returning to her chair, she sat down and looked the dean in the eye.

"Business is not simply a curriculum to study or a way to make a living," she said. "At least, not to me. To me, business is the wave of the future. America needs a bedrock of good financial planning to stand on. Sure, we're the world leader now, but who knows what the future holds? Japan, with its teamwork and dedication, is closing in fast. Western Europe has always been a major economic competitor. We need to move now to stay ahead. Take advantage of our technology, our resources, and our greatest asset, our minds."

She sipped the coffee and felt her words pulsing against her chest, aching to get out. Mr. Thornby, his office, the beautiful grounds of Berkeley just beyond his window disappeared, and she was alone with her dreams.

"The way I see it, the leaders of the economy shape this country in every possible way. They rule all of our lives without our even knowing it. Think about it. They dictate how high inflation can go without hiking interest rates and thereby determine how comfortably we live. They control, to some extent, the supply of goods, lowering or raising the demand and, with it, prices. They decide who can afford a home, how much service prices can rise, how long recessions last without their interfering, cost of living raises, and how much a company is worth. The power they wield is unbelievable and still relatively unknown. I want to be part of that. I'm intelligent and driven and willing to give everything I have to this school and then to my career."

Alex came back to herself, to the room, to the dean sitting still, watching her. She set her coffee cup down and folded her hands in her lap. Quietly, but still with the intensity burning inside her, she said, "Mr. Thornby, I will be the biggest asset to the business department that Berkeley has ever known."

Wendell Thornby leaned back in his chair, and Alex thought she saw him smile.

"You've inherited your father's vitality, I see. Tell me more, Alexandra." And for an hour and a half, Alex did.

• • •

Megan had perfected a way of turning her head to the side just enough so that Alex and Clementine still thought she was listening, but couldn't see her eyes. It took the pressure off. That way, she didn't have to keep her eyes bright and excited, the way theirs were, and she was free to watch the other students pass by on their way to the cafeteria or their next class.

With the hum of her friends' voices beside her, high-pitched and jittery as when girls were talking about a boy who had just winked at them, Megan let her mind wander. It never wandered far. Their senior year was almost over, only four months left, and Alex and Clementine were wishing every last second of it away. Alex had been accepted to Berkeley. She got the acceptance letter two weeks after her interview. Clementine had plans for a full-time modeling career now that she was doing so well with her contract at Saks Fifth Avenue. She might even sign with an agency back east. With plans like that, what did they need the rest of piddling old high school for?

Well, Megan needed high school. Her tenth-grade year had been swallowed whole by Tony. Then there was eleventh grade, passed in an unfeeling, unthinking blur. Now she was a senior, finally alive again and ready to enjoy what were supposed to be the best years of her life.

And her two best friends were doing everything they could think of to rush the days past her.

All they ever talked about was college and careers and what life would be like ten years down the line. But what about now, she wanted to ask, right this second? What about dances and proms and football games and year-books? Alex had had her fill of dates. She didn't even bother anymore. Who needed boyfriends, she said when-ever Megan broached the subject. She was devoting every ounce of her energy to preparing for college and con- quering the business world. And Clementine, the model of the future who had vowed to change the world, was the talk of the town. She'd done a few local catalogues and runway shows already. That left her, Megan, the one who just wanted a normal, happy life. Simple pleasures—a home, husband, family, camping on sum- mer vacations with the kids. Was that too much to ask? Wasn't it her turn now?

Of course, they had no idea she felt this way, and she insisted on keeping her feelings to herself. If Alex be- lieved that life had passed her by, the way it had with Megan, she'd stop it cold, change course, and squeeze every second of pleasure out of it. And Clementine . . . Well, Megan couldn't imagine Clementine's ever wanting to savor things like prom corsages and dating—too juve- nile, she'd say—but if she did, she'd be as up front about it as Alex, letting nothing stand in her way.

Megan rested her chin on her hand and sighed. She watched a few sophomores walk by. You could always tell the sophomores from the seniors just by the way they walked. The seniors dangled their torn textbooks at their sides, papers stuffed into their folders haphazardly, and strode like royalty through their kingdom. The sopho- mores, new and still scared, painfully aware of their infe- rior status, clutched their notebooks to their chests, followed out-of-the-way paths to avoid getting in anyone's way, and had looks on their faces that seemed to be beg- ging for them to be allowed to return to something more familiar, easier.

Megan tuned back in to hear Clementine say, "I sent my photos to Eileen Ford, John Roberts, and a smaller agency, Smiles International. That was a week ago. Don't you think I should have heard something by now?"

Alex bit into her candy bar. "I doubt it, Clem. It might not even have gotten there yet. You know the mail. Getting all the way to New York could take a week."

"Yes, I guess so. God, it makes me nervous. What if they take one look at it and laugh? Maybe I'm not the right type. Maybe they want sunny blonds or exotic brunets. I'm right in the middle. Although I have noticed a few red and blond streaks in my hair. See? What if . . . ?"

Megan closed her eyes when the sharp pains, like boxer's fists, began their rhythmic beating above her eyes. Thump, thump, thump, thump. They'd come off and on for the last few months. Mostly on. She pressed her fingertips to her temples and massaged her forehead.

Hearing the self-confidence drip out of Clementine's voice was the most ridiculous thing in the world to Megan. Of course she'd be accepted. Any modeling agency would be out of its head not to sign her. She was the hit of San Francisco. She'd been in every one of Saks Fifth Avenue's fashion shows. She'd worked for a few other major department stores and local fashion designers. Her determination and ambition were legendary in the local modeling circles.

And Alex was the hit of Berkeley before she even started there. She'd already been approached by five sororities, and every day, she got some new pamphlet about a club that wanted her to join.

"Megan, did you hear me?"

She dropped her hands from her face and turned back to her friends. "What?"

Clementine laughed. "I said, do you think you'll live on campus at San Francisco State or make the horrible commute? I really think you should live in the dorms. As a sociology major, you won't meet any interesting men. Really, Meg, social work is just not the field to go into, moneywise or manwise. I read an article that said there's only about three men for every thirty women in social science classes. You'll need to take some hard science classes if you want to get lucky."

"Hey," Alex said, "maybe your parents would spring

for an apartment. That would help. You could have parties and dances. Stay up till dawn."

Megan smiled weakly. "I don't know. I'll probably stay
home. It's easier that way."

"Don't you want to meet people?" Alex asked. "I'm
definitely going to live in the dorms, at least for my first
year. They're coed, different floors for different sexes, I
think. I'll get used to the school quicker that way. I think
it would be great for you."

Alex and Clementine began discussing a number of alternatives that would be great for Megan, like the best
classes to take, clubs to join, sororities to try out for, and
so on. Megan turned her head to the side again, ignoring the pains in her head that beat in rhythm to her
friends' voices, and watched a sophomore make a mad
dash for a clear path unpeopled by seniors.

* * * *

He'd been watching her for ten minutes. Clementine
was sure of it. She'd felt his hooded gaze on her the moment she stepped into the tree-shrouded senior quad.
She chanced a quick look in his direction. Sure enough,
his eyes were glued to her. He was standing only twenty
feet away, leaning against the brick wall of the auditorium. His blue jeans were ripped at the knees, but his
T-shirt was angel white. It showed off the solid muscles in
his upper arms nicely.

Clementine had never seen him before. She would
have noticed. He looked like Duke, her father. What she
remembered of him, anyway. Strong, set apart from the
crowd, breathtakingly handsome. Her father had darker
hair and lighter eyes, but the stature was the same. Relaxed yet on guard. Contemptuous yet amused. And
reeking of sexuality, like a cat in heat. A tingle traveled
down her spine, and she tore her gaze away.

She searched the courtyard for Alex and Megan.
Where were they when she needed them? She didn't
want to stand there looking like an idiot, waiting for
friends who never showed up. They were supposed to
meet her for lunch, weren't they? Or was today their
yearbook staff meeting? Why was she so confused? Why

didn't he look away? Could he be feeling the same sensations she was? Of course not. But maybe . . .

She shifted her weight from foot to foot, feeling more awkward and heavy in her tennis shoes than she ever did in four-inch heels. For years, she'd fine-tuned her posture and elegant look down to the exact tilt of her head, and now she couldn't even figure out where to put her hands. They looked so silly just hanging at her sides. He was probably laughing at her. If only Alex and Megan would show up. If only . . .

"Hi."

He was beside her now. She hadn't even seen him move. He was just there, at her side. His arms were stronger than they'd seemed at a distance. The muscles strained against the short sleeves of his shirt. His eyes were brown, with long lashes that softened the hooded lids. His hair was even lighter close up, with streaks of white through the yellow, the strands straight as a board. He smelled clean, like soap. God, he was handsome.

"Hi," she said. He just smiled then, staring at her with curiosity, as if she were a modern painting he had yet to figure out. Clementine pressed down her urge to squirm.

"I'm Connor Douglas," he said at last.

"Clementine Montgomery."

"Clementine." He rolled the syllables off his tongue, like a beautiful French word spoken for the first time, and she shivered. "That's unusual. But pretty."

Clementine was at a complete loss. She thought of the things you said to people you just met, comments on the weather, where they live, who they know, but none seemed appropriate. She didn't know what he wanted from her or how she should act. For once in her life, she wasn't in control.

"Thanks. I like it," she said finally.

He threw back his head and laughed. Clementine jerked away at the sound. What was so funny? What had she said? How could she get the hell out of there and wrest her hormones back under control?

"Look," she said, "I'm meeting friends. I have to . . ."

"Hey, I'm sorry." Slowly, he controlled his laughter, although little chuckles escaped now and then. His eyes twinkled when he talked. "I don't know what my problem is. I was just watching you, and somehow, I knew you were different. And, well, I was right. You're special, Clementine Montgomery. And I guess that just makes me happy."

She stopped squirming and chanced another direct look at him. He wasn't laughing anymore, but his eyes still held a hint of amusement. She wondered if he was making fun of her.

"I really do have to go now."

"Okay. Okay. But how about dinner tonight? I'm new here. My mom and I just moved down from Oregon. I thought maybe you could show me around."

"I'd like that." It was out of her mouth before she could stop it. Why would she like that? Dating was still not included in her master plan. She was devoting every extra moment to modeling. She didn't have time for this.

"Great. How about seven?"

"All right." She wrote down her address and handed it to him.

"See you then." He chuckled as he walked away, shaking his head. What was so damn funny? she wondered. She turned and headed for her next class, forgetting about Alex and Megan. She thought of the appointment with a local fashion designer she'd have to cancel that night and the homework she'd have to make up in the morning, all the while hardly noticing that she was smiling.

• • •

"My old man left when I was two," Connor said. The right side of his face was cast in shadows. Only the single candle on the table illuminated the other side. He had on a tweed jacket over a white cotton shirt and a new pair of jeans. Clementine had learned quickly that evening that if she wanted to concentrate on what he was saying, she couldn't look directly at him. With his gaze on hers, his face and body only three feet away, his words fell on deaf ears, and only her body responded. Much too violently for Clementine's taste.

"I'm sorry," she said.

"Don't be. He wasn't exactly prime father material, if you know what I mean."

She glanced around the small Italian restaurant. She hadn't noticed there were so many people there. She hadn't noticed much of anything since they'd arrived two hours earlier. "Yes, I know what you mean."

Two scarcely touched plates of lasagna sat before them. Clementine had no desire to eat. All she really wanted was to listen to Connor's deep voice forever. It sounded so familiar and comforting, as if she'd heard it before, in the good parts of her childhood. He had the type of voice that made you stop and listen. And smile.

"I kind of took care of things after that," he went on. "My mom tried, but she just didn't have the energy, I guess. I started working when I was thirteen. Paper routes, gofer for an ad agency, that kind of thing. My mom was too busy with her boyfriends to make money. That's why we came here. She followed one of the losers down here, but of course, he didn't last long. That's the usual story. Sometimes, a few of them stay for a while and help out, but usually, they just screw her and then hit the road."

Clementine stiffened, and he brushed his fingers over her hand. She felt his touch in her very bones. "Hey, I'm sorry. I shouldn't use that kind of language around a lady."

She relaxed and took a bite of her meal. "It's okay. I use it myself occasionally."

They were quiet for a while, listening to the conversations of the other patrons, the laughter and business deals, a couple fighting loudly in the corner and warning each other to keep their voices down.

"I've never seen anyone as pretty as you," Connor said suddenly.

Clementine picked up her water and drank it quickly, surprised by the pleasure his words gave her.

"I'm nothing special."

"Come on. You are, and you know it. That's what I noticed about you first off. You didn't look like the type to play games. I can't stand all that flirting bullshit. If you feel something, say it. Want something, get it."

She looked at him and smiled. "Okay, I'm special. In fact, I'm special enough to make it to the top. I'll put in a few more months here, then I'm going to find an agent and soar straight to the top of the modeling world. And from there, who knows?"

"Now that's what I want to hear." He raised his glass, his eyes sparkling iridescent behind it. "To honesty. And to a hell of a lot of success. For both of us."

She clinked her glass against his and gulped at the water. She wanted to leave, to run away from him. To stop this now, when she was still Clementine, with one goal, one thought. Yet he kept her there, chained her to him with his energy, with the life he brought to a new, untried part of her.

"So, tell me," she said, trying to hide behind conversation, "what are your plans now? After high school, I mean."

He sat up straight, and his whole expression changed. The seduction was forgotten. His eyes widened, and his hands kept rhythm with his words.

"Well, I told you earlier I want to be an actor. I'm auditioning tomorrow for the part of Tony in *West Side Story* at the BackDoor in Frisco. I've already auditioned twice, and they keep calling me back. I think I've got it."

"That's wonderful, Connor."

"Yeah. It'll be my first major role. I've been an extra a dozen times and a walk-on, and an understudy more times than I can count. I really need this break. And from there, maybe I'll make my way to L.A. or New York. Broadway would be great, but to tell you the truth, Hollywood is my goal. I want the lights and the fans and the big screen with my face on it."

He looked around the room before focusing on her again. "I've never had anybody, you know," he said, more quietly. "I mean, my mom, sure. But she's more interested in getting laid than in a teenage son. So if I make it, I'll kind of have the whole world, won't I?"

Clementine nodded. She wouldn't have thought it possible that two people, unknown to each other for so long, could grow up with the exact same goal. Determi-

nation filled Connor so completely, she could actually
see it inside of him, consuming him.

"Before you know it, little lady, I'm gonna be a star."

She reached for his hand and grasped it tight. "I know
exactly how you feel."

Their hands burned from the contact. Without thinking, she looked straight into Connor's eyes. She was lost
instantly, swallowed by his power. His pupils were dilated,
without a hint of amusement lingering in them. He paid
the bill and stood up. Taking her hand again, he walked
her quickly to the car.

* * *

Before that moment, Clementine would never have
believed that she'd be where she was, getting ready to do
what she knew she and Connor were going to do. She'd
known him for less than twelve hours. Yet it felt like a
lifetime, as if he knew every part of her, every feeling, every thought, every aspiration that burned inside her.

The hotel was run on a pay-by-the-hour basis, and as
most everyone else did, they signed in as Mr. and Mrs.
Smith. She'd heard of people who did this sort of thing
and had always thought them cheap, out for a quick
thrill. But perhaps, just perhaps, all of the other Mr. and
Mrs. Smiths were like her and Connor; too young to have
a place of their own, yet so completely caught up in each
other, needing so badly to be together, it was like they'd
lose a part of themselves if they didn't stretch out skin to
skin, muscle to curve.

The room was on the second floor, directly behind the
neon Sixth Street Hotel sign, which blinked through the
curtains onto the bed. The carpet was orange, with
brown spots here and there. The bedspread, too, was orange and brown and stained, and the television knobs
were pulled off, as if no channel was good enough to
watch.

Connor closed the door and walked past her to the
bed. He sat down and took off his shoes. After removing
his socks, he looked up at her. She was frozen in the
doorway.

"We don't have to do this," he said. "I'll wait for you."

Tears filled her eyes. She was excited and terrified,

sure and uncertain. She'd been staring at the carpet so that she couldn't see Connor even peripherally, but now she looked at him. His eyes were soft, undemanding but hungry. She'd always thought of her beauty as a vehicle to fame, nothing more; yet knowing that he wanted her made her *feel*, for the first time, beautiful. His magnetic gaze steadied her, gave her strength. He held out his hand, and she walked to the bed and grasped it, sitting beside him.

"You may not believe this," she said, "but I've never been with anyone before."

He stood up and walked to the window. Beyond the neon sign was the busy parking lot, with couples arriving, leaving, winking at each other in comradeship.

"Of course I believe you," he said, his back to her. "I know you, Clementine. You act strong and proud and knowledgeable about everything, but inside you're as scared as the next guy."

She gripped her hands together in her lap and stared at her nails, perfectly shaped and polished, as always. How could he know so much? How could it be that there was one person so perfectly suited to her? It was like the fairy-tale fantasies Megan was always talking about, and yet this one was coming true.

"Do you want to be with me?" he asked, still not turning around. His voice had quivered slightly, the only chink in his coat of steel armor, and suddenly she knew. She needed him. Probably more than anything else in her life, she needed Connor now. She walked up behind him and laid her cheek against his back.

"I want you, Connor."

He turned around quickly and pulled her against him. They were both shaking and held on tightly, as if any weakness in their grips might break them apart forever. Keeping his arm firmly around her, he led her to the bed. They sat down, blinking red in neon reflections, and he lifted her chin with his fingertip.

"Would you think it was crazy if I said I thought I loved you?" he whispered.

She kissed his lips softly, their first kiss, like a butterfly brushing its wings across a flower, testing for pollen, and finding it full, sweet smelling, and delicious. She felt the defenses she'd built up around her, the facade of strength and fearlessness, shed like unwanted skin. With Connor she could simply be Clementine, nothing more, nothing less.

"I'd think it was crazy," she answered, "if you said you didn't."

They kissed again, and Connor's fingertips slid down her throat to her breast. He easily slid her loose-fitting sweater off her shoulders and pressed his hand against her firmly. She sighed in pleasure and pulled him back on the bed with her. She had never been so sure of anything in all her life.

• • •

During Connor's audition, Clementine waited with his mother in the shabby two-room house they rented on the east side of Sausalito. She was supposed to meet with the Saks fashion show consultant that afternoon about the fall premiere, but she'd been too nervous to concentrate and had postponed the appointment until the following morning.

Clementine was still amazed that it had been only one day since she'd met Connor. It seemed like years, lifetimes. She was sure she knew everything about him. His dreams were her dreams. His body had conformed to hers so perfectly, she hadn't known where she ended and he began. He'd gone slow, attending to one part of her body at a time, touching her lightly, kissing, sucking, until she'd thought she would burst with pleasure. Finally, when he'd pushed his way inside her, filling her, clinging to her, his eyes closed, his lips by her ear, whispering her name, she'd felt complete. They'd wasted so much time in the years before they met.

He'd been at the audition for three hours now. What on earth was taking so long? Either they liked him or they didn't. But of course they liked him. How could they not? He was handsome. He could sing. He'd proven that in the car on the way home the night before when he belted out "Maria." What more did they want?

She glanced over at Mrs. Douglas, totally absorbed in the latest issue of *Cosmopolitan*. Clementine had shown up on her doorstep, introduced herself as the girl Connor was out with until two o'clock in the morning the night before, and stuck out her hand. Mrs. Douglas had shaken it for two seconds, muttered a greeting, and returned to the couch and her magazine. She'd sat there ever since, getting up only twice for beers. She hadn't offered Clementine anything to drink, and Clementine hadn't asked. She'd wanted to make a good impression, but there didn't seem to be anyone home in Mrs. Douglas's brain to make an impression on. So she'd taken out a positive thinking book from her purse and read for three hours, not even bothering with small talk. If Connor's mother didn't need it, neither did she.

She couldn't resist surreptitiously studying Mrs. Douglas, and marveled at the powers of nature that produced a perfect child from such an imperfect mother. The body must have some kind of gene sifter, she thought, letting the good stuff in and keeping the bad out. Connor looked nothing like his mother. She was flabby, he was all muscle. His hair was golden, hers was dirty brown. Her face was wide, unimpressive, Connor's was angular and pronounced. The only explanation was that Connor's father was gorgeous and, as with Clementine, had contributed the dominant appearance genes. Thank God.

Connor burst through the door fifteen minutes later. He was breathing heavily and his eyes were red. She stood and waited for him to speak, and waited and waited.

Finally, he said, "I didn't know you were going to be here."

"I wanted to know what happened."

Connor turned toward his mother, now peeking over the top of her magazine.

"Yes. How did it go?" she asked. Her voice was gritty, as if she'd washed the words down with sand.

He looked up at the ceiling, then walked to Clementine's side. He grasped her hand.

"It might take me a little longer than I had planned to get to Hollywood." His voice cracked, and although he was acting tough and untouched, she caught the moisture in his eyes. "Will you wait?" he asked.

She wrapped her arms around his neck. She heard the slap of his mother's magazine as she dropped it on the couch, then the rapping of her footsteps as she disappeared down the hall.

"Yes, Connor. I'll wait."

# CHAPTER 6

$M$EGAN TWIRLED IN FRONT OF THE FULL-length dressing room mirror, filled with delight. The dress was perfect. White-and-pink striped chiffon, a sweetheart neckline, and five layers of ruffles layered from her knees to her toes like marble steps.

"Alex, come look."

Alex stepped into the tiny mirrored room and smiled.

"Finally," she said. "And it only took twelve stores and twenty dresses to find the right one."

"Actually, that's pretty quick for me."

"Well, I just wish I had one of your parents' no-limit credit cards. I don't know how you stop yourself from charging the whole mall and taking it home gift-wrapped."

Megan laughed and twisted from side to side, looking at herself from every angle. Now, this was what life was supposed to be like. If Alex wanted to make a complete turnabout and snub every boy who asked her to the prom, then let her. Listening to her these days was like going to a dull foreign opera, where not a word was understandable and the scenes went on and on, aria after aria, while the audience wilted in the hot, stuffy air of the auditorium. Nothing but details about college, bear markets and inflation indexes came out of Alex's mouth anymore, and it took every ounce of Megan's willpower not to forcibly make her shut up.

And if Clementine wanted to wish the world away while she and Connor made lovebird eyes at each other and talked nauseating baby talk, well then, that was her problem. Megan was going to have fun. She was going to the prom with Billy Weinstein, no matter what Alex and Clementine said about him. For once, she was going to be firm. Besides, Billy had matured since she first met him in tenth grade. He'd traded in the tortoiseshell glasses for contact lenses, and his broomstick body was filling out. He'd always be tall and lanky, but at least she didn't feel like she was holding hands with a skeleton.

The most important reason for going to the prom with Billy, though, was that she'd be comfortable. He was like an old rug, worn thin but with a familiar moldy scent and immovable stains. With Billy, Megan knew she was safe. Safe from harm, from hateful words, from the fluttering of her heart that stole her resolve, her will, her confidence. Every time she saw a dark head of unruly hair or someone with eyes that were nearly black, she realized that safe was the only emotion she ever wanted to feel again.

Alex treated the prom like it was a carbon monoxide poisoning contest. Oh, she humored Megan by going dress shopping with her and coached her on dance techniques, but she refused to take any part in it herself. She didn't see it the way Megan did, as a symbol and celebration of their passage into adulthood. Megan told Alex the prom was a once-in-a-lifetime opportunity, an experience she could tell her kids about. Billy was renting a limousine to take them to the Fairmont Hotel, where they'd eat and dance and laugh and stay up all night long. It was the only night Mr. and Mrs. Sanders would allow their daughter that privilege.

Megan stopped gazing at herself and turned to Alex.

"Are you sure you won't change your mind and come? You know you could go with anyone you want. The guys at school don't know which end is up since you stopped dating. Besides, it won't be the same without you."

Alex sat down on the dressing room stool. An errant kink of hair had sprung loose from her tight bun, drooping over her left eye and spoiling the whole look. She pressed it hard behind her ear.

"I don't think so, Meg. I know how much the prom means to you, and that's fine. And, of course, Clementine is just using it as an excuse to stay out all night with Connor. But for me, it seems pointless. All I want is to get out of school and get on with my life. Time won't move fast enough. I want to be at college already, with students who are at school because they want to be, not because they have to be. I don't want to spend my time with a bunch of overdressed kiddies playing adult games. I want the real thing."

She unzipped the back of Megan's dress.

"But it only comes once in a lifetime, you know. And . . ."

"I know, I know," Alex said. "It's your final farewell to high school, a chance to dance and have fun and look like adults for a night, blah, blah, blah. Joey has been on my case for weeks about it."

"Joey?" Megan's body jerked, as if electricity were racing through it, jingling, sparking, setting things in motion.

"Yeah. Little brother know-it-all. Fourteen years old, and he's got it all figured out. The truth is that he's going steady with Stacy Melhoff, and he thinks the world is full of romance. He won't rest until everyone is as in love as he is."

Megan breathed in quickly and cursed the pain in her chest. It was silly. Yet there it was, an aching sense of betrayal filling her lungs, sucking out the air.

"How long has that been going on?"

"What? Oh, Joey and Stacy? I don't know, a couple weeks, I guess. It's pretty funny. Joey is so conservative, you know? He's so—so old. He's got that wise look around the eyes that drives me crazy, as if he has the answers to everything. God only knows where he gets that from. Anyway, he hardly ever touches the poor girl, and when he does, he looks like he's going to die from embarrassment. Mom and Dad and I give them every chance to be alone, but that only seems to make it worse."

Megan suddenly felt sorry for Joey, so out of place, pushed and prodded, like a starfish in a tide pool at the children's zoo. She could imagine him sitting beside Stacy What's-Her-Name, trying to be a gentleman, trying to do things the right way, while his parents and Alex—with "patience" not a word in their vocabulary—stuck their heads around the corner, urging him on.

Megan slipped back into her jeans and sweater. Living in that house with Alex and her one-of-a-kind parents must be similar to being best friends with Alex and Clementine. Everything you did was overshadowed. Everything you found comforting, they dismissed as dull. For every step you took, they took twenty larger ones. Trapped in the shadow of a star.

* * *

John's car was in the driveway when Clementine reached the top of the hill. Dammit, she thought. She liked being alone when she got the mail, just in case there was a response from one of the agencies. Of all the people she'd want around to watch her reaction, John hit the solid bottom of the list.

It had been two months since she'd sent in her photos. Eileen Ford had asked to see more. That had been three weeks ago. Since then, nothing. John Roberts and Smiles International had yet to reply. But today might be different. Today might change her life.

Hoping against hope that John had forgotten about the mail, she walked to the mailbox and opened it. It was empty, and she slammed it shut. Frowning with frustration, she stared at the gloomy house. She'd just have to make do. If there was a reply, she'd be cool and calm. Simply pick up the letter, take it to her room, and open it slowly. Later, if she felt like it, she could tell John what it said. He'd probably jump for joy if it meant she'd move to New York. Then he'd have Angel, his own personal obedient puppy, totally to himself to wait on him twenty-four hours a day.

Clementine walked in the front door and headed for the kitchen. Wearing a gray suit, John was seated at the table, his back to her, his silvery hair gelled to slimy perfection as always. She held back the usual urge to claw her fingers through it and rub the goo all over his face.

"Hello, John. I didn't know you'd be home this afternoon."

He glanced at her and gave her a weak impression of a smile. He made a better effort at it when Angel was around, but when it was just he and Clementine, he rarely bothered. "It was slow at the office, and I thought I'd surprise your mother. Unfortunately, it looks like she's done the surprising. Do you know where she is?"

"Probably at the grocery store," Clementine said, opening up the refrigerator and taking out a soda. "She goes every afternoon, you know."

"Really? I didn't know that."

Clementine gritted her teeth. Of course he didn't know that. He didn't know about anything except his stupid law practice and golf Tuesday mornings and how to make a vodka martini. He didn't know diddley squat about Angel or her life or how much she did for him every day. And he certainly didn't know anything about Clementine. She intended to keep it that way.

"Did you get the mail?" she asked nonchalantly, running her fingertip along the rim of the soda bottle.

"Oh, that reminds me." He turned around and picked up an opened envelope. "This came from the John Roberts Agency. I'm sorry. It seems that they're looking for a different type right now. They were actually quite polite and—"

"You opened my mail?"

"Well, I knew how much you'd been looking forward to this, and I thought you'd want to know right away."

She slammed the bottle down on the counter. It was amazing how fast her body adapted. One minute it was subdued, attempting to be cavalier, then, *POW*, her blood sped through her veins like floodwaters, turning on all the fuses, tingling nerve endings, making her hands yearn to slap and claw. She marched to the table and yanked the envelope out of his hand.

"How dare you invade my privacy like that? You—you

double-crossing swine. Don't you have any scruples at all? This is my mail, dammit. My life. You had no right."

"Now just hold on one minute, Clementine. I have every right to know what's going on in your life. I own this house. I keep clothes on your back and food on the table. As a matter of fact, I'm the one who paid most of the bills for that contest you entered. And I've been paying for the photo sessions you've had since then."

She felt the bile rising from her stomach into her throat. Her face was burning hot, and a loud thunder roared in her ears.

"You have no right to anything in my life," she said. "Just who do you think you are?"

He stood up. At six feet and four inches, he rose a head above her. Her nostrils flared at the noxious smell of his cologne, so putrid, so unlike her father's.

"I'm your stepfather, that's who I am. I'm here every day. I take care of you as if you were my own. That's a lot more than I can say for your real father. Duke won't even let you know where he is, that's how much he cares. In fact, I'd bet my life that he doesn't give a damn whether you live or die."

Clementine was too angry to be hurt. She stomped from foot to foot, knowing she couldn't hurt him physically. He was twice as strong as she, and he wouldn't think twice about hitting her if she came after him with her fists.

"I hate you," she spat, swallowing the saliva she longed to spit in his face. "I've always hated you. My mother is a thousand times too good for you."

She whirled around and walked to the staircase. She put one foot on the step, then faced him again. "I'll be upstairs packing my things. I'll be out of *your* house tonight."

She took the stairs two at a time. Once inside her bedroom, she slammed the door. The heavy silence of the room pushed the thunder from her ears. All that was left inside her was a high-pitched whistle and a consuming dread. She leaned back against the door and uncrumpled the letter in her hand.

Dear Ms. Montgomery:

We appreciate the opportunity to look at your work. However, at this time we are looking for a somewhat different type. More exotic, darker, more sultry. Had you come along a year or two ago, you would have been perfect. But as it stands now, we are already representing more than enough fair-skinned blondes. Best of luck to you elsewhere.

Sincerely,
John Roberts

She tried to pull her back up straight, but it was no use. She slid to the floor, pulled her knees to her chest, and cried. Like the wails of an abandoned baby who's cold and frightened, Clementine's cries, as rare as June snowfalls, sent a haunting chill up the spine of anyone who was listening, even her stepfather.

•   •   •

Clementine packed only the clothes she had owned before she began modeling. She hadn't realized how much of John's money she'd spent since putting her career into full swing. Leaving the wardrobe behind was one of the hardest things she'd ever had to do. She ran her fingertips over the slippery satins and delicate lace trimmings, then quickly shut the closet door. She didn't want anything from him.

She had only one suitcase of her own, so she used two brown paper bags for her books, a few knickknacks, and the teddy bear Connor had won for her at a fair two weeks earlier. She looked around the room once more, her gaze skipping from the window to the white vanity she'd sat at thousands of times, to the fluffy double bed she longed to lie down on now. She shook only slightly when she put her hand on the doorknob and walked out.

"John, you can't do this. Please." Clementine stood rigid at the top of the stairs and listened to her mother's pleading voice rising from the kitchen. "She's my daughter. Where will she go?"

"How the hell should I know?" John shouted in his lawyer voice. He sounded indignant, outraged to be second-guessed. "Probably to that actor boyfriend of hers. Look, Angel, I didn't order her out. She wants to go. And besides, she'll be eighteen in a few weeks. Maybe she needs a little independence."

Clementine gripped the banister, waiting for her mother's angry denials, the demands that she stay, the aggressive maternal instinct to take hold. Instead, the house grew thick with whispers. Clementine picked up her suitcase and paper bags and descended the stairs. After depositing her things in a heap at the front door, she walked into the kitchen.

"I'll be leaving now." She thought when Angel saw her fearful eyes, she might find her strength and insist that Clementine stay. But Angel only shook her head and kept her hand firmly clasped in John's. She belonged to the man now. Long ago, she'd made the choice to hand her life over to John on a newly polished silver platter, and she'd stick to it. Daughter or no daughter.

"I'll be at Connor's if you need me. You know the number."

She turned and headed for the door. "Clemmie," her mother said. Clementine stiffened and waited.

"Be careful, dear."

She fought the wilting in her shoulders and stood straight. "I will, Mother." She picked up her things and walked out the door.

•   •   •

"I think you're making a big mistake."

"God, will you give it a rest already, Joey?" Alex plopped down in a wing-backed Art Deco chair and flipped through a magazine. "I told you, I'm not interested."

Joey shrugged and stood up from the couch. He moved one of the striped pillows to a new location, then to another, trying to make it look like it belonged, but eventually gave up in frustration. Whoever heard of mixing stripes and florals? As far as he was concerned, everything in the house belonged somewhere else—the pillows, the furniture, him. He walked to the piano and sat down.

Alex jerked her head back in distaste when his fingers

hit the keys, loud and strong, pounding out the tortuous classical music she'd never understand or appreciate. The melody sounded vaguely familiar, but that was no surprise. As far as she was concerned, every one of those stupid pieces sounded alike. They were all too loud, too monotonous, lacking a much needed drumbeat, and much, much too long.

"Oh, please, don't start."

Joey continued. It was his one area of dominance. He had realized the power he wielded over Alex after his first piano lesson five years earlier. A little classical music, and Alex would either be on her knees swearing she'd do anything for him if only he'd stop or be out of the house. Either way, Joey's life vastly improved.

He banged out the music, smiling at the feel of cool ivory beneath his fingers. More than any other composer, Beethoven transformed him. The notes were rich, powerful, burning with energy and strength. Through the electricity in his fingers, his mind expanded, his body strengthened, and he felt alive and at ease. He saw Alex out of the corner of his eye, her fingers drumming on the coffee table. Finally, she stood up.

"All right. All right. What do you want?"

He stopped playing and smiled at her. "I want you to go to the prom tonight."

"Why do you care? Go to your prom in four years if it makes you happy."

"Alex, I mean it." He walked over to her, put his arm around her waist, and led her to the couch. Alex cursed the fates for already making him taller than she. It wasn't fair. Taller people had more power. That was a documented fact. Some people even had the nerve to call her petite to her face and expect to live. Good God.

They sat down together, and Joey brushed a wisp of his blond hair out of his eye. "I don't want you to regret this," he said, looking at the wall behind her instead of straight at her. Nothing unusual, Alex thought. He reminded her of Megan that way. "You act like all you want to do is study and read and prepare for college, but I know there's more to you than that. Why are you trying so hard to pretend you don't need your friends or any part of all the things you used to love so much?"

She sat up straight. "Because I don't. I'm grown up now."

"Well, some day, you'll need them. Some day, you'll be old and gray and fat and alone with all the money you've made, and all your friends will be married and happy with dozens of grandkids running around."

"Grandkids, ugh." Alex turned away. He was wrong about her, of course. What did she need with marriage and picket fences? She would never be lonely. She was sure of it.

"I'm going to become Alexandra the Great," she said. "Cultivated, educated genius. Stop talking like an adult. I can't stand it. You're making everything more complicated than it is. I'm just maturing. What's wrong with that?"

"Nothing, if it makes you happy."

"Of course it does."

"Really?"

"Yes," she said, too quickly. She looked down and picked at a thin line of dirt beneath her thumbnail.

"Okay," she said, reconsidering. "So maybe I don't date anymore. But who needs that?" She closed her eyes and thought of the kisses and strong hands and husky words she'd given up for cold nights reading the stock tables. When she opened her eyes again, Joey was watching her.

"All right," she said. "Maybe I need that a little."

They both laughed, and Alex stood up. "Anyway, I can't go tonight. Who would take me?"

He stood, too, and bowed gracefully. "Joseph Holmes, dignified escort at your service."

She looked him up and down. "Well, I guess you look older than you are, almost eighteen probably, but ... Oh, Joey, this is impossible. I don't have a dress, and you don't have a tuxedo and ..."

"Alex, come on. Since when were you ever normal? You've got a million crazy, beautiful outfits in your closet. Put something together, and I'm sure you'll be the hit of the party. And I can wear that black suit I have. Maybe

it's not a tux, but I can snazz it up a little. Come on. I
want to go. And deep down inside, you do too."

She squinted at him. "If I didn't know better, I'd say
you're doing this more for yourself than for me. Are you
tired of Stacy already? Ready to meet some exciting,
older woman?"

He laughed. "Of course not. I just don't want you to
miss this."

She twirled her hair around her finger, considering.
Why not? She might have fun after all. She'd certainly
surprise Megan and Clementine by showing up. And Joey
was the perfect date. He was handsome and considerate,
and of course, she wouldn't have to worry about fending
off any unwanted advances. By God, she'd go.

"All right," she said. "Let's do it. I'll go up and dress.
If we hurry, we'll only miss an hour or so."

"Great. I'll tell Mom and Dad and meet you down
here in half an hour. Oh, and Alex," he said as she was
hurrying up the stairs.

"What?"

"Sorry, but you'll have to drive."

She laughed and ran to her room.

* * *

The candles cast dancing shadows on the wall. Over-
head, four huge chandeliers were shining dimly, like faraway stars blinking light from millions of years ago. The
banquet room was small, but Lincoln High had a small
graduating class. The one hundred students filled the
room nicely.

Megan leaned back in her chair, out of the candle
light, and blinked away her tears. Out of all the dresses
in the entire world to choose from, ten out of fifty girls
had picked the exact same one as she. She was beginning
to think she was jinxed. For once, she'd thought she
would stand out and be noticed, but instead she only
heard the tail end of giggles as she passed, and saw the
ugly stub of fingers as people pointed out her overused
attire.

Billy wasn't helping any. Yes, she'd gone with him because he was safe. That didn't have to mean dull and em-
barrassing. He'd danced with her once. Count it. Once.

In over twelve dances. They'd stepped onto the floor, he'd pulled her to him, and a minute later he was doubled over in pain. He'd twisted his ankle on a slow dance. "Send in the Clowns" even. Unbelievable. So now he was somewhere in the hotel getting it wrapped, she was the laughingstock of the prom, and all she had left to do was watch Clementine and Connor cling to each other through every song, fast or slow, as if the world were about to end.

Why couldn't Alex be there? Megan wondered. At least then, she could laugh a little. Alex would want to walk around the hotel, check out the rooms, ride up and down the elevator, do something other than sit there all alone with ten look-alike girls glaring at her as if it were her fault they'd all chosen the same stupid dress.

Megan shoved her chair back and stood up. Enough of this. If Alex wasn't there, she'd just have to take charge herself. There was no law against walking around the hotel alone. She held her head up and walked to the banquet exit.

She stopped abruptly when the most striking couple she'd ever seen strode through the door. The girl had her dark hair coiled up on her head. A turquoise silk scarf twisted through it, then floated down past her shoulders. Her gauzy skirt was slim and white, falling to her left ankle and rising to her right knee, while her oversize glittery black blouse was gathered at her hips by a wide belt. The blond princelike boy was dressed in a black suit with a silver sash tied around his waist. Together, they looked like royalty from the Middle East. Megan stepped aside to let them pass.

"Megan? Megan, aren't you listening to me?"

She looked straight at the girl for the first time. "Alex? Oh, my God, Alex. Is that you?"

Alex laughed and curtseyed. "Alex Holmes, at your service. And may I present my most handsome and dashing escort for this evening, Mr. Joseph Holmes."

Megan slowly shifted her gaze to Joey. She was so surprisingly happy to see him, she stepped back, embarrassed. Joey was laughing, bowing to her, and for just a moment she let herself believe she was living in a novel, back in time. She was attending a royal ball, and England's most dashing privateer was bowing before her, reaching for her hand, kissing her knuckles. Then Alex touched her arm, and the spell was broken.

"Where's Billy?" she asked.

Megan tore her gaze away from Joey's face. She'd been fascinated by the way the dimmed lights softened his already gentle face. He looked British. In a previous life, he must have been English nobility, she was sure of it. He belonged in a country estate in Berkshire County, with bloodhounds and horses and formal gardens. He'd wear a cape when he went riding, of course. And . . .

"Megan, aren't you listening to me? I asked where Billy was."

"Oh, sorry. The oaf twisted his ankle. He's getting it wrapped."

Alex's mouth hung open for a second. She tried to control herself, but the rumbling laughter in her stomach overtook her, and she threw her head back. Joey chuckled, too, although he tried to cover it up.

"Megan, I'm sorry," he said. But Megan, despite it all, was smiling too.

"Come on, kiddo," Alex said, putting her arm around her shoulders. "You've got me and Joey now. Let's go sit down."

Joey appeared at her other side and slid his arm around her waist. Through lowered lashes, Megan stared at his fingers pressed at her side, so long and well manicured and clean. When they reached the table, he held out her seat for her.

"I just want you to know," he whispered in her ear as she sat down, "that no matter how many girls are wearing your dress, you look better than all of them put together."

Megan smiled brightly. She hardly noticed when Billy came limping back to the table.

• • •

"Hold me tighter, Connor," Clementine whispered. They'd been out on the dance floor for five songs in a row, and no matter what the tempo, they stayed wrapped in each other's arms.

Connor squeezed her and buried his face in her hair. God, she smelled good. Not ordinary or store-bought, like roses or perfume, but with a scent all to herself, a mixture of the ocean, sunny spring days, and sex.

"Is that better?" he asked.

"Yes, much."

Some of the time, actually most of the time, Clementine wished she could stay wrapped in Connor's arms forever. It went against everything she'd ever believed in, everything she wanted to accomplish in her life, but she didn't care. She'd known when she'd left her mother's house that she could go to him, no questions asked. He was her harbor. He loved her without doubts. He wouldn't leave her. For the most part, that was enough.

Yet, of course, there was still the dream. It had dimmed a little when she first met Connor, but only temporarily. His newness, his touch, his kisses had made her forget about hot lights and magazine covers. Now that he was more familiar and human, with bad morning breath and immature pouts when she had to do a fashion show rather than be with him, her determination was back stronger than ever. She loved him. She wanted to be with him. He gave her the will to go on when she wavered. But Connor or no Connor, she was going to be a star.

Through the first few weeks of their relationship, she'd shared every thought, every goal with him. He'd shared all of his with her too. Lately though, she'd noticed a subtle change. Too much talk about *her* career, and he'd have to run an errand. Too many discussions on modeling agents and New York City night life, and he went to bed early. He could go on for hours and hours about *his* acting, hot prospects, the auditions he was working on, Hollywood, but change the topic to her, and the brightness in his eyes faded.

They'd come together so fast, like meteors crashing in space, that Clementine was only now getting a feel for him. He wanted to come first. He had to. His father had left him. His mother didn't care. It was time to be number one. At first, she'd thought it perfect that they shared the same history and needs. It was becoming clear to her, though, that trying to merge two people who both needed total attention and devotion and top billing was like riding a collision course with disaster.

She tried to understand him. She knew he hadn't been getting the breaks he wanted. He'd had a few more bit parts, even a couple of speaking roles, but never the lead, never the piece that would skyrocket him to Hollywood. And she was learning to live with rejection, as well. She hadn't heard from Eileen Ford or Smiles International. Connor propped her up when she was down; she was strong when Connor was weak. Of course, they'd both make it to the top eventually. Clementine just wondered who would do it first. And if it was she, would that leave any hope for them at all?

For now, at least, she had every night with him. After a few days of hashing out the details with Connor's mother, Beverly, Clementine had adjusted quite nicely to living with them. Beverly insisted they occupy separate bedrooms, which Clementine found amusing, considering the openness with which Beverly flung herself from one man's bed to another. But as long as Beverly went to sleep early enough to give them time together, the situation was manageable. Clementine just waited until the light went out under Beverly's door, then slipped under the covers with Connor. When she was lying next to him, goals and dreams, modeling and acting, drifted like dust out the window. All reality except his hands and lips and touch on her skin disappeared.

They had no definite plans for life after graduation. Connor would continue auditioning, and she would wait for responses from New York. Until then, they were together, and if they could only hold each other tight enough, everything else would work out.

•   •   •

"Would you like to dance?"

Megan had been waiting half the night for Joey to ask that question. He'd danced with Alex once, then had returned to the table, where he and Megan watched Alex steal the show, as usual. Once she'd decided to set her college plans aside for the night, she put her whole heart into having a good time. So much for the immature boys she wanted nothing to do with, Megan thought. Alex must have danced with twenty of them by now.

"Sure," she answered Joey.

He held out his hand. When she took it, he led her to the dance floor. His palm was warm and dry. Obviously, she thought, he didn't feel the same way she did. God, what was wrong with her? All night she had been fantasizing about this . . . this boy. She couldn't stop staring at him, thinking about what he'd look like walking beside her on the beach, when his lips met hers, when he was telling her she was the most beautiful woman he'd ever seen. He was only fourteen. He had a girlfriend. He was her best friend's little brother. She was crazy.

He smiled at her before putting his arm around her waist. Well, for fourteen, he was certainly tall enough, she thought. She came only to his chin. And even though he'd been quiet most of the night, with no one but Alex and her to talk to, he hadn't seemed out of place. He just sat in the shadows and watched. Megan had often tried to do that, look like she belonged even when she was alone, but instead, she figured she always ended up looking lost.

"Are you having a good time?" Joey asked.

"Oh, sure."

He leaned back and looked into her eyes. "It probably isn't what you expected it to be, is it?"

She smiled and glanced away. "No. That's always my problem. I fantasize about something so much, no matter how good it is, it can never live up to my expectations."

"Too many novels," he said.

She pulled away abruptly. "How do you know that?"

He laughed and pulled her back to him. "Don't get upset. It's just that the same thing happens to me. I read mystery novels and end up thinking life is fascinating and complicated, filled with eccentric characters and intrigue and excitement. Then I look around and feel sort of cheated and depressed when I realize that the world is filled with normal people, working normal jobs, going home to normal houses and apartments, period. They struggle every day just to make ends meet. Tell me when they have time for intrigue."

Megan laid her head against his shoulder and closed her eyes. "I read a lot of romance novels, and I end up thinking that men are gallant and handsome, and when they find the right woman, they'll do anything for her. But instead, my date sprains his ankle and sulks over his dessert for the rest of the evening. Some romance."

Joey chuckled. "I'm sure there's romance somewhere. Just like there's intrigue somewhere. We're just not in the right place to find it yet. But don't give up. Don't ever give up."

She lifted her head to him. "Have you found some of that excitement with Stacy? Alex tells me you're going steady now."

She could have been reciting the alphabet, her words were so smooth. Not even a quiver, she congratulated herself. And the music drowned out her erratic heartbeat.

Joey looked away. "I don't know. Stacy is nice. She's pretty and smart. I like her well enough, but we're not making any plans for marriage, if that's what you mean."

Megan smiled widely. Although she tried to hide it before he looked at her again, he saw the smile and laughed.

"Jeez, Meg, you don't have to look so happy about it."

She blushed and pressed her cheek against his chest. "I'm sorry. I didn't mean to." Still, pleasure surged through her, tingling her skin. She knew she shouldn't be this happy. It didn't mean anything. Nothing would ever happen between her and Joey. He would always be four years younger. He would only be in ninth grade next year when she started college. Still, she smiled.

Joey laughed again and held her close when the music stopped. They stayed together until the band picked up another song.

"You're something else, you know that, Megan Sanders?"

They danced for three songs straight, and with Joey's arms wrapped tightly around her, Megan believed that what he said was true.

# CHAPTER
## 7

$T$HE SUMMER AFTER HER HIGH SCHOOL
graduation, Clementine realized she was inherently different from other people. Time passed at a different rate
for her. What felt like two months to Alex and Megan
trudged past like two years for her. She couldn't appreciate anything in the moment, not the warm summer
nights or buttery popcorn or sunsets or a good, tearjerking movie. She was never there, in the present time,
experiencing it. Her mind was always far ahead, dreaming up star-studded fantasies and millionaire lovers. She
dedicated her every waking moment to her future and
didn't think twice about sacrificing the present.

That summer, she also noticed for the first time that
she wasn't really happy. Normal things didn't move her.
She couldn't care less about going to college or who won
the World Series or what she did on Saturday nights. All
that mattered was what happened to her next year, and
the year after that. That summer, she realized she was
getting older. Age and passing time and mounting disappointments made her think about things that never had
occurred to her before. Time was making her more introspective, something she didn't necessarily want to be.

She sent her pictures and résumés out everywhere. No

longer was she too proud to go beyond the big agencies; she just wanted someone, anyone to notice her. She was old news in San Francisco. Saks had had another young model contest, and the new winner had the lion's share of contracts. Clementine could still get a department store fashion show, but who couldn't? She hardly felt special at all anymore.

Days passed like weeks, and weeks like months. No one said anything directly, but she knew her friends and family doubted her now. She had risked everything when she'd touted that she was going to become a star, change the world. She had bet the house on herself and lost. No one wanted her.

Eileen Ford had finally gotten back to her with a polite but nonetheless devastating rejection. After three days of sulking in bed, Clementine had gone down the list of agencies, sent her work out to the next in line, got it back, cried, retreated once more to bed, then somehow found one more spark of hope in her heart to begin again.

Connor, too, was facing rejections. They were a pair, she often thought, clinging to each other at night, neither of them hopeful enough to say everything would be all right. And one day Clementine said to herself, for the first time, *I may never make it.* The words chilled her, haunted her. What would she be then, if not a model? She didn't have Alex's brains or Megan's warmth. She had nothing except her looks.

Her mail still came to her mother's house, and she went over every afternoon to check it. She didn't know why she did it, acted like a masochist every day, tearing open letters that told her she wasn't good enough. One afternoon in August, she picked up the stack on the counter and saw an envelope from the Walter Budges Agency in Philadelphia. She had even stooped to going out of New York State for an agent. She opened it up, not even an ounce of hope left. The words were no surprise; they hardly even stung anymore.

Dear Miss Montgomery:
    We regret to inform you . . .

She shoved the letter into the disposal and turned it on without bothering to read the rest. The sound was horrible, grinding without the water on, and it masked the sound of the phone. It was already on the fifth ring when Clementine turned off the disposal and answered it.

"This is Arthur Dennison from Smiles International," a man said. "Is Clementine Montgomery there?"

At first, she thought it was a joke. She almost said something, but then the last shred of hope kicked in, and she gripped the receiver until her knuckles glowed white. Small bonfires burned in her head and stomach. Thank God, her mother was out doing her usual marketing, instead of staring at her the way she always did when Clementine had a call, as if privacy was not a word meant for daughters.

She shifted from foot to foot, afraid to speak, afraid to break this moment when dreams still lived, when anything could happen. She knew he was waiting, but she twirled the phone cord around her finger and then wrapped it around her mother's recipe books three times before speaking. She had a painful urge to go to the bathroom.

"This is Clementine Montgomery," she said.

"I'm glad I finally reached you. First of all, I'd like to apologize for the amount of time it's taken me to get back to you. We've been reorganizing, changing staff, and I'm afraid most of the work sent to us by aspiring models simply got put on the bottom of endless piles."

"That's all right, Mr. Dennison," she said calmly, enunciating clearly the way she practiced every day. She was amazed at how easily she could detach herself from her emotions. She'd started doing it when her father left and her mother stopped caring, but she didn't realize what a master she was until now.

"I appreciate your understanding. Now to the point. Miss Montgomery, I was most impressed with your work. Most impressed. I'd like to arrange a meeting and set up a photo shoot. I'm almost positive you're the model we're looking for. You've got some local experience, which is helpful, and we've had our eye out for someone new and special, nothing like the hundreds of girl-next-door blue-eyed blondes you see everywhere you turn. Of course, we'll pay all your expenses. Can we set up something for next week?"

It was funny, she mused, the way a dream that had been wished for for years finally came true. Where were the fireworks, the parades? Why were there no signs of it at all, except for the adrenaline pumping through her veins and an ecstasy that nearly overwhelmed her? She looked around the kitchen. It was the same as always. Her mother's cardigan was draped over the back of the chair. A pound of ground beef sat thawing on the counter. She saw her reflection in the toaster and was surprised that she looked no different. Yet here it was. She was going to be a model. The words bounced through her mind, threatening to knock her out with their force, but the joy stayed trapped inside her. If she could find a way to transfer this energy to matter, she might light up the world.

"Of course, Mr. Dennison, I'd like that very much." She said it so smoothly. What an actress. She was better than she thought. Movies couldn't be far away now. Wait until Hollywood found out about her.

"Terrific," he said. "I'll make the reservations and let you know. By the way, you're not married, are you?"

"No," she said, her future with Connor dismissed as easily as students on the last day of school.

"That's good. We like our models single. No commitments to break, no jealous husbands to deal with. You understand. Well, I'll be in touch tomorrow. When is a good time to call?"

She told him during the afternoon and, after settling a few final arrangements, hung up. She stood still. Only her eyes moved as she looked around the room. Something had changed. It wasn't obvious, but the light was brighter. The sun was in the same place in the sky, no stronger than before, but the room was nevertheless warmer. She was finally going to get what she wanted. She'd wished, dreamed, cried, screamed, worked, and sweated for this, and now, when it was real and laid out before her, she felt that she'd had nothing to do with it. Fate had its own schedule and rules. It insisted she be at the end of the line, willing to give up totally, to accept defeat, in order to gain success.

She walked to the table and sat down. She wasn't smiling yet. That would come later, along with the phone calls she would make, the pride that would burst out of her. Now, feeling only relief that she wouldn't have to make excuses for herself anymore, Clementine put her head in her hands and cried.

•   •   •

Of course they were happy for her. As Clementine packed her suitcase, she remembered Alex's and Megan's responses, their "Congratulations" and "Isn't that wonderful?" Still, she couldn't quite match their words to their faces.

Alex was almost sincere. After all, she had her own successes to compare to Clementine's. When she'd told Alex the news, Alex had hugged her and said she was proud and pleased. But she'd dismissed the details with a wave of her hand and changed the subject back to herself, to which dorm she'd be living in her freshman year. Clementine knew she was mentally calculating their future potential salaries, wondering if she could make as much through real estate and stocks as Clementine might make through modeling and acting. Still, deep down, Clementine was certain that Alex harbored no real resentment toward her. If anything, her success would only spur Alex to do better herself.

Then there was Megan. Clementine had told her a week earlier over dinner, and Megan had done all the right things. She'd smiled and hugged her, yet she'd been unable to hide completely the bitterness in her eyes. *Why not me?* she seemed to be thinking. *Why do you have all the luck?* Throughout dinner, Clementine had tried to be sympathetic, to play it down, telling Megan it wasn't for sure yet and she might very well come home without an agent. They both knew that wasn't the case, though. There was no way in hell Clementine was going to get this far and then blow it.

Clementine had felt sorry for Megan at the time, but since then, anger had surfaced. Sure, Megan had had some rough times, but that was no reason to wish Clementine unhappiness. The more she thought about it, the more it infuriated her. Why did she have to pretend she wasn't ecstatic? Why did her success have to be measured against her friends', not allowed to be greater or lesser without hard feelings? Why couldn't the three of them wholeheartedly support one another? They all loved one another. Beneath it, though, there was always a tally card, with wins and losses and point totals. Clementine slammed the suitcase shut and added up their scores. It was obvious she was ahead, all things considered. Trying to hide it, even from herself, she smiled.

Connor saw her off at the airport. He was quiet during the drive over, and once they were in line at the ticket counter, she finally gave up trying to break him out of his shell.

When she'd told him the news, she hadn't been sure how he'd take it. His moods had been erratic for weeks. He could be her most steadfast supporter one minute, and then the next minute, he'd be furious with her because she was more interested in her own career than his. Clementine, however, no longer had the time or the inclination to soothe his hurt feelings. She didn't know when her passion for him had cooled, or why. She still loved him. But she wasn't going to let him stand in her way. If he was happy for her, great. If he felt like being a male chauvinist stick-in-the-mud, well, that was his problem. So when she told him, lying in bed the same night she heard from Arthur Dennison, she was hardly surprised by his tight smile and strained kiss on her cheek. She didn't go after him when he grabbed his jacket and went out for a two-hour walk.

All the following week, he was withdrawn and moody. When she asked him outright if he was happy for her, he said yes. When she asked him what was wrong, he said nothing, he was just tired. Finally, she left him alone. She wouldn't let his foul mood douse her enthusiasm. She was going to New York. New York City, home of the wealthy and powerful and glamorous.

Clementine had only one suitcase to check in at the counter, and after that, they walked to her gate. Early boarding of children had already begun.

"I can't believe it, Connor," she said, unable to curb her excitement for his sake any longer. "I feel like I'm walking in a dream."

He looked away from her, out the airport window.

"Aren't you happy for me, at least just a little?" she asked.

He turned back, and she was jarred by the agony in his eyes. Her love for him flooded back into her strong and heavy, like in the first days.

"What is making you so miserable? Tell me."

He put his arms around her, holding her tightly.

"I want to marry you, Clem," he whispered in her ear.

At first, she thought he was joking. She started to laugh, but stopped quickly when she saw his serious expression. Her laughter turned to fear, unreasonable, uncontrollable fear, hardly the emotion she thought she would feel after a marriage proposal. Marriage, though, would ruin everything for her.

"I don't understand," she said.

"What is there to understand?" His voice was high-pitched, unfamiliar. It reminded her of her mother's when she was apologizing to John for something he insisted she'd done wrong. Clementine stepped back.

"I've been thinking about it all week," Connor said. "I love you, and I want to marry you. I thought you felt the same way."

Her gaze flitted over to the boarding gate, which passengers were walking through to the plane. Why did this conversation seem out of place, as if it was pulled from one movie and inserted into another?

"Connor, I don't think this is the time. I mean—"

"I want to marry you," he said loudly, drawing the stares of nearby passengers. "Why aren't you saying yes? Why aren't you thrilled like you're supposed to be? I thought you loved me."

She glanced once more at the boarding area. More than anything she wanted to be through those gates and away from him. She hated herself for it, but couldn't help it. Every instinct told her to run. It didn't matter that she loved him. He was trying to trap her, keep her from her dreams. She couldn't let that happen.

"Look, Connor, this isn't a simple thing you're asking. Let's wait until I get back, and then we can discuss it."

She kissed his cheek and headed for the gate. He caught up to her just before she entered and grabbed her wrist, whirling her around.

"I have to know. You can't go without letting me know."

She stared at him, trying to see through the mask of this pleading child to the man she loved. She put her hand on his cheek, and at her touch, his eyes softened.

"I love you," she said. "Isn't that enough for now? I'll be home in four days, and we can talk about it then."

He jerked away from her and set his jaw hard. "Fine. Go to New York. Of course, that's more important than me."

She flung her arms in the air, not knowing how to deal with him. He didn't understand. Success was everything, what the world judged you by. Fame would make her live forever. She had to have it. Even if it meant sacrificing what they had. Where was the man who understood that, who spoke of houses on both coasts, a Hollywood mansion near the studios where he'd work and a New York penthouse for her? Why, when she thought he was so different, was he acting like such a . . . a *man*? She glanced at the flight attendants getting ready to close the boarding chute.

"I promise, Connor, we'll discuss this seriously in four days. And you know you're the most important thing in the world to me. But I have to get on that plane."

She tried to kiss his lips, but he jerked his head away, and her lips grazed his cheek instead. She sighed before turning and hurrying through the gate, and relief at finally getting away from him released ten pounds from her shoulders.

She located her window seat on the plane, slipped past an older woman already dozing, and sat down. Staring out the plane window, she spotted Connor still standing in the terminal, his face pressed up against the glass, his eyes searching for her.

She had thought he wanted her to succeed as much as she wanted to herself. She would have been thrilled for him if he had landed a part in a film. But it was obvious he was turning out like every other man. Oh, sure, he acted liberal and fair-minded, but when it came right down to it, *he* was the one who was supposed to succeed, or at least succeed first. To him, it would always be Connor Douglas first, Clementine Montgomery second. If at all.

She tapped her fingers on the armrest. Enough, she thought, and like a teacher snapping her fingers to bring her class to attention, she banished all thoughts of jealous boyfriends and envious friends. She turned her mind to modeling instead, to what lay ahead, to lights and photographers and makeup. Let Connor sulk like a baby and Megan and Alex hate her for being more of a success than they were. She was going to New York. And she damn well was going to be excited about it.

•   •   •

Arthur Dennison had told her he would meet her personally at the airport. She walked off the plane and searched the faces of the people gathered at the gate, not realizing until that moment that she had no idea whom she was looking for. From the sound of his voice, she pictured him as older, maybe fifty or sixty, grayhaired, distinguished.

Instead, a thirtyish-looking man dressed in corduroys, running shoes, and a short-sleeved blue cotton shirt disengaged himself from the crowd and approached her. His sandy brown hair fell in a clump over his matching brown eyes. Clementine's heart sank.

"Miss Montgomery, I would have recognized you anywhere. I'm Arthur Dennison." He held out his hand, and Clementine shook it dejectedly.

There was no doubt in her mind that this was all a big hoax. She didn't know why she had let herself believe it could be real in the first place; nothing good ever happened to her. There was no way this man could be serious. Not when he met his prospective clients looking ready for a backpacking expedition. He probably used his tacky apartment as his agency, dangling stardom as the bait to get young, naive models into his bed. Well, if he thought for one minute that Clementine was one of those innocents, he had another think coming.

"You must be tired," he said. "Come on, let's get your luggage."

They walked to the baggage claim area. Arthur talked constantly, about his plans for her, about the business, his other models. Clementine hardly heard him. She just wouldn't get in the car with him, that's all, she told herself. Success wasn't worth pornography or, worse yet, rape. She'd pay her own way home if she had to.

She spotted her suitcase, and Arthur picked it up for her.

"Is this all you have?" he said. "Thank God. You should see how much luggage some of the other models bring with them."

Clementine doubted he knew many other legitimate models, but she played along with his game anyway. She'd sweet-talk him until they got to the car, then she'd grab her bag and run. Or, if she had to, she'd forget the bag. Her money was in her purse. That was all she needed.

His pace was brisk as he headed for the nearest exit, and even with her long legs, Clementine nearly had to run to keep up with him. He probably had a hard-on, she thought, while he imagined using his slimy lines on her. He probably didn't even have a photographer. He'd pretend to take pictures of her, and of course, he'd need to see more cleavage, more leg, more . . .

"Here we are," he said, stopping beside a black limousine parked in front of the airport.

Clementine couldn't stifle her gasp of surprise, and he laughed. "Summer in New York is miserable, Miss Montgomery," he said. "So I wear light clothes. And I like to be comfortable. But that doesn't mean I'm not a professional. I can still travel in style."

Clementine remembered the reason she had sent her pictures to him in the first place, the glowing reviews of his agency in *The San Francisco Chronicle.* She should have thought of that before she became so suspicious, but it was all so unreal to her. She was certain there was a mix-up: either they'd asked for the wrong girl, or Arthur was a con artist. It just didn't seem possible that fate wouldn't swoop down and take everything away from her.

She blushed, embarrassed by her thoughts about him, and he laughed again.

"I can see I was definitely right about you. What a face. You blush magnificently."

Her embarrassment was lost instantly when she realized he was teasing her. She stood up straight.

"Shall we go?" she said icily.

He opened the door for her. "By all means, Miss Montgomery. By all means."

•   •   •

"Turn to the right a little more. Right there. Hold it. More teeth, Clementine. Yes, that's it. Perfect. Come toward me a little. Stop. Head back. Yes. Excellent."

Only once in her life, after a two-hour aerobics class, had Clementine ever been this tired. She smiled just the same. And obviously she hid her exhaustion well. Pierre hadn't even noticed the bone-weary shaking in her legs.

"Perfection," Pierre Martineau said, stepping away from the camera. "A couple more rolls, and I think we'll have it."

Clementine kept smiling, then collapsed into a chair as soon as he left the room to get the film. The man was inexhaustible. But then, all he had to do was command and click. She was doing the work.

She stretched out her legs in front of her. The lights on either side of the set sizzled through her skin, warming her insides. She loved the feel of the heat on her body, although she wished her sweat glands, pouring tidal waves out of her armpits, would agree.

A four-hour photo shoot might not sound like much, but for those four hours, she'd been constantly moving, dancing, smiling, laughing, twirling, anything and everything Pierre wanted. He was good. She'd known that instantly. She could almost see herself through the camera's eyes, sexy one minute, innocent the next. Pierre had photographed the best. Brenda Halsley. Karyn Samstead. Supermodel Jill Isaacs. He'd done an incredible layout of Barbra Streisand. He worked freelance, and Arthur had sought him out specifically for her portfolio. Clementine knew she should pinch herself to see if she was dreaming, but she was afraid she might wake up.

Pierre returned, and she jumped to her feet. Pushing the exhaustion to the back of her mind, she vowed to make the most of every second she had with Pierre. He could teach her much.

"Now, Clementine, I've saved the best for last. We'll do the romance shots now. You can even sit for some of these."

She laughed, grateful that he understood. He changed the background from stark white to an air-brushed pastel and had her sit on an oversize cream-color pillow in front of it. After turning on a fan, he returned to the camera.

"Now, my dear, I want you to think of something soft. Some warm and tender memory that makes you feel melancholy, bittersweet."

The breeze from the fan blew her hair back, and she laid her chin on her hands. At Pierre's words, she had thought of her father. It had been so long since she'd seen him. Seven or eight years at least, and then only for a day, when he'd bothered to stop in to see her while he was in town. One trip to the Denver Zoo, dinner at Howard Johnson's, a good-night kiss on the cheek, then he was gone. He was a tornado whipping up her memories, shredding her orderly life with one look, one touch, before he disappeared into the clouds. The only sign he'd been there was the windblown mess he left behind. Last she'd heard, he was living in Seattle.

Her earliest memory was of Duke. She could recall a stubbly face poised above hers. She looked up into eyes exactly the color of her own, the lightest of blues. The eyes twinkled brightly, and the man smiled at her. She remembered the way he picked her up, his arms wrapped around her so firmly, she knew she would never be dropped or harmed as long as he was near. He nestled her face in the hollow of his neck, where she drowned happily in the odors of him, content to stay there forever. Then he hummed. "Amazing Grace." She remembered it clearly. The resonance of his baritone, the rise and fall of his chest, the scratch of his chin against her head when he stopped for a breath, the love in his voice, his hands, his laugh.

After that, her memories grew hazy. All she remembered was the happiness, the absolute certainty of the goodness in the world when he was close by. And the blinding ache that consumed her when he was gone. He brought the sunshine with him, and darkness fell when he left.

Pierre suggested poses at first, but soon his words died away. Clementine had been aware of the clicking of the camera for the first few shots, but now her thoughts overpowered all else.

Duke's face was right in front of her. His smile was her smile. His eyes, her eyes. In fact, she seemed to have inherited his genes almost exclusively. She smiled, thinking of the strength she'd inherited, his humor, his overwhelming personality and heart-stopping looks. But of course, she might have inherited his cruelty and selfishness, as well. He'd left without saying good-bye. He'd kissed her forehead, hopped into his pickup truck, and waved as he turned the corner for the last time, as if he were leaving only to pick up a carton of milk. His eyes had been bright and happy, incapable of regret. She knew he'd forgotten her as soon as she was out of his sight.

The tears started, tears Clementine hadn't shed for years, but she didn't stop them. She hardly realized anymore that Pierre was there.

Arthur was there, too, having walked into the room unobserved. He saw the tears glistening on Clementine's cheeks, saw Pierre clicking away like mad, and he knew his instinct about Clementine had been right on the mark. She was going to be a star, bigger than even she could imagine. Her face, her entire body, even her most subtle movements, revealed emotions so deep and raw, he almost turned away. But her beauty was riveting. The lines of her face were so well chiseled, so soft and smooth, it was like looking at the face of heaven. She had a way of making you feel for her. Her sadness was heartbreaking, her joy contagious.

He watched for fifteen minutes, until the shoot was over, then he walked over to her. She still sat on the pillows, almost in a trance, and he kissed her cheek.

"You're going to make it," he whispered before he left with Pierre.

Clementine sat alone in the studio long after Arthur and Pierre had left. Both of them were sure of her future, she realized. And she believed them. She never had to doubt herself again. Still, it was funny the way an image, a memory of a strong face with twinkling eyes, could make everything else, even her dreams, insignificant. She had only to think of her father, and suddenly she was a child again, her arms outstretched, waiting to be picked up and held. Nothing but getting his love really mattered.

•    •    •

The next four days passed in a whirlwind. Arthur showed her the city, introduced her to more editors and fashion designers than she'd ever remember, and spent hours with her discussing the image he wanted to create for her. But the highlight of her stay was the two parties he took her to. They were like scenes from a racy novel. The women were all dressed in glitter and sequins, the men in white ties and tails. The trays carried by elegantly dressed waiters held oysters and caviar and champagne.

Clementine met oil tycoons and old money jet-setters. At one party, she even thought she spotted Elizabeth Taylor talking to a princely looking man in the corner, but she couldn't be sure. Handsome young actors, Broadway stars, beautiful models lent the parties flair and style, and Clementine could hardly believe she was included among them. She overheard snatches of conversation about plays under consideration, books to be published, the latest news from Hollywood. This was where things happened, she thought. The people at these parties were the ones who pressed the buttons, paid the big money, made the decisions about who became a star and who didn't.

On her last night in New York, Arthur took her to the Russian Tea Room. They were escorted to a nondescript table in the back, past Henry Fonda and golden boy producer James Nolan, both seated at tables center stage. Clementine glared at the maître d', but Arthur simply shrugged him off.

"Don't worry," he said once the man had left. "One day, we'll walk in here and they'll shove people out of their chairs to give us the best table in the house."

Clementine smiled, wondering if she'd have the time, once she was a star, to settle all the scores she was accumulating. Disrespectful waiters and maître d's, condescending men, every person who ever stood in her way. There were far more than she'd anticipated.

When their waiter arrived, Arthur ordered two glasses of chardonnay and two Caesar salads.

"How did you like the hotel?" he asked.

He'd booked her into the Waldorf Astoria. It was the second hint she'd had, and an overwhelming one, that no matter how lax his dress code was, Arthur Dennison was a successful professional. Staying at the Waldorf was like living in a rich, luxurious fairy tale. How could she not like it?

"It's been perfect, Arthur."

"Great. They treated you well? Gave you all your messages from the heartbroken boyfriends you left behind, I trust."

He was kidding, but his words were more on target than he knew. Connor had called twelve times in four days. Eleven of those times she'd been out, and the one time they did speak was a disaster. His only purpose in calling her was to whine that he was lonely and then, changing tones quickly, to shout that he was still angry at her for leaving without answering his proposal. When she told him she was too tired to listen to his tantrum or make any major decisions, he blew up completely, threatening not to call again—a thought which Clementine found quite appealing—and telling her that maybe he wouldn't be at the airport to pick her up.

"Fine, I don't even want you there," she yelled back. "I'll call Megan or Alex. At least, they'll be interested in what happened out here."

He hung up in a rage, and she felt horribly guilty, yet she didn't call him back. She had too many other things to think about, like the work Arthur was trying to line up for her and stardom. Maybe the separation would be good for her and Connor, she told herself. They'd been together so much, they'd become almost part of each other, symbiotic, and she found the thought of that suffocating. Now that she'd gotten a breath of air, a taste of independence, she wondered how she'd stood his binding hold on her for so long.

"To the task at hand," Arthur said, unfolding his napkin. "You've done beautifully, my dear. Just beautifully. Everyone at the Steinems' party was enthralled with you. In fact, I've had four calls today from people wondering what my plans are, which way we're headed, and so on. It's quite heady, isn't it?"

Clementine nodded and eagerly gulped her wine when it arrived. It was all moving so fast. One day she was sitting across from Connor, dressed in her ragged bathrobe and working on the crossword puzzle, and the next she was wearing a thousand-dollar dress on loan from Arthur's studio and sitting beside Norman Mailer at *the* party of the year in New York City, talking about his new book. It was everything she'd wanted, even more, and yet . . . it was unsteadying, like getting up too quickly and losing your balance.

"So, here's the plan," Arthur went on. "You go home, get your stuff together as fast as possible, and let me know when to book you back out. Meanwhile, I'll find you a sublet, something modest but nice, and start getting you work. I've already got a layout for Fast Fashions set for next month. Remember Ronald Percy at the party? Short guy, balding. He . . ."

Clementine leaned her head back against the rich red cushions. Arthur watched her, noticing for the first time the dark shadows beneath her eyes, her pallor. He reached across the table and covered her hand with his.

"It's going to be fine, you know," he said softly.

Clementine started at his touch. His hand was smaller than Connor's, cleaner, more professional, with perfectly rounded nails. Yet it was masculine and warm.

"I'm sure it will be," she said after a moment. "It's just a lot to take in at once, that's all."

He squeezed her hand, then let go. She was surprised at how cold and empty her hand felt without his on top of it. She moved it to her lap.

"Look," he said, "if you need time, I'll give it to you. Go home, relax, get your things together slowly. We can wait a month or two to get started."

His understanding smile made her see herself as he saw her—anxious, scared, and weak. She noticed her posture—tilted forward, legs crossed, arms ground into her sides, fists clenched. She thought of her life, her hard work, her determination throughout the years, and let the memories suffuse her with strength. Enough. If ever there was a time to be strong, to push the insecurities to the pit of her stomach and seal them there, this was it.

She pulled herself up straight and tall, physically transforming herself into the woman she wanted to be, had to be. A woman with guts and nerve and strength, no matter how scared she was on the inside. So what if she had to leave home and her friends and Connor? You always had to give up something to achieve greatness. Alex and Megan would understand. And Connor would see that she simply couldn't marry him now, not when she had this chance held out before her like sweet candy just waiting to be grabbed and eaten. They could still be together long-distance. They'd keep in touch by phone, and she'd make enough money to go back to California and visit.

She smiled and sipped her wine. What had she been so afraid of? This was all she'd ever wanted. She was going to conquer this town. Whoever said New York was tough hadn't met Clementine Montgomery yet.

"I'll get my things together and be back in a week," she said. "Is that soon enough?"

Arthur chuckled. He'd watched the change and admired her courage. "How about two weeks? Give me some time to find you a place to live, all right?"

"Fine." She raised her glass. "Here's to success."

"Hell, yes. More than either of us ever dreamed of."

# CHAPTER 8

*JACKSON HOLLYWELL POSSESSED AN AURA* of sensuality that threw its mesmerizing shadow thirty feet in all directions. Lined up beside the other UC Berkeley heartthrobs, from sportsmen to physics majors to student body presidents, he would never have been voted the most attractive. His facial features were too angular, his lips too thick, his dark hair too messy. His clothes were typical college casual, his height not extraordinary, only five feet eleven. His body was compact, stocky, animallike. Jackson Hollywell was just an ordinary man, an aspiring architect and artist, with a solid sense of humor, no commitments, and no attachments, having left his mother and stepfather and the shadowy figure of his father behind in Ohio years earlier.

Still, not one woman at Berkeley thought him commonplace in any way. With only a smile, a light tap on their shoulder, a wink, he stole the strength from their legs and coherent thoughts from their minds. It had always been that way for Jackson. No woman was immune to his charms.

Of course, the women at the university acted differently from the girls he'd known in high school. No more were they silly, giggling cheerleaders who asked their friends to ask him if he liked them. These were grown-up, independent women of the world.

Some were aggressive and obstinate, determined to prove they had the same God-given rights as a man. They asked him out boldly, and never tired of discussing equality and sex.

Other women practiced what they thought was the art of subtlety. They maneuvered themselves beside him in his architecture classes, pushing poor foreign exchange students out of their chairs with about as much nonchalance as dynamite, then doing their best imitation of surprise when their fluffy angora sweaters just happened to brush across his chest when they bent forward to pick up the notebook they'd accidentally dropped at his feet.

Still other women flirted openly, insinuating mysterious adventures in dark, sultry apartments steaming with the flavors of Italian food and wine. These were the women Jackson understood. They weren't looking for marriage, as so many others were. They wanted sex. They wanted fun. They wanted to be young. More than anything else, so did Jackson.

In the midst of all these women, however, there was Alex Holmes. Beautiful, brilliant, distant-as-the-Far-East Alex. It was only a coincidence that he knew her at all. He was a junior, she a freshman. She was a business major, he studied architecture. It was only a fluke, a crazy, fated fluke, that they were enrolled in the same biology class—a class he hadn't been able to fit into his schedule during his freshman and sophomore years. Alex was the first person he noticed when he walked into the room, and the only woman he noticed after that. She was seated in the front row, makeupless, her hair in a ponytail, a pair of black-rimmed glasses perched on her nose while she studied for another class. One look and Jackson hadn't been the same since.

He manipulated the professor into assigning them as lab partners. When the teacher called out their names, she looked at him over the rim of her glasses, not smiling. Her eyes sized him up quickly, looking for intelligence and dissecting techniques without even a flicker of interest in his dating potential. That had been four weeks ago, and he still knew nothing more than her name, her major, and her infuriating habit of getting the highest grade on every exam. He didn't know any of the things he longed to know, like who her favorite singer was, where she liked to go at night, what made her happy, and whether she liked him at all.

Alex didn't flirt. She didn't drop notebooks. She didn't brazenly ask him out. She didn't do any of the things other girls did. Instead, she came to class every day thoroughly prepared, with rewritten notes and journals and related books she'd discovered on her own. She sat in her seat, put on her glasses, and concentrated on the professor's lecture as if her life depended on it. She insisted on running most of their experiments herself, taking his advice only as a last resort. She was never seen with a boyfriend and actually took her teachers up on their offers of study conferences.

Yet beneath her austerity and dedication, Alex was warm. She laughed heartily when he told her the jokes he'd picked up from friends just for the pleasure of seeing her smile. She helped him with his studies whenever he needed it. And she moved out of the way when an amorous-looking woman approached, obviously aware of his lively dating life and yet wanting no part of it herself. She listened attentively when he told her bits and pieces about his life—about growing up in Chicago, his mother, stepfather, and half-brothers and sisters living in Ohio, his interest in architecture and art, his job as a part-time drafter for Baron and Jakonovich, his two-bedroom apartment in the city.

In return, though, she offered little of herself. A comment here and there about her two best friends, her brother, her parents. She was an enigma, and day by day, Jackson found himself more drawn to her, fascinated by her poise and character. He wanted to know her, every part of her. He wanted to be . . . her friend.

That amazed him most of all. He'd never been any girl's friend. He had never seen a purpose in that. He had men for friendship and women for sex. Cut-and-dried. But Alex broke every stereotype. She inspired him. She had the qualities he wanted for himself—dedication, warmth, and humor. She was piercingly intelligent, always asking the questions in class he wished he'd asked himself. Even more, she was comfortable to be with. When he thought of Alex, Jackson was reminded of his little league baseball team. The hot summer days, the friendships, the competition, the laughter in the dugout, the camaraderie that pushed even the most blatant error out of the team's mind an inning later. Jackson was the pitcher and Alex the catcher. They had the signs down so well, they were perfectly in sync, blowing batters away and laughing about it over hot dogs afterward. They were building a friendship on that dusty diamond that would last a lifetime.

• • •

After the professor finished his lecture, Alex stuffed her books into her backpack and pressed her glasses back up her nose. Since she'd started at Berkeley, few men had approached her. When they did, she stuck her head deeper into her book and mumbled monosyllabic replies until they went away.

Her metamorphosis from the most active dater in junior high to the biggest bookworm at Berkeley suited her fine. She didn't dwell on the hollow feeling in her stomach when the laughter of men and women drifted up to her dorm room on Saturday nights like exotic music. Sacrifices were to be expected. She knew in her gut that she was headed in the right direction. ONWARD WITH NO WRONG TURNS OR SIDETRACKS. She had that printed in bright red letters on a huge sign that hung over her bed.

She picked up her bag and was about to leave the room when she noticed Jackson still hunched over his book at his desk. Jackson Hollywell. A name that couldn't be spoken by any woman on campus without a wistful sigh following it. He thought she didn't notice his looks, but she did. When God had set out to make a man who could instantly take a woman's breath away, he'd created Jackson. No matter how hard she tried not to, Alex still found herself staring when she should be reading. It wasn't that she wanted him, she told herself, but more that he was unique and striking, like a good photograph or fine wine that should be appreciated slowly.

When the professor had put them together as lab partners, she'd been sure she was in for it. No one with looks like that could think too. He'd surprised her. Biology wasn't even one of his better subjects, and still he'd done well, giving his fair share to their team. And he was a nice person, to boot. Jackson Hollywell was a too-good-to-be-true package wrapped up in ribbons. Alex couldn't help watching him warily, waiting for the catch.

It came fairly quickly. It was an uncomfortable strain hidden just beneath the surface of their friendship. The kind of strain that developed between men and women who hadn't yet ironed out the game plan. Friends, lovers, or acquaintances? She didn't know what he wanted from her. And frankly, she wasn't sure what she wanted of him, either.

"Hey, bookworm," she said. He looked up, and she was met by the headlight flash of his eyes, fresh green, like newly sprouted leaves. "Are you going to stay here all day?"

Jackson stood up and stretched. He had the most ideally contoured body she had ever seen, as if Michelangelo's fingertips had personally smoothed out the ripples. Not that she was looking, but still it was impossible not to notice the solid biceps that pressed against his shirt sleeve, the chiseled, hard-as-logs legs when she spied him running around the track in the early morning. He was one of those men you saw on health club commercials, sweating gloriously while pumping hundred-pound irons. Alex had a quick jealous flash of what he would look like beside Clementine, both so unforgettable, Jackson with his dark skin and unruly hair, Clementine with her model bones and fairness, and both with their unbelievable eyes. The flash brightened for only a second, then faded to the recesses of her mind.

"I was just trying to get in some studying for my Arch 101 midterm tomorrow," he said. "I have to get at least a B. It is my major, after all."

"You'll do fine, I'm sure."

"I wish I had your confidence."

"Jackson, look, what you need is . . ." She stopped and

laughed. "There I go again. Telling people what they need. My friends give me a hard time about that."

"I'd like to hear what you have to say."

She slung her backpack over her shoulder. "Okay. But just remember, you asked for it. What you need is a cup of coffee and a slice of Millie's apple pie, my treat. Then I'll tell you everything you need to know to be a success."

He picked up his book and waved his hand toward the door. "You've got yourself a deal. Lead the way."

. . .

"What was it like living in Chicago as a kid?" Alex asked. The scoop of vanilla ice cream Millie had piled on top of her apple pie was oozing down around the crust, soaking it. Alex liked it best when the warmed pie had been turned into ice-cold ice-cream mush. In the meantime, she sipped her coffee and looked at Jackson sitting on the orange vinyl seat across from her.

"It was like anywhere, I guess. Except Tulvaris, Ohio, where I moved with my mom and stepdad after my dad was killed. Nowhere is quite like that."

"I didn't know your dad was killed," she said softly. "I'm sorry."

He stared at her hard for a second, his expression hurt and bitter as he searched her face for sympathy. A moment later, as if it never happened at all, he was smiling and his eyes were bright.

"It's okay," he said. "It sounds harsh, but I think he probably deserved it. I don't know the whole story, but from what I heard through my mom and stepdad's bedroom wall, the guy was a low-level hood. He didn't know a lot, but what he did know was too much to let him walk the streets when he decided he'd had enough of the mob for one life. He was shot through the head right outside our front door."

"That's horrible."

"For him, yeah. But my mom got out of an abusive marriage and married Stanley, my stepdad, who for some reason she really loves. They had three kids together who I never really got to know because they were so much younger than me. And I got to move to Tulvaris, Ohio, population twenty, if you count the cows."

Alex chuckled and smashed the ice cream farther into her crust. "Were you ever scared when you were little? Living with the mob always right around the corner?"

"Not really. I mean, I didn't even know my dad was a hood. I thought he was a banker."

She laughed loudly, and the sound was so contagious, it sent a wave of smiles and giggles through the restaurant.

"Besides," Jackson went on, eating the last bit of his pie and shoving the plate aside, "Chicago was great. Suburban kids always think cities are scary, with no place to play, but that's not true. Hell, when you're a kid, alleys and condemned buildings are great hiding spots for hide and seek, trash makes terrific base pads for baseball, and violence, well, violence just makes you tough."

"And did you get tough?"

"Hell, yes. I was the biggest seven-year-old shit to hit Chicago since Al Capone."

She laughed again. Jackson leaned back against the vinyl cushion and watched her.

"And what about you? Wait, don't tell me." He closed his eyes and smiled. "I see a dark-haired little girl wearing overalls, never dresses, and with the biggest, dirtiest mouth in the entire kindergarten class. You always told the other kids what to do, were team captain of every sport, group monitor, line leader, and class president."

"Am I that transparent?"

He laughed, and Alex was surprised by how happy his laughter made her. She'd asked him to Millie's on the spur of the moment, startling herself, but now she understood her motivations. Jackson made her smile. She didn't feel that she was better than he, as she did with so many of the other, immature boys pretending to be college men. She didn't feel inferior the way she did when standing beside the brilliant professors of Berkeley. Jackson was her equal.

"I just can't see you taking a backseat to anybody, not ever," he said. "I see a cute little girl with kinky hair that refused to stay in a neat braid. A girl who left her hand in the air after she answered a teacher's question, because she knew she'd know the answer to the next one too. The girl everybody was jealous of, yet the same girl they fought long and hard to be friends with because they thought you had some kind of magic power. You were good in sports, good in math and science, maybe not so good in English, but that only made you work harder to be the best. You never knew what it was like to be last or worst or left out."

Alex had stopped eating and set her fork on her plate. She leaned her chin on her hand.

"How do you know so much about me?"

He smiled. "How do I know so much? Easy. Because I was the boy who hated your guts. The boy who got in trouble every day, bullied the other kids, snapped the girls' bras, stuck peanut butter in your coat pocket. I was the boy who sat in the last row and aimed my paper airplanes directly for the back of your prim little head in the front-row seat."

She resumed eating. "I can't imagine you like that."

"Oh, I was. Believe me. It wasn't until high school that I realized school really did have relevance to the rest of my life, just like my mom and all those teachers and counselors were always telling me. And I knew I had to make some changes if I wanted to get the things I'd been dreaming about."

"Did you always want to be an architect?"

"Hmmm. No, not really. Art is my love. I was drawing before I could walk. I painted on anything. Paper, walls, appliances. My mom hated my guts, I think. But I couldn't help it. It's in my soul, an extension of me. It's strange, but I don't feel whole without a brush in my hand."

"That's not strange at all," Alex said, thinking of her love of business and numbers and money, the way she felt alive and completely vibrant only when she was involved with it.

"Well, the world thinks so," Jackson said, placing his fingertip on the tines of his fork and snapping it up and down. "Art is for eccentric, homosexual men who don't mind going without food for years so they can be discovered after they die. All I hear from my family and friends is reality, reality, reality. Things like bills and rent and food. 'Artists are poor and starving' and 'You'll never make a living as a painter' and on and on. So I decided on architecture to make ends meet until I can prove them wrong."

Alex reached across the table and touched his hand. "All they say may be true, Jackson, but life isn't worth a damn if you don't have a dream to work toward. What's the use of being a millionaire architect if you're miserable? If you can't do what makes you happy, you might as well shrivel up and die."

He squeezed her hand. "I have no intention of shriveling, pretty lady. Never. I paint every night. My bedroom is more like a studio. I've got four easels set up at once because I never know what mood I'm going to be in. I only lay the air mattress down when I'm ready to go to sleep, and usually then, I'm cramped between canvases and paint. Now my roommate hates my guts."

She offered him the rest of her pie, and he took it gladly, releasing her hand. She pulled her feet up beneath her and watched him eat until he wriggled beneath the weight of her stare.

"Is something wrong?" he asked.

She shook her head. "No. Not really. It's just that, well, you don't look like a painter. You're too—too normal. Too tough. Your eyes focus on what's in front of you, not on abstract images and fairy tales."

"Yeah, I know. If the kids back in Chicago knew, they'd beat me to a pulp. But I like it that way. Throws them off guard, you know. I am what I am. Period. It doesn't matter what I look like. I don't see why an artist needs to look like a wimp. I see nothing wrong with combining art and fitness. In fact, I don't see how a painter can live without exercise. You spend so much time in your mind creating, that you end up mentally exhausted and physically stunted. Every night, after I'm through painting, I have to jog or lift weights, something."

"I've never been very creative," Alex said. "My brother, Joey, plays the piano. Beautifully, I suppose, although that classical shit drives me up the wall. And my mother is an art curator. I got my dad's genes. The ones for school and math. Solid, tangible things like that."

He finished her pie and sat up straight, staring into her eyes. "Does it bother you? Do you wish you were more artistic?"

"Honestly? No. I'm practical. That's who I am."

He nodded. "Good for you. And now that we've avoided the subject for an hour, I think it's time you told me your secret."

She raised her eyebrows.

"Remember?" he said. "Everything I need to know to be a success."

"Oh, that secret." She picked up the check and walked to the cashier, where she paid the bill. Jackson opened the café door for her, and they walked out into the bright afternoon sunshine.

"I don't feel so sure anymore about how successful my techniques would be for you," she said. The street was lined with poplars, shading the sidewalks, diluting the strength of the sun. They continued slowly, in step, as if they had nowhere to go for hours.

"I mean, we want such different things," she went on. "I *am* going to be a success in business. I know it. It's like I have no choice. And I'm not kidding myself about how hard it will be, either. I know I'll have to work my way up the ladder and probably forgo marriage and a social life to get what I want, but that's worth it to me. In the meantime, I've developed a way of plowing through the mud until I reach dry land."

"And that is?"

"I put every ounce of strength I have into reading and studying and learning. I can almost feel my brain stretching, I use it so much. I'm up at five in the morning and in bed at midnight, with constant studying during all hours in between—unless, of course, I'm meeting a handsome man for pie."

He laughed, and without thinking, she slipped her arm through his. He wrapped his hand around hers as they strolled on, along a street of two-story, upper-middle-class homes, fallen leaves crackling beneath their feet.

"And I've taught myself new ways of thinking," she continued. "I have positive self-talk statements stuck all over my dorm room, and I never allow a negative, scared thought to enter my mind. The key, I think, is that I'm learning to act the way I want to be some day. So that when I finally get there, to the top, I'll already be accustomed to the success, totally confident and in control."

"I don't see that you'll have much problem with that," Jackson said. He hoped he'd be around when Alex did make it, so he could see the world's reaction to this incredible, inexhaustible woman.

They kept on walking, quiet sometimes, then talking about college and dreams and art and business and love and laughter. They kept their arms linked tightly, walking in step and laughing in sync. And inside, both were thinking how wonderful, how warm and cuddly it was to have found a new friend.

• • •

Alex and Jackson had dinner together three times a week. Alex had tried to adjust her palate to bland and fattening dorm food, but when Jackson offered his specialty of stir-fried anything he could find in the refrigerator, she unhesitatingly accepted.

They talked long into the night. Even with Megan, Alex had never felt this free. Something about the newness of Jackson, his total interest in what she was saying, his maleness, made their conversations different. He had a unique, masculine perspective that she found fascinating.

"I have this feeling I won't ever get married," she said one night.

It was a few weeks before Christmas and the windows of Jackson's apartment were frosted white. Exactly as he'd said, his easels covered almost all the floor space in his bedroom and were creeping toward the living room. Alex had been dumbfounded when she first saw his work, a cornucopia of colors and textures and images that burst from the canvas. From what she'd learned from her mother, she knew Jackson had talent. It was raw, untutored, unrestrained, but nevertheless fresh and exciting.

"Of course you'll get married," he said. He was working with acrylics in the corner, trying to capture Alex on canvas and occasionally shouting at her to keep still. "Everyone gets married."

"I'm not everyone," she said, moving again, this time lying down on the air mattress that was wedged against the closet door.

"Are you comfortable now?" he asked.

"I think so."

"Try to stay still, okay?" He stared at her until he'd decided on his approach, then dived into his paints again.

In her whole life, Alex had never remained motionless
for more than a few minutes at a time, and this night was
no exception. She sat up and Jackson groaned, pushing
his paints aside.

"Sorry," she said.

"Don't worry. I'll get this picture some day." He sat
down on the windowsill. "I'd rather hear why you think
you're so unlovable."

"It's not that. It's just that when I try to picture myself
at fifty, I don't see someone standing beside me. I close
my eyes and see me in my house, reading by the fire, a
dog at my feet. I look around the room, but there's no
husband there, no man watching television or reading
beside me. Do you think that's a premonition?"

"Maybe. Does it bother you?"

She looked out the window. "Only at night, when my
eyes are burning so bad, I can't read anymore and the
clock ticks as loud as a time bomb. Things are different
then, in the darkness. Heavier. Harder. The rest of the
time, if I keep busy, I don't think about it."

"Well, then, keep busy. Run yourself ragged. Who
needs introspection, anyway? I may never marry, either,
and that's fine. There's a lot more than love in this
world. Everyone makes it out to be better than it is."

"Yes, but you date. You have your pick of women. For
some reason, I can't go halfway. If I fell in love, I'd fall
completely. And the thought of losing myself like that
terrifies me."

"I hate to break this to you, sweetheart, but you're
confusing poetry with reality. Take a look at the couples
around you. Most fight like cats and dogs. Love ain't no
paradise."

He was right, of course. Every relationship she knew
of had its problems. Love never seemed to make anyone
happy, at least not for long. Better for her to stay alone
and make her own happiness.

She stared at Jackson's watercolor of the twilight behind the San Francisco skyline. It was beautiful, enchant-
ing, her favorite of his pieces.

"I told you about Megan," she said. "She's always tried so hard for love. Even now that she's in college, it's like school is just a detour for her before she finds Mr. Right. One minute I think she's crazy, and the next I wonder if she knows something I don't. And then there's Clementine. She says that even though she's in New York, concentrating on getting her modeling career off the ground, Connor still calls her and whines about how she's ignoring him. When I hear that, I thank God it's just me in my life. I don't have time for all that nonsense."

Jackson walked over to her and pulled her up. Grabbing his coat, he led her to the front door.

"I say we forget all this crap about love and marriage," he said. "Let's just be friends, have fun, get through school, and conquer the world."

He flung open the door and was walking out before Alex pulled him back. Her hand was on his wrist, and she could feel his steady pulse beneath her fingers. She raised herself up on her toes and kissed his cheek.

"Thanks, buddy," she said. He put his arm around her, and they walked out into the night.

• • •

It was natural that they move in together. Jackson's roommate eventually had his fill of easels and canvases and paints, and moved to his own place in the city. After a year of dorm life, Alex, too, was ready for a home of her own.

Of course, everyone assumed they were a couple, and in many ways, they were. Alex loved him, and she knew he loved her back. They supported and took care of each other. She made a mean chicken soup when he had a cold, and he stayed up late into the night quizzing her for tests. Every aspect of what a couple should be materialized between them except for that first kiss, that initial romantic touch that broke the intimacy barrier forever. Alex had waited. Jackson had waited. But the moment never seemed right, and there was always the chance that by becoming lovers, they would cease being friends. It was a risk neither was willing to take.

Often, though, especially in those first weeks after Alex moved her bed and self-talk posters and stereo into his apartment, she wondered why it hadn't happened.

She wouldn't have minded his arms around her when it was cold. Sometimes she stared at his lips while he spoke, wondering what he tasted like. But she never mustered enough nerve to find out. If she moved toward him, a million repercussions would flash through her mind. First they would spend more time together, maybe cut a few classes to go to the beach instead. Then her grades would slip, she'd settle for a bachelor's degree instead of a master's, then a paper-pushing job instead of top management. One kiss and she would sacrifice everything, the way Megan had for Tony and Clementine had for a while with Connor. Alex was too smart—or too stupid, depending on how you looked at it—to let that happen.

So she held back, he followed her lead, and they remained just friends. They both longed for success, and both were tough enough to pay the price for it.

•    •    •

Clementine's pictures started appearing in women's magazines about a year after she moved to New York. Arthur wanted to proceed slowly, Clementine wrote in her letters to Alex. He had a plan. Pique the nation's interest with bits and pieces. A side shot in this magazine, a mysterious silhouette in another. There was a need for self-effacing models willing to play themselves down, and Clementine was going to fill that need for a while. She'd create an aura of mystery, never allow the public to know everything. Arthur taught her to hold back, to keep a side of herself hidden. At least until he had the magazines and advertisers salivating for more.

It didn't take long. After a few months, the occasional phone calls from a few photographers and advertisers turned into a steady stream. Still, Arthur held out. He didn't want to turn Clementine into just any model. She was going to be a star. She was going to be the person everyone thought of when asked who the most beautiful woman in the world was. She would use her modeling platform to jump to the movie world. He already had her enrolled in John Daniel's New York acting class. And after making movies, she would launch her nationwide lecture tours, helping women grow to independence. Clementine was still as determined as ever to change the world.

Alex sat on her bed and read Clementine's most recent letter. Her contract with Amour Perfume was sealed. The campaign would begin in October, with ads in *Cosmopolitan* and *Vogue*.

"The pictures are so daring," Clementine wrote. "The one that's coming out in *Cosmopolitan* has me lying on my back on a rock. We shot it at Nantucket. God, it was cold, and the ad is supposed to suggest summer. Anyway, I'm wearing this gold one-piece suit. Low-cut chest, high-cut legs. My back is arched and my eyes are closed. It's fabulous, really. Seductive, if I do say so myself. I have a feeling it will be a hit. Arthur thinks so too."

There was always a mention of Arthur, Alex mused. Arthur said this. Arthur wants me to do that. Clementine rarely, if ever, spoke of Connor. Ah, love. What a pain in the ass.

Every time Alex read one of Clementine's letters, or saw a magazine ad, or read another "promising young star" quote Clementine sent her, she had to try hard not to let the jealousy swallow her up. Clementine didn't even have to try. She just flew to New York and jumped on the fast track to stardom. Back at Berkeley, Alex merely studied and studied, trudging her way through another of her six years of college.

Before she could wallow any further in self-pity, the phone rang. She hurried to the living room and answered it.

"What are you wearing tonight?"

Alex laughed and sat down on the couch. "Jeez, Meg. Not even a hello, how are you?"

"Sorry. I just never know what to wear. I always end up looking like an overdressed peacock or something the cat dragged in."

"Stop worrying. We're only going to Salizar's. It's very casual. And, Megan, it's not like you're meeting the queen of England. It's only Jackson. Believe me, he's not that exciting."

Jackson had walked into the apartment, and he glared at her. She stuck her tongue out at him.

"What time are we meeting again?"

"Seven-thirty. See you then, Megan."

Jackson had snuck up behind her, and as soon as Alex hung up the phone, his fingers were under her arms, tickling her. They fell to the floor, laughing and wrestling. Jackson was strong, but Alex was quick, and occasionally she got in a good punch in the groin.

She kicked at his knees until he loosened his grip, then she worked her way on top of him, pinning his arms beneath him.

"All right, Mr. Hollywell, you asked for it." Before he could stop her, she lifted up his shirt and slid her hands up his ribs. She tickled him until tears rolled down his cheeks.

* * *

Megan arrived at the restaurant first. She always did. She couldn't be late for anything—dinner, dates, dentist appointments. The waiter escorted her to the table, and she sat down alone.

Knowing that Alex's idea of casual could mean anything from shorts and a tank top to an evening gown, Megan had chosen something in the middle—a pale yellow wool dress tied at the waist with a white sash, and a single string of pearls around her neck.

She was unreasonably nervous. She was only having dinner with Alex, after all. And Alex's roommate, Jackson. Someone she had heard so much about she practically knew him already. Still, her palms sweated and her heart raced. Meeting new people always did that to her. It was so important to make a good first impression, and she had only one chance to do it.

She heard Alex before she saw her. It was the laugh. The rich, full-bodied laugh that made everyone around her smile. Megan turned her head to the restaurant entrance along with everyone else. Alex and Jackson were walking toward her.

"Goodness, you look pretty," Alex said, kissing her cheek. She stood aside, and Megan had her first clear view of Jackson.

"This is my best friend, Megan," Alex said. "Megan, this is my other best friend, Jackson."

"It's so nice to finally meet you," Jackson said, shaking her hand. "I've heard so much about you."

Megan wondered if he noticed she was trembling. She was sure her whole face was quivering like jelly, but it couldn't have been, or Alex would have said something. She should have expected Jackson to be handsome. More handsome than any man she'd ever seen in her life, in fact. Alex wouldn't live with just anybody. But then, Alex had told her they were only friends and that she didn't want a relationship. Megan wondered how Alex could live with him and not want a relationship.

Jackson sat down on one side of Megan while Alex took the opposite chair. He wondered why Alex hadn't mentioned how pretty Megan was. How soft. From what Alex had said, he'd pictured Megan much differently. Plump, rougher-skinned, definitely not the beauty she was. He knew Alex cared deeply for her friend, yet she often made Megan sound small, insignificant, as if her quiet acceptance of life made her less important to the world.

As Alex and Megan started talking, he took the opportunity to study Megan. Her hair was golden even in the dim light. He caught only glimpses of her blue eyes, for she avoided his gaze. It was funny, he mused, but though he'd just met her, she already affected him, made him feel taller and stronger, like the hero at the end of a movie. And it was funny how nice the feeling was, how it seemed impossible that he hadn't missed it before.

"The fish is really good here," he heard Alex say. "Especially the halibut. How about a bottle of wine?"

He and Megan agreed, and they ordered. When the wine arrived, Jackson poured each of them a glass and offered a toast.

"To old friends and new friends."

Megan chanced a direct glance at him and found herself swallowed up in the depths of his eyes. She pulled the glass to her lips and drank. The wine slid down her throat, and still she couldn't look away.

Jackson stared at her, his mind shifting data, refiling, trying to determine if maybe some of his ideas about avoiding relationships had been wrong. He could imagine Megan, comfortable in one of his work shirts, her hair down around her face, her arms out to him, needing him to love her. He had a sudden desire to be needed.

Alex watched Jackson and Megan and sighed. She had known they would hit it off. Despite Jackson's insistence that he could get along quite well without a woman, deep down he needed someone to love him. And God knows Megan needed someone to love.

As Alex looked at Megan and saw the possibilities dance in her eyes, she knew there was no greater thrill than those moments before anything had happened, when everything was still possible. A new man, and suddenly the world was fresh again for Megan, as if someone had sponged the dirt off the windows and made them sparkle. She was wondering if he would call and what she would say and when their first touch would come and how it would feel. Briefly, with an intensity that sucked the breath right out of her, Alex felt an aching desire to be in Megan's chair. To feel her heart race, to be ingenuous enough to give up her soul for love.

Thankfully, the feeling subsided, and she was Alex again, strong, confident, alone. She closed off her mind to any and all unwanted thoughts, as if she had all of her emotions sorted into separate cabinets and could lock certain ones up when she was tired of looking at them.

She watched the two of them stare at each other, and wondered what was bothering her about the picture. She wanted them to be together; that was why she'd set up this dinner. Still, something was wrong, some ingredient missing that she had yet to identify. They were obviously attracted to each other, but Alex felt uneasy. Megan had been through so much already, and she didn't want her to be hurt again. Yet there was nothing she could do. The die had been cast, and Megan and Jackson had fallen for each other. Alex set down her glass and cleared her throat.

"Shall we order?"

# CHAPTER 9

*Up until the night she met Jackson, Meg-*
an was running a treadmill, getting nowhere and bored
with the scenery. College life at San Francisco State University was the same thing day after day—notes, studying,
tests, lectures, on and on. Alex said to give it time. Pretty
soon, Megan would feel like she belonged there. She had
only to catch the ambition bug, then each day of learning something new and moving closer to her career goals
would be exciting and stimulating.

If Megan caught anything, though, it was only the out-
of-place, want-to-go-home flu she'd been plagued with all
through high school. Only now, instead of head cheerleaders and football captains surrounding her, there
were future brain surgeons and political activists, all with
a sense of purpose and promise. And then there *she* was,
still leading the life everyone else thought she should
lead, pretending to enjoy herself for her parents' sake,
and wondering what her version of happiness was and if
she'd ever find it.

Her grades were mediocre, but she had no desire to
improve them. She simply wasn't motivated. The idea of
becoming a social worker and helping people sounded
appealing, but the drudgery of getting there, plodding

through four years to reach a bachelor's degree, then another year for a master's in social work, stretched out before her like a teenager's summer vacation with her family—excruciatingly dull and lifetimes long.

Alex told her to visualize her life ten years down the line. She should imagine herself in her office, black-framed diplomas on the walls, working with troubled teens or abused children, then going home in the evening satisfied that she had made a difference. Megan's next question always was, *"What am I going home to? Is there someone waiting on the other side of the door? Am I living in the country, in a ranch-style house behind a white picket fence where the sun shines most every day, or am I still in Sausalito, driving home in the fog to my parents?"* For one of the few times in her life, Alex had no answer.

Alex and Clementine encouraged her to move out of her parents' home, find an apartment of her own, or at least move to the dorms at San Francisco State. Megan saw little point to that. She didn't want to live alone, and there was no one from college she knew well enough to live with. As for the dorms, she hated school enough as it was. She wasn't going to add insult to injury by actually living there.

So she plowed through, her head down, pressing forward into the wind. She attended classes, studied, occasionally went out with Alex, sometimes for coffee with classmates, and answered Clementine's letters with a minimum of hostility. "I'm thrilled that so many wonderful, too-good-to-be-true events have happened in your life," she would write, slamming the pen down after every sentence. She'd get the letter out of the house and out of her mind as fast as possible. She loved her friend, and she didn't understand why her success was such a bitter pill to swallow. Perhaps it simply drove home the point that all women were not created equal, that happiness was not doled out in equal portions.

Megan ate sporadically, watched television, read seven romance novels a week, and slept. She was only nineteen. She knew there should be more. She should be feeling more, doing more. Life wasn't meant to be like this—barely getting through, with no hope, no future goals, no shiny prospects on the horizon. There had to be something out there that excited her, that made her come alive with energy and desire and motivation. When she met Jackson Hollywell, Megan discovered what it was.

• • • •

Jackson wasted no time asking Megan for a date. He got her number from Alex and called her the day after they met, inviting her to meet him the following Saturday in Golden Gate Park in front of the museum. Megan had hoped he would call, had willed the phone to ring with every fiber of her body. Yet when it did, she had been so shaken, she'd almost lost the nerve to pick it up. When Jackson asked her out, his voice was soft, and she'd imagined he'd sent his breath through the receiver into her ear, tickling her, standing her hairs on end. She took a deep breath and steadied herself, and of course she said yes.

She arrived at the park early. Again. She'd spent the better part of the morning getting ready. She had to wear just the right amount of makeup. Not too much, in case they were going to spend the day outside, but not too little, in case he wanted to walk through the museum, where the lights were dim.

And then there were the clothes choices. September afternoons could be cool, although when she looked out the window in the morning, the sun was bright and strong. She decided on pleated beige pants and a dark green short-sleeved sweater. She stared at herself in the mirror before she left. After all she'd gone through, it was the brightness in her eyes, not the blush or eyeshadow, that made her look attractive. It was amazing, she thought, what a little excitement could do for one's complexion.

She sat down on a bench in front of the museum and waited. The park was bustling with people. Tight-lipped parents and hyperactive children headed for the museum and planetarium. Couples, men and women and men and men, held hands and talked in hushed voices as they walked through the wooded paths. Long-haired, time-warped hippies sat on the lawn playing guitars, and old men studied their chess sets with hardly a blink or a thought to the time speeding by while they pondered their moves.

Megan closed her eyes to everyone around her and turned her face up to the sun. Its warmth was magical, penetrating her skin and suffusing her with the joy that comes only from love's first days, when butterflies live in stomachs, colors are vivid, emotions are raw, and the world seems endless with possibilities. She smiled without opening her eyes.

Jackson stood against the wall of the museum, watching her. It seemed impossible that only a week ago he didn't know her, had never seen her, had never felt the wild feelings inside of him. They must have met before, known each other in another lifetime. They were connected, able to read each other's thoughts without words. When he had turned to look at her at dinner the other night, she had been looking at him. When she had laughed, he'd smiled at her happiness. When she had left, he'd felt lifeless and empty, as if a part of him had left with her.

From what Alex had told him and what he'd learned the other night, they were nothing alike. Megan was shy, easily frightened, uncertain. He was outgoing, a risk seeker, and sure. As he looked at her, though, with her face tilted up to the sun, capturing the rays in her hair and skin like golden sparkles, none of that mattered. Megan made him feel alive. Strong, whole, completely a man. Nothing else, not incompatible dreams, histories, or passions, seemed important when compared to that. He walked toward her.

"Hello," he said. She opened her eyes quickly and stood up, self-conscious, as if he'd peered into her mind and caught her in a romantic daydream.

"Hi."

He smiled at her, and the trapped-animal look in her eyes disappeared. Her shoulders relaxed.

"I thought we could just walk for a while," he said. "And talk."

She nodded and slipped her arm through his when he offered it. They headed down the steps to one of the tree-shrouded paths.

"I'm glad you could come," he said softly when all sounds of people and guitars and children's cries had disappeared and they were left alone with the wind and the birds.

"Me too."

He glanced at her, then turned his eyes forward again. "This may sound strange, Megan, but I feel like I've always known you. Like without even talking, I know what you're thinking and you know my thoughts. Isn't that crazy?"

When he spoke her name, Megan shivered. If only she could hear him say it every day, when he came home from work and kissed her on the mouth; when they lay in bed, coiled around each other after making love; in the morning, when she woke up beside him. Being with him felt so right. How could she ever have thought that what she had with Tony was the real thing? That was child's play, a pretend kind of love with no backbone or substance. This was real. Jackson was kind and warm and honest. He wouldn't hurt her.

"No, I don't think it's crazy," she said finally, inhaling the cleanness of the trees, the dust splattered off their leaves by the rain the night before. "I feel that way too."

Jackson smiled, delighted, and held her arm tighter against his body. "Well, then, I want to spend the whole day with you. Doing everything. First lunch and then anything you'd like. A walk on the wharf, Chinatown, shopping, whatever. So long as you're happy."

It seemed impossible that he was serious, that of all the things he could be doing, of all the people he could be with, he wanted to be with her. Yet his spring-green eyes were serious, locked on her with no quick side glances to see what he was missing. They headed to the street where his car was parked. Megan was sure everyone was staring at them, marveling at the happiness that must have been bursting out of her skin like moonbeams. It was difficult not to smile at the strangers she passed, wanting to share her joy. Let the world think she was a little off kilter, she thought. She was falling in love. That explained everything.

• • •

At the end of the evening, they sat in the dark cocoon of Jackson's car, silent. Outside, a few men jogged by, a mounted policeman steered his horse out of sight around a corner, and the moon hid like a prison escapee behind the clouds. Megan's car was parked a few feet away.

Jackson reached over and took her small hand in his. He'd held her hand earlier, when they ran for the cable car, but this was different. There was no excuse for their touch now.

She remained silent. She had talked and laughed most of the day, as delighted by the flowers he bought her and the ice cream they shared as a child finding an Easter egg stuffed with candy. On the cable cars, she'd held the railing and leaned out the side to catch the wind on her face, laughing. He'd been shocked to learn that although she'd lived in the Bay area her whole life, she'd never been on them before. But that was part of Megan's charm. She'd lived and yet not lived, been a part of her world and somehow never experienced it. He felt like her teacher, instructing her on the finer points of life, how to enjoy it, how to squeeze every pleasure out of it and meet each moment head-on without fear.

Over hamburgers at lunch, she told him about her parents, with their most expensive house on the most expensive hill in Sausalito. While they walked along the wharf, she told him about college, her lack of enthusiasm, her dull life that had run on and on without any signs of letting up until she met him. She actually said that—until she met him. In the car, he waited for a pair of headlights to pass, then squeezed her hand.

"You had fun today?" he asked.

"Oh yes," she said, turning toward him.

"That's good."

An awkward silence followed. They both looked straight ahead, focusing on cars, teenagers lurking in the woods, anything but each other. Megan bit her lip, wondering where the ease they'd shared all day had gone. Why couldn't they just skip this phase, the awkward, groping, hand-tangling phase, and move on to a peaceful, friendly companionship, the kind couples shared in books and sitcoms? She sighed.

"Do you want to go home?" he asked.

She jerked away, pulling her hand out of his grip and scooting toward the door. "Okay. Let me just find my keys." She bent down for her purse on the floor, but Jackson grabbed her shaking hands before she could reach it.

"Look at me, Meg," he said softly. When she kept her eyes averted, he released one of her hands and turned her head toward him with his fingertips.

He said nothing, just looked at her, until he saw the moisture in her eyes.

"I don't want you to go," he said.

She seemed to melt then, right before his eyes, the layer of fear coating her face dissolving. "You can trust me, you know."

Megan nodded, afraid to speak, afraid that if she made even the smallest movement or sound, he would fade away like the last remnants of a hazy dream. He leaned forward. His lips touched her cheek delicately, almost as if he was afraid of damaging her. She closed her eyes, and he kissed away the moisture at the corners of her lids.

"Oh, Megan," he said. She encircled his neck with her arms and held on tightly. "I've never felt like this before. You make me feel so good."

Megan burrowed her face into his neck, inhaling his scent of grass and leather and rubbing her cheek against his collar.

"Please, don't let me go," she whispered.

He clasped his hands around her back and locked her hard in his embrace.

"Never. Never, Megan."

•   •   •

Megan drove home slowly. She hadn't had a drop of alcohol, yet she felt drunk and had to keep her hands locked on the steering wheel. She smiled at the passing motorists, though in the darkness they couldn't see her.

Megan Hollywell. She ran the name over her tongue, enjoying every syllable. Mrs. Megan Hollywell. She'd wear white, of course. A few months ago, she'd seen the gown she wanted on the cover of a bridal magazine. It had embroidered lace around the collar, twelve layers of ruffles in the skirt that fell over a petticoat to the floor. She liked the feel of Jackson high above her, so she'd wear white satin ballerina slippers. And, of course, a blush veil for Jackson to lift ever so slowly before he kissed her and sealed their vows.

She laughed as she started over the Golden Gate Bridge. The lights of the bay were glorious, a thousand candles lit especially for her. Clementine would tell her not to jump the gun. Slow down, get her bearings, play it cool until she knew exactly where she and Jackson were heading. Well, that was all very well and good for Miss Montgomery, queen of the models who could have any man she chose. But a Jackson Hollywell came around only once in a lifetime, if ever, for someone like Megan. If she didn't grab him, she'd never get another chance. She just wasn't special enough to attract someone like him twice.

Besides, it was impossible to play it cool when he was nearby. She fit so perfectly into the hollow of his shoulder, like the final piece of a puzzle. He was strong enough for both of them, and with him by her side she'd never have to fear anything again. Most amazing of all, his feelings for her seemed just as intense. He'd held her so tightly before saying good night that, for a moment, she hadn't been able to breathe. The lack of oxygen had made her dizzy, yet she'd never wanted him to stop. Every sign pointed to a relationship, a lasting relationship. And yet . . . And yet he went home to Alex.

Megan cleared the bridge and headed through the windy Sausalito streets toward home. She loved Alex with all her heart. But dammit, could Megan never have someone free and clear of her? Alex had been with Tony first. And despite their rocky start, Clementine and Alex became friends instead of Alex's leaving Clementine for Megan. And now Jackson. Megan drummed her fingers on the steering wheel as she headed up the steep hill to her parents' house. Okay, so she never would have met Jackson if it hadn't been for Alex. Still, did he have to

live with her? Would he talk to her about their date?
Would Alex tell him it was a good idea, a bad one?
Would he take one look at Alex and wonder what the
hell he was doing with her?

Megan parked in the driveway and slammed her fist
on the steering wheel. "Enough. Enough. Enough." For
once, she'd have to have faith in herself. Self-confidence
and determination, like Alex and Clementine had.

"I'm special enough to keep him," she said to herself,
stepping out of the car and slamming the door. She
walked to the house and let herself in, deliberately ignoring the gnawing doubt that tickled her stomach.

• • •

Alex was sitting on the living room couch studying her
economics textbook when Jackson walked in. He looked
at the clock on the table beside her—one forty-five AM—
and took off his coat.

"What are you, my mother?"

She closed her book and retied the sash of her bathrobe. "As a matter of fact, I have a big test tomorrow in
Hansen's class."

"Yeah, sure." Jackson walked to the kitchen and took
a soda out of the refrigerator. He opened the can and sat
down on the couch beside her.

"Truth?" he asked.

"No. Can I help it if I'm curious?"

He laughed and kicked off his shoes. "That's better.
What do you want to know?"

"Everything, you idiot. Did you get along? Was it what
you expected? Are you going out again? Did you elope,
what?"

He took a long sip, then set the drink down on the table. Turning toward her, he laid his arm on the back of
the sofa and rested his chin on it.

"She makes me feel like a man, Alex. Don't laugh. I
know it's a cliché, but it's true. Megan is so soft and fragile. I want to cradle her in my arms and make sure no
one ever hurts her again."

Alex ran her hand through her hair, untangling it.
"And how does she feel?"

"The same, I think. I mean, she has the same look of urgency in her eyes that I do."

"God, this was only your first date." She stood up and circled the room. "Why do you have to make it sound like it's now or never?"

"It's not all like that. We laughed a lot. We did touristy things. The cable cars, Chinatown, stuff like that. We were like kids again. I felt so comfortable with her. I was reminded of an old married couple who knew each other so well, they didn't need words anymore. They felt each other's thoughts."

Alex stopped pacing and whirled to face him. She opened her mouth, then closed it again.

"What?" he asked.

"Nothing."

"Alex, you were going to say something."

"You won't want to hear it."

"Try me."

She returned to the couch and sat down, taking Jackson's hand in hers.

"I was just thinking that I wished I had a tape recorder. When you finally come out of this love haze, I'd like to play back your words. You wouldn't believe it."

"Why do you say that?"

"Because you don't sound like you. 'Reminded of an old married couple.' Good God. What about a new married couple? What about excitement and love and passion? You make it sound like Megan's already in the rocking chair and you're in the recliner. Is that what you want? Since when were you interested in becoming a comfortable old fuddy-duddy?"

"Hey, it's my life."

"Of course it is. But don't screw it up. Don't start going in a direction that's totally wrong for you."

Jackson pulled his hand away and stood up. He walked to the doorway of his bedroom and turned around.

"I thought that you, of all people, would be happy for me. God, you'd think you'd want us to be together."

"I don't give a shit whether you're together or not," Alex said, getting up too. "If she makes you happy, finc

But you're not seeing things clearly. You're right, Megan is fragile. She needs a life in the country with some homebody man and two-point-two kids. I'm not putting that down. All I'm saying is that man is not you. Your kind of love is different from hers."

"What the hell do you know about love? You're so scared of it, you don't even want it close to you. You're afraid it will rub off on you and make you weak and human like the rest of us."

Alex stiffened her shoulders. "I know enough, Jack. I know that kind of life might sound appealing. It even sounds nice and comforting to me sometimes, believe it or not. You've been looking for meaning in your life, and now you think you've found it in Megan. But just tell me what happens in a few years when Megan is happily raising a family, tending her garden, and you're pacing around your easels stuck away in a corner of the basement wondering where your dreams went."

Jackson stared at her, anger building up, then, just as quickly, subsiding. He walked over to her and touched the back of his hand to her cheek.

"I don't want to fight."

She drew a deep breath and put her hand over his. "I know."

"Let's just take it one day at a time, okay?"

She nodded. Crossing the room, she picked her economics book off the sofa and headed for her bedroom.

"Alex?"

"Yes," she said, not turning around.

"Still friends?"

She picked up his shoe from the floor and turned in a flash, throwing it at him and hitting him hard in the stomach. "Hell, yes," she said, and closed her door.

• • •

There really was no dating. At least none that Alex could see. Jackson and Megan met, they fell in love, and they got engaged. All in less than two months.

She learned to hold her tongue. After that one conversation with Jackson, she never brought up her fears to him again. It took only a single discussion with Megan, too, to make her realize that Megan was as unwilling to listen to reason as he was.

"I think you're going too fast," Alex had said two weeks after Megan and Jackson met. They'd been sitting on Megan's bed as they'd done so many times before, talking about the same subject—boys, now grown to men.

"Why?" Megan had said, not really listening. Instead, she got up and began searching through her closet for the perfect outfit to wear to dinner with Jackson that evening.

"Because you hardly know him and already you're talking marriage. Megan, shouldn't you give it some time to see if you're really compatible?"

"No, I don't think so." Megan tossed two dresses on the bed and squinted at them. Shaking her head, she returned to the closet.

"Dammit, listen to me," Alex said, jumping up and stomping to the closet. She closed the door and pulled Megan back to the bed. "Sit down."

"What's wrong with you?"

"You and Jackson are what's wrong with me. Listen to me. I think this is a mistake."

Megan turned her head to the side, away from her. "You're just jealous," she whispered so quietly Alex couldn't hear.

"What?"

"I said you're jealous."

"That's ridiculous. Jackson is my friend. Period. Hell, I introduced you two."

"All right. So maybe you're not jealous of me, but you're jealous because I'm in love."

Alex breathed deeply and sat down. "I'm not jealous, Meg. Really. If you're truly in love, then I'm happy for you."

Megan turned toward her. "Really?"

"Of course."

Megan hugged her. "I'm so glad. I want to share this with you. With Clementine so far away, I need you so much more."

"You've got me. But you know I always say what I feel.

I can't pretend that everything is perfect when I don't think it is."

Megan nodded and smoothed down one of the dresses she'd discarded, rethinking her decision. "Fine. Go ahead and tell me."

Alex shook her head, watching Megan's interest drift back to clothes and makeup choices. She spoke her thoughts anyway.

"It's just that you're charging ahead like a freight train, not looking where you're going. Have you thought about the future? Have you two talked about your goals, what you want your life to be like ten, twenty years from now? Do you understand Jackson's need to paint, and does he understand how family-oriented and old-fashioned you are? Are you sure your ideas mesh?"

With a wave of her hand, Megan dismissed Alex's words. She returned to the closet and opened it, picking through the clothes again. "Oh, Alex. Just because you're a planner doesn't mean the rest of the world has to outline their lives down to the smallest detail. I love him. Plain and simple. And he loves me. It's enough."

That had been three weeks ago. Two weeks later, Jackson had proposed. Without a thought or concern or iota of trepidation, Megan had accepted. They scheduled an engagement party for the following week and the wedding for April. And there was nothing Alex could do but be happy for them.

Alex put on her coat and walked out to her car to pick up Clementine at the airport. Clementine had insisted on flying in for the party. She couldn't wait to meet this Jackson fellow, she'd said, who had stolen both of her best friends' hearts. Jackson had booked early dinner reservations for the four of them—himself, Megan, Alex, and Clementine—at Clancy's for the following night. From there, they would go to Megan's parents' house for the engagement party.

Alex headed for the freeway, thankful that once Clementine arrived, she'd have another neutral person to talk to. Someone not clouded by visions of picket fences and starry-eyed love that supposedly lasted a lifetime. Clementine would understand.

• • •

"I think it's cute," Clementine said as soon as Alex had explained all the details. They were in her car, driving home. "Really, Alex, don't worry so much. People change. If this Jackson thinks he wants a wife and kids, then maybe he does. It's his life."

"But it's not him," Alex said, maneuvering through the rush-hour traffic back toward the city. She glared at a teenage boy who cut her off. "I've known Jack for over a year now. He has dreams. He wants to be a painter. He'll never be satisfied with a life like that."

"Look, some people change. They fall in love, and the picture gets a new perspective."

"That didn't happen to me or you."

"Well, we're different. We won't let it happen. Even when you were dating every boy in sight, you still put school first. You put your life first. The same goes for me. I meandered a little with Connor, but thank God, I'm back on course now."

Alex stole a glance at her friend and noticed the tight, determined lines around her mouth. This was a new Clementine. At least on the outside. Alex had almost laughed out loud when she first saw her walk off the plane, her lips red, her eyes expertly made up with shades of coral, her cheeks contoured perfectly with rose blush. Seeing the people around her, though, staring at Clementine as if she were a god sent down from heaven, Alex had realized just how beautiful Clementine was. She'd had her hair cut blunt at the shoulders, and Alex noticed a few auburn streaks that hadn't been there before. She was wearing a navy suit—slim-fitting skirt, white blouse, tailored navy blazer, and a white hat. She looked like English royalty, but with an added sexuality that took your breath away.

Alex had stood stiff, not knowing what to say to someone so different and unapproachable. Then Clementine had seen her and smiled, and she was just Clementine again.

"How is Connor?" Alex asked now.

Clementine shrugged and looked out the window at

the cars that surrounded them on all sides, some honking as if noise would make the gridlock go away.

"Please don't bring him up. Do you know how awful it is to try to break up with someone who still loves you? I can't bring myself to cut the ties completely. He's flown out a few times. The first visit was all right. I was lonely, I guess, and he was a present from home. But since then, each trip has gotten more difficult. He's become so demanding. He was up for a part in Hollywood, some romantic comedy film, and he got through the third audition before they said no. He took it hard, went on a three-week drinking binge, then expected me to pick up the pieces."

"Does he still want to get married?"

"Actually, he hasn't mentioned it much lately. It's funny, but I kind of miss his proposals." She shook her head and changed the subject. "God, I missed this city," she said, staring at the one-of-a-kind skyline over the bay. "New York is great, but it has no character. Someone just clumped a bunch of buildings together, threw some trash and homeless people around, and said, 'Here you go. The Big Apple.' "

Alex laughed and patted her hand. "It's good to have you back. At least for a little while."

Clementine smiled. "Thanks. And really, Alex, don't worry about Megan. I'm sure she's doing the right thing. You'll see."

• • •

Megan and Jackson arrived at Clancy's restaurant half an hour before Alex and Clementine showed up.

"Clementine always did have to spend an eternity fixing her makeup and hair," Megan said. "I can't imagine what she must be like now after modeling for over a year. Twice as bad, I'm sure."

Jackson kissed her cheek and sat back in his chair. He was happier than he ever could have imagined. He had a beautiful woman beside him who belonged to him and would become his wife in a few short months. Megan had taken to wearing her hair up, tied with a ribbon in the back, and he liked the look. He could see her face more clearly, the contour of her cheek, her blue eyes.

She was happy. He could see it in her posture, her bright smile, her easy laugh.

"You've missed her, haven't you?"

Megan nodded. "Yes. I didn't realize how much until she agreed to come back for this party. It was really sweet of her. I'm sure she must be very sophisticated by now. Her perfume ad came out this month in *Cosmopolitan.* I've heard a lot of people talking about it, wondering who she is. One of the guys in my psychology class says he keeps it taped up over his bed. Things are really going her way."

"Things are really going your way too," Jackson said, leaning over and kissing her nose. "Or have you changed your mind about me already?"

She smiled. "Never."

They were kissing when Alex and Clementine walked in.

"Excuse me," Alex said, clearing her throat. "I don't care if you're getting married or not. No groping at the table."

Megan laughed and stood up. She hurried past Alex to Clementine, who looked more regal and self-possessed than Megan remembered, and hugged her.

"You look beautiful," Megan said. And Clementine did. She'd chosen a silver silk pantsuit, the color reflecting her eyes, making them appear more see-through than ever. Her hair was swept away from her face and clasped in the back with a silver comb. A few men had stared at Megan when she entered the restaurant, but with Alex and especially Clementine there now, their gazes were riveted on their table. Megan tried not to notice.

"I want you to meet my fiancé," she said. "Jackson Hollywell, this is Clementine Montgomery, my other best friend."

Jackson stood up and held out his hand. Clementine kept her smile steady, the acting classes doing her more good than she'd realized, and took his hand in hers. It was warm and solid. She shook it once before extracting hers.

"It's so nice to meet you. My heartiest congratulations to you. You're getting a wonderful woman."

They sat down, and Jackson inched his chair closer to Megan's.

"Yes, I know," he said.

"When's the wedding again?" Clementine asked. She would simply keep the conversation moving, she told herself, leaving no time for crazy thoughts or the pitter-patter of her heart.

"April nineteenth. Only six months away."

"You must have a lot to do."

"Goodness, yes," Megan said. "The dress, the church, caterers, flowers, you name it. But you know my mother. She'll handle everything perfectly. Sometimes, I think she's more excited than I am."

Jackson ordered a bottle of champagne and hid behind the pouring duties while Megan spoke of the guest list and honeymoon plans. He waited until he was sure the women were busy in wedding talk before stealing a glance at Clementine. He'd seen the ad in *Cosmopolitan*, as well. Alex had shown it to him briefly, and he'd looked at it more closely when he was alone. It was incredibly seductive, a picture you couldn't tear your gaze away from. In it, Clementine's skin was golden, glimmering with water beads, and her light hair fell down the side of the curved rock she was lying on. The ad had nothing whatsoever to do with perfume, but he'd heard that sales for the Amour line had skyrocketed since it was released.

He had hated himself for it, but his first thought after seeing the ad was, How had Megan managed to get a best friend like that? Not that Megan wasn't wonderful, too, but Megan was honey, and Clementine was dark molasses. Megan was an orange eaten in sections after the skin was peeled away, while Clementine was a rich ripe peach oozing with juices and aching to drop from the tree.

The more he'd looked at the photograph, however, the more Jackson had realized it was only an illusion. People never looked as good as they did in print ads, where artists spent hours airbrushing faces to perfection. It was a good thing he had the real thing beside him in Megan.

The only problem with his theory was that Clementine was sitting across from him now, real, alive, flesh and blood, and looking better than she had in the ad. He lost control of his thoughts again and found himself imagining what it would be like to be sitting beside her, her slim hand in his, with everyone talking about their wedding. He hated himself for it, and yet he couldn't stop. Every nerve in his body was on edge, tingling to touch her just to see if her skin was as soft as it looked.

He'd heard so much about her from Alex and Megan—her lifelong dream of being a model and the way she'd gone after her goals with every ounce of energy she had. Her determination to succeed reminded him of himself. He had tried to explain his obsession with art to Megan, but when she turned her head to the side, thinking that he couldn't see her gaze wander in search of something more interesting to lock onto, he'd realized she didn't care. After a few efforts, he stopped trying.

Now he had a sudden urge to talk to Clementine about his love, his dreams, his resolve to make it, no matter what. In his gut, he knew she would be interested. She would understand and want him to succeed as a painter or nothing else, just as he did. She would never say that he could simply be an architect if things didn't work out, the way Megan did, as if it were only the weather column in the newspaper they were discussing rather than his soul, his life.

He watched Clementine openly now while she talked to Megan about music choices for the ceremony. She sat straight, the way mothers wished their children would sit. She didn't cower. When the waiter asked for their orders, she looked straight at him.

Finally, Jackson tore his gaze away and looked at Megan. She seemed even softer, when flanked by her two best friends. She was glowing, so in love and thrilled to be marrying him that all of his doubts disappeared. He leaned over and kissed her cheek. Clementine was for men with power and prestige. Men who wanted to live the high life, conquer all they saw, jet-set around the world. Jackson only wanted a happy life. A comfortable life. He'd work a little, paint a little, and love a lot. Megan grasped his hand beneath the table and held it tightly. The band of the diamond engagement ring he'd given her pressed against his finger and felt solid and comforting.

"We have something to ask both of you," Megan said to Alex and Clementine after they'd finished the meal. "It may sound a little strange, but I think it's perfect."

She sat forward and smiled. "We love you both, you know that. So we were hoping that Clementine would agree to be my maid of honor and because you're so close to both of us, Alex, you would be Jackson's best man, best person, whatever. Best everything."

Alex laughed. "I like best man. It suits me. Of course I'll do it. All right with you, Clemmie?"

Clementine wrenched her gaze from the man across from her. She'd taken a chance and looked directly at him when Megan had started talking, and had instantly wished she hadn't. She'd never seen anyone like him. He had only to look at her, and her insides felt queasy and unsteady. She saw now what Alex had been talking about, her doubts about his marriage to Megan. He had a fire that burned so brightly in his eyes, it was unbelievably cruel to stifle it in suburbia. Yet he was choosing that life. It was obvious he loved Megan. She should be happy for them, Clementine thought, and smiled at Megan.

"Of course I'll be your maid of honor. Maybe I can even come in a few days early and help."

"I'd love that," Megan said.

Clementine saw the happiness that radiated from Megan's eyes. She held out her hand, and Megan grasped it.

"I'm thrilled for you, Meg. I mean that."

"I know," Megan said, looking at her husband-to-be. "I think I must be the luckiest woman in the world."

# CHAPTER 10

*CLEMENTINE SAW PLACES SHE'D NEVER* dreamed of. The undersides of bridges, torn-up railroad tracks, country barns, penthouse suites, Fifth Avenue at three in the morning, the only time the crew could convince the NYPD to let them close down the street and shoot half-naked women in next summer's hottest fashions. She went where she was told, wore bikinis when it was freezing and furs when the sun beat down, smiled until her teeth ached, and wondered why on earth she'd ever wanted to be a model in the first place.

This was not glamour. Being told to turn and sit and laugh on command made her feel like someone's poodle. Photographers blasted her, told her her nose was too long, her hips too wide. Advertising executives said she didn't wear their clothes well, was not a convincing enough salesperson. Camera crews, makeup artists, hairstylists, the whole lot of them, when they weren't criticizing, didn't see her at all. They saw through her, to sales figures and hair products sold. She didn't feel like a commodity to be used so much as a nothing, a blank canvas that was meaningless and ignored until they began to paint her, making her into the product they wanted to see.

Needless to say, it was not what she had expected. At first it was exciting, seeing her picture in glossy magazines. This was success, after all. Well, not all-out, wow-the-world success, but a start. She'd been in *Cosmopolitan* and *Vogue*. Arthur's phone rang consistently, if not for cover photos, then at least with requests that she be one of ten girls in a jeans ad. But the excitement faded quickly. The shoots were all pretty much the same—long, exhausting, boring. And she was no different from any of the other models in the magazines. Nothing about her made her stand out from the crowd.

She was far from writing her own ticket. She was still eating meat loaf instead of thick, tender steaks. Oh, sure, she wrote home to Alex and Megan and made it *sound* like she had everything she'd ever wanted, but those were just words used for effect. Long ago, she learned that no one listened unless she had something spectacular to say. And she wanted to be heard so badly, a little stretch was no crime.

Arthur, at least, was a comfort.

"Give it time," he said almost daily. Time. As if her face would stay this smooth forever. As if she could survive the nights in the bathroom, vomiting up the chocolate cake that would otherwise show on her stomach the next morning. As if people would wait forever for her to become famous like she promised, instead of smirking at one another and saying, "Ha! I always knew she'd be a disappointment."

"You'll make it," Arthur said so calmly and surely, she wanted to bottle the words. She believed him because she had to, because she had given up the life she knew, her mother, her best friends, even love. Two weeks earlier, she had ended it completely with Connor. He'd said he was going to fly out again, and she'd known it was time to tell him how she felt.

"I don't think so," she'd said to him.

"Why not?"

She curled up around the phone in her bedroom and took a deep breath.

"I think we should just say good-bye, Connor. It's been

over between us for a long time. We should stop fooling ourselves."

He was quiet for a long time, and she was amazed that the same physical sensations occurred both at the beginning of a relationship and at the end, as if they were just two sides of the same coin. Her heart pounded hard, her palms grew damp. She was as nervous about hurting him as she had once been about meeting him. Finally, he spoke.

"If I were a star," he asked softly, "would it be different?"

"Oh, Connor, no. I loved you for you. It's just too hard to stay together now. We're too far apart."

The line was quiet again, and then, a minute later, she heard the gentle click of the receiver as he hung up. Only one tear fell before she pushed him out of her mind. It was for the best. It had to be for the best.

It was stardom or nothing. She would do everything—forgo love, stand for a shoot for five hours without complaint, change her hair, fill her bloodstream with diet pills, vomit—whatever it took to make it.

That meant showing up in dives like this. Clementine stared at the worn gray building in a not-too-comforting part of town, then back at the address in her hand. The two matched.

"It's a layout for Spielman Casual Wear," Arthur had told her.

"Not another catalogue," she'd complained. She had dressed in enough clothes she would never be caught dead in to last a lifetime.

"Yes, one more."

And, of course, she was here. Arthur was the boss. He was a good agent. He got her work most every day. He had found her a nice apartment uptown that she could afford, which was far better than the hovel in Brooklyn she'd been living in for the year and a half she'd been in New York. He was even a good friend. It was he who held her hand when she fell into melancholy over her friends left behind in California, over breaks that went to other models.

She still smiled when she remembered thinking he

was a sex pervert. Some pervert. He never even kissed
her. She knew he wanted to. She'd learned to read that
look in men's eyes long ago. But he never acted on it.
They were good friends who had good laughs and a sensational business relationship, and perhaps he was afraid
of spoiling all that. Sometimes she was thankful. After
Connor, she needed a breather. Other times, she
thought his lips on hers were just what she needed to
make this whole damn struggle worthwhile.

She walked inside the building and looked around. It
was dark, lit only by a murky yellow light at the top of the
stairs and the cloudy daylight that snuck in under the
door. She had the strangest feeling that she shouldn't be
there.

"Miss Montgomery, is that you?"

She looked up to see a man and woman she recognized as the owners of Spielman Casual Wear standing at
the top of the stairs. The woman smiled down at her.

"I know it's not what you're used to, but we're just
starting out, and this was the best we could do. We use
two adjoining rooms up here for our studios."

Clementine swallowed the last remnant of her pride
and smiled back.

"It's fine," she said, walking up the stairs. This was a
job, and that was what mattered. Not the roaches that
skittered across the floor or the draft that would chill her
or the condescending look Mr. Spielman gave her, as if
he was doing her the biggest favor in the world by letting
her play dress-up in his clothes in this hellhole. Only the
work mattered.

She spent seven hours in the cramped apartment, posing in everything from evening dresses to lingerie. The
clothes weren't too horrible, but nothing incredibly
fresh, either. The Spielmans would put out just another
junk-mail catalogue that ninety-nine percent of Ameri-
cans threw immediately into their garbage.

Clementine sat and knelt and smiled and pretended
to throw a beach ball in front of tacky airbrushed back-
grounds that would fool no one. They paid her—or
rather they would pay Arthur, who paid her, minus his fifteen percent commission—forty dollars an hour. Two

hundred and eighty dollars. Two hundred and thirty-eight for her, she figured in her head with the speed of a woman to whom money meant everything. At midnight, when they were finally through, she dressed again in her own clothes, her bones raw, her stomach craving food, her mind starved for words other than "turn," "smile," "no, not like that," and thought that it wasn't nearly enough money.

The Spielmans and their photographer asked her out for coffee, but she declined. All she wanted was to take a cab to her new apartment on the Upper West Side, make herself a colossal turkey sandwich, and soak in a bath for hours.

"Lock up then, will you?" Mrs. Spielman asked.

"Yes, of course."

They left, and Clementine gathered the remainder of her things. She locked the studio's four locks as she left and walked down the steps. She was almost to the door when she heard the creak of the floorboards behind her.

She turned around slowly, or at least that was how she would always remember it. Every action for the next two hours took days, years to complete. He was standing right behind her, his dark hair in his eyes, his mustache hiding his mouth, a knife gleaming in his dirty hands.

"What—What do you want?"

He stepped closer, so that she could smell the sewer odor of him. Her gaze darted up the stairs, behind him, to the sides. She slid her foot back toward the door until she hit it. She spun and dived for it, but he was on her before she'd even turned the knob. He slammed her into the wall and held the blade at her throat.

"Think you're a real snake, don't you?" he said.

*Don't cry,* Clementine told herself. *Whatever you do, don't let him see you cry.*

He smiled at her, revealing yellow teeth, one of the front ones missing.

"Saw you come in. A model, ain't ya?"

She said nothing and focused on the wall behind him, on the speck of blood or feces that someone had smeared there.

"Answer me!" he shouted, shaking her.

"Yes."

He smiled again. Stepping back, the knife still held out in front of him, he looked her over.

"Not bad. No Marilyn Monroe, but not bad."

"What do you want?" she asked. "I don't have much money, but you can have it. Just take it and go."

He picked up her purse and took the few bills she had out of her wallet. He slipped out her credit cards and took those too.

Then he moved close to her again and slid the dull end of the blade along her cheek. It was ice-cold, and she closed her eyes.

"Never had me a model before," he said.

He pressed his knee against her leg, and her eyes flew open. The pressure felt like thousands of ants crawling over her. She started shaking and heard a strange sound in her head, like a high-pitched whistle.

"What's your name?" he asked.

The whistle got louder and the shaking worse. She tried to lift her hands to fight him, to do something other than stand there and let him press his sickening leg against hers, but except for the shaking, she was paralyzed.

"Your name, dammit. What's your name?"

She opened her mouth, but nothing emerged. He drew the knife back and stabbed it into her shoulder. The pain tore at her, shooting down her arm and out the ends of her fingertips. She screamed as blood spilled out, dripping onto the floor, but he clamped his free hand over her mouth.

"What the fuck is your name?"

Tears slid down her cheeks. She felt dizzy, and she thought there was too much blood for just one cut.

"Jane," she said. "Jane Doe."

He looked her in the eye, then grabbed her injured arm. He clamped down on the wound, squeezing the blood out, and pulled her with him toward the back of the building. He opened a door and yanked her into the alley. A wino sat along the far wall, but when the man glared at him, he ran away. Clementine called after him for help, but the man only laughed.

"This ain't no cop show," he said. "No winos are gonna rescue you."

He threw her against the hard brick wall, and her head reeled. She thought of tomorrow's shoot and what she would wear and whether they would take her with her shoulder bleeding so bad. Then she realized how crazy it was to think of something like that at a time like this, and she laughed. The laughter came from deep inside her, and it sounded alien and sick, not even a part of her. The man stepped toward her again.

"You like that, huh? A little roughhousing turns you on?"

He aimed the knife for her chest. He had to be moving in slow motion, for in the few seconds it took for the knife to reach her, she thought of Duke and her mother, and how much she loved them both, no matter what they did to her. She thought of Connor and how the love had built and exploded and died, like a supernova, and how much she had hated saying good-bye. And Arthur and all his kindnesses and, despite his good looks, how she didn't feel anything for him but friendship. And her career, which meant so little now, when everything was magnified so greatly. And Megan and Jackson and how she wished them happiness. And Alex, and how disappointed she would be to know that Clementine hadn't been able to fight, had been like every other woman too scared to kick and scream and find a way out. "She really was nothing special after all," Alex would say. And she would be right.

She watched the knife lunge forward, waiting for that last pain calmly, almost resigned to it. It didn't come. All she felt was the snap of the top button of her blouse as the knife ripped the fabric away.

"No," she said. "Not that."

He didn't listen. He ripped the blouse in half and stared at her breasts, milky white in the darkness. Involuntarily, her gaze fell to his pants, to the hardness pressing against his fly.

"You want it, don't you?" he said.

As if a demon had been let loose inside of her, Clementine leapt at him. She didn't care about the knife. She would rather die than let him rape her. She didn't even feel the blade as it grazed her stomach. She only wanted to rip his tongue out so he could never speak again, grab his penis and chew it to pieces and spit it back in his face. His violence had invaded her, and the black images were no longer cruel or disgusting, only what she had to do to survive.

She dug her nails into his face, drawing blood. She kicked at his groin, pummeled his ribs with her fists. He screamed only once, then came back at her with the same fury she'd unleashed on him. Only he was stronger. He slammed his fists into her stomach, and the air rushed out of her. She fell to the ground, and he was immediately on top of her, pinning her. He held her until she ran out of steam, until her mind was the only thing left fighting him.

He unzipped his pants and then hers. He pulled hers down roughly, and her butt hit the cold, muddy pavement of the alley. He wedged his knee between her legs and, smiling, rammed himself inside her.

Clementine struggled for only a moment before she knew she couldn't win. Her insides were being ripped apart, torn away. Her blood was sliding out of her. She cried without making any noise. He was so intent on beating himself into her, leaving his mark, that he didn't notice her slamming her head against the concrete again and again until finally, mercifully, she passed out.

•   •   •

Clementine sat in the bathtub and let the boiling, bloody water turn tepid. She drained it three times without getting out, refilling it again with more fiery water. She had scrubbed herself hard, over and over, but she could still smell him. She would probably always smell him.

The phone disturbed her twice, ringing seven times before the person finally gave up. She thought it was Him, but of course, it couldn't be. That was only her imagination.

Her head and stomach had stopped bleeding, but not her shoulder. She held a washcloth on the wound, but that did little good. The blood trickling out was black now, as if she'd used up all the outer lighter blood and was draining her inner arteries.

She had woken up five times in the hour and a half that he'd raped her. Each time, she had opened her eyes, seen his maniacal face, which would haunt her the rest of her life, felt his thick, slivering penis shooting in and out of her, and faded out again. The sixth time she'd woken up, he was gone.

She'd crawled to her knees and felt his semen dripping out of her. She had taken off her ripped blouse and wiped it off her, out of her, disgusted that any part of him might still be alive inside of her. Getting up slowly, she found her pants and put them on, then walked back into the building. She feared he might still be there, waiting to start again, but he was not. She found a sweater in her bag and put it on. In the inside pouch of her duffel, where he hadn't bothered to look, was ten dollars. Enough for the cab ride home.

The cabbie said nothing about her appearance. It was two in the morning, and as long as she paid him, he didn't give a damn. She made it inside her apartment building and leaned heavily against the elevator door as it rose twelve stories to her floor. She got out, unlocked her apartment door, relocked it behind her, and collapsed.

She woke up an hour later, her blood staining the gray carpet, and crawled into the bathroom. She didn't know how long she'd been in the tub, but from the sunlight pouring beneath the door from the living room, she estimated it was noon, twelve hours since ... Him. She knew she would now relate her whole life to that moment, "before" and "after," events from the one not even comparable to those from the other.

Someone pounded on the door, and she shot up. Oh, God, her name was on her credit cards, and he'd looked her address up in the phone book. She curled into the corner of the tub. She would drown before she let him touch her again. She would die before letting anyone touch her again.

"Clementine, open up. It's Arthur. Are you all right?"

She breathed again, then sank beneath the water so

she couldn't hear him, leaving only her nose and mouth and eyes exposed to the air. He only wanted her to work, and she knew she would never work again. She would never get out of this tub.

She stayed beneath the water, listening to the almost complete silence as she swished waves around herself. She knew now why babies didn't want out of the womb. It was safe there, insulated. Sounds were muffled, far away. No one could penetrate it, or hurt you.

Just as she was closing her eyes, the bathroom door burst open and she jumped up. Arthur strode in, heading for her. But in her mind it wasn't Arthur. It was Him again, smiling, telling her she wanted it. She splashed at him, screaming. She reached for her razor, but he caught her hand in time. He held her down, wrapping his arms around her and letting her scream. She didn't stop. She couldn't.

• • •

An hour later, Arthur lifted Clementine out of the tub. She was quiet now, like a scared child. He bandaged her shoulder, but it was obvious the wound needed more than his amateur ministrations. After bundling her into her robe, he picked her up again and carried her to the sofa.

Her gaze fell on the dead bolt on her door, still locked. He answered her unasked question.

"When you wouldn't answer your phone or the door, I crawled out on the fire escape and pried open your bedroom window. I knew something was wrong. You wouldn't miss a shoot."

*Oh, yes, I would,* Clementine thought, but she said nothing. Now that she'd stopped screaming, she couldn't speak. She went from one extreme to the other without warning or control, she thought. Inaction to mania, screams to silence. One night, and she had lost all traces of herself. One night, and she was altered forever.

Arthur sat beside her. He took her hand, and she yanked it away. *Don't touch me,* she wanted to say, but her lips wouldn't move.

"Who did this to you?" he asked.

He hadn't asked anything while she was in the tub.

Now he watched her closely, as if he would find the answers in her face. She knew he was thinking of police and justice and manhunts, but none of that would change anything. It would be like being raped all over again, the questions, the medical examination, the pushing, the probing. And they would never find Him. He was the kind that melted into the cracks, walked through the streets unnoticed, faceless.

She said nothing, only stared through the doorway to her bedroom window. She would get bars first thing. And alarms. And Mace. And a gun. Oh yes, she would get a gun. With hollow-point bullets to rip a man's guts out.

"I have to take you to the hospital," Arthur was saying. "Your shoulder is still bleeding."

Still she was silent. What would words do? Arthur stood up and paced before her.

"Let me help you," he said. "I can't stand to see you like this. I love you. God, do you know how much I love you? I'll kill the son of a bitch who did this to you. I swear it. Clementine . . . Clementine?"

The tears fell, and she couldn't stop them. She opened and shut her mouth in a pantomime of speech, but only grunts came out. She kept hearing his words, "I love you, I love you." She wanted to tell him, *Don't love me. I'm dirty.* Nothing came out.

Finally, he held her again, and she sobbed into his shoulder.

"You're safe now," he said, but she knew she wasn't. Never again. That man had taken security away from her. He had made her small, defenseless, frightened forever of shadows and darkness and men.

"I'll take you to the hospital," Arthur said.

She nodded and stood up. That was all there was left now, just the physical scars. The doctors would stitch them up, and that would be that. They would tell her she was cured. It would be as if nothing had ever happened.

•   •   •

Arthur stayed with her for five days. He cooked and cleaned and shoved food down her throat and canceled her shoots. He slept on the couch and ran in when she woke up screaming. He learned not to touch her, but to sit by her side and talk softly instead.

Clementine lay in her bed day after day and knew this was what hell was—memories that played like reality, again and again, slowly, quickly, backward, forward, but always with the same ending. He raped her. Raped. Raped. Raped.

It was a payback, that's what it was. For every time she'd swished her hips or worn tight jeans or flirted or winked. God was saying, "Hey, you slut. See what you get? That'll teach you."

She heard Arthur in the other room, talking on the phone. He had been wonderful, but he made her uncomfortable, being so close. She wrapped her arms around her stomach and thought of Megan and Alex and the days they'd spent gossiping and laughing, with such certainty that life would always be good and pure. More than anything in the world, she wanted those days back.

"Arthur?" she called when he was off the phone. He came into the room quickly, so eager to help that she wished she could change for him, could be all better so that he would feel he'd made a difference.

"Yes?"

"I want to go home."

He sat down on the far edge of the bed, careful not to touch her.

"I thought this was your home now," he said.

"Not anymore. I want to go back to California. I want to see my friends."

He turned away, and she knew he was thinking about lost revenue, the shoots she would miss.

"Do you know who that was on the phone?" he asked.

She shook her head. She didn't care. She didn't care about anything except getting out of there.

"It was the advertising director for Amour Perfume. He's finally made up his mind. He wants you and a few of the other girls for a new television commercial."

He looked at her, his face triumphant, waiting for her excitement and gratitude. All she could think of was that He probably had a television. He would see her and come after her again. Her hands shook, and she hid them beneath the covers.

"It's a once-in-a-lifetime opportunity," Arthur went on. "No lines, but think of the exposure. They'll start off local, I think, but the plan is to go national eventually. They made up their minds to go with models instead of actors, looks over substance, I guess."

He laughed, but Clementine could think of no reply. He inched forward, and she scooted away. He drew a deep breath.

"This is the chance we've been waiting for. You can't go home now, honey."

"Don't call me that."

He stood up and walked to the window.

"I may not know what happened to you, but I know it was bad. If you'd just let me help you. If you'd just confide in me, then maybe . . ."

*Don't cry*, Clementine told herself. That was the only thing she could control now, her tears. If she fought really hard, she could hold it all in, pretend it was all right, and people would think she was still the same Clementine Montgomery.

Arthur sat down on the chair beside the bed. He reached for her hand, but she jerked away.

"I'm a nice guy," he said. "I really am. Other agents would have slammed the door in your face if you hid in the bedroom for a week the way you have."

"I didn't ask you to do me any favors."

He ran his fingers through his hair. "I know that. I wanted to help you. I still do. But you've got to think of your future. Your career. You just won't get another chance like this."

She pulled the covers up to her chin.

"I can't," she whispered. "Not now. I can't do anything until I see my friends."

He walked to the door. When he turned back to her, she could see the confusion in his eyes. He was a man of business, straightforward, analytical. Every problem he'd ever encountered had a solution. Until now.

"I've got to go to the office for a while," he said.

She nodded. She waited for him to leave, but he just stood there.

"I wish I could make you see that work's the best medicine," he said.

He was trying to help, but he was miles from understanding her. She wished she could explain things to him, but there weren't words enough in her vocabulary.

"Think how much better you'll feel after you do this," he said, "when you get the success you've waited your whole life for. Just think about it, okay?"

When she said nothing, he turned and walked out. She heard him rummaging around in the living room, then he opened and closed the front door and was gone. The apartment was still and lifeless, with only traffic noise to keep her company. Clementine pulled the covers up over her head and curled up in darkness.

• • •

The three of them sat on the lawn outside Megan's parents' house, staring at the bay. It was a perfect day, cool, just barely breezy, with only specks of clouds in the sky. Megan was babbling on about her wedding plans, and Clementine thought her voice sounded beautiful, perfectly feminine and sweet and harmless.

She had flown in the day before. When she had seen Megan and Alex standing there at the arrival gate, waving, so happy to see her and so much as she remembered them, there'd been no thought in her mind but to hold on to them as tight as she could. They'd hugged her back, all three of them looking like blubbering idiots, crying and clinging to one another, but Clementine hadn't cared. She was safe again, home again.

They wanted to know everything, about her apartment, her jobs, the commercial she'd mentioned.

"I don't know if I'm going to do it," she'd told them on the way to Megan's.

"You're crazy," Alex had said. "You have to. This is what you've been waiting for."

She was right, of course. But as they sat on the grass, just like the girls they used to be, except that they weren't as naive or hopeful anymore, Clementine didn't want any part of New York ever again. She wanted to force herself back in time, to live again in those years when everything was simple and easy and innocent. She wanted . . .

"How's Arthur?" Alex asked.

Clementine snapped out of her reverie and shrugged. "Oh, fine. Angry that I'm here and not drooling all over him for getting me this commercial."

Megan reached out and took her hand. "Why are you here, Clem?"

It had been so easy, with Arthur, to hold the tears in. Here, with the two people who knew her better than anyone else, she felt there was no place to hide. They could almost read her mind. From the moment she had stepped off the plane, they had hovered close to her, looking at her strangely, as if they knew what was wrong.

She had planned a number of excuses. She was lonely. She needed a break. Her mother was sick. The words were almost out of her mouth when Megan squeezed her hand, and she knew she couldn't lie to them.

"Something happened," she said quietly. Alex inched closer, and they formed a circle. Clementine looked down at the grass while she spoke. "A week ago, a man . . . he raped me."

All was silent except for the distant sound of a ship tooting its horn. Clementine waited. It seemed she waited hours, but she knew it was only seconds. Then their arms were around her, and she couldn't tell whose tears were whose. She clung to them, thanking God for giving her these two women who could feel her pain, help her carry it.

Later, when the details were out, most of the tears had been shed, and they were sitting in the kitchen drinking coffee, Clementine rested her chin on her hands, exhausted.

"I can't imagine how you'll get over this," Megan said.

Clementine looked at her. "I doubt if I ever will. I can close my eyes and see him so clearly, it frightens me."

Alex paced around the room, angry. She kicked the cabinets as she passed.

"What gets me is this—this scum is going to get away with it. Are you sure you won't go to the police?"

"I'm sure. They won't catch him, and I don't want the publicity."

"God, it just makes me sick," Alex said. "I'd give anything to get him in a dark alley and ram something up his—"

"Alex!" Megan said.

"Oh, come on. We can talk about what a man can do to a woman, but not the other way around? I'd just like to give him a taste of what it's like."

Staring at her friend, Clementine knew that something like this would never happen to Alex. Alex would find a way out, fight until the death, somehow prevent it. God, she wished she were Alex, or at least had part of her spirit, her guts.

"What do you do?" Clementine asked her. "How do you keep from being frightened?"

Alex sat down and thought about it. Finally she said, "It's not that I'm not scared. When I have to walk alone at night or I hear someone come up behind me in the dark, I get as scared as the next person. But I've always been able to ignore certain feelings if I want to and concentrate on others. So, in the dark, I think about light and strength and power. I keep walking and whistling like nothing's wrong, like I don't have a care in the world."

"What do you think I should do?" Clementine asked.

"I'll tell you exactly what to do," Alex said. "You go back to New York, make that commercial, and don't let that trash get the better of you. The only thing you change is your insides. You harden up. You go out and buy a gun, and whatever you do, don't show your fear. Fear attracts crime like a magnet. You hold your head up and walk right past the nut cases, knowing that if one of them makes a move, you'll blow his fucking head off."

Alex made her feel strong again. Almost normal. Clementine reached for her hand, then Megan's.

"I don't know what I would have done without you two."

"Oh, Clementine," Megan said, "I'm so sorry."

Clementine nodded. "I know. Me too."

• • •

Clementine stood on the Virginia Beach shore, sand covering every inch of her, as well as all of the other models. This commercial, she decided, would be the most ridiculous thirty seconds ever to hit the airwaves.

When they were finished—if they ever finished—the spot would show Clementine and the three other girls running down the beach in bikinis two sizes too small and stealing beach balls from four of the most handsome men ever to roam the planet. The men chased them into the water and then wrestled them to the ground. At that point, a voice-over said, "Amour Perfume: for women who love men. And Amour Cologne: for men who love them back."

Clementine thought it was the biggest piece of crap fed to the American public since Watergate. The funny thing was, the onlookers on the beach were loving it. The Amour marketing director, who looked like an idiot walking among the sunbathers in a suit and tie, said everyone couldn't wait to get out to buy the perfume. Either they were just trying to be nice, or the sun was way too strong.

Still, Clementine was there, making five hundred dollars minus fifteen percent equals four hundred and twenty-five dollars a day to brave the chilly ocean. More than that, Amour had tentatively scheduled three variations of the same silliness, and they wanted all the models back to film them. Better than anything, Clementine was back at work, acting normal, not showing her fear.

Returning to New York had been the hardest thing she'd ever done, but Alex had been behind her, pushing her all the way.

"Stand up straight," she'd said at the airport. "Don't let the bastards get you down."

That image of Alex's fearless face, her thumbs-up sign, kept Clementine's head up and her pace steady whenever she had to walk alone. And the memory of Megan's tears kept her fighting. Getting better wasn't only a personal thing. She was doing it for all of them.

On her first day back, right after the call to Arthur— who had practically hooted with joy when she told him she would do the commercial—she had walked twelve blocks to the nearest gun shop.

"I want the best handgun you've got," she'd said, "and the bullets that rip your insides out."

The man hadn't questioned her, and after her permit had been granted, she had walked home tall, her hand in her purse, wrapped around the butt of a .357 Magnum. She had met the stares of the men on the street, almost daring them to make her use it. She had no doubt she could fire it easily.

She knew she was healing. The first time John, the model she played off of, wrestled her to the ground, she froze. The whole horrible scene played out again. Her struggles accomplished nothing. He was closing in, pushing inside her. From far away, she heard John's voice asking if he'd hurt her, then everyone came running. Arthur knelt down beside her.

"Talk to me, Clem," he said.

She looked up, those goddamn tears sneaking into her eyes, and he shielded her from the rest of the crew.

"It's just a commercial," he said softly. "It's not real."

She stood up slowly, blinked back her tears, and stared at the worried faces around her. She couldn't blow this, she thought, not after she'd come so far. She dug deep inside herself and brought out a smile.

"I'm fine," she said. "Just got the wind knocked out of me."

They all laughed and went back to their places. John looked sheepish and apologized.

"I'm really sorry. I'll be more gentle next time."

Now, eighteen still-not-perfect shots later, John's touch didn't faze her in the slightest. "It's not real," Arthur had said. Whatever happened, it wasn't real. She knew without a doubt that she would go into acting, into a world where nothing could harm her, where it was all make-believe. The stage, the camera, would be her haven.

She began to enjoy herself, even laugh. She had three best friends now. Alex, Megan, and the camera. Alex and Megan had got her going, but if it hadn't been for this commercial, she didn't think she would have made it.

She would have gone insane, never let a man touch her again. Make-believe had saved her life.

Arthur walked up to her and smiled.

"You having fun?" he asked.

"It's a living," she said, and smiled because they both knew it was a lot more than that.

"You're doing great, you know."

She could see in his eyes that he meant more than just the shoot. She wondered how much he knew, how much he'd guessed. She would have liked to tell him, but despite their friendship, he was a man, and that made all the difference.

"I know," she said.

"I think it's a go-ahead for the other commercials."

"Great. But we still need the time off to go to California. I can't miss Megan's wedding, and I can't think of anyone else I'd want more as my date than you."

He smiled. "Don't worry. We'll be there. Anything for my little star."

He walked away, whistling, and Clementine wished they had been lovers in the "before" period of her life. Any chance of romance was ruined now. Perhaps if they had broken that boundary when they first met, she could bring herself to kiss him now, or even just hold his hand, as his eyes begged her to.

"Clementine, let's try it again," the director said.

She walked into the water and washed off the sand. In front of the camera, at least, she was perfect. No obvious traumas or scars. Makeup covered the stitches on her shoulder. She was the woman men wanted, but could never reach. A perfect arrangement.

# CHAPTER
## 11

*CLEMENTINE FLEW TO CALIFORNIA ON THE* Monday before the wedding; Arthur would fly in the following Friday. Both Megan and Alex were at the airport again to pick her up, smiling and hugging and all of them feeling, for a moment, thirteen instead of twenty and certainly not old enough for marriage. They had planned an all-girls' day, complete with final dress fittings, lunch, and man talk.

"I'm going to look stupid beside you," Alex said to Clementine when they stood in front of the mirror in the dress shop's dressing room. Reflected at them were two pink taffeta gowns, but the same dress had completely different results on their different bodies.

"That's not true," Clementine said.

"It is. They make these dresses for tall, perfect size-six women like you. I look like a fat midget."

Megan giggled and fixed the bow over Alex's bustle. "You do not. Anyway, Clementine will be beside me and you'll be beside Jackson. Don't worry."

Alex twisted from side to side, wondering how anyone in her right mind could have picked this dress. Even Megan, with her old-fashioned tastes, couldn't possibly find this promlike monstrosity appealing. Alex had seen a gorgeous silver twenties-style dress on the way in. All it needed was a hat and long gloves, and boy, would she make an impression. But it was Megan's wedding, and she'd wear this damn pink taffeta and look like an over-dressed dog if it killed her.

"So, what color is Jackson wearing again?" Clementine asked as Megan unzipped her dress.

"White. I wanted to be the only one in that color, but he has this crazy notion that it's his wedding too."

"Figures," Alex said. "He always was a little too high and mighty for my taste."

"And the honeymoon?" Clementine asked.

"Just a couple of nights up in Mendocino. Jackson still has to graduate. He can't miss too many classes. And then he's going to start full-time at the architecture firm."

Alex put on her pants and sweater and knew she should hold her tongue. As usual, she couldn't.

"What about his art? When will he paint?"

Clementine walked to the corner of the room, out of the line of fire. She was wondering the same thing, but she thought it was for Megan and Jackson to work out.

"Maybe in the evenings," Megan said offhandedly. "It's more important that he make a good impression at the firm. Even though I've got my trust fund money coming after the wedding, we need to make our own way in the world. And you can't do that as a painter."

Alex opened her mouth to say more, but Clementine scooped up their gowns and opened the dressing room door.

"Come on, girls," she said. "I'm starving. Let's go to lunch."

Megan put one arm around each of her friends and hugged them tightly. "Oh, it's so good to have both of you here. My best friends."

Clementine glared at Alex, old friends together again and back to normal, as they walked out of the store.

●　　　●　　　●

"So, have you slept with him yet?" Alex asked.

Megan had just swallowed a spoonful of clam chowder and almost spat it back out. "Jeez, what a question."

"Why? It's straightforward. Sex. You know, S-E-X. Bodies and sweat. The number one topic of conversation for every living soul, except me."

Megan blushed down past her shirt collar, and Alex laughed.

"Well?" she asked.

"No," Megan whispered into her soup. "I want to wait until we get married. I think that's important."

Alex opened her mouth to bring up Megan's past with Tony, but Clementine kicked her beneath the table.

"Ouch!"

Clementine scowled at her, then smiled at Megan. "Well, that's fine. Although I'm sure Jackson isn't all that pleased."

"Actually, it seems all right with him too. He understands me."

Clementine thought back to the night of the engagement party, the electricity Jackson had emitted at dinner and at the Sanderses' house during the party. He'd stolen the show that night, completely winning over Megan's parents and their friends with his vitality and humor. Clementine had watched him, his eyes magnetic and his grin always flirtatious, whether he was talking to Megan's eighty-year-old grandmother or a woman destined to be an Oakland Raiderette. It didn't seem quite possible he wouldn't want sex at the earliest possible moment.

"Jackson is so boring now," Alex said. "He comes home, does his homework, and goes to bed. He certainly isn't the Jackson I met two years ago."

"Well, I think it's great that he's trying so hard," Clementine said. "When some men get married, they figure they can go on being the jerks they've always been. At least, Jackson realizes he'll have to change a little."

"He told me he wants to do everything right," Megan said, staring at her ring. "When I said I wanted to wait to make love, he respected me for that. And he's really making an effort in college now, much more so than before. I know he'll put that same energy into his job, and in the meantime I have enough money from my trust fund for us to live on. He's following all the rules, planning every little detail. He works day and night so that our marriage will be what I want it to be."

Alex set down her spoon and leaned forward. "I'm going to say what I want to say, so don't you dare kick me again, Clemmie."

"Fine, say it. But Megan's life is her own business."

Megan looked from one to the other. "What's going on? Am I missing something?"

"Alex is just being a pest again," Clementine said. "She isn't happy unless she's got her nose in everyone else's business."

"Megan's life is my business," Alex said. "She's my friend. And Jackson's my friend. I only want them to be happy."

"Hey, she's my friend too."

"Yeah, but—"

"Would you two please stop acting like I'm not even here?" Megan said. "Tell me what you're talking about."

Clementine looked away. Alex shrugged, then said, "I just don't understand, that's all. Marriage and love are supposed to be spontaneous. I'm not saying it's all wine and roses, but it shouldn't be something you have to work at every second. Isn't love just supposed to happen? Your dreams and desires and habits mesh, and every day is like a vacation, certainly not like slaving over a job you hate."

They were quiet, and Clementine refused to look, afraid to see Megan's reaction. Finally, dying of curiosity, she turned to find Megan staring at her hands, twisting her ring around her finger.

"What do you know about love?" Megan asked. "Just because you've decided to be a frigid intellectual who doesn't care about anything but test scores doesn't mean the rest of us don't have feelings."

Oh, great, Clementine thought.

"That's an awful thing to say," Alex said. "And it's not even true. I just have different priorities. I don't want to throw my life out the window for some man who might end up not loving me anymore ten years down the line. What will you have left if that happens?"

Megan stared across the restaurant. "You don't think I'm good enough for him, do you?"

"Oh, God, Meg, that's not what I meant at all." Alex scooted her chair closer to Megan's. "Really. You're more than good enough for him."

"Then why don't you want us to work? You're always acting like we're bad together when you know we love each other. Why can't you see that?"

Alex looked to Clementine for support, but she was nodding in agreement. "Yeah. Why, Alex?"

"Oh, you be quiet." She turned back to Megan and saw her eyes watering. Alex handed her a napkin.

"Look, it's not that I don't want you two to work. Really. It's just, oh, I don't know. I'm afraid, that's all. It doesn't feel right somehow. I have a feeling in my gut like something's wrong, but I don't know what it is or how to fix it. I know everything seems perfect now, but I worry about what will happen later on."

Megan dried her eyes and lifted her head. "That's not really your concern, is it?"

Alex jerked back as if she'd been slapped. Their lives had always been each other's concerns. Until now. She slid her chair away. "No, I guess it isn't," she said quietly.

The waiter took their bowls and brought their lunches. Clementine looked from one to the other, then started drumming her fingers on the table.

"Come on. We're hardly ever together anymore, and we need to enjoy it. It's been a hell of a few months for all of us. Part awful, part wonderful. But how often do any of us get married?"

Alex thought of her life, dark on all sides except for one spotlight straight ahead, where her career lay. She tried to imagine herself in Megan's seat, her head filled with guest lists and flower arrangements, but couldn't. It wasn't that she didn't want to be there, or that she would mind getting showered with gifts and attention. In fact, it all sounded nice and normal and domestic. She just didn't see it ever happening to her.

Clementine shivered once, thinking of His hands. She wanted to make marriage seem terrific for Megan's sake, but just the word unnerved her. If being touched by a man felt like poison, marriage, with sex demanded night after night, would be like death.

Only Megan smiled, appeased. Marriage, after all, meant everything. She was going to be with the man of her dreams until death parted them. Perhaps she wasn't as smart as Alex or as glamorous as Clementine, but she was the only one wise enough to realize that love was all that mattered.

• • •

Jackson stood at the window of his apartment like a statue. The heat of his breath painted the glass white in rhythmic intervals, the only sign that he was alive. No matter how hard he tried, he couldn't see this day as anything but an ending. An end to freedom; an end to fun; an end to the awesome dreams only the young have enough hope to believe in; and, of course, an end to his life with Alex. Outside, it was raining cold and hard. It was his wedding day.

Alex was whirling around her bedroom like a hurricane, slamming doors, muttering, cursing the curling iron, which never fixed her hair the way she wanted it to. She never had learned how to dress quietly. Jackson smiled. Even when his legs were leaden, his heartbeat erratic, and his doubts so strong he wondered how he ever could have thought he was ready for marriage, Alex made him smile.

He walked away from the window and sat down on the couch. He had been dressed and ready to go for forty-five minutes, and still he and Alex didn't have to leave for the church for two hours. His mother had called from her hotel early and woken him up. She'd disregarded the map enclosed in the wedding invitation and needed directions to the church and Megan's parents' house for the reception. That was his mother. Careful till the end. But it was nice that she'd come. And especially nice that she'd left Stanley, her insurance salesman husband, at home.

"Dammit," Alex muttered from the bedroom.

"What's wrong?"

"This damn dress is what's wrong. I was trying to pull the sleeves down a little on the shoulders, try to make it look halfway decent, and now I've ripped the damn thing. Damn. Damn. Damn."

"Come here."

She walked out of the bedroom. Her hair was twisted in a knot on her head, with only a few curly kinks falling down along either cheek. The pink dress swished around her, and just as she'd said, there was a rip along the left shoulder.

He stared at her, so out of place in frills and feminine lace that he laughed.

"Oh, sure," she said, "go ahead and laugh. You get to look like Humphrey Bogart, and I look like Barbie's worst nightmare."

"I'm sorry, Alex. I really am. It's just that I never thought I'd see you quite so out of place. It's kind of a nice change, actually."

"Shut up. Just look at this rip and tell me what to do."

He stood up and ran his fingers over her shoulder.

"Take it off and bring it here. I got an A in sewing class in junior high school, you know."

"You took sewing?"

"Of course. You know I'm a crusader for equal rights." She raised her eyebrows.

"Okay. So I also got kicked out of wood shop for stealing the saws."

"Figures." She slipped the dress off her head, revealing a thigh-high slip underneath, and handed the dress to him.

"The sewing kit is in the hall closet," he said.

"I didn't know we had one of those."

"Didn't you know that when you're studying your brains out in your bedroom, I sneak out here to do some needlepoint or knitting? I'm afraid I'm a closet tailormaniac."

"God, you're weird." She found the box in the closet and handed it to him.

He smiled and sat back down on the couch. After threading a needle, he turned the dress inside out. Alex sat beside him.

"You're nervous, aren't you?" she asked quietly.

"Nervous? No, not really."

"What then?"

He smoothed the dress out and started on the rip, sewing carefully, making sure each stitch was even and unnoticeable.

"I don't know, Alex. I guess I just don't feel like I'm supposed to. I should be happy, right? Thrilled about my new life?"

"I don't think that's true. My guess is that most people are scared to death on their wedding day. No matter how much you love someone, it's still traumatic."

"Yes, but . . ."

She touched his cheek. "But you're not totally sure, right? You love Megan. She's wonderful and kind and soft and gentle, but you wonder if that's really what you want. It all went so fast. Dating and then, pow, you asked her to marry you. Maybe you're thinking that you didn't think things through."

He laid the dress down on the coffee table and turned toward her.

"After I met her, it felt so right, you know? And I was afraid that if I didn't act, I'd lose her or the moment or the feeling of belonging and strength that she gave me. I wanted so desperately to keep all of that. Do you understand?"

"I think so," Alex said softly. "Megan was the first woman you wanted to be with forever. Megan was your first *love*. And that can make you rash and impulsive, even a little crazy."

"Sometimes I think you can look right into my mind."

She smiled. "You're my friend. Sometimes my best friend. I know you."

He grasped her hand tightly. "I want so badly for this to work. It's got to. Marrying Megan is what life should be like. A devoted wife, some kids, a house in the suburbs."

"Who said life should be like that?"

"Everyone."

"Come on."

"All right. Me. My mother, I guess. After my father died, she wanted everything to change. She was going to lead a normal life if it killed her. And she did. She met

Stanley, changed her name, changed my name, had some more kids with him, and settled down in Dullsville, Ohio, to rot. All my life she drummed her feelings into my head. Routine is the essence of happiness, she'd say. Be normal, comfortable, secure, and in the end, you'll look back at your life and be pleased. No regrets. I rebelled against that my whole life until I met Megan. Then, suddenly, everything my mother had ever said made perfect sense. I didn't want any regrets."

Alex stood up and walked to the window. Jackson watched her. The gray murky light penetrated her ivory slip, silhouetting the curve of her waist and hips. Not since he'd first met her, when there was still a possibility they might choose the lovers route rather than being just friends, had he noticed how curvaceous she was. He looked away.

"I'll say this only once," she said, her back to him. "I promise. Then I will forever hold my peace."

"Go ahead."

She spun around, and he was awed by the picture she made. The smoky light smudged the contours of her face, shadowed her eyes and lips and cheeks. He imprinted the vision on his mind, knowing this was how he would paint her some day. It would be his going away present to her. A thank you for her friendship. He needed no model. Alex was so clear to him, he could call up her image at any moment.

She was still thinking, choosing her words, and he had a moment more just to look at her. Her silhouette was beautiful. Why did he have a feeling that every woman other than Megan would be beautiful today?

"I think you'll regret marrying her," Alex said at last. "I know that's a harsh thing to say, but I feel it as strongly as my love for you both."

He looked down at the dress and toyed with the stitches he'd made.

"I understand what's happening," she went on. "I know you love her. I don't doubt that at all. And God knows she loves you. Megan isn't capable of anything less. But neither of you is willing to step out of the fog for a moment to see reality, to see what life is going to be like for you together. In fact, I think deep down inside both of you agree with me and are scared to death of what you'll see if you bring your heads out of the sand for even a minute."

She looked at him intently. "You don't know her, Jackson. Trust me. You know nothing."

He got up abruptly and walked over to her, standing so close, Alex had to tilt her head back to see him. She studied his face, hard and stern and yet with a hint of desperation in it. He placed his hand on her shoulder, then slid it behind her neck.

When he lowered his head to hers, she didn't turn away. He kissed her as she remembered being kissed when she was younger, when tongues and lips and tastes were new and exciting and the only outlet for passion. She twined her arms around his neck, clinging to him, feeling for the first and only time what it was like to love Jackson as a woman. His lips were warm, and his tongue quick and expert. He kissed her cheeks, her forehead, her nose, her neck, every inch of her face, breathing in her fragrance. His mouth met hers again, demandingly, with a sense of lost time and a hunger for a life that would never be. Their tongues circled quickly at first, then the passion died as they woke up to the day, the moment, the sun breaking through the clouds outside the window, and the thought of a woman standing in a church dressing room in Sausalito, thrilled to be getting married that day. They broke the kiss at the same time, but kept their arms around each other.

"At least," Jackson said, "I won't regret never doing that."

Alex smiled. "I've always wished you would. Just once. I'm not so cold, you know. I want love too."

"I know, Alex."

She breathed deeply. "You know I love you, don't you?"

"Yes. And you know you'll always be my best friend, no matter what happens with me and Megan?"

"Yes."

They were silent for a long time, staring at each other.

Alex finally released her grip around his neck and stepped back.

"Be happy with her," she whispered before hurrying into her bedroom and closing the door.

Jackson nodded and returned to the couch to finish her dress. He thought, though he couldn't be sure, he heard her crying.

• • •

Megan's mother was in her element orchestrating the wedding. While she was never much interested in Megan, seating charts, flower arrangements, and menu planning were definitely challenges that inspired her. Megan had never seen her so alive, so forceful, so *interested* in anything. But it made sense, really. This was Ginny Sanders's chance to show off her good taste, her riches, her poise, to several hundred of her closest friends.

Now that the day was here, Ginny was panicking over every perceived flaw. Ten minutes earlier, she had stormed through the church, reprimanding the florists for the sixteen rose-and-orchid arrangements that were definitely not the shade of pink she had ordered. Couldn't they see that the flowers were coral? Coral, not pink. Clementine walked behind her, mimicking her finger-pointing and vein-popping facial expressions, making the six florists laugh hysterically until Ginny left the church in disgust.

A dozen times, Ginny bustled in and out of the dressing room where Megan and Clementine were getting ready, asking Clementine to check this or find someone to do that, completely oblivious to the fact that every arrangement was already taken care of. The flowers were lovely, whether pink or coral, the caterer had arrived at the house and was setting up for the reception, the organist was at the church, Megan was beautiful, Alex had called and said she and Jackson were on their way, and all they had left to do was wait out the final hour. But Clementine humored Ginny all the same, saluting her whenever she left to do her bidding.

Megan sat on a stool in front of the dressing room mirror and stared at her reflection. Her veil had two loops of pearls that dangled over her cheeks, and she toyed with them, certain they weren't quite even and everyone would notice. The petticoat she'd been so determined to wear made it difficult to sit, and she had a sudden urge to go to the bathroom—an almost impossible feat in hoops and slips and garters and hose and gadgets wrapped around every square inch of her body.

"Jack and Alex just arrived," Clementine said as she returned to the room, having completed the twelve tasks Ginny had given her. "Your mom met them out front and gave them each a typed list of their responsibilities. Alex lunged for her, but Jackson managed to restrain her."

"What did Jackson do?"

"He burst out laughing, of course. Your mom stomped away, as usual."

Megan giggled and looked at her reflection again. She maneuvered a few bobby pins that were holding the veil in place until the pearl loops evened out. Clementine pulled up a stool and sat beside her.

"You're the model," Megan said. "Tell me truthfully, how do I look?"

Clementine eyed her thoughtfully.

"Stand up," she commanded. Megan did so, and Clementine looked her over from head to foot.

"Truthfully, Meg, I wouldn't have chosen that style dress for me, but on you it's perfect. The dark makeup on your eyes balances the white. Your hair is perfect with the veil, the curls fit just right beneath the pearls, and the hoops add height as well as width. You are a perfect bride."

Megan hugged her. "You've always known just what to say. Really. Alex would have told me I looked all right and to stop making such a big deal of it."

They laughed. "Yes, well, there is a kind of charm to Alex's bluntness, I guess."

Clementine parted the curtains over the window to look out at the parking lot. A few early guests were arriving, driving up in Mercedes-Benzes and vintage Jaguars, and greeting Ginny and Richard Sanders with air kisses.

"Any of your friends coming?" Clementine asked.

"A few. From college and high school. Jackson invited

some of his friends from school and the firm. The rest
are my parents' acquaintances. My mom told me not to
worry about not knowing anyone. 'Just think of all the
presents,' she said."

Clementine shook her head and watched a group of
young men, handsome and athletic and obviously Jackson's friends, arrive.

"All that matters to me is marrying Jackson," Megan
went on. "Not how packed the church is, which my
mother seems to think is the key to a successful marriage."

Alex burst through the door, the left shoulder of her
dress fixed flawlessly. She slammed the door shut, sat
down on the stool, and spoke without pausing for a
breath.

"Jackson is driving me crazy. I don't know why you
want to marry him, Meg. He's the biggest pain in the ass
I've ever known. And this is the last time I'm a best man.
Men are as jumpy as hooked fish."

"He isn't having second thoughts, is he?"

Megan's face had lost its color, and Clementine hurried to her side to put her arm around her.

"Of course he isn't," Clementine said. "Isn't that
right, Alex?"

Alex stared at Megan, her body rigid while she held
her breath. Alex stood up.

"Hell, no. He just wants to get it over with so he can
start his life with the most wonderful woman in the
world."

Megan heaved a huge sigh of relief, and Clementine
stepped away.

"I'm going to find your mom and tell her the bakery
sent the wrong cake. Just for fun."

Alex watched Clementine leave, not knowing at all if
she was doing the right thing by holding her tongue, but
determined to stick to the vow she had made to Jackson.
She walked over to Megan.

"Happy?" she asked.

"More than I ever thought I could be."

"I'm glad."

"You don't think it's wrong anymore?"

Alex looked out the window. "I just want the best for both of you."

"This is best, Alex. I know it. I feel it. Jackson gives me everything."

Alex turned back to her, putting her arm around Megan's waist and hugging her tightly. "Do you remember when we were in second grade? You liked that boy you met when you went to Florida with your parents, and I liked Bill from the skating rink."

Megan laughed. "Of course I do. Jason ... Jason ... I can't believe I don't remember his last name. I thought he was the most gorgeous boy who had ever lived, and we had the romance of the century. Two seconds of hand-holding on the beach was big-time back then. I was depressed for weeks after we came home from vacation."

"Remember all those nights we spent talking about them?" Alex said. "You were sure you'd never love anyone but Jason, and I was devastated because Bill had never come back to the rink. Night after night, we sat in the gazebo behind your parents' house facing the direction we thought they lived, giggling and gossiping and trying to send our thoughts to them through the air."

"Yes. And when the phone rang, we raced to the house, sure that they had heard us and were calling us back."

They grew silent, each remembering so many once forgotten little things—Monopoly games, movie star crushes, hopscotch, and make-believe—that, when stacked side by side, made up the whole of their friendship. Megan closed her eyes to stop the tears.

"We were always there for each other," she said. "You were so much more reliable than any boyfriend turned out to be."

Alex glanced at the floor. "You'll have a husband now."

"Oh, Alex," Megan said. "You won't lose me."

Alex turned to her quickly, ready to deny that that was what she was feeling. Instead, she squeezed Megan tighter.

"Promise?" she asked.

"I promise. We're blood sisters, remember? Best friends forever."

Ginny burst into the room, clapping her hands.

"Come on, my dear. The ceremony can't wait forever. Alex, you should be with Jackson in the back room, and Megan, it's time for a last minute check on your makeup. Hurry. Hurry. We haven't got all day."

Alex walked to the door, then glanced back to find Megan's gaze on her. They smiled at each other once more, childhood friends with a lifetime of memories and a bond stronger than lost loves, misunderstandings, and sometimes even husbands.

• • •

At the time, she hardly noticed it. Years later, though, when the music and the smell of her bouquet and the murmurs of the guests as she walked down the aisle had faded bitterly from memory, the only thing about her wedding ceremony that remained clear in Megan's mind was the way Jackson's hands shook as he slid the ring on her finger. Her eyes had focused on them, the fingers that were usually so sure and steady, like a surgeon's hands, that trembled uncontrollably when Alex handed him the ring. Megan had even placed her hand over his to help calm him.

She'd thought little of it, assuming it was nerves. So many people watching, so many changes to deal with all at once. A few years later, lying beside her husband and watching him sleep, his face so smooth without the tense lines that had become a second skin to him during his waking hours, she wondered if perhaps he had known all along that their marriage would turn out the way it had.

The reception was held in the Sanderses' expansive backyard. The rain had stopped early in the morning, but the grass was still soggy, and the guests' feet left imprints as they tromped between the gazebo and dance floor and house. Alex suggested Megan forgo a guest book and tear out the grass instead, with everyone signing by their footprints.

All her life, Megan had waited for the moment when her new husband would take her hand, lead her onto the dance floor, put his arms around her for all the world to see, and dance with her. That afternoon, when the band struck up the music, Jackson appeared at her side just as she had imagined. She slipped her arm through his, and they took their places in the center of the rented wood dance floor.

He'd left his trembling behind at the church. His arm was tight and secure around her waist, and he held her close. She couldn't see his eyes, but the feel of his body, which was now hers to touch and cuddle and love, was enough. She could hear people saying, "Lovely couple" and "Isn't it wonderful?" It didn't seem fair to all of the people still searching for someone to love that she could be this undeniably happy.

"I love you," she said, pulling away and looking up at her husband. Her husband. The words made her giggle.

Jackson stared into Megan's eyes. He had avoided doing that until now, afraid of what he might see there. He wanted her to have at least a little doubt, some insecurity about whether they were doing the right thing. He needed to know that he wasn't the only person in the world who felt like running as far and as fast as he could on his wedding day. But as he had expected, she felt nothing of the kind. Her eyes radiated absolute confidence in him, in their marriage and future happiness. He focused on a spot beyond her shoulder and whispered, "I love you too."

"I'm so happy. Can you believe this day is really here? It seems like I've been waiting for it forever. Oh, Jackson, you are my fairy tale come true."

Not trusting his voice, he pulled her to him, crushing her in his arms.

"I know," she whispered, running her fingers through his hair. "It's overwhelming right now. But we're together, and that's all that matters."

He stared over her head, and his gaze locked with Alex's. The tears in her eyes were a reflection of his own. She turned and walked away.

• • •

Clementine had assumed she could find a plausible way around dancing at the wedding. For months now, she'd refused to consider anything that involved touching a man. If she failed, and an image broke through of thick, hairy arms encircling her, holding her down, she couldn't breathe. It all happened again, and paralysis took hold, just like before.

Now Arthur was standing in front of her, holding his hand out, smiling like any normal man, expecting her to dance with him. Clementine's smile froze on her lips. Her skin felt prickly again, as if covered with ants. Arthur shifted from one foot to the other, then let his hand fall.

"It's only a dance," he said softly.

She shook her head. It wasn't only a dance. It was the whole idea of touch, of a man's holding her, invading her, taking away her power. She knew it was only Arthur and that he would never hurt her. But the memories hurt, and Arthur, along with every other man, triggered them. She could pretend it was all right for a man to touch her when the cameras were on, but when that red light went off, she was helpless again.

She turned away and squeezed her eyes shut until her tears retreated. When she let herself think about it, she knew she wasn't getting any better. She tried not to show her fear, tried to act normal, but she still made wide loops around men in the street. She couldn't even look at lovers kissing in the park. Their embraces revolted her, literally turned her stomach. Today, when Jackson had leaned over and kissed Megan at the end of their vows, she had to turn her gaze away.

The worst part was, she could not imagine this ending. If anything, every day the fear and revulsion got worse, as if it were entrenching itself inside her with steel and concrete reinforcements. She began to fear the fear itself; she began to fear everything.

Arthur sat back down in his seat beside her.

"I shouldn't have asked," he said. "I'm sorry."

She shook her head again. "Of course you should have asked. It's completely normal to ask a woman to dance. I'm the crazy one."

He reached out to comfort her, then remembered himself and retracted his arm. At Clementine's back were the dancers, and in front of her were tables of couples holding hands, laughing. People had no idea what they had, she thought, how much a simple touch meant, when it didn't sicken you.

"You're not crazy," Arthur said. "You're healing."

She looked at him. "You know that's not true. I can fake things for the camera, but not in real life, not with you."

"No one wants you to fake anything. When you're ready, when the memories of whatever happened fade, then you'll be all right again. You've got to give it time."

"Time," she repeated softly. No, she knew there wouldn't be enough time in her life for her to ever let a man in again, let him touch her.

They were silent then, and Clementine looked around. A horde of well-wishers surrounded Megan, dotting her with orange and pink and red lipstick, cattle brands from the lips of women she didn't even know. Clementine searched the masses for Jackson. She'd hardly seen him at all since the first dance with Megan. She scanned the yard and finally caught a glimpse of white at the opposite end of the lawn. He was walking alone, head down, beyond the rose garden overlooking the bay.

Arthur followed her gaze and sighed. "I'm no expert, but I'd say that's one man who wasn't quite ready for marriage."

Clementine breathed again, thankful the subject had changed from her.

"You think so?"

"Did you see how nervous he was during the ceremony? He looked as if he'd rather be anywhere but there beside Megan."

"I'm going to talk to him."

"Leaving me for another man already, are you? I knew it wouldn't last."

Clementine stood up. She wanted to say so many things, like thank you for not asking what happened and for being so supportive, but the words wouldn't come. It would be so nice if she could lean over and kiss him, but when she got even close, Arthur's eyes changed to His, his smile turned grotesque and mean. She stepped back and clenched her hands.

"There are no other men," she whispered.

Arthur watched her walk way. "Not yet," he said. "Not yet."

•     •     •

"Hey, Mr. Married Man," she said when she reached Jackson. His back was to her, and he spun around quickly.

"Oh, hi, Clementine." He smiled, but his eyes looked moist.

"I'm sorry," she said quickly. "You'd rather be alone."

She had pivoted and taken a step away, when he grabbed her arm. For a moment, as his fingers prickled the nerves on her skin, sending one goose bump after another up to the back of her neck like dominoes, she didn't think of Him at all. Then the magic dimmed, Jackson became only human again, a man, and the horror rushed back in. She jerked her arm away.

"Sorry," he said, seeing her face. Of course, he had no idea what had happened to her, but he seemed to sense something and stepped away from her. "Please stay."

Clementine concentrated on her breathing. In-out-in-out. Relax, everything's fine. When he kept his distance, she could think straight. Too close, and she felt opposite forces fighting for supremacy in her brain: one, making her think of Christmas mornings in front of a fire and whispered words until dawn, and the other, making her remember always the feel of hot, unwanted, steely flesh inside her, ripping her apart.

"Is everything all right?" she asked, shaking her thoughts away.

"Oh yes. Sure." He stared out at the water, now reflecting the sun's inconsistent light like a cracked mirror. Clementine studied his profile, noticing how his eyelashes stood out long and curled, framing his eyes.

"Actually, no," he said, turning back to her and smiling sadly. "But I'm sure it's just wedding-day jitters."

She nodded. "You'll be fine once you're off on your honeymoon. Mendocino is always beautiful. The redwoods and the ocean. Very romantic too."

"Yes. Megan's paying, you know. I wanted to handle it, but of course, I'm just a part-time draftsman in an ordinary architecture firm and her parents have all this." He waved his hand around him. "We'll just use her trust fund money."

Clementine looked back toward the reception and spotted Megan laughing with Alex. Talking to Jackson was perfectly harmless, she told herself. There wasn't an ounce of betrayal in it, yet she moved beyond the corner rosebushes to where Megan couldn't see her. She ignored the guilty tension swirling in her stomach and convinced herself that she only wanted to understand Jackson's point of view, make him feel more comfortable while he was there on Megan's turf, surrounded by mostly Megan's family and friends. She knew nothing of him. He knew nothing of her. He had married Megan. She would never marry. But from the first moment she'd seen him, she'd felt a bond formed on nothing, only the air between them, yet unbreakable nonetheless. Standing beside him, she never wanted to leave. He made her feel that she had come home.

"Well, I'm sure you'll still have fun," she said, pushing her loyalty back toward Megan. "Your wife certainly looks happy."

"Yes, I think she is," Jackson said. He sensed Clementine's sudden unease and decided to lighten the mood. "Are you having a good time? I didn't see you out there dancing with your date."

She smiled. "I'm not much of a dancer. Besides, Arthur's notorious for making a fool of himself on the dance floor. I didn't want to be dragged into that."

"Arthur's your agent?"

"Yes. And my friend."

And what else? Jackson had a burning desire to ask. God, it was hard to talk to this woman and not touch her, not reach out and run his hand over her skin. Every inch of her radiated sexuality, yet she hardly seemed to notice it. He knew he should avoid her, get out of this conversation immediately, and always make sure in the future that he was never alone with her. The desire to stay there with her, though, was too strong to ignore.

"How's the commercial coming along?" he asked.

"Fine. It's a lot of fun. A lot of hard work too. But the exposure should really help my career."

"I'm sure. I'll look for it when it comes out."

Clementine nodded, and they fell silent again. She toyed with a few flecks of imaginary lint on her dress. This was the time to leave, she thought. They had nothing to say. They were awkward as hell with each other. But she couldn't move. She was beginning to believe Jackson had some kind of magnetic force field that had trapped her in its claws and wouldn't let go.

"Well," she said, "I just wanted to tell you congratulations. I'm happy for you."

He looked at her, and their gaze locked once again, their eyes understanding so much more than their words could say.

"Really?" he asked.

Clementine knew the right answer, but it refused to pass her lips. The hum of the crowd faded, and she was aware of only the two of them. He stepped forward, to within two feet of her, and she wasn't scared.

"Jackson, I . . ."

"There you are," Megan said, her skirts swishing loud as ocean waves. As she walked around the rose garden, Clementine took a quick step back, as if she had invaded the space around a man where only his wife was permitted to go. "I've been looking all over for you."

She put her arm around Jackson's waist and kissed his cheek. "Mother says we should cut the cake now. And, Clem, I want you and Alex standing right in front when I throw the bouquet."

Clementine shook her head. "You're pushing your luck with us old spinsters." She turned her attention back to Jackson and saw that his gaze was still on her, intense and burning. She wondered if Megan noticed.

"It was nice talking to you, Jackson."

"You too."

Clementine walked back toward the party, her chest feeling strangely empty. If Megan hadn't interrupted, what would she have said? No, Jackson, I wish you weren't marrying her. I wish we'd met first. I wish . . .

She shook the thoughts out of her head. Rubbish, she

told herself. She was acting like a ridiculous schoolgirl, jealous of Megan's happiness. She wouldn't allow herself another moment of self-pity. She had New York. She had a budding career. Megan only had Jackson. So why did it seem that her friend was getting a better deal?

• • •

Alex caught the bouquet. She had never been able to pass up a competition, no matter what the prize. She dived for it actually, shoving three young girls out of her way and landing facedown in the grass. It was only after she lifted the bouquet high above her head, like a trophy, that the implications sank in, and then the flowers weighed down on her. No matter what the old wives' tale, she would not be the next woman to marry. She had analyzed and discarded most every man on the Berkeley campus. None inspired, challenged, or intrigued her. She couldn't help it that she was who she was, that her parents had taught her never to settle for anything mediocre, always to hold out for something better. She just wasn't made for love, and she could never be any different.

She stared at the orchids in her hands. They were merely an extraneous adornment; she had no use for them. She walked up to one of the girls she had pushed out of the way and handed her the bouquet.

After changing into their going-away outfits, Megan and Jackson said good-bye to their guests on the front lawn. A white limousine, stocked with champagne and caviar, was waiting in the driveway to drive them up the coast to Mendocino, courtesy of Megan's parents. After the farewells were said and the guests started back toward the food tables and dance floor, Jackson stepped into the limousine, leaving Megan alone with Alex and Clementine.

"Take lots of pictures," Alex said.

"Yes, and remember to find me a seascape," Clementine said. "The local artists in Mendocino are wonderful. I'll reimburse you."

"Of course. Of course."

"And we'll have your apartment spotless by the time you get home," Alex said.

"I told you not to do that," Jackson said, popping his head out of the limousine sunroof. He was uncorking the champagne.

"We want to."

The three of them hugged tightly. Never mind the pomp, the smiles, the celebration. It had all dwindled down to just the three of them, best friends closing out a chapter, ending the only way of life they'd ever known. No matter how happy this day, it was tinged with sadness. Their friendship would never be the same again. Jackson would be first in Megan's life. She would no longer need her friends for comfort or support; Jackson would supply all that. As Megan crossed a bridge into a world Alex and Clementine had no access to, it seemed as though the richest, sweetest part of their friendship was over.

"I love you both," Megan whispered. "It meant so much to me to have you in my wedding."

"Just be happy," Alex said, trying to cover up the shaking in her voice with a laugh. "Run him ragged. Don't let him watch too much football, and be sure to have a headache at least once a week. That'll keep him guessing."

"Hey," Jackson said.

"Be quiet. This is girl talk," Alex said.

They huddled together, not wanting to let go, to grow up, until they heard Ginny clapping her hands. "Hurry, Megan. It's a three hour drive, and you don't want to be exhausted by the time you get there. Get a move on."

Megan saluted, and they laughed. She stepped inside the car and snuggled next to her new husband, waving one last time before the chauffeur closed the door. Jackson and Megan were kissing as the limousine left the driveway and drove out of sight around the corner.

Alex released a long sigh, wiped away only one tear, and held on tight to Clementine's hand.

"I hate being the one left behind," she said.

Clementine nodded. "Let's get drunk."

"Start pouring, girl."

# CHAPTER
## 12

$A$LEX LIFTED THE BLANKET OFF HERSELF and slid out of bed. She grabbed her robe and tiptoed to the door, then looked over her shoulder to make certain he was still sleeping. His chest rose and fell steadily, as if he were dreaming of the tides, and she smiled. Ben was wonderful when he slept. Innocent, quiet, warm. It was too bad he had to wake up. Alex closed the bedroom door and walked into the living room.

She flipped on the television, turned down the volume, and checked the time. Nine-fifteen. Six months earlier, Clementine had finished filming her latest commercial for Amour Perfume. Tonight at nine-thirty was its West Coast debut, and Alex put on her robe and settled into the couch to wait.

Her feet resting on the coffee table, she mentally recounted all three of Clementine's previous commercials, from the first Amour Perfume ad two years earlier with the models on the beach, to the second one, where the group was skiing and falling over one another, to the most recent, where they were sitting around a fire in a mountain cabin, snuggling and looking too perfect even to be human.

Clementine could probably make a career out of lightweight commercials if she wanted to, but Alex doubted that she did. She could hear the hunger in Clementine's voice when they spoke on the phone, the frustration over how slowly things were moving, how the commercials had not propelled her to the top of the modeling ladder as she had hoped. She was doing well, had a fairly recognizable face, and was making a decent living, but as Alex knew, when a career was all you had, it had to be top-notch or nothing.

The two of them often talked on the phone late at night, when the rates were low and neither could sleep. Alex thought it strange how close she was now to Clementine, even more so than to Megan, who since her wedding two years ago had plunged so deeply into married bliss, Alex saw no traces of the girl she'd once been. More than anything, Alex wanted to have her oldest friend back, to talk and laugh with her, but it seemed Megan's all-out love for Jackson had canceled out most of her love for her friends.

Alex tried not to be hurt, tried to justify it. Being married to Jackson was Megan's dream come true, after all. Megan wouldn't be Megan unless she put everything she had into her marriage. Still, it wasn't fair. Friendship and marriage were two separate entities; one should have nothing to do with the other. One certainly shouldn't drain the life from the other, suck the strength away until only the shell remained. But that was exactly what had happened.

So Alex was thankful for Clementine. She, at least, was still there. She still wanted to listen. She understood when Alex told her about waking up six months earlier and suddenly needing a man again, any man, to balance the blandness of the rest of her life. Clementine understood about the loneliness, the struggle to make it, the burning ambition.

"There are so many sacrifices," Alex had said to her a few weeks earlier. "Not only love, but fun too. Finding some horny college boy for a night sounds good at the time, but then I get him here, and all I want him to do is go home."

"Do you think we'll always be this way?" Clementine

had asked. "Didn't you used to assume you'd get married like everyone else?"

"No. I always felt different. Even when I was little, I knew I'd end up alone."

"Oh, Alex."

And so it went. They bolstered each other, cheered on each other's careers, then late at night wondered why they weren't happy. Why, when they talked to Megan, she sounded so perfect, as if she had life all figured out, while they, who were doing what all the magazine articles and self-actualization books told them to do, were still limping along in the dark.

"I want to prove to Megan," Alex had said to Clementine the previous week, "that I'm doing the right thing."

"What does Megan have to do with it?"

"You can't deny that the three of us are always competing. She seems so certain that getting married and having a family is the only way to go, and I know in my heart that it's not. Maybe our way isn't easy, but that doesn't make it wrong."

"Megan is just Megan," Clementine said softly. "I think she's trying as hard as we are to prove that her way isn't wrong, either. It's like we think we have to justify our lives to one another, when the truth is we're all envious as hell of the lives the others lead."

"I know," Alex said. "I miss her."

The words came out before she could stop them. She didn't want to admit it. She felt ridiculous even feeling it. Most women grew up and got married, and their friends accepted that. So why was it so hard to let go, to resign herself to the fact that their friendship had to change? She could not be number one in Megan's life forever. What hurt was that she didn't even know if she was on the list anymore.

"I miss her too," Clementine said. "But I want her to be happy. We have to let her have her happiness."

•   •   •

The clock read nine-thirty, and Alex sat down on the floor in front of the television. Clementine had said this latest commercial was different from the others and left it at that. Alex turned up the volume when the ad came on.

It was the beach again, a throwback to the first ad, which had done so well. Clementine and a long-haired, extraordinarily good-looking man were playing Frisbee, both wearing stone-washed, tight-as-rubber jeans. Clementine was laughing, diving for the Frisbee and throwing it back to the man like a pro. Then the man threw it over her head toward the water, and she caught it behind her back. She smiled seductively before she unzipped her jeans and unbuttoned her blouse. She took her time sliding off her clothes and revealing a tiny white bikini underneath. She smiled once more at the man, then ran into the ocean. The last shot captured her hand flinging the bathing suit back toward the shore as she disappeared beneath the waves. The scene cut back to the man sitting on the beach, smiling. A voice-over said, "Amour Perfume: for women like Clementine and men who'd do just about anything to be with her."

Alex laughed as she turned off the television. It was a small but enticing variation on Amour's usual slogan. She hurried to the phone and dialed Clementine's number.

"So you've gone solo and gotten a name now," she said when Clementine answered.

"I knew it was you, Alex. And yes, finally. It was Amour's idea. They've used the other girls in their own commercials too. We're all so excited. We feel like real people again."

"I loved it." Alex lowered her voice and mimicked the voice in the commercial. "For women like Clementine and men who'd do just about anything to be with her."

Clementine laughed. "That's great. But honestly, do you think I'm getting typecast?"

"As a sex goddess? God, what I would give to be thought of as a sex goddess."

"You know what I mean. Do you think I'll never get a serious movie role because of all this?"

"Are you thinking of movies?"

"I've always wanted to act. It's so boring sitting around

and posing all day. I told you I'm still in acting school. It's coming along well. And I want out of New York."

"I know, Clem."

"I'm not as scared anymore. I can even walk at night again, as long as I've got my hand on the gun in my purse. It's just that I'm not getting anywhere here. It's obvious that I'll never be Jennifer O'Neill or Tracy Lloyd or any of the other supermodels. I don't even think that's what I want to be."

"Well, you make your own breaks. When yours comes, get your ass out to Hollywood and pound the pavement."

Clementine laughed. "You have a crass way of putting things, but you're right. Don't get me wrong, I love the commercials. They're fun, but not exactly challenging."

"I'm sure you'll rise above it at some point."

"Yes. By the way, how's . . . um, Henry, I think his name is?"

"Henry?" Alex repeated, the name familiar but unplaceable. Finally, she remembered. "Oh, yeah, Henry Schwartz. He's gone. After him, there was Mike and Steve and now Ben. Ben's okay."

"Back to the old Alex, I see."

Alex twisted the cord around her finger. Funny that people thought of her like that, almost as two people— the young, carefree Alex who had fun with the boys, and the old, crusty Alex who put work first, as if the two were mutually exclusive. Alex would have loved to have both. It ate at her every night, lying beside some man she couldn't care less about. Why couldn't she have both? Why wouldn't her heart turn on when her brain was working? Why did every man touch only her body, not her soul?

"I met Ben at my work at Goodman and Associates. He's a young CPA. Wants to take over the world or something."

"Sounds like a match made in heaven."

"I doubt it. But he's fun. In bed, at least. And he doesn't demand anything."

"Oh, Alex."

"Don't 'oh, Alex' me."

"I just worry about you, that's all. I know you said you

only wanted some companionship, but that can be hard, jumping from man to man. You need continuity."

"I get continuity at college and at work. And it's better than living in a make-believe convent like you, afraid of even the most innocent kiss."

Clementine was quiet, and Alex immediately felt guilty. Why did they do that to each other? Say things they knew would hurt? Sometimes, they were like old lovers that way, past the point of being careful with words, as if their time together had given them a license to be mean.

"God, I'm sorry," Alex said. "I didn't mean that. I just get frustrated with my life, and you're the only one I have to take it out on. What you do with your love life, or what you don't do, is your business."

"I'm just too busy," Clementine said too brightly, and Alex knew she was lying. As far as Alex and Clementine had come as friends, Clementine still had her boundaries. Whenever Alex hit a sore subject, her defenses went up. Perhaps, Alex thought, they all had boundaries. Even the closest friendships could go only so far, then you had to keep the rest for yourself, hide a tiny piece of your heart and mind away so that you always had at least one secret left.

"Of course," she said. "We working girls don't have time to have the romances of the century, like Megan has with Jackson."

"Are they still being disgustingly cute?" Clementine asked, relief in her voice that the conversation had moved on.

"From what Megan tells me, yes," Alex said. "Jackson is busy being an architect, and hating it from what I can gather from him. But as far as Meg is concerned, their lives are perfect. They bought the house in Concord, she's got her garden, and she's trying every conceivable method to get pregnant. Ovulation predictors, standing up, sitting down, upside down, you name it. It's so homey, it makes me want to spit."

"Well, she's happy."

"Yes." She paused. "Well, congratulations again. Keep in touch."

Alex hung up and sat back down on the couch. She didn't want to return to Ben . . . Ben . . . what? God, she couldn't even remember his last name. Was that the way it was to be then?

She searched out men, tried to force herself to fall in love with them. But with each one, there was always some overwhelming flaw that turned her stomach. They were too frivolous, too macho, too serious. Too human.

Yet despite all the failures, Alex kept trying. At the very least, she had discovered sex again. For that one moment of exquisite pleasure, the man beside her was perfect and she loved him. For just that moment, she saw what she was missing, and that kept her coming back for more like a bloody prizefighter with too much pride to stay down.

Alex stood up and walked back into the bedroom. She might as well wake Ben up. At the very least, he was good for something.

•  •  •

On that same night, Megan lay awake in her bed staring at the ceiling. The living room light shone through the bottom crack of her bedroom door, tempting her curiosity. Jackson sat up in the living room until two or three o'clock every morning, painting or drawing, excluding her. Every once in a while, she heard the scratch of his charcoal pencil.

She'd read that two years was the cutoff point for newlyweds. Two years of love, then you were brutally woken up from the honeymoon stage and metamorphosed into a normal fight-a-lot, ignore-each-other-the-rest-of-the-time married couple.

The only problem with the theory, so far as Megan could tell, was that she and Jackson had never had a honeymoon stage to begin with. Sure, the three days in Mendocino had been nice. She and Jackson had gone out to dinner at a couple of country inns, had sat beside crackling fireplaces sipping wine and savoring duck specialties. They'd taken a picnic to the rocky coast, hiked through redwood forests, and browsed the shops in town, where Jackson had found a gorgeous seascape painting for Clementine and Megan had asked other tourists to take pictures of them.

Thinking back, Megan tried to concentrate on those romantic moments and forget the remaining hours of their honeymoon, when Jackson was occupied by painting. She couldn't believe it when he'd unpacked his suitcase and revealed three canvases and a set of acrylics and brushes. Without a word, he set up his workstation in the corner of their hotel room and proceeded to paint, from memory, the most beautiful, intriguing picture of Alex she could imagine. He said he wanted to give it to her as soon as they got home.

All right, so it was a nice gesture, but did he have to spend a little over half of their entire three-day honeymoon painting the damn thing? Couldn't it wait a few days, until they got home? When he finally did take a break and they settled down to making love the way Megan had always dreamed of—as a married couple committed forever—he smelled so much of turpentine, he gave her a headache.

Still, it had been a memorable vacation, all in all. In fact, Megan could have lived with his painting and smells forever if she and Jackson could have stayed there, soothed by the roar of the ocean and awesomeness of the forest, away from the world. But, of course, they had to come home.

True to their word, Alex and Clementine had polished their new apartment spotless. They had shined the dark chestnut furniture Megan had inherited from her parents, aired the linens, even set vases of fresh-cut flowers on the tables, and left two long-stem red roses on the bed pillows. Megan had been delighted.

It was unbelievable that this was *her* home. She had chosen it, set up the furniture, hung the pictures. *She* decided where the dishes went, prepared the meals *she* chose, watched the television programs *she* wanted to see. A whole passel of insecurities she didn't even know she had melted away as she passed through the gate into adultland, where she was equal with the rest of the world—a competent, decision-making person, without a mother and father to set the rules and tell her what to do.

If Jackson had felt the same way, everything would have been perfect. As they walked into their apartment for the first time, though, he hardly seemed to care at all that this was where they would start their life together. He left the suitcases in the foyer, stomped through the living room, tossed the red roses into the wastebasket, then lay down and fell asleep almost instantly.

Later, during their first dinner at home, he set down his fork and stared at her.

"Coming home," he said, "makes me feel like this is the start of the horrible world of reality. From now on, I have to work every day, whether I want to or not, bring home a paycheck, and pay all the bills. I can never slack off or relax or just be me again."

Megan stopped eating and took his hand. "I see it more as the reality of being with you every day. It's what I've been waiting for."

"And what about money?"

"You don't need to worry, Jack. We can always use my trust fund in case of an emergency."

He yanked his hand away and stood up. "I didn't say I couldn't handle it. I'm the husband, you know. I don't need your charity. I can support us just fine." Then he grabbed his canvas and paints and was gone for the next four hours, leaving Megan to cry herself to sleep. Megan woke up the next morning after Jackson had already left for work, and the first thing she did was invest her quarter-of-a-million-dollar trust fund in mutual funds and the stock market. To date, she had increased her savings to close to three hundred thousand dollars.

More than two years had passed since they'd first walked into their apartment. As Megan saw it, those years could easily have crossed the border from disappointment into happiness, if only they had let them. There was no wall shutting them out. Jackson graduated with honors from Berkeley and was promoted to associate architect at Baron and Jakonovich. A year later, they bought this two-bedroom house in Concord with a ten-by-ten-foot garden area in the front and three fruit trees in the back. She cooked Jackson's favorite meals, wore the perfume he loved, fixed her makeup flawlessly every day even though she rarely saw anyone but him. She did everything, goddammit, and still he stayed up until two o'clock in the morning drawing and painting his stupid pictures instead of lying beside her and holding her the way a satisfied husband should.

Sometimes, Megan thought he hated her. It was a harsh and crazy thought, but in her gut, that was what she felt. He never did anything to imply it. He certainly never said it. He kissed her when he left for work in the morning and when he came home in the evening. He praised her cooking. When he made love to her, he did so methodically, without passion, but she sensed no pain or anger. It was only around his eyes that she could tell. She'd be knitting something for the baby they would have some day—a craft she had taken up with the hope that subconsciously it would penetrate her body and help her to conceive—and she'd look up to find his eyes piercing through her like daggers. He'd turn away quickly, but not before she was chilled to the bone.

What had she done? She read articles on how to have a happy marriage, how to make love, how to be a good wife. She was doing everything she possibly could to make him happy, and sometimes, when he chose painting or paperwork over her, a blinding rage suffused her, so strong and terrifying and alien, she was sure it would eat her up alive.

When something around her was bad or ugly or painful, she often simply closed her eyes, refusing to acknowledge its existence and thinking instead of carousels and happy children and ice cream. Earlier that night, though, when they had watched Clementine's commercial together, she hadn't been able to ignore the way Jackson's gaze stuck to Clementine's image like glue. He'd watched so intensely, Megan was sure she could have taken her clothes off and he wouldn't have noticed. Was that what he wanted? A woman who didn't care if she got sand down her pants? Well, Megan cared. She couldn't help it, she cared.

She heard Jackson's scuttling, the clicking of his

brushes as he set them back in their cans beside his easel. She tried to be understanding about his art. Although his need to express himself creatively was alien to her, she didn't deny him that right. She let him keep his easels in the living room, even when they had company over and the guests had to weave around them to reach the sofa. She didn't say a word when he spent extra cash they could have put into a savings account on brushes and canvases and supplies. She had even offered to let him use some of her money to buy the things he needed, but that suggestion had only led to another fight.

Many times, feeling misunderstood and abused, she almost told him what she really thought—that he'd never sold one damn thing his whole life, that there were a million artists in the world and fewer than one percent ever made a living out of it, and that this late-night life-style of his wasn't normal. He and she weren't like the Croswells with two kids next door, or Ruth and Wayne across the street, who watched the news at eleven and then went to sleep together. Didn't he know how hard it was to lie to Alex and Clementine about how "great" their life was? She couldn't admit to Alex that Alex had been right, that Megan and Jackson weren't compatible at all. Oh, why couldn't he be normal? Why couldn't he be the man he was supposed to be?

The light in the living room finally dipped off, and Megan lay down quickly before the door opened. She watched Jackson walk through the dark bedroom. His silhouette was as perfect as ever. Wide shoulders, hard-as-a-rock chest, muscled legs. He took off his shirt and pants and got into bed naked, as always. She kept her head turned away from him.

"Meg, you awake?" he whispered.

She remained silent. He sighed deeply and turned on his side away from her. She waited until his steady breathing told her he was sleeping, then cuddled against his back. When he was asleep, she had him. For those few hours, at least, Jackson was completely hers.

•   •   •

Clementine lay down on the sand and closed her eyes. She wrapped the blanket tighter around her, guarding against the November chill that came so suddenly to Martha's Vineyard. Only an hour earlier, no more than three clouds had littered the sky. Now, the sun was hidden behind a blanket of smoky plumes and the air smelled moldy, like old rain.

The cry of the gulls saddened her, as if they, too, had agonizing fears and disappointments and were shouting their frustration to the gods. Their screeches made her long to hear Arthur's carefree voice, his easy laughter, and she sat up. She spotted him a quarter mile away strolling along the sand, his corduroys rolled up, the water lapping over his feet. Even from this distance, she knew no smile was tugging at his mouth, no joke or gag was waiting to pounce. He stared at the water and then, sensing her gaze, turned toward her. She tucked the blanket under her chin as he approached her.

"Do you want to go back to the cabin?" he asked. "It's getting awfully cold."

"I'm warm enough."

He nodded and sat down beside her, cross-legged. Picking up a handful of sand, he let the grains slide out between his fingers.

"Why don't you just say it, Arthur," she said. "You're angry."

"I'm not."

"Of course you are. I said I'm leaving, and you're angry."

He turned to her, smiling, prepared to pull a joke or snappy retort from his bag, but this time the bag was empty. The smile faded, and he pulled the blanket up around himself too.

"You're right. I don't want you to go. I feel like we're just getting started, both with your career and with us personally."

She looked away. "I've been in New York for four years. Too much has happened. Too little. Let's face it. I'm never going to be a supermodel. The commercials were great, but not enough. I have to try my luck in Hollywood. Now. Before my chance is gone."

Arthur drew pictures in the sand.

"And us?" he asked. "There's no hope for that, either?"

She put her hand on his arm. "It's not you. If I could be with anyone, it would be you."

"Don't give me that crap," he said, standing up. His sandy hair slapped in his eyes as the wind rose on the swiftly approaching storm. "Do you think explanations like that help? Every day, I try to think of a new way to make you love me, to get rid of the haunted look in your eyes, but nothing works. I thought for sure when you agreed to come to Martha's Vineyard with me that this would be it. But still, nothing's changed."

Clementine stood up, dropping the blanket. Her heart was breaking for him, for herself, but that wouldn't alter her decision. She had come to Martha's Vineyard in the hopes the fresh air and sandy beaches would make it easier for them to say good-bye, but it was no good.

"Arthur, I . . ."

He took off for the water, running hard until he reached it. He waded into the waves, the icy water soaking his pants up to his knees.

"Damn you!" he shouted, the force of his words lost in the wind, like a distant echo. He kicked at the water, sending sprays of silver tinsel five feet in the air.

"Do you think I don't know what happened?" he yelled back at her. "Did you think I never figured it out?"

She looked up and down the beach, her stomach hollow, scared. He couldn't know. No one but Alex and Megan knew. It was their awful, dirty secret. She walked toward him warily.

"I don't know what you're talking about," she said.

"For God's sake, why can't you confide in me? Do you think all men are like that slime? Do you think I'm like that? Do you think we're all looking at you, thinking about how to do it, how to—"

She clamped her hands over her ears. "Stop it! Just stop it!" she shouted.

"No, I won't stop it." He grabbed her hands and held them. "I'm going to tell the truth because one of us has to. I knew from that first day, Clementine. I pretty much guessed what happened, but that night you talked in your sleep. Screamed really. I never said anything because I wanted you to come to me. I wanted you to trust me. But you didn't."

"Don't," she said; tears streaming down her cheeks. "I can't talk about this. Not with you. Not with any man."

"You can. You didn't do anything. He was the one who raped you. You're the victim. You—"

She pulled away. "I didn't fight hard enough!" she screamed. She was sobbing now, and every nerve was pulsing, painful. "I let him do it. That's not a victim. That's an accomplice. Don't you see? I didn't fight until it was too late."

She ran away, toward the cabin in the trees. It was raining now, but she didn't notice. She ran as fast as she could, thinking only that he knew, that he'd always known, that he'd looked at her and thought, *That's Clementine. The rape victim.* That was how he defined her.

He had tricked her into trusting him, into feeling safe when she was with him. She'd even come to this cabin with him for the weekend as his friend. God, she had been a fool.

She listened for his footsteps behind her, but they didn't come. Inside the cabin, she locked herself in her bedroom. She felt sick, violated all over again. Megan and Alex were different, they were her friends, they were women. Just the thought of Arthur's looking at her and knowing made her shiver. His knowledge stripped away the veils she wore, the painted smile. It left her naked and vulnerable, and that was something she was never going to be again.

•   •   •

When Arthur didn't return to the cabin for over an hour, Clementine's anger vanished. She was only sorry it had to end like this. She decided to leave right away, instead of in a month, as she'd told Arthur earlier. She couldn't stay with him knowing what he knew, with all of her defenses shattered. Every time she looked in his eyes, she would remember.

Arthur entered the cabin and knocked on her door. She dried her eyes and opened it. They stared at each other for a moment before Clementine turned around and walked back to the bed.

"I know an agent in Los Angeles," he said. "Will Holoman. He's good. Very professional. A real go-getter. I'll call him tomorrow."

She nodded, and Arthur leaned against the door.

"I'm sorry if I upset you," he said. "It wasn't my intention. I only wanted to show you that it doesn't matter, that—"

"Doesn't matter?" she repeated, looking up. "Doesn't matter? A man rapes me, and that doesn't matter?"

"That's not what I meant."

"Yes, you did. That's why I couldn't tell you. Because you and every other man would act exactly the way you're acting. You think you can pat my head and tell me it's been three years now and why aren't I over it yet? You think, hell, it's only sex. People do it every day. What's the big deal?"

"Clementine . . ."

"It's not about sex," she said, her voice rising. "It had nothing to do with sex. It was about power. He stuck his penis inside of me, and he knew he owned me. You're a man, Arthur. You can't possibly understand what it feels like to have something foreign and unwanted and dirty rammed inside of you."

He closed his eyes. "Don't," he said.

"Why not? You want me to deal with it, but you can't stand the rough language?"

He looked at her again. "Fine, tell me."

"I will." Her voice was angry, hard. "Do you want to know how big his dick was? Do you want to know how bad it hurt? Well, I'll tell you." She clenched her fists, forcing herself to hold his gaze. "It was huge. It was fucking huge, and I bled for hours afterward. It hurt like hell. I kept banging my head against the ground while he was doing it, just banging it and praying to die."

Arthur moved quickly to the bed and grabbed her hands.

"All right," he said. "That's enough. You were raped. It was vile and disgusting, but there's not a damn thing I can do about it. All I can offer is my love, and you won't take that. But you can't let this rule your life. You're going to have to come out of it sometime."

She turned away. "You know now," she said quietly. "But that doesn't make you understand."

"No, I don't understand. But I love you, and I don't want you to go."

She sighed. "I have to. Not just to try my hand at acting, but to forget. It's my only hope."

He stood up and took a deep breath. "All right then. I can't fight your memories."

He walked out, and she was alone.

"Neither can I," she whispered.

• • •

Will Holoman was short, fat like the Pillsbury dough-boy, and balding. He was happily married, with two kids to round out the picture, and Clementine couldn't have been happier. He stirred no memories. This time, she would be all business. Hollywood, a blank canvas to her, was going to see the new and improved Clementine Montgomery. No traumas, no commitments, no past.

She and Will hit it off immediately. He described his life in two paragraphs. Wife named Laurie, two daughters, Jessica and Janet, one ulcer, and a heart condition. Yet he refused to slow down.

"Work *is* my life," he told her as he drove from the airport through the sunshiny Southern California streets toward the San Fernando Valley, where he'd found her an apartment in her price range. She would have to live off her savings for a while, while Will hunted down work for her.

"I'd rather have the health problems and work," he went on, "than be totally fit and lying like a bug around the house. I'd go crazy."

Clementine agreed wholeheartedly. In fact, as she breathed in the smoggy air and gazed at the expensive cars plowing down the freeway around her, she felt free for the first time in ages. She'd been too stubborn, too determined to leave her mark on the modeling world, to get out of New York earlier, even though she'd known it was killing her. Not only the memories, but the rising crime rate, the callousness, the distance from her friends. Los Angeles wasn't much of a safe haven, of course, but the openness appealed to her. She'd buy a car, take long drives along the coast, get a tan. She would start from the ground up, build a new Clementine.

"What about your wife and kids?" she asked Will as they headed up Mulholland Pass, the gateway to the valley, with green rolling hills on either side of them. "Isn't it hard to combine family and career?"

"Not when everyone understands that career definitely comes first."

She nodded and leaned back in the lush leather seat of Will's Mercedes-Benz. Yes, she and Will were going to get along just fine. During the remainder of the drive to her one-bedroom apartment in Studio City, he filled her in on his plans for her. He thought he could land her a couple of commercial auditions to start. She had the experience. A few casting directors might even remember her face from the Amour ads.

"We could try the horror film route," he added. "It's no piece of cake, either, but still easier to get into, considering everything."

"No, definitely not. I'd rather starve."

He laughed. "Well, you just might. I don't want to burst any bubbles you built up in New York, but you can't just walk into this town and take over. Everyone's done commercials here. I'm afraid you're nothing special. You're gonna have to pay your dues like everyone else."

I've already paid them, Clementine thought, but she only nodded.

"Arthur told me you were good," Will said, "so you'd better be. I only represent serious actors, the ones willing to work their butts off for a walk-on. If that's you, we'll hit it off great. If not . . ."

"Believe me, that's me," she said. "I'll do whatever it takes. This is all I've got now."

He glanced at her, then stopped in front of a pink stucco five-unit apartment house.

"This is it," he said. "Home sweet home. I'll let you get settled in today, but tomorrow we start banging down doors. Commercials, walk-ons, one-liners, whatever. You up for it?"

She smiled widely. "Hooray for Hollywood!"

• • •

She tried Alex's number first. Clementine could talk to Alex for hours about life and dreams and goals and the pitfalls of men, while Megan wanted to talk only about Jackson and negative pregnancy tests. No matter how hard she tried to be interested, five minutes was the limit of Clementine's patience with Megan.

Alex didn't pick up, though, so Clementine gave in and called Megan. She had to tell someone about her apartment, her plans, her excitement. Megan answered on the third ring.

"You are talking to the future queen of the big screen," Clementine said.

"Who's that?"

"Very funny. You wouldn't believe my apartment, Meg. It's so cute. It's got a great loft that will look perfect when I get a loveseat and a waist-high bookcase for it."

"Sounds wonderful."

"It is. It's perfect. And it's so warm here. Jeez, two weeks ago I'm waiting for a cab in the middle of a hailstorm, forty degrees out with a wind chill of like minus two, and now I've got all the windows open and it's got to be at least seventy degrees. November in Los Angeles. I love it."

She heard sniffling at the other end of the line and sat down on the floor.

"Meg, are you all right?"

"Me? Oh, of course. I've got a little cold, that's all."

"Sure?"

"I'm sure. I'm really happy for you, Clem. Really. Are you all right about Arthur, though? I thought you two would get together some day."

Clementine sighed. Leave it to Megan to bring up the one part of her life that she had made a complete disaster of.

"You know what happened. I can't be with any man. Not even Arthur."

"It's been three years now. I thought maybe you were over it."

Clementine looked out the window. Over it. As if the memory were just a hurdle on a track and all she had to do was jump it.

"The more time passes, the worse it gets," she said. "The fear is entrenched inside of me now. It's like my mind is making the memory worse than it was. I guess life isn't that simple after all."

"Yes, I know."

Her voice was sad and strange, prompting Clementine to ask again if she was all right. "You can talk to me, you know," she added. "I want you to talk to me. Is it Jackson?"

Megan looked around her living room and breathed deeply in and out, trying to steady herself. Jackson's canvases, dozens of them, were ripped to shreds and scattered across the floor, all of his work for the past year destroyed. Splattered paints dripped down the walls, creating psychedelic panoramas before they sank into the carpet. She still gripped the knife, and the skin on her palms was raw and stinging. She couldn't stop the shaking.

"Everything is fine, Clem," she said. "I'm right in the middle of making dinner, that's all. Could you call me back tomorrow?"

"Of course. Take care."

Megan hung up. She pried the knife out of her hand and set it down on the counter. She'd been crying, but she hadn't noticed until now. She slid down along the wall to the floor and pulled her knees up to her chest. Very softly, like a child, she hummed a lullaby.

# CHAPTER
## 13

*JACKSON WAS THE FIRST PERSON OUT OF THE* hotel development meeting. He was hoping that if he got a head start, his boss, Gary Pulacman, who sweated and huffed just moving his size-forty-eight belly to the refrigerator for another beer, wouldn't be able to catch up. He knew Gary was after him. Every week, he said the same thing. Where was Jackson's enthusiasm? What had happened to his creative ideas? What was his problem?

Jackson dashed around a water fountain, hopped over two supply cartons, and headed for the drawing room. He hated this goddamn job and all of its goddamn rules and tedium, that's what his problem was. How was he supposed to get excited about designing the same goddamn four-walled store or house every goddamn day?

He reached his desk—a drafting table amid twelve other drafting tables separated from one another by chest-high white plasterboard walls—and sat down. Sooner than he'd thought possible, Gary, stomach first, appeared beside him.

"Jackson, we need to talk," he said in the same slobbery way he did each time he'd spent an hour or two kissing clients' self-satisfied behinds and taking credit for Jackson's ideas.

"What about, Gar?" he replied.

"Come on, Jack, you're a good architect. One of the best. Why do you have to do this? If you wanted it, I'll bet you could have my job one day and probably even a partnership with Jakonovich."

"And what if I don't want that?"

That threw Gary, as Jackson had known it would. It was ridiculous to Jackson the way Gary and everyone else at Baron and Jakonovich thought the sun rose and set over architecture. They never tried anything else. They never thought of anything else. Their world consisted of drafting boards and layouts and plumbing schematics. They had one goal, and that was to make it to the top of this firm at the expense of all else. Jackson, on the other hand, hated the office. He hated the work. His most important short-term goal was to make it to Friday and get home to his paintings.

"Look, I don't know what's going on with you," Gary said, pulling himself up as high as his five-foot-six-inch frame would allow. "But I do know that I don't like your attitude. You presented your ideas for the Wonders Hotel project like a robot. You practically insulted Mr. Hendricks with your condescending attitude, and you know damn well that he's one of our biggest clients and likes to think he's running the show. You stomp around the office like a spoiled brat, and I am sick and tired of it. Do you hear me?"

Jackson snapped shut his briefcase and felt his emotions shutting off, too, like automatic sprinklers done for the day. He looked around the room, at the cubicles with the same people doing the same things they'd done for years, and he shook his head. It was all so clear now. There were two choices, always two choices. Live for today and be happy, or live for tomorrow and suffer. Sure, you sometimes had to sacrifice now for later, but there was a point when you said enough was enough and started living, taking the consequences of poverty or ostracism while you sucked up every ounce of pleasure life had to offer. Jackson had never set a deadline for how long he would stay at this rotting firm, but he knew his time was up. He grabbed his briefcase and walked to the door.

"Don't you walk out on me!" Gary shouted. "Just where do you think you're going?"

"Out. I need some air."

"If you walk out that door, Mr. Hollywell, I will not guarantee you a job when you come back."

Jackson stopped at the door and turned around. The other architects were all watching, peeping over the walls like giraffes at the zoo. Jackson shook his head and laughed.

"Well, thank God for that," he said.

•   •   •

As far as Jackson was concerned, nothing was quite so wonderful as being outside on a Wednesday afternoon while the rest of the world was typing, massaging aching heads, pouring the seventh cup of coffee, or taking conference calls. He had the city to himself. He left his car in the parking lot and hopped on a bus heading for Fisherman's Wharf. There wouldn't be many tourists on a weekday in November.

He got off at Ghirardelli Square and strode toward the planked sidewalks of the wharf. A few passersby stared, as if a man in a business suit and carrying a briefcase was more outrageous than the long-haired hippies and tattooed women who claimed Golden Gate Park as their home. He looked at his reflection in the window of a personalized T-shirt store, wondering just what it was the world saw in him.

Staring back at him was the quintessential business man. Meticulously combed hair, clean shave, dark navy suit, white starched shirt, red tie. If the man in the glass had been only a portrait, rather than his own reflection, would he have recognized himself? Where was the naively hopeful light in his eyes? Where were the blue jeans he'd sworn in high school never to part with, no matter what job he got? Or the flannel shirts he'd kept for years, despite unsightly rips. Last he remembered, Megan was stuffing them in the back of the bottom dresser drawer.

He had come so far from what he'd intended to be. At eighteen, he'd been determined to conquer the world his way. Now, at only twenty-four, he had no dreams left untarnished. A few still sputtered for life, but the rest had died, some slowly, some exploding instantly on impact with reality. Jackson took a long, hard look at himself, at his life, at how he had unknowingly let the best in him perish and the worst thrive. He'd gone from free spirit to middle-class conformist. From artist to imitator. Passion to apathy.

He yanked at his tie until it hung loose around his neck. He opened the briefcase and dumped his plans and drawings into a nearby trash can. A man was playing the harmonica a few feet away, a coffee can for money set in front of him. Jackson handed him the briefcase.

"It's leather," he said. "Cost me close to two hundred at Saks. You could sell it for seventy-five, easy."

"Thanks, man."

Jackson nodded and walked on. He felt lighter, younger than he had in years. Tonight, he'd find those old flannel shirts and wear his blue jeans. And he would paint. Anything and everything. He would go home and set up four canvases, enough to capture all the images in his mind. Everything he'd stood for, believed in, and wanted to be couldn't be lost completely. There was life inside him yet. He'd buried it beneath three-piece suits and conformity, but he'd find it again. He'd have to. If he wanted the rest of his life to be worth living, he'd have to.

He glanced at his watch. Three-thirty-five. Megan would expect him home in three hours. Three hours. When was the last time three hours had seemed brief? When he was painting, but that was all. A minute at the office felt like an hour. And at night with Megan, when she rambled on about petunias and her weekly, outrageously expensive visits to the fertility doctor, the minutes felt like days. He kept waiting for it to get better. Instead, every morning, the day spread out before him like a scorching desert extending beyond the horizon. And every day, he had to cross it.

Ah, but at this moment, he was free. Free. He didn't give a shit about the job. Actually, he was surprised he'd put up with it for as long as he had. If it weren't for

Megan ... Well, if it weren't for Megan, a lot of things would have been different. Anyway, he was sick of being proud. Either he'd find another job he could enjoy while he strengthened his painting techniques, or hell, he might even take Megan up on her offer to use some of her trust fund money. He'd take a vacation. Yes, a vacation. That's what he needed. He and Megan could fly to Aspen, do a little skiing, rekindle the sparks. He'd tell her how he'd been feeling. Why hadn't he ever thought of that before? He'd been so busy trying to be the responsible, dependable husband he thought she wanted, he'd never taken the time to tell her he was unhappy. She would understand.

Up on the corner, a lingerie shop caught his attention. A faceless mannequin was wearing a silk negligee he would love to see on his wife, instead of the cotton pajamas and nightshirts she usually wore. She would look perfect in it.

She didn't think he knew how hard she worked at her appearance, but he did. It was just that by the time he'd worked eight hours at a job he hated, then driven for an hour to a suburb of indistinguishable stucco houses he couldn't like no matter how hard he tried, he didn't have the energy to tell her her lipstick matched her nail color perfectly. And when she started getting on his case about the glop of red acrylic paint he'd accidentally dropped on the carpet, or the brushes he'd left in the sink, or the dinner party she was planning for their idiot neighbors who had nothing better to talk about than lawn fertilizers and the high cost of day care, he stopped seeing her, stopped listening, stopped, for all intents and purposes, being her husband.

He walked into the store and looked closely at the negligee. It was a soft coral pink, its sleeves edged in antique lace, and the satin skirt fell to the floor. Megan really would look lovely in it. The color was perfect for her. He loved her in roses, creams, pastels—enhancements to her softness. He loved it when her blond hair fell over her cheek when she slept, like silken threads. God, he loved her.

Jackson closed his eyes. Had they really been married

for almost three years? When they were fighting, it seemed like a lifetime. Yet sometimes, when he realized how easy it was to hurt her and how very little he really knew of her or she of him, it seemed like only hours. He had no idea who his wife was, what she wanted, what she needed from him, what she thought, what she felt. All he knew was that she was on one course and he was on another, and for three years they had been traveling full speed in opposite directions.

"Can I help you, sir?" a middle-aged saleswoman asked.

Jackson opened his eyes and ran his fingers over the negligee again.

"Wrap this up, will you?" he said. "It's a present for my wife."

. . .

The smashed petunias in the garden were his first clue. Every day, the yapping poodle next door tromped through Megan's garden and destroyed a section of her flower bed. By the end of the day, though, Megan had new ones replanted, or at least the old ones removed. That day, when Jackson walked up the concrete path to his front door, the flattened blue-and-white petunias looked like dirty blueberry pancakes.

He tried to open the front door, but it was locked. That was the second clue. The third was when he walked to the window to look in and call for Megan, and found the drapes closed tightly. Megan never closed the drapes. Her plants needed optimum sunshine, she said. And she hated the feeling of being closed in. Later on, Jackson would put everything together and wish he had prepared himself. At the time, he only searched through his pockets and found his keys.

As he walked inside, he lost his breath the way he had in elementary school when someone kicked a soccer ball full force into his stomach. The prettily wrapped package dropped out from under his arm. He leaned back against the wall and banged his head on it, again and again.

A bomb had exploded in the living room. That was the only explanation. His oils, his watercolors, his sketches, everything was destroyed. A few of his older, more amateurish pieces were probably safe, out of harm's way in the back of the closet, but these . . . these had been the essence of him.

The past year had been the best of his life artistically. The unhappiness within him had been exorcised through his painting, reincarnated into creative energy that kept him up until the early morning working feverishly. He'd continued doing landscapes, but he'd also begun a series of more abstract work, plucked from his subconscious, his heart. He hadn't said anything to Megan, but he was going to try to interest a gallery in showing the new paintings. For the first time, he had been certain his work was great.

He kept pounding his head against the wall. It felt good, the blunt jabs of pain smashing his brain. He threw his head back harder and harder, seeing white lights now, sparkling flickers in his eyes. He didn't notice when Megan approached him. He only felt her fingers gouging his arm, pulling at him.

"Stop it. Stop it, Jackson!" she yelled.

He shook away the lights and looked at her. She'd been crying. Red circles rimmed her eyes. Her mascara had stained her cheeks and chin.

"What—what happened?" he asked.

She dropped her head. That was when he looked down at her hands, at the paint under her nails. A second soccer ball, harder than the first, rammed into his stomach. He bent forward.

"You did this," he whispered. He waited for her to deny it, ready to believe any outrageous explanation just so he'd be able to look at her again without hatred.

She nodded, and Jackson fought for breath. It was strange that that was his only feeling, the lack of oxygen. He expected the anger, the need to fight down his fists, but there was only the struggle for air, an eerie lightheadedness.

He walked through the room, looking for something to salvage. There was nothing. He picked up a corner of what had been his favorite seascape, painted a few months earlier when he'd driven to Carmel for the day.

A cypress had stood in the foreground, and beyond it was the extraordinarily calm sea. He'd left it on the windowsill for inspiration, to fill him with peace when his life had little of its own. Megan had cut it into dozens of pieces, sliced it like a delusion-plagued serial killer on a rampage.

His paints were overturned, the oils decorating the carpet like gaily colored lollipops. In the years he and Megan had been married, she'd never let the house go for more than three days without a full floor-to-ceiling cleaning. And now she'd done this. He thought of the portrait of Alex he'd painted on their honeymoon, still one of his best pieces. Thank God, Alex had it with her. It was a small consolation, but it was something. He rubbed his forehead, then looked over his shoulder at Megan.

She was crying silently, still standing by the door.

"Why?"

She shook her head.

"Dammit, why?" he yelled, kicking at the destruction around him.

"I don't know," she whispered.

He shook his head and laughed bitterly. The two of them seemed to be acting out a scene from a soap opera, exaggerated, ridiculous, overly dramatic.

"You don't know," he repeated. "That's rich." He stomped through the wreckage, kicking again.

"You destroyed my work," he said louder. "Dammit, Megan, you destroyed my life. This was all I had, the only thing that made me happy. You knew what it meant to me, and then you took it away."

"All I know is that it means more to you than I do," Megan said. She'd found her strength again. The tears stopped, and she walked toward him, driving the paints deeper into the carpet. "It's been eating me alive, the way you ignore me, the way you look at me like you hate me. Every time I see your art, I see something that you love more than you love me. It was driving me insane!"

She paced around the room, the scrunching of the canvases beneath her feet sounding like nails on a chalkboard. "When life gets too much for you, you paint. But what can I do when it gets too much for me? I don't have anything. I have to lie through my teeth to Alex and Clementine. Alex would have a field day if she knew the truth. 'I told you so,' she'd say. Oh, she knew it. She knew you'd never be happy with boring old Megan."

"Meg." He reached out his hand to her, but she jerked away from him.

"Goddammit, it's not fair." She shook her head violently. "When I need you to hold me, you ignore me and hold your damn paintbrush instead. I hardly see you, and when I do, I could be dead for all you care. All I know is that you married me for some reason even you don't understand, and now you're trying to figure out why and get the hell out."

"That's not true."

She faced him. "Like hell it isn't!" She'd never known how much power she had until she looked around the room and saw what she'd done. "I do everything for you. I cook. I clean. I let you paint. I support your career."

"I hate my career."

She turned away.

"I hate it, Meg. I know you want the perfect nine-to-five husband, but that kind of structure makes me miserable. I need art. It's inside of me. Everything around you . . ." Jackson closed his eyes, the full force of what was lost hitting him hard. "Everything here was me. You destroyed me."

She whirled around to face him, and for once, Jackson was the first to turn his gaze away. "All I wanted was a happy life," she said. "A husband, a house, a baby. Why is that so hard for you to give me?"

"I'm not some kind of wind-up toy that you can manipulate however you want. I'm a person. I have my own dreams and ideas. Doesn't what I want matter to you at all?"

"You're not being fair," she said, crying again.

"I'm not fair? I'm not fair?" He grabbed her arm, his fingers digging into her skin. She flinched, but he held on tightly.

"You act like a maniac, ripping apart my life's work, the only thing that gives me any peace, just because it bothers you to look at it, and then you have the nerve to say I'm not fair. God, you've really twisted the picture, haven't you?"

"Maybe I have," she yelled. "But you were never around to tell me I was wrong."

He let go of her arm and walked to the door. The package still lay there, and he picked it up.

"Where are you going?" she asked.

"Out."

"Where, Jackson? You can't walk out on me now. This is our marriage we're talking about. Please, we need to talk."

He turned around. "Right now, it seems to me the only thing we need is a divorce. I'm going to take a walk and try to change my mind."

He slammed the door. Megan wanted to throw herself on the floor and sob, punch the walls with all her might, but she didn't. Instead, she took a garbage bag out of the kitchen cupboard and returned to the living room. It was surprisingly easy not to think when she was cleaning. She'd been doing the same thing for three years, putting herself into automatic, voiding all thoughts of the sham of her marriage and focusing on which cleaner would work best on which stain.

She bent down and opened the bag. Piece by piece, she picked up the mess.

•   •   •

Alex dug into Millie's apple pie with a vengeance. She rarely had a chance to eat anymore. Work on her master's degree took up five days a week, from eight in the morning until at least eleven at night, and the other two days were spent at Goodman and Associates working on the books. None of the men who passed through her life were interested in feeding her, and frankly, she didn't think she'd be able to make enough conversation with any of them to last through a two-hour dinner.

So she grabbed a soda here, a candy bar there. The perfect diet. She'd lost ten pounds in the last three months without even trying. Why should she care about nutrition when she was thin and gorgeous?

She laughed out loud, finally capturing her date's attention. He had been staring out the window for ten minutes, ignoring his blueberry pie.

"What's so funny?" Jackson asked.

"I was just thinking about what a gorgeous, sexy woman I am."

He smiled. "And modest too."

She sipped her coffee, watching him over the rim of her cup. His face was pale and lined. His dark hair, usually attractively messy, was too far gone now even for him. His flannel shirt was creased and wrinkled, as if he'd forgotten to take it off and had slept in it.

"You, on the other hand," she said, "look like shit."

He leaned back against the vinyl cushions of the café booth and rubbed his hand over his stubbly chin.

"Thanks."

"I'm serious, Jack. It's been four months since you and Megan started counseling. That's supposed to be helping, remember?"

"Helping. Ha!" He picked up his fork, then set it down again and pushed the pie away.

"Can I have it?"

"It's amazing you don't get fat. Megan won't even eat one bite of pie without . . ."

"Without what?"

"Do you realize that's the first time I've used her name in everyday conversation? That almost sounded like she was my wife."

Alex picked up the bill and stood. "Forget the pie. I'm paying, and we're going for a walk."

Returning from the cashier, she pulled Jackson out of his seat and slipped her arm around his waist. They walked outside into the warm late spring day.

"Do you love her?" Alex asked immediately.

"God, can't you start with something a little easier?"

She stopped and turned Jackson toward her.

"That should be easy, Jack. That should be the easiest question in the world when you're married."

"Where do you get off being so judgmental? You don't known a damn thing about love and marriage."

Alex whirled around and stormed off down the hill.

"Alex, wait!"

She picked up her pace and turned the corner, heading back toward the Berkeley campus. Jackson ran after her and, when he reached her, grabbed her arm.

"Alex, I'm sorry."

"Everyone says those things and then says they're sorry, like I'm a punching bag that always bounces back."

"Of course you're not. And I am sorry. Really. That was shitty. I'm shitty. You're my best friend. Please forgive me."

She messed up his already messy hair and smiled.

"Fine. Forgiven. But that's the last time. Now, come on. Let's get back to the campus."

They walked the mile to Berkeley quickly, talking about their old college days, their apartment, anything but the present. It was much easier for Jackson to take refuge in the past than to deal with reality, the way he had to every Monday and Wednesday night with the marriage counselor. Four months earlier, he had realized his and Megan's only choices were counseling or divorce. Despite how far apart they'd grown, he didn't want to admit defeat and lose Megan completely.

But God, he hated those sessions. He hated the counselor's pointed questions, which always seemed accusing, laying the blame on him. He hated Megan's tears, which began, without fail, five minutes after they arrived. He had taken to setting his watch by them. And he hated himself for his duplicity. For wanting to be free again or, worse, forgetting Megan was even a part of his life at all. An hour before each session, he had to work up enough energy to go, to fight, to pretend that this marriage was the most important thing in the world to him, the way it was to Megan.

He and Alex reached the south lawn of the campus and sat down in the sun. Jackson lay on his back and stared at the thin lines of clouds that streamed across the sky like factory smoke.

"I love her," he said softly. Alex nodded and wrapped her arms around her knees. "I love her because she's my wife. Because over three years ago, I met her at the altar, believing we could work together."

"And can you?"

"It sure doesn't look that way, does it?" He sat up abruptly. "Counseling *is* supposed to help, but it's only making things worse. Dr. Chadwick tells us to talk about our feelings, let them out in the open, but all we learn from that is how little we actually know about each other. Megan is saying things I can't believe."

"Like?"

"Like I'm supposed to work in a real job. She can't stand it that I'm trying to make a living as an artist. She wants me to crawl back to Jakonovich like a spineless wimp and ask for my job back. It's like she has this image of what I should be and doesn't give a damn what I'm really like, as long as she can squeeze me into this mold of hers."

He ran his hand through his hair, cringing when he felt the oil that was accumulating there. When was the last time he'd taken a shower? Days? Weeks?

"It doesn't matter that she's got all that money in the bank," he went on. "Money that she once offered to me. No, now she says that money is only for investments and, in the meantime, I'm supposed to support her."

"That doesn't sound like Megan."

He stopped and looked at Alex. Her eyes were closed, her face turned up to the sun. Her dark kinky hair fell halfway down her back; she hadn't cut it for three years. It was as wild and unmanageable and completely Alex as ever.

"Well, that's the essence of what she says. She's different now, Alex. She's stronger. Something kicked on inside her the day she ripped up my paintings."

He clenched his fists. Standing, he ran to a thick-trunked tree a few yards behind them and swung on the lowest branch.

"You're still mad at her for that?" Alex asked.

"Yes. No. I don't know. I think of all that was lost, and I want to kill her. But then I think of the work I've been doing lately, trying to compensate, and in a way it was to my advantage. It spurred me on to work harder and do more."

"Come here," Alex said, turning around and watching him swing one-armed like a monkey. "Come on, you idiot, I want to be serious for a minute."

He walked back and sat down beside her.

"You're not being fair to her, you know," Alex said.

"How can you say that? She's the one who trashed my paintings. I'd say I'm being extraordinarily fair about that."

"I'm not talking about your paintings. I mean emotionally."

Alex picked at the grass blades, laying them in the palm of her hand according to size. "You should hear Megan when she calls me. She raves about the progress you're making in counseling. How well your marriage is coming along. She's sure you're working out your differences and everything will be fine. And then, ten minutes later, you call me from a phone booth, yelling and screaming, telling me how miserable you are. You two are worlds apart from each other."

"What am I supposed to do? Burst her bubble? Burst her whole world?"

She dropped the blades of grass and stared straight at him. "Yes, dammit. She's living in a world that doesn't exist, and one day, whether it's tomorrow or five years from now, she's going to find that out. Try to imagine how devastating that's going to be for her. You have your painting and your dreams. But Megan only has you. Be honest with her, Jack. Tell her you don't think it's working. Tell her you're scared. Tell her the truth for once."

Jackson looked away. A few students were exiting the buildings and lying down on the lawn for a between-class tanning session.

"Megan doesn't want honesty, Alex. She wants a Norman Rockwell painting, a page out of some psychologist's book on how to have a successful marriage. Every time I try to bring reality in, she slams the door."

Alex stood up and brushed the grass off herself. She held out her arm to Jackson and pulled him up. "Well, then, you'll just have to pry the door open again, now won't you?"

•  •  •

Clementine stared at herself in the full-length bedroom mirror. The satin brushing against her legs felt like baby's skin. She ran her hands down her hips and turned from side to side. The coral negligee fit her perfectly.

She'd almost sent it back after she'd received it six months earlier. The card had read:

To Clementine,
    Thinking about you.

                                    Love, Jackson.

She still remembered the feeling she'd gotten from those words. It was similar to the jarring cold of the ice cubes a cousin had slipped down her back when she was five years old. Cold, slippery, shivery chills that made her body tense. For a moment, she'd easily forgotten Megan and their marriage and the miles that separated Jackson from her. She'd imagined him thinking of her, daydreaming about things that might be, some day, if their lives could only change course. He was the only man who had ever made her feel awkward and uncomfortable, and yet so completely, totally at home.

But then she'd seen her face in the mirror, the haze in her eyes like a smoke screen, the color in her cheeks, and she'd stiffened. Her heart was betraying her. It had no idea how far she still went to avoid physical contact. How, when a man was ringing up her groceries at the market, she made him put her change down on the counter instead of into her hand. How, in line at the bank, she never stood closer than three feet to the man in front of her.

Whatever feelings she had for Jackson would have to stay buried with the rest of her emotions. That was her only defense against the memories, to keep everything—fear, anger, love, hate—locked away inside. It was the only way she knew to survive.

Besides, she was married to her career now. Will had gotten her auditions for movies of the week, and she'd landed a guest appearance—a four-liner even—on an ABC Sunday Night Movie. Still, it was slow going and much more difficult than she'd thought it would be. She had to fall back on her modeling skills and do a few catalogue spreads to help make ends meet, but that didn't daunt her. If she had to go backward to eventually go forward, then she would do it. She couldn't let Jackson Hollywell sidetrack her now. She would simply put him out of her mind.

At first, too busy to get to the post office to return it, she had left the present unopened on the coffee table, where she stared at it every morning and evening. After a week, unable to stand the curiosity any longer, she'd opened it. She had wondered what it might be—an album she may have mentioned, a book. When she saw the creamy negligee beneath the white tissue paper, her heart had stopped. She'd lifted it out of the box and held it against her cheek.

The tears had started easily then. She wasn't sad, not really. She'd just felt a pain in her chest and head, a loss of something she had never experienced and probably never would. If only things had been different, she'd thought. *If only I were someone else.*

Megan had mentioned her problems with Jackson, but Clementine doubted they were serious. Megan called once a week to give her a run-down of the counseling sessions, how much closer she and Jackson were getting, how wonderful it was now that they were being completely honest with each other. During the calls, Clementine stood with her back flat against the wall, pressing hard as if hurricane winds were coming straight at her, holding her there. It hurt, Megan's soft words, the details of the way he touched her, wanted her, loved *her*. It was ridiculous. She hardly knew him, had barely seen him, been with him. Yet at times, she thought she would give everything she had to be in Megan's shoes for just one day. To be touched by a man like that without terror or memories, to stretch out beneath him, rub her leg along his, feel him inside her and not scream. Just one day to be normal, to be loved.

It would never happen. Megan and Jackson would work out their problems and go on, married, together, devoted. And Clementine would have . . . her career. Yes, she would always have her career.

She'd almost taken the gift back to the post office right then. Stationery, a pot holder, maybe even a scarf she could understand, but not a negligee. She'd put it back in the box, marked it "Return to Sender," and was almost out the door when she stopped. What if Megan opened it? Clementine couldn't imagine that she knew about the gift. Despite the harmlessness of it, Megan would be hurt and jealous. Clementine turned around and slipped the package under her bed, deciding to give it to Jackson personally, when she was in the Bay area or he was in L.A.

That time never arrived. And now here she was, six months later, wearing it for the first time. With the package beneath her bed, she hadn't been been able to stop thinking about Jackson. She'd slip the negligee out at night, run her fingers over the ribbons, rub the satin, and wonder what had possessed him to send it to her, how much he knew about her feelings for him. Looking at herself in the mirror, she knew all the answers.

Jackson had sent it to her because he felt the same thing she did, an undeniable attraction, an irresistible need to keep in contact. It was almost as if his hands had touched the fabric, caressed it, and now his touch could penetrate the miles and massage her. Jackson's hands weren't dirty or rough as His had been, but smooth and delicate, artist's hands, painting portraits on her skin, setting her nerves on fire.

Somehow, despite the small amount of time they'd spent together and the distance between them, Jackson knew exactly how she felt. He knew that when she allowed herself to think of a man, of loving a man, she thought of him. He knew that despite her love for Megan, her thoughts betrayed their friendship. Her mind ran wildly out of control, like a villain's. She hoped for problems in their marriage, separation, maybe even divorce. It was horrible, and yet she couldn't help it.

She didn't care that even if he were free, she still had her fears of intimacy. She hit a wall every time a man came near her. She didn't care that she knew nothing about him, aside from what Megan and Alex told her. She knew only that her feelings for him were completely irrational and time had not dulled them at all.

As she gazed at herself in the mirror, running her fingers along the satin that clung to her waist and hips, imagining her hand was his, his face was staring back at her, she knew her fantasies grew more vivid, more believable every day. Despite all her resolutions, all her fears, if he wanted her, she would give herself to him. The only question was whether it would ever come to that.

# CHAPTER
## 14

*A*LEX HAD THE CORNER OFFICE. ALL RIGHT, so maybe it was a really small corner, no bigger than a closet really, with no secretary out front and furnished with only a rickety desk and chair, but it was on the twenty-third floor of the Bank of America building in the Financial District, with a smashing view of the city and the San Francisco–Oakland Bay Bridge beyond. And it was hers, completely hers.

Going the extra two years and getting her master's degree in business administration had made all the difference to her career. No longer was she pouring coffee and conquering the oh-so-challenging work of keeping the books straight at Goodman and Associates. She was an assistant investment consultant with Rock Solid Investment Company, making the not-too-shabby starting salary of thirty thousand dollars a year.

She'd known from the start that she was qualified for the job. One of her professors had even put in a good word for her. The problem had been convincing Brent Gibbons, the chief executive officer of Rock Solid, that she was good enough. Alex had heard of him long before she applied for the job. His name was whispered with awe at power lunches, his quotes common in *The*

*Wall Street Journal.* He was the leading instigator of the takeover bid for Metro Enterprises, and it was rumored he'd had a hand in the Walshman buyout. Meanwhile, quickly and quietly, he had bought Rock Solid Investment Company and raised it from a second-rate, five-employee business into one of the leading stock brokerage houses on the West Coast.

From what Alex had learned through her research, Rock Solid leased out three floors in the B of A building, had more than two hundred employees, and was the favorite investment company of the San Francisco/Los Angeles elite. The firm had a six-month-old branch in New York and was in the final stages of opening an office in London. Rock Solid had branched into every aspect of the financial services market, but specialized in what many considered risky, high-yield investments, volatile stocks and mutual funds. Yet Brent Gibbons's rate of return for his clients was remarkably high. The clients told their friends who told their agents and business partners and wives and husbands, and the business grew, outperforming even the company's expectations.

Alex never expected to meet Brent Gibbons personally. CEOs were busy with marketing and management, not employee interviews. She had a lot to learn about the way Mr. Gibbons ran a successful company. When she arrived at the corporate headquarters for her interview, the secretary informed her that Mr. Gibbons handled all personnel interviews himself. Alex swallowed the gum she'd been chewing and sat up straight. She could do this, she told herself. He was just a person, like her. Same blood, same bones. When the secretary told her he was ready for her, Alex sat for a moment gathering her strength, fighting dizziness and butterflies, then stood up and entered the office.

The room was dark, like a kindergarten class at nap time, and lush, stocked with thriving plants and Expressionist paintings. The bookcases on the side walls were lined neatly with encyclopedias, dictionaries, and economics books by the masters. The far wall was glass from floor to ceiling, with a magnificent view that extended across the Bay Bridge all the way to Oakland.

Brent Gibbons was on the phone, his head turned away, so that all Alex could see was the tip of a Greek angled nose and a head of gray hair. She walked to the front of his desk and waited, mentally gluing her feet to the floor so she wouldn't fidget. She had a better view of him here. He was what she had expected, the epitome of the hard-nosed investment broker. Dark suit, red power tie, ringless hands. Either he was married and cared not to advertise that fact, or a wife just didn't fit into the picture. Listening to his voice rise, caught up in the passion of a purchase, a possibility of making a killing, Alex was certain his devotion to business was complete. The richness of his baritone voice and the authority he commanded alleviated her nervousness for the moment. He was all she wanted to be.

At last, he finished the call and stood up. He was tall, close to six feet, making her uncomfortably aware of how small she looked beside him. His handshake was firm, and Alex had had time to wipe all traces of sweat from her palms onto the sides of her skirt.

"Sit down," he said. He reseated himself and picked up her résumé. He looked it over for a good three minutes, nodding, making notes in the margins. Alex had never wanted to know anything more than what he was writing down.

"This is very nice, Miss Holmes," he said. "It is Miss, isn't it?"

"Yes, sir."

"Fine. A remarkable GPA. Three-point-eight. Impressive. The work experience is a little thin, however. We usually look for someone who has worked in the investment field directly. In fact, we've got two more interviews lined up today with young men who have spent the last five years on Wall Street."

With his eyes piercing hers, Alex realized she had already been unfairly categorized. Brent Gibbons had decided the moment he looked at her that she was too young, too fresh, too . . . feminine. Damn this skirt and blouse. She should have worn the pantsuit. She turned her head to the side, angry and frustrated. She was a fool to think she could get the job. She was only twenty-four,

fresh out of college. And she was a woman. No matter
what anybody told her about equal rights, the men in
charge, the Brent Gibbonses of this world, still believed
a woman couldn't hack the pressure of business. They
talked big, but that was only talk. Get a bunch of men
alone together, and you'd find out they still thought of
women as the pea-brained, good-for-one-thing-only babes
and chicks they'd pulled around by their hair in the
caveman days.

It was true, unfortunately, that she had only pushed
papers in accounting at Goodman. And she'd met one of
the other interviewees in the lounge, and he most definitely was qualified. Boring, but qualified. She had to
think fast, talk fast. She wrung her hands together on her
lap.

"Mr. Gibbons, I realize I may not have experience precisely in the investment business, but I don't think that
should rule me out. What does the job of investment consultant really entail? Number one, developing a trusting relationship with clients that will make them feel comfortable
leaving their money in our hands. And let's face it, a
woman generally induces trust more quickly than a man
and is better at developing personal relationships. Number
two, I'd be working with your brokers, learning the stocks,
the trends, knowing when to advise, when to jump on it,
and when to get a second opinion. You wouldn't want
some hot shot from Wall Street who thinks he knows everything in here making multimillion-dollar mistakes for your
clients, would you?"

Gibbons was watching her hands, loosed from her lap,
gesturing animatedly. "As I see it," she continued, "an investment consultant should have a light but firm touch,
an all-around sense of how to make money, and the ability to soothe people's frazzled nerves. She should have a
way with words and enough brains and charisma to get a
hesitant investor to take the plunge."

"And I assume you have all that?"

He was smiling condescendingly, but Alex's only
choice was to continue. This was her only chance to
make all her years of college worth something.

"I do," she said. "I'm a businessperson, Mr. Gibbons.

I think, eat, sleep, and dream stocks, bonds, mutual funds, cash flow, and corporate takeovers. I've studied the rules, the game plan, every aspect of this business for six years, and although I know that's not the same as actual experience, it gives me an upper hand, an overall sense of where things are headed in the economy."

He sat back in his chair. "You talk pretty, Miss Holmes, but I don't need pretty. I need tough. I need savvy."

Alex clenched her hands into fists. She hadn't felt this outclassed since she first met Clementine. She knew she was as good as gone, but she still couldn't give up. This was the only job she wanted, the kind of job her parents had told her to fight for.

"I am tough," she said. "The truth is, I've given up everything for business. I've never done anything halfway in my life, and this is no exception. If you hire me, you'll get more than a full-time employee. You'll get a lifetime employee. How many people can offer you that?"

Gibbons stood up and walked to the window.

"You remind me of a young man I once knew," he said softly. "He was as fiery as you, as idealistic about his future."

"What happened to him?"

"He grew up. Got married. Got jaded."

He turned and stared at Alex, and she felt her face grow warm. Though her outfit was almost androgynous—slim gray skirt and jacket, white blouse, black pumps—this man somehow made her feel feminine.

"You?" she asked.

"It doesn't matter. The point is that this is a cold business. The people you work with will pretend to be your friend, and then they'll stab you in the back as soon as you turn your head. Clients are nervous, edgy. They take it out on you."

"I know all that."

"Most of our employees have no social life. There's no time for it. This is a twenty-four-hour-a-day job."

Alex didn't blink. "I know."

"And you still think you can handle it?"

She leaned forward. "I know I can."

Brent Gibbons sat back down and looked at his calendar. Alex held her breath.

"Is a week from Friday at eight all right?" he asked.

"Excuse me?"

"For now, you can go to employee relations down the hall, they'll fill you in on our insurance and benefits package. You'll start tomorrow at eight, then next Friday, if you're free, I'll take you to dinner. I always like to take my new employees out. We're not so big yet that I can't still add a personal touch. It's a celebration of new beginnings and a damn good tax write-off."

His smile changed his whole demeanor. His gray steel eyes turned smoky, his face softened, and he looked distantly familiar, like an old neighborhood friend. All you had to do was look closer, lift the layers of wealth and years away, and beneath you found the same awkward, dream-filled kid from down the street.

Alex let his words sink in, let the shock of surprise and happiness fill her, before she smiled and hurried to the door.

"You won't regret this, Mr. Gibbons."

He looked at her pointedly. "No, I don't think I will."

Walking down the hall toward the employee relations office, her adrenaline pumping and her mind racing ahead to tomorrow, Alex rammed straight into a woman turning the corner with a foot-high stack of folders in her arms. The papers scattered like leaves through the hallway.

"I'm so sorry," Alex said, and immediately bent down to try to put things back in order.

The woman shook her head and got down on her knees. The first thing Alex noticed was her bright red nailpolish and pointed, triangular nails. When she glanced at the woman's face, she almost jumped back at the sight of bright clownish makeup slopped over pale skin. The woman's straight black hair was hairsprayed to a sticky death. A secretary, Alex thought.

"I truly am sorry," she said again. "I just got a job, and I was so excited, I guess I wasn't watching. I'm Alex Holmes." She extended her hand.

The woman sat back on her heels and slowly, as if it

were taxing every ounce of her energy, shook Alex's hand.

"Maxine Waterdell. Just which job were you offered? Certainly not coffee monitor, I hope."

Alex ignored her sarcasm and stood up, straightening so she was as tall as she could make herself. "Actually, I'm the newest investment consultant. And yourself?"

Red anger flickered in Maxine's eyes for a moment before she composed herself and stood, as well. She took the remaining papers from Alex.

"I'm Mr. Beerson's secretary," she said. "But not for long. I've got big plans."

Alex supposed Maxine wanted her to be impressed, but she doubted if secretaries ever did climb out from behind their dictation machines and make it all the way to the top of the company, the way they did in rags-to-riches movies.

"Well, that's nice. I'd better be on my way. It was nice meeting you."

Maxine nodded and walked away, not a single strand of her black hair budging. Alex shook her head. She hadn't even started working, and already she felt she had an enemy. Oh, well. She didn't have time to worry about a disgruntled secretary's attitude. She was on her way to becoming the investment consultant of the century.

The following morning, Brent Gibbons showed her her office and briefed her on the details and responsibilities of her position. When he finished three hours later, Alex sat back in her chair and wondered what she'd gotten herself into. Before her were five six-inch stacks of client portfolios, three stock analyses, twelve lists of possible investments and trading reports to memorize, and four notebooks on employee procedures. In her dreams of a big-time job, she was always busy, but her fantasies had never included quite so much paperwork.

She sat at her desk, closed her eyes, and thought of all the adjustments she'd have to make. This was a whole new life-style. There would be no more loafing days. She couldn't cut work the way she had a few college classes, when the beach or a drive up the coast was infinitely more appealing. She'd have to be up by six-thirty every morning, in the shower by seven, and at the office by seven-forty-five.

And she'd need to fill out her wardrobe. Turquoise silk pants and scarfs and sequined dresses were great for the single life at dance clubs, but not for here. She'd need at least three suits, four slim skirts, and God knows how many blouses. Her hair needed a trim. Two minutes after she pulled it back, tweaks around her cheeks and forehead escaped again. And no more fooling around with just anybody. She had a name to protect now, a career. She was going to be sophisticated, dedicated, completely and centrally focused on only one thing. Rock Solid Investments.

And yet . . . And yet when she had gone to sleep the night before, she hadn't dreamed of bonuses and promotions, but of a gray-haired, aristocratic man. "He got married," the man said as he drifted away from her.

"You?" she called after him. "Are you married?"

He smiled and was gone.

All during the week, as Alex read client files and portfolios, she looked for Brent Gibbons in the hall but never saw him. She was with the riffraff now, the lowest-level new employees and secretaries, nowhere near the CEO's office. Except for a date on his calendar for dinner, he had probably already forgotten her.

\* \* \*

They went to Molita's on Western Avenue near Market Street. The dress code was formal, jackets required. Alex was grateful she'd chosen a white, tea-length dress, subdued yet elegant. That was another section of her closet she'd have to fill out—tasteful elegance. Sometimes she hated being an adult. She slipped off her coat when they sat down, revealing the draped U-shape neckline in both the front and the back.

"You look lovely, Alex," Brent said, and ordered a bottle of champagne.

Tasteful elegance, Alex thought, did have its good points. "Thank you, sir," she said.

He laughed and took his cigarette case out of his jacket pocket. "At least for tonight, you can call me Brent. All right?"

"All right."

Alex looked around her. The room was dark, too dark. The single candle at each table hardly seemed adequate for eating. Maybe they didn't want you to see the food too clearly. She watched the waiters coming and going quickly through the back room. It was a wonder they didn't trip over the chairs.

"Are you preoccupied, Alex?"

She snapped back to attention. "No, I'm sorry. I have this terrible habit of imagining the worst possible thing that could happen everywhere I go."

He smiled, revealing slightly yellowed but large, straight teeth. "And what do you imagine here?" he asked as the waiter filled each of their fluted glasses with the bubbly liquid.

"Oh, just that they keep it this dark so we can't see the things crawling around in our food."

"Madam," the waiter said, indignant, "I can assure you there is nothing crawling in our food."

"She was only kidding," Brent said. "Really. Please don't take offense."

The waiter looked at Alex suspiciously, then nodded and walked away.

"I'm sorry," Alex said. "I never quite learned how to hold my tongue. It's just that people can't take a joke, you know? The world needs a sense of humor. Just the other day, in fact ..."

"Are you nervous, Alex?" he asked softly.

"No, of course not. I'm never nervous."

He lit his cigarette, staring at her.

"All right," she said. "A little."

"Why?"

She shrugged. "Because I don't know why I'm here."

"I told you why."

"The real reason."

He blew a gust of smoke over her head, then lifted his glass of champagne and clicked it against hers. The bubbles tickled Alex's nose as she drank.

"Didn't you believe me when I said I always take my employees out to dinner to celebrate?" he asked.

"No."

Brent threw back his head and laughed. He had a young laugh. A young face. A young body. Only his hair revealed his age.

"You're wonderful, Alex. Really. I don't think I've ever met a woman quite like you."

"Are you married?" she asked. The question rushed out before she could stop it. She couldn't play the games Megan played, flirting and pretending and hoping you got the information you wanted by the end of the evening. Alex didn't have the patience for that, or enough hope to waste on a lost cause.

"Yes," he said.

She took a deep breath and looked away. So that was that. At least she could stop those silly fantasies right away, before they became too entrenched. Of course he would be married. He was too perfect not to be married.

"Her name is Carlotta," he said. "We met when I was in Spain on a business trip fifteen years ago."

"Any children?"

"Yes. One thirteen-year-old son. Peter."

Alex sipped her champagne. She had no right to be disappointed. It was just that this was the first time in years that a man had inspired her to fantasize, to wonder. *What if he kissed me? What would it feel like? What do his legs look like, or the muscles in his back? How warm is his skin? Is any of this possible?*

But it wasn't.

"And you?" he asked. "Are you married?"

"No."

"But you'd like to be?"

"No." The word came out too loudly, sounding too desperate. Sometimes, her own voice betrayed her. "No. It doesn't fit in with my life. Not now."

He nodded and flicked the drooping ashes from his cigarette into the ashtray.

"I think that's wise," he said. "Not because marriage is no good, but because you really can't have it all. Men get closer to it, because they're not expected to raise children, but women have a devil of a time."

"That's what I tell my friends and family, but they think I'm making excuses. They say things like, 'Well, why can't you get married, have babies, and work part-time?' As if my career were only a sidelight."

He nodded. "My wife is perfectly happy being a housewife and mother, and I respect her for that. But if she suddenly decided she wanted to be a brain surgeon, we'd have a serious problem. There aren't enough hours in the day to be all you want to be and all your child needs you to be."

"And what about you?" Alex asked. "What sacrifices have you had to make?"

"Time with Peter," he said softly. "He's a teenager now, and I'll be damned if I remember the day he got out of diapers or rode a bicycle for the first time. His voice is deeper now, and I don't know when it changed. He's even got rock star posters taped up on his wall, and for the life of me, I can't recall when he took the clown faces down."

"That's too bad."

"It's worse than bad. It's foolish. Somewhere along the line, I got my priorities confused, and now it's too late to change. I made my choice to be a businessman, and Carlotta has resigned herself to my schedule, but it's not as easy with Peter. He doesn't understand."

"You have the company, though," Alex said, trying to lighten the mood. "You've made it the most successful house on the West Coast."

Brent looked at her. "Do you think that makes up for it?"

"It would for me."

He shook his head. "Perhaps you're different, but I don't think so. I felt much the same way at your age. I was going to take over the world, be independent, no commitments. Then I met Carlotta and, well, I lost myself. After Peter, I mellowed. Every day, I find that the things that used to consume me, the deals, the stress of the stock market, the rush of a big killing, those things just don't mean as much anymore. But when I go home and see my son, hear his laughter . . ." He smiled. "That means more than words can say. Age, I suppose, has a way of putting life in perspective."

They talked of other things after that, of plays and art

and literature. Alex drank her champagne, enjoying the dry smoothness of the restaurant's most expensive bottle. Brent was right. She had been nervous. As they talked and laughed, the anxiety disappeared, her shoulders hung naturally, and her sweat glands relaxed. Not since Jackson had stopped their weekly lunch dates and applied himself full force to a last-ditch effort to save his marriage had she talked to someone so easily, felt so comfortable, so *equal* with a man.

After a while, Brent raised his hand, and Alex was amazed at how quickly the waiter appeared, despite her insults.

"Would you mind if I ordered for you?" Brent asked. "I know you're a woman of the world, but I'm quite an expert on this particular menu."

She smiled. "I think I can live with it just this once."

"I'd like an order of stuffed mushrooms to start and then two lobster Florentines," Brent said to the waiter. "Two spinach salads, and a basket of warm sourdough bread. And be sure the bread is warm this time, Randolph. We don't need a repeat performance."

"Yes, Mr. Gibbons."

Alex smiled at Brent as the waiter scuttled away. "You come here often to terrorize the poor man?"

Brent stubbed out the remainder of a cigarette and refilled each of their champagne glasses. "Occasionally. And it was you who terrorized him, not me."

She pressed the glass against her lips and stared at him. Certain men paled with time. At first glance, you thought they were handsome. But then, you noticed chicken pox scars and uneven razor stubble and hairs sticking out of their ears. Other men appeared at first to be nothing extraordinary. The more you looked, though, the stronger the set of their jaw became, the brighter the eyes, the more intriguing and handsome and beguiling their features. It seemed impossible you hadn't noticed at the very beginning how overwhelmingly attractive they were. Brent was that kind of man.

"So, do you really take your new employees out to dinner?" Alex asked. "Or am I special?"

He smiled at her. "You are very special, Alex. And no,

I don't always take my employees to dinner. Only when I'm intrigued."

"Doesn't Carlotta mind?" Her heart pumped like mad as she asked.

"Carlotta is . . . a very understanding woman. A lot has happened in the fifteen years we've been married. You can't expect to stay passionate about the same woman forever. She has her life now, her friends, and I have mine."

"And your life includes taking women out to romantic dinners?"

"Is this romantic? I hadn't noticed."

Alex stared at her glass, embarrassed. God, she was no good at this anymore. Being a flirt in junior high school was one thing, but trading sexual innuendoes with a sophisticated married man was so far out of her league, she should probably just get up and leave. Still, her body was leaning toward him with ideas all its own, while her mind kept screaming, *He's married, you idiot! What the hell are you doing?*

"I'm sorry," Brent said, brushing his fingers over her knuckles. "That was unkind. The truth is that I enjoy women. I always have, and my wife knows that. What harm does a little innocent flirting do?"

He smiled again, but Alex's heart told her this was not innocent, at least not for her. If she were Carlotta, she would not want her husband out with another woman, caressing her knuckles.

Brent pulled his hand away when Randolph returned with their mushrooms.

"You see?" the waiter said, looking at Alex. "Nothing is crawling."

She laughed, the tension broken for the moment. "Yes, I see. I'm sure it's wonderful."

He smiled smugly and left. Alex turned her attention back to Brent.

"Tell me about your son," she said, hoping that was a safe topic.

"Peter. He's wonderful. On the soccer team now. His grades could be better, but I can remember myself at his age. There are too many exciting things to do and see to sit around studying all day. He's got his mother's good looks, thank God. Black hair, brown eyes. He'll knock the girls out in a few years."

Alex popped a mushroom into her mouth and closed her eyes for a moment to appreciate fully the savory, garlicky taste. It wasn't every day she was treated to a hundred-dollar-plus dinner. She opened her eyes again and smiled.

"He sounds perfect," she said.

"Not perfect. But mine."

She had planned to discuss the portfolios she'd reviewed, but Brent was so interesting and talkative, business slipped her mind. Throughout the extraordinary dinner and dessert, he told her about his house on Russian Hill and the one in Palm Beach, his knack for chess and tennis, his college days at Harvard. She told him about her life, her dreams, her friendship with Megan and Jackson, her weekly phone calls with Clementine in Los Angeles.

"And don't you dare tell me she's the most beautiful woman you've ever seen," she said to him three hours later as he drove her back to her apartment. "That's all I hear since everyone saw her in those silly commercials. No one can even believe I know her, let alone that she's one of my best friends. It's like she's some kind of goddess who can't socialize with us normal folk."

They had pulled up in front of a Victorian town house, whose third floor was the site of her new apartment. Brent leaned over to kiss her cheek, and his cologne danced like flames around her, smelling so good.

"You, my dear Alex, are the most beautiful woman I've ever seen. And to tell you the truth, I can't say I've ever seen one of your friend's commercials."

Alex opened the door and stepped out. Turning back, she bent down and said, "You keep on saying things like that, Mr. Gibbons, and I won't be responsible for my actions. We single girls are suckers for sweet talk."

"I'll take my chances."

She closed the door and watched him drive away. After he'd turned the corner, she ran full speed up the stairs and into her apartment. She grabbed the phone and fell back on the couch, smiling. Wives and possible infidelity were meaningless right now; she was too happy. She had to call Clementine.

•   •   •

Megan put her clothes back on and walked into the doctor's office. She had longed to get pregnant from the day she married Jackson five years ago, and had made her way from the examination room to the doctor's office dozens of times. It was always the same result: no pregnancy.

She sat down in the leather chair inside the cool office and leaned her head back. If only. That was all she ever thought of. If only she could get pregnant, everything would be fine. She knew that with all her heart. Jackson wanted a child as much as she. He'd never said so directly, but she knew it was true. He would make a wonderful father. And a child, their child, would bind them together forever. If he couldn't love her for any other reason, he would love her for giving him a baby. He would take care of her for nine months, hold her hand during delivery, then the three of them could go for walks in the park, on boat rides in the bay, to the children's museum. Their love would be real. Not forced and strained and awkward the way it had been for a year, ever since they'd started counseling.

Not that Jack wasn't trying. She knew he was. She knew he had never tried harder in all his life. He worked every day. He wasn't making as much money as he had at the architecture firm, but he certainly seemed happier working as an assistant to Alex's mother, Jo, at the San Francisco Museum of Art. And he painted for only a few hours every weekend, and only when she was working in the garden or grocery shopping. And he made love to her every Friday and Saturday night, at eleven-thirty, after the news. It took two and a half minutes, exactly. It was no wonder she didn't get pregnant. No child in his right mind would want to be born out of an act like that.

Yet despite all his efforts, all his words of love, his praise for her cooking and cleaning and gardening, their life together had an air of unreality about it. His touch was stiff. His words sounded hollow, forced out of his throat with superhuman effort. The only time the honesty broke through was after they made love, when he turned away from her without a kiss or a hug and fell asleep, leaving her alone while she cried. She knew then that she had never loved anyone as much as she loved him, and no matter how hard she tried or how much effort he put into their marriage, he would never love her like that in return.

Dr. Harding, a fiftyish man with gray hair and glasses, walked into the office. He closed the door behind him, and Megan felt a rock settle into her stomach. The doctor walked around his desk and sat down. Resting his chin on his hands, he looked at her.

"Why didn't you tell me about the abortion, Megan?"

She couldn't breathe. She gulped at the air until it filled her lungs again.

"We've been wasting so much time," the doctor went on. "Fertility drugs and sperm count readings won't do very much good when scar tissue is blocking the sperm's path."

She leaned back in her chair and closed her eyes. He said it so easily, *abortion*, like he'd say *sugar* or *candy*. Unconsciously, she clutched at her stomach.

"I keep trying to forget," she said, opening her eyes.

Dr. Harding nodded and looked away from her. She felt he could read everything in her face, see every scene as if he were watching a movie. Tony, Alex, that cold office and the doctor who'd smiled right before he ripped the baby out.

"Abortion can be very traumatic," Dr. Harding said, glancing at her charts. "But you can't fool yourself into thinking it didn't happen. Didn't it ever occur to you that your infertility might have been due to that abortion? Or that I'd figure out what had happened with this last physical?"

She shook her head. It hadn't occurred to her. She didn't want it to occur to her. She wanted to pretend it never happened, pretend that there was only Jackson and her and their house and their love. If she could just build a strong enough wall around them, all of the past and its horrors would fade.

The doctor waited until she dried her eyes.

"Well, let's forget about that," he said. "The real issue now is surgery. You'll need to have that scar tissue removed if you want any shot at pregnancy. It's blocking the sperm's path to the egg and the egg's path to the uterus."

"I'll do it," she said instantly.

"I'm glad. But unfortunately, I won't be able to perform the surgery."

"What? Why not?"

"I'm leaving tomorrow for France, remember? Sort of a six-month swap of knowledge and doctors. My colleague from France is coming here in my place."

"I don't want him to do it."

"Megan, he's a fine doctor."

"I don't care if he won the Nobel Prize for Medicine," she said, standing up. "This is my body. My future baby we're talking about. I want someone I can trust. Someone from this country, someone you know well and can recommend without any reservations at all."

Dr. Harding picked up a pencil and scribbled a name on a piece of paper. "All right then. My first choice is a man by the name of Dr. Lawrence Mendelsohn. He's one of the premier gynecologic surgeons on the West Coast. Unfortunately, he's based in L.A."

"That's fine."

"You'd have to go there for the operation."

Megan thought of Clementine. It was understood that her door was always open for Megan and Alex, just as their doors were open for her. It was one of the most comforting feelings in the world, knowing there was always a place you could go.

"Fine," she said again, clutching the paper in her fist. "Don't you see? I'd go anywhere if it meant I could have a baby. I have to get pregnant again, Dr. Harding. I have to."

•   •   •

Jackson was sitting on the living room couch reading the paper when Megan got home. He smiled at her when she came in. If it weren't for that smile, she might have been able to distance herself from him, lessen the love.

Perhaps then the ease with which he pulled away from her, the quick way he hung up the phone when she called, the kisses that he always ended first, wouldn't hurt so much. But every day, he smiled. And every day, she was filled with the hope that this would be the day he'd fall in love with her.

"How was the doctor?" he asked, setting down his newspaper and looking at her.

She dropped her purse on the table and sat down beside him. "I have to go to L.A. next week."

"I beg your pardon?"

"Dr. Harding found the reason why I can't get pregnant. Scar tissue is completely blocking the sperm's path. Since he's leaving tomorrow for France, he recommended a doctor in L.A. to perform the surgery. I'll stay with Clementine. I'm sure it will be fine."

"Wait a minute. Scar tissue? From what?"

Her eyes widened in horror, and Jackson grabbed her by the shoulders, thinking she was going to faint. White terror colored her face.

"Meg, tell me. Don't ever be afraid to tell me anything."

Megan focused on his pants, his pleated beige cotton pants. Each crease had been meticulously ironed. Jackson always had been a stickler for neatness. Every night, he was up with the iron, pressing and steaming.

"Megan," he said, shaking her. "What is it? I have a right to know, don't I?"

She looked at the open window, at the lace curtains blowing in the late afternoon breeze. Through the sunlight beams, she could see the dust floating in the room. So much dust. She'd never be able to clean it all.

She stood up and walked to the window. The memory was still there in the back of her mind. She couldn't hide it completely behind the gauze of normalcy. She had been so stupid. She'd never told the doctor or her parents or anyone except Alex and Clementine about the abortion. She'd certainly never told Jackson. Why would she have? It would only have been another strike against her. Another fault for him to add to his already long list of reasons not to love his wife. How could she have been

so careless? She should have told him it was cysts or be-
nign tumors, anything but scar tissue.

"Meg," he whispered. He was right behind her, his
chin resting on her shoulder so she could feel his breath
on her cheek. There was no way out of it now. She
couldn't take it back. She couldn't lie. She would tell
him, and he would hate her, and that would be that.

She tilted her head back until it rested against him.

"There was someone else before you, when I was fifteen. His name was Tony. I was stupid then. I didn't use
birth control, and he made it clear after I told him I was
pregnant that he didn't want anything to do with me. I
had an abortion."

As she spoke the words, she felt it happening again.
She felt the doctor's hands on her, ripping into her. The
anesthesia didn't numb her completely, and she felt the
warm blood that gushed between her legs and turned
ice-cold as it soaked into the towels. She screamed, begging him to stop, and her nails bit into Clementine's
arms. Clementine's face was above hers, crying. She'd
never seen her cry before. But Clementine's tears spilled
down onto her while Clementine shook her head, as if to
say there was nothing she could do. Then Megan fainted
and floated in and out of dreams of Tony and their baby,
and nightmares about knives cutting the life out of her.

She didn't realize she was screaming, until she felt a
man's arms tighten around her and urge her down to
the floor with him. She pounded her fists against his
chest, thinking he was Tony, then the doctor, then Clementine, who had let him do it, let him hurt her, let him
take away the one thing that had been truly hers.

"It was my baby," she cried, her fists aching and tiring
and finally dropping to her lap. Jackson nodded and
held her tighter, his tears soaking through her shirt to
her shoulder. "I saw it. It was a baby, my baby."

She curled up inside her husband's arms and let him
rock her. She stopped crying long before he did.

"I love you, Megan," he whispered. She curled closer
to him in response. "I love you."

# CHAPTER
## 15

*CLEMENTINE STOOD JUST INSIDE THE DOOR* of the bar, smoke penetrating her clothes and hair, men smiling at her and walking too close as they passed. She clenched her hands and fought the image of His face and the horror that always accompanied it. Head held high, she reminded herself why she was there. She was going to see her father. For him, she would stand there forever.

She hadn't seen him in fourteen years, not since she'd been ten years old. Fourteen years! It ripped at her when she thought of how much they could have meant to each other in that time, all the things they could have done. Their separation had always been a weight on her mind, but since she'd moved to Los Angeles two and a half years ago, she had been trying harder than ever to track him down. She called old friends, went to the library and searched phone books in every town for his name. She couldn't help herself. She could be composed at auditions, cold and stoic in front of men who approached her. But when she thought of Duke, all her facades fell away. Some bond had formed in those early years, when he was godlike and she was still unformed, and she couldn't break it.

She'd always felt he was the key to her, the reason she was the way she was. As time passed and success came slowly, if at all, and the rape remained too vivid in her mind, Duke took over more and more, until he was all she thought about. If she could just see him, everything would be all right. Her faith in love would be restored. She believed that with all her heart.

Finding him seemed a lost cause, however, until an old neighbor from Denver mentioned hearing from a friend that Duke was in Las Vegas. Clementine had gone back to the library, grabbed the latest phone book from Las Vegas and, miracle of miracles, found her father's name. All she had to do was convince him to come and see her.

The first time she called him, he was hesitant, wary, as if she were a telephone salesperson instead of his daughter. She said, "Duke, it's me, Clementine," and he couldn't think of one word to say.

"I've missed you," she went on shakily. "I tracked you down to Las Vegas and . . ."

"You need something?" he asked. "I ain't got any money to give you."

The wind rushed out of her lungs, and she fought back tears. Why did things always work this way? Why, when she loved someone so much that she could hardly stand it, did he not love her back at all? Why did the people she could easily do without care about her? Why didn't people ever love the right people at the right time?

"I only want to see you," she said. "I'm living in Los Angeles now. I was hoping you could come out to visit."

He made some excuse, she couldn't even remember what now. Clementine walked to the bar and took a stool. She ordered a glass of white wine and lit one of the few cigarettes she'd smoked since high school. Her hand shook as she tossed the match in an ashtray.

She had called him four times in three weeks. It was as if she had lost control of her own actions. She wanted to be strong, the way she appeared to everyone else, but then she'd think, *He's my father.* That was enough to make her a child again, to make her want him beside her so badly, it hurt.

On the fourth call, sounding worn down and willing to do anything to get her off his back, he finally agreed to drive to Los Angeles to meet her. She ignored his hesitancy and focused only on the anticipation of seeing him again. They would sit and drink, then go out to dinner, and she would tell him everything. He would make everything better. That's what fathers did.

She had waited half an hour, smoked three cigarettes, and drunk two glasses of wine, when he finally arrived. She knew he was there before she even turned around. She could feel him searching the room for her, and the hair on the back of her neck tingled. She straightened her shoulders and turned around. He took her breath away, just as he used to. He was tall, roguishly handsome, dressed in jeans and a light sweater. Her eyes met his. She rose to meet him. All she wanted to do was run and throw herself in his arms, but his gaze drifted past her and he grinned.

Clementine turned to see a young, beautiful darkhaired woman rush out of her chair and into Duke's arms. He kissed her loudly, causing most of the customers to stare. Clementine was stunned and embarrassed, watching her father slide his hand down over the woman's behind.

"Gloria, you're looking good," he said too loudly.

Clementine was halfway between sitting and standing, not knowing what she was supposed to do. She waited for him to push the woman aside and hurry to her, but he seemed quite content to run his fingers all over her body, mindless of the stares he got. Finally, when Clementine thought she wouldn't be able to stand it any longer, he and the woman walked over to her.

"Hey, Clementine," he said, not hugging or kissing her, only standing awkwardly by her side, holding tight to the woman. "This here's Gloria."

The woman smiled brightly, and Clementine felt tears sting her eyes. She blinked them back and lit another cigarette.

"Nice to meet you," Gloria said, filling in the silence.

"Duke told me he wanted to meet you while he was in L.A. visiting me. I think it's great the two of you want to stay close."

Clementine looked at Duke, her eyes pleading for answers, denials, but he wouldn't meet her gaze head-on. He ran his hand up along Gloria's torso, brushing the outside of her breast.

"He's staying with you?" Clementine asked. She had thought he would be staying with her; that had been the implication, anyway. She'd had images of Duke sleeping on the sofa in her loft and the two of them sharing coffee in the morning, catching up on everything.

"Of course," Gloria said. "Didn't you tell her, Duke?"

Duke ordered a straight Scotch from the bartender and finally looked at Clementine. She didn't know what she saw in his eyes, fear, avoidance, guilt, anger. She only knew it wasn't what she wanted to see, wasn't what she needed from him, wasn't even close to what he saw in hers.

"I guess I forgot," he said. "I thought it would be easier, staying with Glory here. She's got more space. And I'm sure you're a swinging single now. I don't want to get in the way."

Clementine nodded. What else could she do? The three of them drank while Gloria chattered on about her job as a flight attendant, and how she and Duke met on a flight to Dallas, and the crazy things they did in bed that first night they met. If it wasn't so sad, Clementine probably would have thought it funny the way her father bragged to her about his sex life, poking her in the ribs as if she were one of his poker buddies. She watched him, studied his hair, which was graying slightly, his white, white smile. He looked like the man she remembered. His voice was the same. But nothing else was right. She couldn't reach out and touch him. At the end of the evening, he wouldn't take her in his arms and soothe her fears. He wouldn't hum in her ear. He would take Gloria home and do crazy things to her and probably never think about Clementine again.

"Would you both like to go to dinner with me?" she asked, trying to salvage her pride and what she could of the evening. "We could go someplace in Hollywood, my treat."

Gloria looked at Duke, her eyes telling him in no uncertain terms that dinner with his daughter was not what she had in mind. Clementine sat up straight, her chin out, hoping that just this once a parent would take her side. Duke only squeezed Gloria tighter.

"Sorry, kiddo," he said. "Me and Gloria already made plans. But it was good seeing you. We should have done this sooner."

Gloria told her it was nice to meet her, and the two of them turned to go. Then Duke stepped back, and Clementine caught her breath. He bent down, the aroma of his cologne washed over her, and he kissed her cheek. His lips did not frighten her; they were soft, harmless, father lips.

"I probably won't get another chance to see you this weekend," he said. "Gloria wants to go to the beach, maybe do Disneyland. You understand. I haven't seen her for a couple of years."

Clementine nodded and didn't watch him as he left. She asked the bartender for another wine, then another. She smoked cigarettes and watched the ashes fall. She'd thought there was no love as strong as that of a parent for a child. That was what all the talk-show hosts said. She hoped they were lying, but she knew inside that it was only her parents who were different. She must have done something to make them stop caring. All her life, she'd felt like she was dancing for them, never stopping for a breath, twirling until she was dizzy and sick. Still, they didn't notice, were not proud of her. Or did they think she didn't need their praise? Was that why no one but her friends ever helped her, because she pretended to have all the bases covered, her world completely under control?

She ground out her cigarette and stood up. The room wavered, and she gripped the edge of the bar. The bartender caught her eye.

"I'll call you a cab," he said.

She nodded. "Call me an idiot while you're at it," she said, then broke down into giggles.

• • •

Clementine closed the last page of the script and leaned back against the gnarled trunk of the oak tree. She was sitting on the grass in a small neighborhood park, two blocks away from her apartment. She often came there to read, especially in the few weeks since Megan had arrived and had her surgery. Clementine had to get away from the constant blare of the television set, which Megan had on from nine in the morning until three in the afternoon, a day full of beeping, buzzing game shows and farfetched soap operas.

She ran her hand over the bound pages, reminding herself that it was real, that the part was open to her, against tremendous odds, but open just the same. Will had somehow managed to get her an advance script.

"The rumor's out that the studio might be willing to go with an unknown," he'd told her. "They're talking big name, but that's just talk. They want to keep the costs down."

The screenplay was written by Tyler Holbrook, a young playwright who'd burst onto the Hollywood scene a year earlier with the smash hit *Loving on Empty*. He'd won the Pulitzer first and then an Oscar, and had since holed up in his Hollywood Hills home to churn out two more screenplays. Clementine could hardly believe she was holding one of them in her hands.

*Guilty Verdict.* After years of worthless scripts full of butcher-wielding mass murderers and air-headed call girls, this was like a breath from heaven. She had come to the park in the morning, figuring she'd read for an hour or two at best. Instead, she'd been enthralled by the script, reading straight through until she was finished at three-thirty, six and a half hours later.

*Guilty Verdict.* The story of an ordinary woman—a wife and mother—betrayed by her husband's brazen affair with a nineteen-year-old college student, then wrongly accused of murdering the girl. Throughout the harrowing trial, which results in a guilty verdict and a thirty-years-to-life prison sentence, Melissa Marlow (the heroine) maintains her innocence. After serving five years of her term, she proves her case with the help of the sympathetic lawyer she falls in love with.

The film would cover all the angles—the traumas Melissa faces in prison, her determination to keep in contact with her children, her divorce, and her battle to regain some semblance of a normal life when the ruling is overturned and she is released.

Clementine pulled her knees up to her chest and rested her chin on top of them. It was a tough movie, raw, even harsh in the prison rape scenes. At least, she could call on her own emotions for that. Oh, but it was an actress's role. Melissa had depth and fire and strength and fear and desires, everything. Tyler Holbrook was a genius. He'd given the character complexity and reality, three full and varied dimensions that made her more human than many of the people Clementine knew in real life. God, she wanted this role.

Will had explained she'd have to test at least twice for the part, probably three times if she got that far. But he had an in with the casting director at Lancolme Studios, where the picture was to be produced, and was certain he could get her at least the first reading. From there, it would be up to her. Her only other screen test had been for the guest role in the ABC movie, and that was nothing compared to this. She'd be just another face in the crowd to the casting director. Somehow, she would have to make herself stand out. Landing a role like this was the future of her whole career. This movie could make her. She couldn't even imagine life going on if she didn't get this part.

Clementine stood up and brushed the grass off her. She'd have to get to work immediately. She'd go see Will that afternoon and tell him she loved the script and would read anytime, anywhere. And from now until then, she would study like crazy. She'd memorize, rehearse, research prison environments and murder trials. She'd do anything and everything she had to do to land this part. Megan would just have to get along without Bob Barker for a week or two and be Clementine's audience instead. A new star was rising on the horizon.

• • •

*All My Children* was Megan's favorite soap opera. No one could top Erica Kane. She was ruthless and powerful and went from man to man quicker than even Alex managed. Megan watched her for inspiration, then squared her shoulders and called Jackson at the museum. But at the sound of his voice, like an old song that brought back bitter memories, she lost her facade of strength and became only Megan again, the loving, devoted, miserably lonely wife.

She pulled the blanket tighter around her and turned the volume up on the television. Clementine had gone out to read hours ago, during *The $10,000 Pyramid.* Something about a script to read. Clementine had left her alone a lot since the operation two weeks ago, and Megan was grateful. Not that it wasn't nice to have Clementine around. After all, it was Clementine's apartment, and staying with an old friend was like being back in your mother's arms, safe, sheltered, all scents and sounds familiar.

And Clementine had been wonderful to her. After the surgery, when the doctor ordered her to do nothing but rest for a couple of weeks, Clementine had given her the remote control, the number of the Chinese and pizza places that delivered, and a stack of trashy novels she'd found in her closet. Still, whenever Clementine was around, there was a look in her eyes that made Megan uncomfortable. As if Clementine didn't quite approve of Megan's bonbon/potato chip/Erica Kane method of recovery.

Megan slept on the couch, ate her meals on the couch, read and watched television and called Jackson on the couch. She wondered if there was a category in the *Guinness Book of World Records* that she could break. Number of hours lying on a couch straight, excluding bathroom trips. There might be something she was good at, after all.

The key turned in the front door lock, and Clementine walked in. Megan noticed the look of repulsion that crossed her face when she glanced at Megan and the mess around her. Megan sat up straight.

"I guess you're getting a little sick of me just sitting around, aren't you?" she said.

"Of course not, Meg," Clementine replied, setting the script down on the kitchen table. She picked up three half-full glasses of water and a crumb-filled plate from the coffee table and took them to the sink.

Megan flung the covers off her and stood up. "Stop it. Please, Clem. I can do that. I can do something."

Clementine looked at Megan, still in her nightgown, as she had been continuously since the operation, with her blond hair flying around her head as if the wind had caught it. She took Megan's arm and led her back to the couch.

"It's easy, isn't it?" she asked.

"What?"

"Doing nothing. Thinking nothing. Watching screaming contestants, devious women, and unfaithful men. It's easier than facing things."

"What's there to face? I came here for an operation. I had it, and soon I can go home."

"How soon can you try to get pregnant again?"

Megan smoothed down her hair. "Dr. Mendelsohn said in anywhere from six weeks to three months, depending on how fast I heal. I'll have to go for a checkup to that French doctor that took over for Dr. Harding, and if all is well then, Jackson and I can start trying again."

"Jackson must be happy about that," Clementine said, toying with the edge of the blanket.

Megan was quiet, and Clementine noticed the tears pooling in her eyes.

"What is it, Meg?"

Megan shook her head and scooted back on the sofa. She grabbed a pillow and hugged it to her stomach.

"It's not at all like I said it was," she whispered. "We haven't been happy at all. Every day is a struggle. I'd fight to the death to make him love me if only I knew how to fight."

Clementine leaned her head against her friend's. "Why didn't you tell me?"

"I don't know. I wanted to prove to you and Alex that

Jackson and I were right for each other, that my kind of
life was as good as yours. I couldn't admit that we . . ."

She started sobbing, and Clementine held her. Clementine thought of all the stilted phone conversations
over the past year, when Megan merely said she was fine.
She hadn't pushed the issue and she should have.
Friends pushed to get to the truth.

"You don't have to prove anything to me and Alex,"
Clementine said. "We love you."

Megan dried her eyes and sat up straight.

"I don't understand Jackson," she said. "He should be
happy. Any normal man in a normal marriage would be
happy. So why isn't he? Why does he hate me? Why does
he sound like he's got a million things to do whenever I
call him? Why didn't he come with me when I had this
operation? Why isn't he here with me now, holding me,
pounding down the door to take me home and make
love with me? Why, Clementine?"

Clementine picked up the remote control and turned
off the television. Standing, she walked behind the fan-
backed rattan chair and leaned her elbows on it.

"Have you ever asked him if he wants a baby?"

Megan wiped away her tears and shook her head.

"Megan, this takes two, you know. Maybe he just wants
to be with you. Maybe the thought of being a father
scares the hell out of him. Maybe he's not ready."

"Or maybe he doesn't love me and doesn't want another tie binding him to me."

"Why don't you ask him?"

"And risk finding out?" Megan asked in horror.

Clementine nodded and picked up her script again.
"It's your life. I have to go to Will's to try to set up a
reading. This film is wonderful, everything I've been
looking for."

"That's great," Megan said, but her voice was flat.

Clementine studied her, one hand on her hip.

"Listen, Megan. I love you to death. You know that.
And you can stay here as long as you want. But if you
want my opinion . . ."

Megan shook her head, cutting her off.

Clementine rapped her fingers on the table, then walked to the door.

"I'm going to give it to you, anyway," she said. "If you're so damn scared that he doesn't love you, you're as good as divorced. What kind of marriage is that? You don't know if he loves you. You don't know if he wants a baby, and meanwhile, you're doing everything you can to get pregnant. Granted, I'm no expert on love and marriage, but I can tell you one thing. I would never, ever, put up with the insecurities and miscommunication you're living with. Call the man, for God's sake. Tell him to get his butt down here and to hell with work. Tell him you love him and if he doesn't love you, then he should get the hell out. Stop crying and act like a woman, Megan."

By the time Megan looked up, Clementine was gone. It was getting to be quite a chore, she thought, listening to Alex and Clementine make these unforgettable speeches about *her* life, about what *she* should do. When Megan tried to say something like that, something profound and intense, her tongue twisted in her mouth and nothing but a spoonful of saliva came out. She pretended she didn't care what they said. But ten minutes after Clementine left, she put her hand on the phone. Half an hour later, she dialed Jackson's number.

• • •

Alex and Jackson met at the airport cafeteria. Jackson smiled when he saw her. She was dressed in a dark gray wool suit, her hair coiffed to perfection, her makeup understated and elegant. He studied her as he would a difficult puzzle he had three minutes to solve.

"What is your problem?" she asked.

"I was just trying to find the wild and crazy Alex I know somewhere beneath that Elizabeth Arden face."

She laughed as they walked through the cafeteria line. She asked for a hamburger, onion rings, and a milk shake.

"There she is," Jackson said. "She's hiding in your mouth, scarfing down grease and fat. Good old Alex."

They paid for their meals, Jackson choosing only a cinnamon roll and coffee, and walked to a corner booth that faced the runways. An American 747 was rolling toward the boarding chute.

"As a matter of fact, smarty pants," Alex said, after taking a huge bite of her hamburger and wiping the grease off her chin, "I almost never get to eat anymore. I always skip lunch, and dinner is usually a frozen burrito in the microwave."

"Mmmm."

"That's the corporate life."

"And you're loving every second of it."

Jackson was enthralled by her smile. She'd always been happy, carefree, and easy to laugh, but this smile was complete and whole, as if her life were full of wonder and she'd found happiness far beyond her wildest dreams.

"Oh, Jack, it's better than good. It's great. I'm making a difference. I know I am. I haven't even been there a year yet, but already clients are requesting me. They like my style, I guess. Low-key but informative and friendly. And I bring them results. I've formed a network of contacts on Wall Street, and I'd say my ratio of winners to losers in stocks has been close to ten to one. Brent says he's never seen anyone take to this job as fast or as well as I have."

"And what Brent says matters to you."

Alex turned away to hide her smile. She shouldn't be smiling, she knew that, but she couldn't help it. Sometimes late at night, when most of the building was empty, Brent came to her office and looked over her work. When he praised her, the world could end right then, she was so happy. It was strange and unnerving, wanting, even needing someone's approval so badly. But it was lovely, exquisite when he gave it to her.

"You've made yourself indispensable to this company," he had told her just two weeks earlier as they walked to the elevator together.

"No," she'd said, her arms and legs tingling as if he'd touched her. They reached the elevator, and as the doors opened and they walked inside, Brent placed his hand at the small of her back.

"Okay," he said. "Indispensable to me then."

Thinking about that now, Alex smiled.

"It matters," she said to Jackson. "He's married, so it won't go any further than a business relationship, but I respect him more than I do anyone else."

Jackson watched her face, full of secrets, and wondered if she knew how much emotion she showed, and if Brent picked up on it. She was falling for the man like she'd never fallen for anyone, and she didn't even know it. He was suddenly very scared for her. She acted tough as nails, but strong shells often had tender insides. Alex had never given her emotions full rein; she had no idea how powerful they were. She was probably the most vulnerable woman he knew.

"Be careful, all right?"

She stared at him. "This is Alex you're talking to, remember? I'm no starry-eyed teenager. There are men in my life when I need them and not a moment longer. I know better than anyone that there's no future with Brent. I'm content to be his friend."

She smiled and dug into her hamburger, but Jackson was not convinced. She was different, he realized, as if she had been altering herself microscopically day by day until, before he had even understood what was happening, she was a foreigner he didn't recognize. She was more businesslike than ever, yet somehow softened, too, as if the cutthroat world she lived in had worn away her edges. More than anything, he wanted her to be happy, but he didn't think she truly understood what happiness was. He doubted any of them did.

Alex glanced up from her hamburger and saw Jackson staring out the window. He was looking better, she mused. For a while there, when he and Megan were going to counseling two nights a week and he was trying to be the model husband, the circles had darkened like mud beneath his eyes and, despite his still stocky build, he'd looked gaunt and hollowed out. Today, he was tanned, the circles were gone, his eyes were bright, and his dark hair was combed. Yet a trace of tension remained; his mouth was drawn into a line as taut as wire. She offered him an onion ring.

"You need it," she said.

"Hardly. Since Megan left, all I eat are Big Macs and frozen pizza. I crumbled up her list of the four food groups she kept on the refrigerator door and shoved it down the disposal."

"Well, thank God for that. I wouldn't know the four food groups if they were staring me in the face."

Jackson toyed with his cinnamon roll before abruptly turning his attention to Alex.

"I asked you here for a reason," he said.

"I figured that."

"After I get to Los Angeles today, I'm going to have a talk with Megan. About us."

Alex swallowed hard and pushed her plate away.

"You're going to ask her for a divorce, aren't you?"

He nodded, not looking at her, focusing instead on the salt and pepper shakers sitting in a pool of catsup. He cleaned up the mess with his napkin.

"Why now? What made you decide?"

He sighed, the burden of his decision lessened by confiding in Alex. Talking with her was always an instantaneous catharsis, the weight of hidden feelings and unsaid words shooting off his shoulders in a blaze of fireworks.

"Since she left for the operation three weeks ago, I've had the house to myself. God, Alex, you wouldn't believe it. I can paint all night if I want to. I can leave the dishes in the sink without her telling me to put them in the dishwasher. I can walk in the rain without her warning me about pneumonia. I can spread my easels out all over the house and lose myself in them without hearing her sighing in the other room or crying when she thinks I've forgotten about her."

"You want to be free," Alex said.

"Yes and no. I wish I could have both. I wish I could paint and live and breathe and love all at the same time. But I can't. At least, not with Megan. I'm not saying she's wrong. It's just that she needs so much, and I don't have enough to give. It's not fair to her."

"Well, I'm glad you've found a line of reasoning to assuage your guilt."

He stared at her. "I thought you didn't want us together."

"Why does everyone always say that? It's not true. I wanted you both to be happy. But this is going to devastate Megan. I just want you to know that. And don't give her any of this 'it's for your own good' crap. That's to help you sleep at night, not her."

"Why are you so angry?"

"Why? Why?" Alex rapped her fingernails on the table, not noticing when the longest one cracked. "Because she's my friend, dammit. Because her pain is my pain. Because you've been leading her on for almost five years, especially recently. You made her think you could work things out because you were too chicken to be honest with her. I wish you'd figured this out a long time ago."

"So you're saying it's wrong to try to love someone?"

She shook her head and watched a slim, private European jet land on a distant runway.

"Because I did love her, Alex," Jackson went on. "She's the essence of everything I should love. She's fragile and soft and kind. She loves cooking and gardening and wants desperately to raise children. I wish that I could make her right for me. I've tried for almost five years to somehow wedge her into the right slot in my life. But it won't work."

Alex wrapped an arm around her stomach, feeling sick, feeling the pain Megan would soon feel and wishing she could keep some of it for herself, so that it would be weakened by the time it reached Megan.

"Look," Jackson said softly, "my life is not awful. In fact, I could probably stay married to her forever, and that would be okay. She'll finally get pregnant, we'll have our two kids, she'll join the PTA, and everything will look perfect on the outside. But inside . . ." He grabbed Alex's hand and held it tightly. "Inside, it will kill me, Alex."

She nodded. "I know. But if you want me to say, 'Great, go ahead and divorce her; I give you my blessing,' I can't do that."

"I don't want that. I just wanted you to know. I'm so afraid of losing you. I can just see you and Megan and Clementine forming this female battalion and coming after me with a brigade of fully loaded tanks. I couldn't stand being the villain in your eyes."

She squeezed his hand. "The only real villain is the dreams that don't come true no matter how hard we wish for them. I know you tried, but Megan tried even harder, and I don't think she's willing to give up. Not yet. She loves you so much, Jack."

"Too much," he whispered. "Much, much too much."

•   •   •

Jackson parked along the sand in Zuma Beach, near Malibu. Megan had packed a picnic basket with wine and cheese and crackers and grapes and turkey sandwiches. The four food groups.

They spread the blanket on the dry sand close to the water. Down the shore, wrapped in fog, an old man searched with a metal detector for coins in the sand. Megan handed Jackson the bottle of wine and a cork-screw, and he opened it.

"You're looking well," she said, smiling at him. "You got a tan."

"Jo sent me to Mendocino for an art show. They held it outside, and it was a beautiful, sunny day."

"I wish I could have been there."

He took two plastic cups out of the basket and poured some wine into each. He looked at Megan's profile as she stared out at the gray sea.

"Really?" he asked.

"Of course. Anything to be with you."

She said it quietly, almost a whisper, but the words ripped through Jackson, making him feel tiny and worth-less and cruel. He set his wine down.

"We need to talk, Meg," he said, shifting to face her. She kept her eyes averted, watching the waves foaming like detergent when they hit the sand.

"I've been doing a lot of thinking," he went on. "Since you've been gone, I've had time to be alone, time . . ."

Megan stood and hurried toward the water. Rolling up her jeans, she waded in, letting the chilly foam lap up to her ankles. She steeled herself, waiting for Jackson to ap-pear behind her. She thought of diving into the waves and swimming away, out of listening range, the way she had when she was young and unafraid of riptides and sharks. But she wasn't young and fearless anymore. She felt Jackson's presence behind her and turned to face him.

"We really do need to talk," he said.

"Yes. But I'd rather not."

He nodded. Bending down, he picked up a smooth brown rock, glossy in the water but dull and lifeless when dry. He side-armed it out past the breakers, watching it skip two times before it sank.

"Impressive," she said.

He turned to her and smiled, a boyish smile, and she caught her breath. He moved closer to her and put his hands on her shoulders.

"I think you're the most wonderful woman I've ever known," he said. She laid her head against his chest, waiting, hoping she was wrong. He was quiet for a long time, and the hope began to grow and spread, warming her despite the misty cold air.

"But I can't be with you anymore," he said. "I just can't."

This was when she was supposed to sob, pound her fists against his chest, beg and plead with him not to leave her. But Megan didn't feel anything. It was like after she'd lost her baby, the hollowness, the pressure on her chest that kept her from breathing. She lifted her head away and stepped back.

"You want a divorce," she said, hugging herself.

"Yes. I've thought about it a lot, like I said. It's not that I don't care for you, it's—"

She held up her hand, silencing him. "Tell me this. Did you ever love me? Really?"

Her eyes pierced his, like daggers drawing blood. They were so clear and blue, so honest, they made Jackson feel that everything he was was bad, and everything she was was good.

"I think so, Megan. I don't know. I thought I did. I wanted to."

She nodded and looked out at the ocean once more. A twinkling pleasure boat was heading back toward the harbor. It was strange, she thought, the way the world went on, unaware and indifferent to her grief. How could there be joy for some and sorrow for others? If she strained hard enough, she could almost hear their laughter.

She walked back to the blanket and sat down. She picked up her plastic cup and dumped the wine into the sand, staining it red.

"Megan, please let me explain," Jackson said, following her.

"Explain what? That you don't love me? That your painting is more important to you than I am? That you need your freedom? That you were never happy? I know all that already, Jack. Inside, I've probably always known it."

"I know I've hurt you."

For the first time, Megan reacted to his words. She sprang up, pointing at him, her face infused with color.

"You don't know anything, Jackson," she said, and began throwing the food back into the basket.

"I know you were a great wife. I know how hard you tried and—"

"Shut up! God, what are you trying to do, destroy me completely? Do you think I need to hear this? How great I was? How wonderful and kind? What I need is a husband, dammit. Not some guilt-ridden jackass who thinks he can take away the pain by telling me how cute and sweet I am."

She picked up the basket and blanket and ran toward the car. She threw the supplies on the sand beside it and started walking along the street back toward the Pacific Coast Highway.

"Megan, where are you going?" he yelled.

"Home to Clementine's," she called over her shoulder.

"You can't walk there."

"Like hell I can't."

Jackson ran to the car and threw the basket and blanket in the backseat. Scrambling into the driver's seat, he started the car, then hurriedly drove up next to Megan. He rolled down the window.

"Meg, please get in."

She ignored him and kept walking.

"Please. Come on, you've just had surgery. You'll hurt yourself."

She stopped and stared at him. "Call me a cab."

"What?"

"I said call me a cab."

"Be serious. It'll cost a fortune to get you back to the Valley."

"I am serious, Jack. You want a divorce, fine. I'll give it to you. Now I want a cab. I'd say that's the least you could give me."

He looked at her for a long time, trying to see past the stubborn determination in her eyes to the emotions hidden inside. But her veneer was impenetrable. She placed her hands on her hips and squared her shoulders, like a body builder showing off his physique. He shook his head and put the car into gear.

"I'm sorry," he said.

Her face crumpled for a moment, then she composed herself.

"Well, good for you."

"Meg . . ." But she had already walked away. She sat down on the sand with her back to him. Jackson sped away to find a phone booth.

•   •   •

After calling a cab company, Jackson waited in the car twenty feet from where Megan sat. She was so still and lifeless, she could have passed for a statue. He couldn't tear his gaze from her back, curved forward, or her hair curling like Medusa's snakes in the salty air. His mind was flipping through memories of their married life. He wished he could remember a day when she was completely happy, but he found it hard to picture her smiling.

The taxi arrived half an hour later, and Jackson waited until Megan was safely inside before he left. He had planned to follow them and make sure she got home all right before he looked for a hotel. When he merged with the traffic on the highway, though, he changed his mind abruptly. Pushing down on the accelerator, he sped past the cab. He wanted to beat Megan home, to have a moment to tell Clementine in his own words what was happening, why he wanted out of his marriage. Why hadn't he thought of that before? If Megan got there first, she'd twist the picture and turn Clementine against him. Clementine would have no choice but to side with Megan.

He had to make sure Clementine didn't hate him, that there was some hope left for them to . . . to what? Jackson didn't know. He just had to beat Megan home.

But the taxi driver, knowing the canyons and passes better than Jackson, was quicker. Jackson slammed his fist against the steering wheel when he saw the cab in the parking lot of the apartment building. At least, Megan hadn't gone inside yet. She was paying the driver, then she waited at the bottom of the stairs for Jackson.

"What are you doing here?" she asked. They walked up the steps to Clementine's second-floor apartment.

"I—I wanted to drop off the picnic basket before I left. And maybe talk some more."

"I don't want to talk anymore today," she said in a monotone. "And you forgot the picnic basket."

He looked down at his empty hands, then hurried back to the car. By the time he returned, Megan was inside the apartment and Clementine was holding her.

Jackson met Clementine's eyes over Megan's shoulder. He couldn't tell what he saw there—pity, relief, anger. She held his gaze for a long moment before turning her head away.

"Come on, Meg," she whispered, guiding her to the couch. "Sit down, and I'll make us some tea, okay?"

Megan nodded, hardly noticing that Jackson was standing five feet away from her, awkward and forgotten, holding a sandy picnic basket and blanket. He set them down on the table and walked closer to Megan.

"Can I call you tomorrow?" he asked.

She raised her head, and in the light he saw that she was crying, probably had been crying throughout the cab ride home. Maybe it was his punishment that he would always be the villain and no one, especially Megan, would ever know that he was hurting too.

He stepped back, unwittingly glancing into the kitchen. Clementine was standing in front of the stove, her gaze fastened on him. She was as beautiful as he remembered, if not more so. He wondered what she'd done with the negligee he'd sent her, the one he'd bought for his wife and then sent to the woman he really wanted to see in it. She'd never acknowledged it, but then, she hadn't returned it, either.

He lost himself in her eyes, thinking he saw desire and understanding there, then realized he was seeing what he wanted to see. Still, she didn't look away. He wondered if she felt as he did, that they needed to fill their minds with the picture of each other, so that they could part again and live on only memories until the next time.

The kettle whistle blew, and Clementine jumped. She poured the water into two mugs and stirred the tea. She brought one to Megan and returned to the kitchen. Jackson could smell her perfume as she passed.

She glanced at him once more from the kitchen, and he wondered what she was thinking. He knew he was horrible, standing with his back to his wife and staring at the woman who haunted his dreams. But he couldn't stop himself.

She picked up the other mug and walked to the couch. Sitting down beside Megan, she put her arm around her shoulders. Without looking up, she tilted her head toward the door.

"I think you'd better leave," she said.

Jackson looked from her to Megan, who was sitting with her head down, then back to Clementine. He nodded and walked to the door. Although he could have imagined it, he thought he caught a quick, sympathetic smile on Clementine's lips as he left.

# CHAPTER

## 16

*THE PAPARAZZI HAD BEEN LINED UP OUT*-side the Beverly Hills Hotel for hours, each vying for the best location. In Hollywood, they could always catch a glimpse of *someone, somewhere.* An Academy Award nominee entering a glitzy restaurant, or a shot of a certain TV star's wife leaving with a certain someone else's husband could be counted on to net a quick thousand from the *Enquirer.* But this night was special. Anticipation hung in the air as thick as the Indian summer smog. Pictures and interviews from the *Guilty Verdict* end-of-production party were heavily sought after.

Months before the cameras even started rolling, *Guilty Verdict* was making headlines. First, there were the rumors of Jane Fonda and Paul Newman in the leads, then the unheard-of decision to use the roles as vehicles to bring two new faces to stardom. The casting had taken six months, final touches on the script another three, and then the shooting schedule had expanded to seven months after the director quit and another had to be brought in. Three months had been devoted to postproduction, and for the past several weeks no one who was anyone had talked about anything but the upcoming Christmas opening at Mann's Chinese Theater.

Will had advised Clementine to show up an hour late, to assure that she would have the photographers' and reporters' full attention. They'd gone shopping together, she and Will, on Rodeo Drive, and picked out the pale yellow chiffon dress from Giorgio's she was wearing. It was all image, Will kept telling her. Getting the lead in *Guilty Verdict* had certainly been a major battle, but emoting the right image of sophistication and mystery was the war.

Clementine sat in the back of the limousine the studio had supplied and let the humidified spray from the air conditioner cool her face. October in Los Angeles and 103 degrees. A record. She'd hardly even noticed the temperature. Heat waves only affected the regular world, people in old cars without coolers or houses equipped with broken-down fans. Clementine Montgomery traveled in style, in limousines with fully stocked bars. She looked out through the tinted window and noticed a carload of teenagers trying unsuccessfully to peer through the one-way glass to see who she was. She put her fingers in her ears and made the most ridiculous face she could think of. Yes, world, Clementine Montgomery had finally made it.

Her mother used to say, "It's darkest before the dawn." It was one of those stupid things mothers say that go in one ear and out the other. But now, with an eerie sense that many of the things her mother had said were more astute and on target than she ever would have imagined, Clementine was beginning to wish she'd paid closer attention to her.

A year and a half ago, it had seemed the whole world was against her. First, Megan was in the midst of her divorce. Not that it was Clementine's problem directly, but she and Alex and Megan had never quite learned how to separate their joys and sorrows from one another. And with Megan still living in her apartment and sobbing until three o'clock every morning, Clementine was sucked into the line of fire whether she liked it or not.

Megan was like a woman lost at sea. She didn't know what to do or where to go. She remained on the couch, for only Bob Barker could make her forget her pain for a little while. Most unnerving of all for Clementine was her guilty thought that she had somehow been a part of their breakup. She should have sent the negligee back. She shouldn't have stared at Jackson the way she had when he and Megan returned from the beach. She should have helped Megan work on her marriage instead of secretly wishing she'd fail so that maybe, just maybe . . .

And there was Duke. When she'd woken up with a nasty hangover and a battered heart the morning after the bar incident, she'd vowed to write him out of her life for good. She had caught a glimpse of the real man that night, and she wanted no part of him. Three weeks later, though, sitting unobtrusively on top of the stack of bills in her mailbox, was a letter from him. With shaking hands, she'd torn it open and read it.

> Clementine,
>     Sorry about Gloria. When I told her I was coming to LA, she went crazy. Wanted to make up for lost time. Not that she's anything special to me, but she's a nice girl, and I couldn't disappoint her. You understand.
>     Left Glitz Town and got a new job. Doorman at a dance club. It's fun, and I get to meet a lot of great-looking babes, but let's face it, it's not a lot of cash. So I thought, since you said you're doing so good now, you could loan me a little (500 is about what I need) just to tide me over until I get on my feet again. You always were a good girl. I'll see you soon.
>                                                                        Duke

She realized then that she hadn't called him "Dad" since he'd walked out on her and her mother. She didn't love him less. It probably wasn't possible, no matter what he did to her, for her to love him less. Still, "Dad" was meant for men who hug and protect and tuck you in at night. "Dad" was someone special, someone who loved you back.

Clementine took out her checkbook and wrote the check immediately. He was using her, of course. She knew it was wrong, pathetic even to let it happen, but she didn't care. She was willing to cling to any thread he dangled before her. She was connected to him now. Perhaps once he got the money, he'd call her, ask her to come out to ... to ... She looked at the return address. Dallas, Texas. Come out to Dallas, Texas, to visit. She tried to stop herself from hoping, to hold her head up like the adult she was, but it was no use. She could be ninety-three, and she would still be his child.

Three weeks later, after the first check was cashed, another letter came. He needed five hundred dollars more. Rent was due, the boss had stiffed him, and he was sure Clementine would help him out once again. She hesitated only a moment, then wrote the second check. If nothing else, when he looked at it, he would think of her. She would make him smile.

As the letters continued arriving every few weeks, Clementine was able to pretend the two of them were normal father-and-daughter pen pals. She sent him little notes with the checks, updates on her career, and he gave her pieces of himself with his requests, tidbits about life as a doorman, women that he met. In the end, five months later, when the letters stopped without a warning or thank you or good-bye, Clementine had sent him three thousand dollars. She would have sent three hundred thousand, no matter how much Megan and Alex protested, if only to stay in contact with him. But he didn't give her the chance.

Lastly, darkest of all before the dawn, was the uphill, nail-biting, claw-scratching battle for the part in *Guilty Verdict*. Will had secured a reading for her, but as Clementine recalled it, she'd been the forty-fifth actress to read that day and the studio had already set its sights on Jane Fonda for the lead. Clementine had overheard a conversation on the way into the studio, between an assistant producer and a bit player, about the contract negotiations with Fonda, and that had been enough to kill the butterflies in her stomach, filling it with red-hot rage instead. She waited until the casting director, a chain-smoking middle-aged woman, and her assistant, a pimply faced boy who couldn't have been more than fifteen, called her in, then she let them have it.

"I would like both of you to know," she said, throwing her script on the desk, "that I have been working my tail off for the last month researching this part, learning every line so that I could be prepared for anything. I have turned my life upside down so that I'd have a shot at this role."

Gwen Raspian, the casting director, puffed on her cigarette, then spoke without removing it from her mouth. "That's fine, dear. Please read from page three hundred two."

"No, I will not read from page three hundred two. You can't turn my life inside out when you already know damn well that you want Fonda for the role. You have to have some kind of ethics."

"Listen, Miss . . ."

"Miss Montgomery."

"Miss Montgomery," Gwen said. "We have not decided on Jane Fonda absolutely. Yes, we'd love to have her, she's an asset to any picture; but no contract has been signed, and she hasn't agreed to the part yet. Should some young, talented, easy-to-work-with, and I stress *easy-to-work-with*, actress come along who knocks us off our feet, we wouldn't hesitate to sign her."

That blew the wind out of Clementine's sails. Gwen yawned behind her smoke screen, and the boy squeezed a pimple on his nose.

"Fine," Clementine said. "I just wanted to be sure I still had a chance."

"You have about three minutes' worth of chance left," Gwen said, glancing at her watch. "I've got seventeen actresses behind you, and I can't afford to get backed up listening to an amateur's tirades."

Clementine bit back a sarcastic retort and flipped the script open to page 302. She knew the scene well and had just enough time left to do it. Closing her eyes, she focused on the emotions, transporting herself from her own life to Melissa Marlow's. She knew the character perfectly, every subtle shade and dimension. Instantly, Clementine lost herself completely. When she opened her eyes and turned to the teenage boy who would read the part of Melissa's son, she could see the prison bars behind him, feel the chill on her arms, smell the urine that permeated everything.

"I am innocent," Clementine/Melissa said wearily, tired of having to say it over and over again.

"But the jury said . . ."

"I don't care what the jury said or what the judge said. I don't give a damn what your father, your friends, or even you say." Melissa walked over to the boy and squeezed his arm. "I am your mother. No matter what anybody ever says, I will always be your mother. And I say I'm innocent."

"But—"

"But nothing," she said, her voice rising, her fingers pressing into his skin. "Didn't I love you? Didn't I teach you right from wrong? Didn't I fix your breakfast every morning and tuck you in at night? More than your father, more than anyone else in the world, I loved *you*. I'm a part of you, Jamie."

She released his arm and put her hand on his cheek. "I'm a part of you, just as you are a part of me. We have the same blood and bones. All I'm asking is that you think for a minute if you have it in you to kill someone."

He looked into her eyes and shook his head. "No, of course not."

"Of course not," she said, wiping away the tear at the corner of his eye. "Because you're my son. Because we have the same mind. Deep inside of you, whether you admit it to me or not, you know that I'm just as innocent as you are." She hugged him tightly before the prison guard came to take her away again.

Clementine finished the scene and stood up straight. She closed her eyes once more, bringing herself back into the present, and when she opened them, she was almost shocked to see the four white walls and three chairs rather than her jail cell.

"That was great," the boy said, his pimples forgotten.

Gwen shushed him and nodded. "Yes, fine. Please leave your papers with the secretary, and we'll call you if we decide on a second reading."

"A second reading?"

"Of course. Probably even a third. You must know that."

"Of course," Clementine said, then thanked her and walked out. She handed the secretary her bio and left the studio, kicking herself for every wrong move she'd made, certain she'd pushed the part just a hair beyond her grasp.

Clementine still couldn't believe that Gwen had called her back and let her read again, then a third time, and then offered her the part. After years of darkness, of silly commercials and exhausting photo shoots, of heartache and bitterness and violence, the dawn had finally arrived. And what a dawn it was. Every day of shooting she'd been pampered like a star. These last three months had been especially intoxicating, watching the picture come together with music and sound effects and editing. It was over now, and this Christmas, 1981, *Guilty Verdict*, starring Clementine Montgomery as Melissa Marlow and Randy Fallini as Wesley Cross, attorney-at-law, would be coming to a theater near you.

The limousine pulled up in front of the pink hotel. Cameras clicked like bat wings, and questions were shouted at Clementine from beyond the red-roped walkway as she strolled toward the entrance. She answered a dozen or so of the questions, smiled at a young, much too attractive valet standing near the hotel doors, then curtsied once for the photographers and walked inside. As she crossed the lobby, she passed a few production crew members, wearing tuxedos instead of their usual T-shirts and jeans. Each of them stopped to say hello or smile. It seemed everywhere she went now, people wanted to talk to her, ask for her autograph, or just look at her. She was somebody now. It was funny that inside, despite the glitter and seventy-dollar haircut and the inane conversation she would make that night at a five-hour champagne-and-caviar party, she still just felt like Clementine.

• • •

Alex and Jackson flew into Los Angeles together during the second week of December for the opening of *Guilty Verdict*. Alex had called Megan six times, making sure it would be all right for her to bring Jackson as her date, though privately Alex thought it was exactly what Megan needed to snap her out of her depression. Alex couldn't ask Brent, of course, though she wanted him by her side more than anything. Living without him, watching his exotically beautiful wife, Carlotta, kiss him and take him home with her every night, was something she was learning to cope with. It was like living outside a candy store, with her face pressed up to the glass, watching everyone else eat the chocolates.

Jackson was the only other man she wanted to be with. Her lovers had dwindled, then faded away completely as she lost interest. None compared with Brent. It was impossible to make love and not yearn to call his name, not wish for his lips on hers, his arms around her.

Yet she was learning that despite what the poets said, love was not necessarily a requirement for happiness. She found that other things excited her, like closing a big deal, or this opening, or being with her best friends again. It wasn't physical or romantic, but something about Clementine and Megan made her feel good inside, safe and warm, no matter where she was. They made her think of things other than what she had and had not achieved. They made her laugh. They were a part of her, her past, and she thought that if one of them died, it would be like having one of her arms cut off. She could be in the middle of a horrible mound of paperwork at the office, thoroughly frustrated and out of sorts, and Megan would call. Just the sound of her voice would make Alex smile again, her troubles forgotten. A smile was a precious commodity in her world, and her friends gave them to her freely.

That was another reason Alex was bringing Jackson. She wanted to give back some of what she'd gotten. She wanted to prove to Megan that she could handle seeing her ex-husband again. Megan was stronger than she thought. It had been a year since the divorce became final. She could deal with it now.

Each time Alex called her about bringing Jackson, Megan said it was okay, as if she had the choice of saying something else without looking ridiculous. What did she care, anyway? She knew it had been a year. She'd crossed each day off on her calendar in bold red ink, patting herself on the back when she managed to get through another one.

Alex and Jackson were staying in two rooms at a hotel in the Valley, near the new three-bedroom home in the Hollywood Hills that Clementine and Megan were renting. It was a nice house, solid. Megan had spotted it first, after she and Clementine realized they'd need a bigger place if they were going to be living together for a while.

After the divorce, Megan had needed time to adjust, to cry, to mourn the loss of everything she had ever wanted to be. As the days passed slowly and painfully, living with Clementine got comfortable, and Megan told Jackson to sell their house in Concord so she could stay on in Los Angeles.

She had expected to move out when the time was right. But the routine she and Clementine fell into became impervious to change. They didn't always get along—far from it. Clementine hated watching television, and Megan loved it. Megan hated the piles of dirty clothes Clementine left around the house. But those things were trivial when compared to the companionship they shared. Clementine had never realized how alone she'd been, always keeping to herself. Megan had never realized how lonely she'd been all those years with Jackson, when the two of them struggled to make the smallest conversation. With Clementine, the words came easy.

They accustomed themselves to each other's habits and nuances, and the right time for Megan to leave never materialized. They signed the lease on the new house and closed for good the discussion on Megan's moving out.

So there they would be Friday night at Mann's Chinese Theater, Megan thought two days before the premiere. Alex and Jackson, Clementine and her co-lead from the movie, Randy Fallini, and Megan. Clementine had told her she knew dozens of men from the studio who would love to be her date, but Megan had declined. She didn't want to suffer through a whole evening with someone she didn't know. She didn't want pity. She didn't even want to go. But she saw no tactful way out of it.

She was going to see Jackson again. Of course she could handle it. No big deal. The only thing that might bother her, just a little, was that the first time Jackson saw her after the divorce, she would be standing alone. She wished she were carrying on a torrid affair, maybe with a gorgeous Latin American hunk who serenaded her and wrote her poetry. What Jackson thought shouldn't matter to her, she knew that. She was living five hundred miles away. She had finally taken Clementine's advice and found a part-time job at a country boutique. She was getting on with her life and doing fine. Just fine.

She hardly even admitted to herself that it still hurt. It was unreasonable, ridiculous, unheard of to love someone a year after he was gone. She knew Jackson didn't think of her every night before he went to bed. She doubted if he thought of her at all. From what she pulled out of Alex, Jackson's social life had never been better.

Once the house in Concord was sold and the profits divided, Jackson moved into the arty Haight-Ashbury District of San Francisco. He worked four days a week with Jo at the museum, painted every night, had friends over until two o'clock in the morning, walked to the bay at dawn and invited some homeless person out for espresso. He was doing everything he'd always wanted to do, living free without any encumbrances. Alex had slipped once and mentioned a woman he was seeing, but when Megan pressed for details, Alex said that the woman wasn't anyone special, only one of the many he saw off and on.

In the light of day, these women friends of Jackson's were clear-cut tramps, but in the melancholy of darkness, Megan pictured them young, dark, and exotic. They were probably liberal college students, fellow artists, or eccentric authors. They were *interesting*. They had lives to talk about, current events that aroused them, thoughts and opinions on everything. Megan was sure none of them worked in a boutique, selling dried flowers and homemade door knockers.

She walked outside and sat on the front porch steps.

Clementine had gone shopping two hours ago, to find a dress for the opening. She'd invited Megan along, but they both knew Rodeo Drive wasn't Megan's kind of mall. She'd probably just dig an old dress out of the closet.

The phone rang, and she hurried back inside the house. A long-ago voice, never forgotten but stored in the inactive file of her mind, said hello.

"Megan, is that you?"

"This can't be Joey Holmes, can it?"

"In the flesh."

"I can't believe it." She sat down on the couch and twirled the phone cord around her finger. "How have you been? My goodness, it's been forever."

"Since you got married."

"And divorced."

"I'm sorry."

"Don't be," she said, and was surprised by how easily the words came, how far away the pain seemed, and how vivid her memories of Joey's arms around her while they danced at her senior prom remained. "It's hard now and then. Actually, it's hard a lot. But I'm getting better."

"I'm glad."

"How about you? Where are you? Are you married?"

He laughed, a simple, honest laugh with a quarter of the force of Alex's. Megan had forgotten how different they were.

"Let's see. I'm fine. I'm living in West Los Angeles, working as a music teacher and part-time private instructor. I even play in a local orchestra on weekends. And no, I'm not married. Never found the right person, I guess."

"But you sound happy," Megan said. She remembered how happy she'd been when he told her he wasn't serious about his girlfriend, Stacy or Sandy somebody or other. When they'd broken up for good a month later, Megan had been ecstatic for a week. It was the same feeling now, giddy happiness with no explanation except that she was glad there was no woman he looked at with love in his eyes.

"I am happy," he said. "I have my music. I have good friends. I'm doing what I want to do."

"I'm glad for you, Joey. Really. I wish Alex had told me sooner you were living in L.A. I would have loved to get together with you."

"Actually, she told me you were here when you first decided to stay after the divorce. I never called because . . . I don't know. I thought you needed time to adjust. And then, well, I guess I didn't have the nerve."

He sounded so nervous and shy, so unlike Jackson, who was always in command. It was a nice change, and it made Megan feel stronger by comparison.

"Well, I'm glad you called now," she said. "Actually, Alex is flying in today for Clementine's opening."

"I know. That's why I called. Well, one of the reasons. Alex suggested it. She said you weren't going with anyone to the film, and I thought—"

"Dammit," Megan said, standing up. "Why do they always do this? Don't they think I can run my own life? Do you know how sick and tired I get of being told what to do and who to see?"

"I'm sorry, Megan."

"They won't accept me for who I am. They want me to be like them, to go out every night. Well, I don't want to. I enjoy staying home. Is that so horrible?"

"I don't think so," he said softly. "I enjoy the same thing."

Megan forced herself to calm down, to let the anger fade away.

"I didn't mean to yell at you, Joey. It's just that I wish they'd let me be me once in a while. Not everyone wants to be a star, or a raging success. I just want to be happy."

An awkward pause ensued, and Megan wondered if she'd ever learn how to act around men. With Tony, she'd been too naive; Jackson had made her feel weak and inconsequential; and now she had yelled at Joey when he was only trying to be nice. What was it about men that their personalities could alter hers so drastically? Was she so raw and undeveloped that the force of their wills could mold her into whatever shape they chose?

"So, I guess that means you don't want to go with me," Joey said.

Megan imagined him sitting in his home, his palms sweating like hers, waiting for her response. Maybe it had been Alex's idea, but it wasn't a bad one. She would be comfortable with Joey. And if it hurt to look at Jackson, of if she cried or had to leave early, Joey would understand. She'd be a fool not to say yes. And she was getting damn tired of playing the fool.

"I'd love to go with you, Joey."

"Great," he said too quickly, too enthusiastically, the kind of response Megan usually made.

"I think everyone is meeting here at seven," she added. "Let me give you directions."

"Alex already gave them to me."

They laughed at the same time. When Megan hung up a few minutes later, she was still smiling. And when she went to bed that night, she completely forgot to cross the day off her calendar.

•    •    •

Clementine hadn't realized how nervous she was until she finally started to relax. *Guilty Verdict* had been playing on the oversize screen for an hour, and it wasn't until that moment that she unclenched her fists. She looked down at her palms and saw the half-moon indentations in the skin, two of them drawing blood.

The audience was deathly silent, holding back whispers and sneezes. She hoped that was a good sign. God, why hadn't Will prepared her for this? She hadn't realized how hard it would be to sit in a theater full of hundreds of people watching her every move on the screen, ready to point out the smallest flaw. She glanced past Randy's golden boy head to the end of the row and saw Mel Robinson, the Los Angeles film critic, jotting a few notes on his pad. Randy turned to her and smiled. When he squeezed her hand, she noticed his palm was sweaty too. That helped.

What definitely didn't help, however, was the man on her left. Jackson Hollywell had taken the seat beside her so naturally, like a husband who belonged there. Granted, Megan was on the other end, past Randy and Joey. Jackson probably just wanted to keep his distance. Still, maybe he wanted to be near her too. She glanced out of the corner of her eye and was disappointed when she realized that wasn't the case. Jackson looked like a cornered criminal, holding his arms close to his body to hide the gun beneath his jacket. God forbid, their arms might touch accidentally.

She focused again on the screen, trying to concentrate. Unfortunately, it was the scene when she and Randy—who played the sympathetic lawyer so convincingly, Clementine found it hard to remember he wasn't really an attorney—kiss for the first time. She had had no trouble kissing him. She had taught herself long ago to differentiate between reality and film work. She simply turned off her emotions, stuffed all memories of Him down into her deepest, darkest corner, and did what she was told. If there was a certain coldness in her eyes, a lack of passion, well then, she couldn't help that. No one had complained so far, so she must be getting away with it.

This particular scene had required twelve takes to get it right. First, they weren't passionate enough. Then too passionate. Then awkward. Then too nervous. Finally, when they had the director's instructions for a closed-mouth, exploratory kind of kiss down pat, Randy changed the game plan. When their lips touched, he instantly opened his mouth and stuck his tongue inside of her mouth. At first, Clementine had thought he'd been caught up in the heat of passion, then she'd felt the burning peppers transferred from his mouth to hers. She pulled away and ran to the faucet, and Randy was laughing hysterically when she returned.

"Very funny," she said. The whole crew was in on the joke, hiding behind cameras and props while they laughed. A moment later, Clementine was laughing too.

"I'll get you back for this, bozo," she said.

"Oh, I hope so."

Jelly in Randy's coat pocket evened the score two weeks later, and tonight Clementine poked Randy in the ribs, remembering. He stuck his tongue out at her, and she smiled. Good old Randy. Gorgeous, six-foot-three-inch, blond-haired, blue-eyed Randy, who had Albert Einstein's mind and Arnold Schwarzenegger's physique, and was one hundred percent homosexual. She hoped the women of America never found out. Let them enjoy their fantasies.

The film ran on, a solid mixture of suspense, drama, and even a little comedy, and by the last few minutes, Clementine had relaxed her body completely. She'd have to be calm and composed for the reporters. There could be no hint of any insecurity about her performance. If she could just get through the quick interviews, she'd be on to dinner at Ma Maison with Alex and Megan and their three dates, with whom, unfortunately, despite what the tabloids liked to think, none of them were romantically involved.

At last, the final shot appeared on the screen. Clementine and Randy were holding each other on the steps of the courthouse as Clementine's ex-husband was escorted inside, the real surprise murderer of his mistress. With one final look between them, Clementine and Randy walked away. The credits rolled across the screen.

When there was no sound from the audience, the past hour of relaxation evaporated. Clementine panicked. The years after Him were outweighed momentarily by all her normal years before Him, when she had been able to turn to someone for comfort when she was afraid. Not thinking about what she was doing, she reached for a hand to hold, and was oblivious to the surprised look on Jackson's face when it was his she gripped. Suddenly, deafening applause exploded around her. The members of the star-studded audience rose to their feet, even Mel Robinson, and looked around until they spotted her and Randy. They clapped louder as the credits finished and the lights came up. Then the applause turned to comments, and Clementine could hear "wonderful" and "superb" as the crowd filtered from the theater. She was still holding Jackson's hand as they stood up. She looked down at their entwined fingers without terror or disgust. How simply beautiful a hand in hers was, she thought. When it was the right person's hand. And when she wanted it there.

"Sorry," she said, finally pulling away. She tried to

laugh off her embarrassment. "I guess I was a little nervous."

"Don't be sorry," he said so quietly, only she could hear. He moved closer to her while they had a moment to themselves, waiting in their row for the crowd to pass. He smiled at her, and she felt the same way she had at his and Megan's wedding—awkward and transparent on the surface, yet warm and snug underneath, as if he had wrapped her in an electric blanket while snow fell around them.

"You were sensational," he said. "Really. I was very impressed."

She opened her mouth to respond, but Alex stuck her head around Jackson's side and jumped in.

"That was fantastic, Clem," she said. "You could have heard a pin drop in here. You blew everyone away."

"What about me?" Randy asked.

"Oh, you were okay," Clementine said, laughing.

They left the theater, running into the line of reporters waiting just outside the doors. Microphones were jammed in Clementine's and Randy's faces, and questions were thrown at them from every quarter, until Randy took charge and pointed to the reporters one by one like the President. Bulbs flashed until they were blinded and seeing purple spots where faces should be. Clementine soaked it all in, never once dropping her most dazzling smile. She watched Jackson, Alex, Megan, and Joey walk into the shadows, leaving her alone in the limelight. *Come back*, she wanted to say. *Share this with me.* But, of course, they couldn't. They were proud of her, thrilled for her, but not a part of her. No matter how hard she fought against it, there would always be some things in life that she had to do alone.

•  •  •

The entrance to Ma Maison was packed with reporters, as well. Clementine and Randy smiled again, answered the same questions again. Yes, they were very pleased with the film. They were thrilled that the opening seemed to be such a success. They blushed and said it was a little early to be thinking Oscars.

The group of six made it through the flashbulbs and

into the beautifully decorated restaurant. Every head
turned as they were escorted to their seats. Middle table,
front row center. Clementine wished Arthur were there
to enjoy the moment with her.

Two bottles of champagne were poured immediately.
Holding his glass, Randy stood up and cleared his throat.

"I'd like to toast my beautiful costar, Clementine
Montgomery," he said.

"Hear, hear."

"And I'd like to add that I wasn't so bad myself."

"Oh, please," Clementine said.

"I wasn't. And finally, I'd like to say how wonderful it
is that Clementine has such good friends. Alex and Jackson, who flew all the way from my favorite town, San
Francisco." He winked at Clementine and laughed.
"And, of course, Megan and Joe, who agreed to join us
for this ridiculously overpriced meal that Lancolme is so
graciously picking up the tab for."

Megan turned to Joey as she sipped her champagne.
He hadn't said much all evening, standing in the background as she did. He had arrived at the house early, before Jackson and Alex, and she had been pleasantly
surprised at the lack of changes in him. He was older
now, of course, completely a man, making the age difference she used to feel so strongly negligible. But his hair
was still the same sandy blond, his eyes still sensitive and
thoughtful, and he hadn't outgrown his tentativeness
and bent for caution. After he'd hugged her and had
taken a step back to look in her eyes, she'd felt as though
she were looking at her own reflection.

When Jackson and Alex arrived half an hour later,
both regally decked out in black, a perfect match, Joey
reached for her hand. Jackson didn't hesitate to approach her. He kissed her cheek, asked about her health
and job, then moved on to Clementine, who grabbed his
attention and held it as if she were a brightly colored
string and he a kitten unable to resist.

Alex was her usual self, unchanged by the stiffness of
her profession. Her glittery body-hugging dress, slit from
her knee to the top of her thigh, had brought stares
from every man at the theater. And, of course, Clemen-

tine was stunning as always, breathtaking really. Living with her every day, Megan had begun to forget the effect she had on people, the way their eyes widened in appreciation, as Jackson's did. Her white off-the-shoulder designer original brought out the clarity of her eyes, the eyes Megan was sure everyone would be talking about after they saw the film.

For once, Megan had felt all right blending into the background behind Alex and Clementine. This time, she had someone to share the shadows with. Sitting at the restaurant, though, with Jackson directly across from her and surrounded by stars and whispers and glitz, Megan felt out of place. She looked around, watching the other customers watch their table. Everyone recognized Clementine and Randy from all the recent publicity, but most, she guessed, were trying to figure out who the others were. Wouldn't they be surprised to know that she and Joey were just nobodies?

Alex sent Jackson a glare from beneath hooded lids one more time, then turned away in disgust. She had lost him the moment he saw Clementine and locked onto her seductive homing device. He had stayed by her side no matter how hard Alex tried to pry him away. When they'd arrived at the theater, despite all her efforts to the contrary, he had managed to sneak in front of her and take his seat next to Clem. And he'd done the same thing at the restaurant. If Alex hadn't interrupted them at the theater after the movie, when she saw Clementine's usually solid defenses crumble, she was sure something would have happened to create a rift between Clementine and Megan forever.

Clementine was talking to Randy, and Jackson and Joey were discussing some new pieces the San Francisco Museum had just acquired, but still Clementine's and Jackson's bodies were leaning inward, toward each other, as if they hadn't the strength to sit straight. Alex chanced a glance at Megan, seated beside her, and saw that her gaze was fixed on them too. She leaned over to her.

"How are you?" Alex asked.

Megan started, then regained her composure and smiled. "Fine. Just fine."

"Are you still mad at me for asking Joey to call you?"

She shook her head. "No, Alex. It's really nice having him here. He makes me feel like I'm not the only person in the world who isn't perfect."

"Meg . . ."

"Alex," Clementine cut in, "tell me about your job."

"Well . . ."

The conversation never stopped. Randy, in particular, kept it lively. He made everyone feel comfortable, taking it on himself to include Megan and Joey. He talked to Joey about music, and was surprisingly knowledgeable. And he insisted that he was envious of Megan's normal life.

"Are you kidding?" he said when she insisted it was boring and mediocre. "Don't ever put down your life, Megan. It's wonderful. You don't need all this crap." He waved his hand around the room. "You can get by on a little happiness, a little excitement, a little bit of everything. Moderation is the key, and you're the only one who seems to have mastered the art."

Joey and Megan were the first to leave. They got up soon after the luscious chocolate mousse dessert was devoured.

"I really have to get home," Joey said. "I've got to give a lesson at nine o'clock tomorrow morning. You can stay if you want, Meg."

"Oh no. I'm tired. It's been wonderful, though."

She walked to Clementine's chair. "You really were great, Clem. I'm so proud." As she leaned over to kiss Clementine's cheek, she could smell Jackson's cologne hanging in the air, wrapping Clementine in its embrace instead of her, and the air left her lungs. She pulled away.

"Nice seeing you again," Jackson said, trying unsuccessfully to capture her gaze.

"Same to you," she said quickly, then hurried out the door with Joey.

They were all silent for a moment, then Alex stood up. "Well, we've got a plane to catch in the morning. Are you ready to go, Jack?"

"Actually, I was hoping to stay a little while longer. It's not very often I'm treated to a meal like this."

"I can take you home, Alex," Randy said. "I'm pretty beat myself."

Alex tried to think of a way out of it. She knew she should do something. Clementine wasn't making any move to stop what was happening. Hell, she was so high on her success, she probably didn't even know what was happening. And Jackson didn't seem to give a damn. Somebody had to stand up for Megan.

"Clem, aren't you tired?" Alex asked.

Clementine toyed with her napkin. "No, not really. You and Randy can take the limousine home. That would be fun for you. Jackson can drop me off later."

Alex shook her head, but said, "Well, I guess you know what's best."

Clementine looked up at her and saw the disappointment in her eyes.

"Don't worry, Alex," she said softly. "I'm a big girl now."

Alex walked over to her and hugged her. "Then act like one," she whispered in her ear. She turned to Jackson. "We leave for the airport at ten tomorrow, right?"

"Finc," he said, squirming a little beneath her mother-hen gaze. Finally, she took Randy's arm and left. And Clementine and Jackson were finally alone.

# CHAPTER 17

"**S**O, WHAT WOULD YOU LIKE TO DO NOW?"
Jackson asked.

They had been quiet for too long after Alex and
Randy left, like ex-lovers searching for words after using
up all the small talk. Clementine looked around, surprised to see that only one other couple was left sipping
coffee in the corner.

"What time is it?"

"Ten to one," Jackson said, glancing at his watch.

"I hadn't realized it was so late. Maybe we should just
go home."

He ran a fingertip along the rim of his coffee cup.
"I'd like to spend some time with you," he said softly, not
looking at her. "We're alone for once. After tonight, I
don't know when we'll get another opportunity to be together."

There it was. Out in the open. Jackson shook his head
at the waiter when he offered more coffee.

"Megan will be wondering where I am," she said finally.

"She'll think you're out with Randy."

Clementine turned on him abruptly. "You want me to
lie to her?"

"Of course not. I'm just saying she won't worry to-night. You can tell her who you were with tomorrow. It's been over a year, Clementine. It shouldn't bother her anymore."

Clementine squirmed against the confines of her dress. The elastic that held the off-the-shoulder sleeve in place dug into the skin along her upper arms, leaving red indentations like railroad tracks. What she really needed was to go home, soak in a tub, think about the film, the critics who'd praised her, the attention she'd received, and bask in the glow. But what she needed and wanted were two different things. What she wanted, most definitely, was to stay with Jackson.

"This dress is really uncomfortable," she said.

"Look, we can go to my hotel, and I'll give you a pair of my sweats to wear. Then we'll just drive. Come on, Clem. This is your night. Don't end it. There's still a few hours left until the sun comes up. Chew every bit of meat from the bone."

Their eyes met briefly before Clementine turned away. Her heart had quickened its pace. Every instinct told her to say no, go home, think of Megan, keep behind the impenetrable wall she'd erected after Him. This wasn't safe. She wasn't in control. But Jackson's will was as strong as hers. He ripped down every stone she put up.

She glanced around her one last time, then nodded. "That sounds nice," she said.

Jackson smiled at her so happily, she couldn't help smiling back. What could a few hours together hurt?

• • •

Clementine walked out of Jackson's hotel bathroom in baggy navy blue sweatpants that hung precariously on her narrow hips and a long-sleeve blue work shirt, the sleeves rolled up to her elbows. Jackson was sitting on the edge of the bed, wearing jeans and a sweatshirt, chuckling.

"Don't you dare say one word," she said, walking to the mirror and wrinkling her nose at her reflection. Jackson appeared behind her and looked in the mirror.

"I was going to say you look wonderful. Really. I like

you much better like this than in what you were wearing earlier."

She smiled at him. "Where to now?"

"How about a drive to the beach? We can put the top down in the rental car and breathe in that famous Los Angeles air."

"How can you afford renting a convertible? I didn't think Jo paid you that well."

"She doesn't. Not that I care. Hell, I'd pay her to work there. As for the convertible, if you hadn't noticed, it's only a beat-up MG, not a Mercedes. Sure, it's a little expensive, but I wanted something special for this occasion."

The night was cool and breezy. The sky was as clear as the air above faraway mountains, dotted with stars and planes. Christmas lights glowed red and green, strung around houses and the tops of high-rise buildings. Jackson pulled out of the hotel parking lot and headed for the freeway. As he drove, he glanced occasionally at Clementine. Her eyes were closed, and she smiled when the wind whistled over the windshield and picked up her hair, spreading it out like a fan around her face.

"Having fun?" he asked as he maneuvered the MG into the fast lane of the freeway. At this late hour, the freeway was devoid of all but a few big rigs and some old cars loaded down with young people.

"Yes," she said. "It's been forever since I've gone driving just for the fun of it. Driving here is such a hassle. It takes an hour to go six blocks. It never occurs to me to do it other than when I have to."

"Do you miss the Bay area?" He had to shout a little to be heard over the wind.

She shook her head. "Not really. I don't think I ever wanted to live there forever. It's too wet and foggy and dreary for my taste. But I have good memories. It will always be the place where my dreams began."

"And is this where they end?"

Clementine leaned against the car door and watched him drive. His dark hair swirled around his face, changing designs and whipping against his skin. He looked right in this car—free, slightly untamed, and young. She thought how wonderful it would be if she had the power to give him everything he wanted—success, respect as an artist, money, love. His happiness was important to her, despite how little she knew of him.

"I hope my dreams never end," she said, turning her thoughts back to his question. "I'll always change them, add new ones, and keep on going. At least, I hope I will."

He smiled at her as they exited on Sunset Boulevard and headed toward the beach.

The street carried them first through the well-to-do neighborhood of Brentwood. Clementine looked at the houses, a mix of traditional and contemporary one- and two-story homes set back behind perfectly groomed lawns. It was close to three o'clock in the morning, yet most of the grounds and the porch lights were lit, as if the owners were awake and restless and fearful of burglaries.

"How about getting a house here some day?" Jackson asked. He slowed down. "That one's nice," he said, pointing to a large wood-sided two-story house set back beyond a lantern-lit garden and lawn. "You could probably even afford it now with the money from the film."

She looked it over, then shook her head. "They didn't pay me that much. And besides, this isn't for me. I don't even think California is for me."

"But this is Hollywood. Home of the stars. Isn't that what you want?"

As Jackson drove, she tried to imagine driving these streets every day on the way home from the studio to her house. Gazing at the lit windows, she put herself on the other side of the curtains, with big-screen televisions, hi-fi stereo systems, maid's quarters, his and her bathrooms, and headaches from worrying about the parties she'd have to plan to get into the society column. She put her feet up on the dashboard and shook her head.

"Nope. I'm not sure exactly what I want, but it's definitely not this. I have this image of myself in the woods somewhere, surrounded by trees, maybe even with a stream running through the property. I see a ranch-style home with old, comfortable furniture and a fireplace in the master bedroom."

Jackson glanced over at her as he stopped at a red light.

"Really? That sounds wonderful, but somehow I always had you pegged as the high-tech Manhattan penthouse type."

She thought about Manhattan and shivered. She would never go back.

"I used to want that," she said quietly. "But not now. Fame is wonderful. I love the reporters and the fans, but I have no illusions about it. It won't last forever. I'll wake up one morning, wrinkly and old and last year's news, and that's when I'll need a safe haven away from the world. A place that makes me feel like I've come home."

He smiled at her and accelerated again down into the canyon.

"I hope *Guilty Verdict* is a smashing success, of course," she went on. "And then I hope I get more good, meaty roles and the movies go worldwide and I make a hell of a lot of money. But then, then I don't know."

The road was a racetrack of hairpin turns now, and the two of them fell from side to side, bracing themselves. They curved past houses and small shopping centers and parks. Jackson increased his speed, feeling eighteen and immortal again, transported back to when grown-up fears of crashing and death didn't exist. Clementine was laughing, young again too. They emerged, finally, at the bottom of the canyon, and the Pacific Ocean sparkled like an endless sea of black diamonds in front of them.

Jackson turned up the coast and drove along the empty highway. He stopped at an all-night convenience store and hopped out of the car. In a few minutes, he was back with two cups of hot coffee and a box of chocolate doughnuts. Clementine took the food and laughed.

"Is this your usual breakfast?" she asked.

"No. I usually have a Twinkie, too, but they were out."

The mischievous smile he wore as he turned back onto the highway was so alluring, Clementine couldn't turn away. He took better care of himself than he let on, she knew. Somewhere in between sitting at a desk in the museum during the day and standing at his easel painting at night, he found time to get some kind of exercise. His muscles were tight, perfectly formed, and solid. His legs bulged hard against his jeans.

Jackson pulled into the parking lot of Will Rogers State Beach and turned off the engine. Clementine handed him his coffee and laid the doughnuts between them.

In front of them, the waves crashed in steady intervals, no more nor less than they needed to be, unaffected by heartaches, death, and world wars. The familiar womb-like, salty scent of the sea wafted over the windshield. Something about the ocean, the incessant roar of its waves, its endlessness, made Clementine feel at peace, re-assured her that some things in life were constant.

"So, what about you?" she asked, taking the plastic lid off her coffee. "Where do you want to end up some day?"

He cocked his head to the side, contemplating her question as he bit into a doughnut.

"Hmmm," he said, wiping the crumbs off his lips. "I've never really thought about it. I guess I never imag-ined that I'd *end up* anywhere. As an artist, I'm always working toward something, a better portrait or land-scape, or showing my work in some small gallery and then a larger one and then ... I don't know. I can't imagine ever stopping all of that and saying, 'Okay, I'm done now.'"

"That must have been hard for Megan to under-stand," Clementine said. "I think ending up somewhere warm and cozy was all she ever asked for."

Clementine had wanted to say that all night. She longed to hear his side. She believed Megan, she even understood Megan, despite how radically different they were. But she needed to know how a seemingly perfect man like Jackson could let his marriage fall apart.

Jackson finished his doughnut. Sunrise was still more than an hour away, but the shoreline was already lighten-ing to a deep purple. A lone surfer walked along the sand in his wet suit, a fluorescent orange surfboard slung under his arm glowing like neon. Jackson pulled one leg up on the seat and looked at Clementine.

"Megan and I were never right for each other," he said. "You've got to know that. You saw it."

"It wasn't for me to see."

"True. What can I say? That I'm sorry? That I wish to God I'd never hurt her? I mean both of those things more than you can ever know, but that doesn't change anything. Megan still can't bear to look at me. I still see the pain in her eyes. I shattered her blissful view of marriage and happily ever after."

Clementine was drawn to his face by the strength behind his words. His green eyes stared at her, intense and penetrating, as if he were trying to see inside her. It would have been so easy to forget the world, the past, her vows of independence, her friendship with Megan, and live only in this place, on the beach with the sun not yet risen, and with this man who had captured her thoughts and mind and emotions completely, without ever coming close to her. All she had to do was reach out to him, kiss the lips that she knew would be warm and passionate and a perfect fit to her own, and she would fall over the edge. She longed to know what he tasted like, what it felt like to cuddle within his arms.

All she had to do was forget that he was a man, that if she let him in, she would be helpless again and he could hurt her. All they had to do was forget that he and her best friend had been married once, then they would be perfect together, a matched set. The love that she used to look for at every street corner was staring her in the face.

"Clementine," he whispered, leaning forward to kiss her.

She glanced down at her body and realized she was leaning toward him too. She sat back abruptly, hitting the door and cringing in pain when the metal handle jammed into her spine. Looking away from him, she watched the surfer run through the waves and jump onto his surfboard, heading out to sea. She measured her breaths to a slow rhythm to steady herself.

"You don't know me," she whispered.

"I do."

She shook her head, forcing herself not to cry, not to

let out any clues. She felt as alone as she would have if he were nowhere near her, if she were the only person on earth.

"Megan is my best friend," she said. The first real friend she'd ever had, she added silently. She couldn't betray her. She and Jackson would never get past his marriage to Megan. He had loved her, he had left her, and that would always be a wedge between them. Even if they could forget, the pain in Megan's eyes every morning and every night would be there to remind them.

Jackson stared at Clementine for a long time, hoping she would look at him again and give him a chance to change her mind. He had waited so long for the time when he could be alone with her, without Alex's criticism or Megan's jealousy weighing on them, yet now that they were there, with no one and nothing between them, she still kept them apart.

"I guess I better take you home," he said when he realized there was no hope.

She nodded, and he started the car. They drove silently along the coast, toward Malibu Canyon, the sun just a glimmer on the horizon behind them. They reached the canyon and headed back toward the valley.

"I had a wonderful time, Jackson," Clementine said as he drove slowly along the turns in the dim canyon.

Jackson nodded, feeling too old all of a sudden. Old, mortal, and very, very tired.

•   •   •

Megan sat in the hard, butt-numbing junior high school auditorium seat, mesmerized. She remembered when Joey played the piano for her when they were younger. Back then, he'd played third-grade study book pieces, not Beethoven's Sonata in C Sharp Minor. And back then, she used to sneak beneath the bench and poke his feet, trying to break his concentration, instead of sitting spellbound, awed beyond words by the beauty of the music and the talent Joey had honed to perfection over the years.

She watched Joey's face as he played, realizing she'd never seen this man who sat at the grand piano, dressed in black tails, his fiery intensity and bottomless pit of emotion a tribute to Beethoven's genius. Joey's eyes were glazed, fixed on a point beyond the side stage. His lips were pressed together as if they were being crushed by a single, devastating ray of gravity. And all the while, his fingers worked their magic, sometimes slow and hypnotic, other times so quick that her fingers ached in sympathy. She glanced around her, pleased and proud to see the spring concert audience rapt and attentive.

The concert—the third Megan had attended since linking up with Joey four months ago at the opening of *Guilty Verdict*—was a mix of Joey's piano solos, which Megan was happy to note got the most applause, and performances by the North Valley Orchestra and Choir. Two hours later, when Megan finally stood up, her legs had joined her behind and tingled, half asleep. She walked outside and leaned against the flagpole, waiting for Joey to come out.

When he appeared fifteen minutes later, he was wearing comfortable white cotton pants and a green sweater. He was smiling shyly again, unable to transfer the confidence he found at the piano to the other parts of his life. He was the thirteen-year-old boy she remembered so vividly.

"I can't tell you how wonderful you were," she said as they walked to his car.

"Really?" His hazel eyes seemed to be pleading with her to agree with him. She laughed.

"I don't understand why you're so unsure of yourself, Joey. You're brilliant. Everyone thinks so. You should have heard the audience talking."

They reached the car, and he opened the door for her before hurrying around to the driver's side. He got in and started the engine.

"Still hungry?" he asked.

"Famished."

They drove to a family-owned diner in West Los Angeles that specialized in country ribs and chicken. The restaurant was loud with the cacophony of clanking dishes, unrestrained laughter, chattering, and parents yelling at their children to behave. Megan noticed a small-town twang to the voices.

"This looks like something that belongs in the Midwest," she said.

"You hate it."

"I didn't say that. Actually, I think it's charming. And quite a change from the stuffy places Clementine likes to go. I'm just surprised that it's here in L.A., that's all."

"Well, all the people who move here from Ohio and Kansas need a place to eat, don't they?"

Megan watched Joey as he looked around, obviously delighted by the people, the noise, and her approval of his choice. She smiled at him.

"It's so easy to make you happy," she said as a waitress showed them to a booth by the window. The waitress handed each of them a menu and poured two cups of coffee. "Clementine is so serious with her acting now. Alex is far away and, I don't know, consumed by her work to the point that we can't even talk. And me, well, with everything that's happened in my life, I guess I just don't smile as much as I used to. But you don't miss a second of what life has to offer."

"That's true only when I'm with you," he said. She tried to look at his eyes to see if he was teasing her, but he pulled the menu up over his face.

They each ordered barbecued ribs and a green salad, then they were quiet, listening to the conversations around them. Someone complained about a sick aunt. Another criticized the Rams' playing tactics. Another thought Ronald Reagan should go back to acting and leave the country alone. Joey stole occasional, quick glances at Megan, but he turned away whenever she met his gaze.

"Are you going to tell me what you're thinking?" she finally asked him. "Or do I have something hanging from my nose?"

He smiled and shook his head. "No, not that." He toyed with the salt and pepper shakers, changing their positions five times until he had them the way he wanted them.

"I was just deciding whether or not to tell you about the crush I used to have on you."

"No."

"Yes." As he laughed, a clump of his blond hair fell over his right eye, and he pushed it back into place.

"I thought you were so pretty," he said. "And soft. So different from Alex."

The waitress brought their salads, but Megan ignored the food.

"Well, as I recall it," she said, "you and Alex never did see eye to eye. Maybe you liked me simply because I was so different."

"No, I just liked you."

Megan grabbed her fork, squeezing it tightly to keep her hand from shaking.

"I had a crush on you too," she said, then instantly regretted the words. She wasn't being careful, and after Jackson, caution was her number-one priority.

"I know," he said. "I remember how happy you were when I told you Stacy and I weren't serious."

"You remember that?"

"Of course. I remember all the times we spent together."

After a pause, Megan said, "So, I guess we liked each other, but neither of us would do anything about it."

"Well, we were young. Or at least I was."

He laughed, and suddenly the tension broke. Megan looked at him and was glad to see he was just Joey again, her friend, not some man she had to play games with. She didn't have to be afraid of him. He couldn't break a heart that was already broken. Besides, she couldn't imagine Joey's hurting anyone.

They changed the subject to Alex. She was still plodding away at Rock Solid. In the nearly three years she'd been there, she'd let the work swallow her up. That was nothing new for Alex, but this time, her devotion was complete. For months, Megan hadn't heard anything about boyfriends or fun or recreation. If she didn't know Alex better, she'd say she was hiding in numbers, behind tortoiseshell glasses and shop talk. But, Megan thought, Alex never hid behind anything.

She had been promoted to investment consultant and then to senior investment consultant a few months earlier and was making more than a good living. But was she happy? Megan realized sadly that she had no idea. Their conversations had been difficult and strained in the last several months. They seemed to have no common ground on which to meet anymore.

"Has she said anything to you about her boss, Brent Gibbons?" she asked Joey.

"No, not recently."

"I thought for a while that they'd get together."

"He's married," Joey said. The word hung in the air, the way Megan thought it must hang over Alex, like thick atmosphere weighing her down. She had a burning desire to blow it away, to change history, to make everything better for Alex. Once, that had been so easy. Alex's worst problem was a broken roller skate, and Megan was a whiz with a screwdriver. When did everything get so complicated? When did their lives become so separate?

"Sometimes," Joey said, taking a corn muffin from the basket and buttering it, "Alex scares me."

"Spiders in your bed?"

"Oh yes. She used to love to do that, and make ghoulish noises outside my bedroom door on cold and rainy nights."

Megan smiled. "She always did have a warped sense of humor."

"What scares me now is the way she tackles life. It amazes me that people are like that, so driven and ambitious and aggressive, when here I am, Joseph Holmes, music teacher, piano player. I wonder if what I'm doing is enough."

"I've always been awed by Alex," Megan said. "Even when we were little. I'd dress my Barbie in dresses and play house, and she'd take her Barbie to corporate board meetings."

Joey laughed and bit into his muffin, dropping crumbs all over the table. "She didn't really do that, did she?"

"No, not exactly. But it was like that. In kindergarten, she was planning what to do in sixth grade. And in sixth grade, she was deciding where to go to college. She's always been an incredible person. High-spirited. Loyal. Driven. And with inexhaustible energy. I love her more than anything. She probably knows more about me than anyone else does. But still, it's hard living in her shadow."

"But you're not. Alex has her own weaknesses. She simply doesn't let them show. And you have your own life. Just because your values are different doesn't make you less important."

Megan looked around the restaurant, seeing people like herself who blended into the woodwork, then focusing on the few who stood out, like blinking electric billboards, like Alex.

"What you say sounds good," she said, turning back to Joey, "but I don't think that's what happens in the real world. You have to be special today. Growing up, getting a job, getting married, and having kids doesn't cut it. You have to be a supermom or a vice president of a major corporation. You have to be Alex or Clementine, or you just get swallowed up."

Joey thought of reaching for her hand, or even sitting beside her and putting his arm around her, but he was too afraid of scaring her off. He would have given anything to make her smile, to make her see herself as he saw her. But she had already pulled away from him. For every step he took forward, she jumped back five. Four dates, and he had yet to even hold her hand.

He had never seen anyone as beautiful as Megan. Every man's head turned when she walked into a room. But years of being first Alex's friend, then Clementine's, and then Jackson's wife, had made her feel subpar, even worthless.

Didn't she know how much she had to offer? Her beauty and warmth and kindness affected everyone. She lifted the world up a step or two; just knowing her made people better and more honest. Damn Jackson for hurting her, for making her so defensive that Joey saw no way of getting through to her. He wished she'd get angry, let her emotions for Jackson die in a volley of verbal gunfire, instead of allowing them to rot and fester inside her. But she didn't. She was too insecure to realize that part of the blame for the failure of her marriage belonged to Jackson.

"Well, I think you're wonderful, Megan," he said,

wishing he were a poet or an orator instead of just a tongue-tied man falling in love.

"I know this sounds horrible," she said, as if she hadn't heard him, "but sometimes I wish I had never met Alex and Clementine. Maybe then I wouldn't feel so mediocre, so much less than what they are. If I had ordinary friends, I'd be equal."

"Did it ever occur to you that people of the same caliber usually stick together? Couldn't it be that Alex and Clementine are your best friends because *you* are extraordinary?"

She set her fork down and stared at him. Her mouth opened, then closed.

"Ah, I see you haven't considered the possibility," he said. "Well, think about it. In the meantime, eat. You're much too skinny."

She smiled, and before the night was over, he had her laughing again. It was never easy, being with Megan. He had to work hard to make her smile, search out restaurants that she would enjoy, find interesting news items and gossip he thought she'd like to discuss. Extracting a laugh from her was like pulling teeth. No, it was never easy being with Megan. But Joey couldn't imagine being with anyone else.

• • •

Clementine sat on a beach chair in her backyard. The September sun was hot, and she reached for the water spray bottle beside her to mist her face. She had her tanning sessions timed. Thirty minutes each side, never more, never less. All summer she'd been cultivating it, disregarding Megan's surgeon general warnings about skin cancer. She liked the way the sun had lightened her hair, streaking the natural light brown color with strips of blond. Along with the artificial touches of auburn, her hair could appear to be any number of colors.

The movie offers had poured in like sweet wine after *Guilty Verdict* came out nine months earlier. Overnight to the world, over a lifetime to her, Clementine went from being a nothing actress to one of the hottest properties in Hollywood. Will screened the scripts and passed along to her the ones he thought deserved a reading. She stayed up late most every night browsing through them. As of now, though, she hadn't been impressed enough with any of them to accept the parts.

And there was the money. Two hundred fifty thousand dollars for her role as Melissa in *Guilty Verdict;* commercial royalties from Amour Perfume, which was cashing in on her success and playing her TV ads all the time; five thousand dollars a pop for photo spreads, if she was interested. As if she wouldn't be. She would have jumped at everything right away if Will hadn't held her back, forced her to play it cool. Coolness, she thought, was for seasoned agents and Katharine Hepburn, not scared little actresses just waiting for the bubble to burst.

Still, everything was going according to plan. Yet when Will suggested she buy a house and settle down, maybe in Hollywood Hills, where she and Megan were still renting, or up on Mulholland Drive, Clementine panicked. She needed a tax write-off, he said, and the image of those places was perfect for her—arty, secretive, not too stuffy, and fun.

Although fundamentally she agreed with his advice, the thought of buying a home and settling into this lifestyle made her shiver. She had money and fame, but she wouldn't call herself happy. A whole side of her was missing. She didn't know if she'd ever be able to find it in L.A., where appearance meant so much. She had to put all of her energy into her facade instead of probing into the meat of her, the way she would have to at some point if she ever wanted to feel normal again.

Settling down would seal her fate. She knew it was crazy, but if she bought a house and moved in, she believed that everything she was at that moment would become permanent, fixed. That would be the Clementine Montgomery she'd have to live with forever. And that scared her to death.

Every day, her desire to change grew. She couldn't continue living like this, half alive. She had the success she'd always dreamed of, but it didn't come close to her fantasies. She still woke up alone. She still had nightmares. She still felt different, cut off, and she hated it.

Nine months since the debut of *Guilty Verdict;* nine

months since she'd seen Jackson. She tried not to think
of him. At first, she'd been surprisingly good at it. She'd
had so many publicity appearances to make for the film,
she'd been almost always busy. But as time went by, instead of fading, the memory became enhanced, like
good wine. She could picture every part of him as if he
were standing right in front of her: the dark hair, green
eyes, strong body, large yet refined artist's hands. At odd
moments of the day, she'd wondered what he was doing,
how his painting was going, if he'd tried to sell anything
yet or approached any galleries. She'd wonder who he
was dating and whether he ever thought about her.

Alex used to keep Megan up to date on Jackson's activities, and Megan relayed those details to Clementine,
complete with her own feelings and opinions. But after
Clementine told Megan about her night at the beach
with Jackson, the confidences stopped. Megan said not a
word about Alex's calls. Not a word about still loving
Jackson. Not a word. Megan hadn't appeared to be jealous at the time. She'd said she understood that Clementine only wanted to enjoy her whole evening and Jackson
had just happened to be there . . . and thanks for telling
her.

Clementine had thought that would be the end of it,
but instead, her night with Jackson, however harmless,
had opened a chasm between her and Megan. Not an
obvious, talked-about one, but uncrossable just the same.
Megan went on as usual—working at the boutique, reading a few of Clementine's scripts for her and giving her
opinion, seeing Joey—but she was always a step beyond
Clementine's grasp. It was as if she were afraid to mention Jackson's name, afraid it might spark Clementine's
interest enough to pursue a relationship.

Clementine hated what was happening to them.
Megan was the one constant in her life, the link between
childhood and the present, always there in the next
room if she needed her. No matter what her own problems were, Megan had always been willing to listen to
Clementine, to hold her and assure her that some day
she would be normal again. Now, however, any and all
volatile subjects were either avoided or the prelude to a

fight. They could barely talk about simple things, like the weather or a humorous magazine article they'd read. They couldn't even make eye contact, as if they each had secrets to hide.

The front door slammed, and Clementine heard Megan walking through the house. She was back from another day spent with Joey. They'd been dating off and on since the movie premiere, but still nothing romantic had happened. Clementine had never seen a more perfect couple. Similar interests, similar temperaments, and obvious respect and fondness for each other. But Megan wouldn't let go of the past, the bitterness. Wouldn't let go of Jackson. Clementine was beginning to wonder if she ever would.

Megan pushed open the sliding glass door and stepped outside.

"It's boiling out here," she said. "And you're going to get skin cancer."

"I'm not. I'm careful never to overdo it. And I'm not that hot."

Megan stared at the sweat bubbles popping out all over Clementine's flat-as-a-rock stomach and shook her head.

"Do what you want, but it's too hot for me."

"Wait a minute, Meg," Clementine said, turning around. "I want to talk to you."

Megan sat down in the chair opposite her and wiped her forehead. She was already sweating.

"How was your date?" Clementine asked.

"Fine. And it wasn't a date. Joey and I just went to the movies."

"What did you see?"

"What does it matter?" Megan's voice was edgy and strained, and Clementine sat back.

"Sorry. I was just curious."

Megan closed her eyes, turning her face away from the sun.

"No, I'm sorry. I'm just defensive about it, I guess. Everybody wants me to start this great romance with Joey, but I can't. I like him. He's wonderful. But I can't be . . . that way with him."

Clementine stood up and grabbed a towel from the table. She wiped the sweat off her neck.

"I understand your feelings. But Alex and I just want you to be happy. It's been so long since Jackson, and Joey seems so right for you."

"Don't you think I know how long it's been?" Megan stood up and walked to the door. "I'm the one that's hurting, remember? And I know how alike Joey and I are, how perfect we would be. You two drum it into my head enough."

Clementine leaned against the patio table, looking down at the ground. "We're only trying to help."

"Well, stop trying. Every day you have to tell me how kind Joey is, how considerate, how much he wants our relationship to move forward, blah, blah, blah. But dammit, it's my heart. My life. *I* make the choices. Can I help it if I still care about Jackson? I love him. I'll always love him. I don't know why, but I do. I can't be perfect and strong like you two, and I wish you would stop trying to make me that way."

She hurried inside the house, slamming the door shut behind her. Clementine put the towel up over her face and held it there. She wasn't hurt by Megan's outburst. Anger was preferable to silence any day. And actually, she was getting used to scenes like this. Although Megan liked to believe she was weak and always would be, in the last few months Clementine had watched her backbone strengthen. It was a slow process, with many setbacks, but all in all, Megan was learning how to stick up for herself. It was annoying as hell, but it was a good sign.

What did bother Clementine, however, was the way her own hopes rose and fell daily. Each morning, she hoped that this was the day Megan would fall in love with Joey. And each night, she was disappointed. She knew she couldn't force Megan to love him. And even if Megan did fall for Joey, that wouldn't take away the awkwardness and pain Clementine would cause by starting up with Jackson. Clementine had racked her brain to think up some way around the guilt, some way to avoid the rift that was bound to materialize between her and Megan if she was with Jackson. But she knew she could do nothing. Being with Jackson would mean the end of her friendship with Megan.

Clementine dropped the towel and turned her face away from the house, as if Megan could look out the window and see into her thoughts. She had always been so sure of herself before, but for the first time, Clementine was beginning to question her priorities, what was most important to her—the past or the future, friendship or the chance for love, Megan or Jackson.

# CHAPTER 18

*IF THIS WAS HEAVEN, ALEX THOUGHT, SHE'D* opt for hell. She looked out the window of her London flat and wrinkled her nose in distaste. Foggy again. Like living in a cloud or on a mystery movie set, with dry ice fuming around her knees. In the distance, bells were chiming. Big Ben probably, although Alex couldn't be sure, what with all the clocks and towers and chimes and churches they had around here. The gates to Buckingham Palace were pearly enough. Throw in a few golden-winged angels, and you'd be set.

She breathed on the glass and wrote her name quickly before the haze disappeared. It didn't seem possible that there could be another place in the world as dreary and terminally damp as Sausalito. And the odds that she would end up living there half the year were overwhelmingly stacked against her. Ah, but here she was. London in October. Fog and rain and smoke and trench coats, day after day after day. Alex turned on her heel and walked into the kitchen.

She poured herself a cup of coffee and sat down at the kitchen table. Spread out neatly in front of her were the latest quarterly figures, which Maxine had sent her

along with a personal note. In red ink—Maxine's unpro-
fessional trademark—it read:

> Dear Alexandra,
>    Don't worry about a thing. Brent promoted me to
> senior consultant, and I've got all the bases covered.
> You'd be amazed at how easily I can handle the whole
> office and how smoothly things run while you're away.
>                                                    Maxine

Alex wadded up the paper and aimed for the trash can
in the corner of the room. She missed by inches. She'd
been watching Maxine slither her way up the ropes, almost paralleling Alex's rise. Alex didn't understand it.
Maxine was not management material, not with those
blood red nails and slicked back black hair and clown
makeup. God only knew why anyone trusted her with
their money. But they did. Her winners-to-losers ratio was
as good as Alex's. And Brent hadn't hesitated to bump
her up into Alex's old spot when he'd sent Alex to London for six months.

Alex had analyzed everyone at Rock Solid and knew
Maxine was her only real competition. Once old Dick
Collins in the front office retired, or died, one of them
would take over. Vice president. More than anything in
the world, Alex wanted those two words after her name.
Alexandra Holmes, vice president. She deserved it, dammit. Not Maxine. She had put in more late hours, more
weekends, given up more dates, more fun, than anyone
in the history of the world. She had given up everything
for this one thing. It simply wouldn't be fair if she didn't
get it.

So much had happened in the four and a half years
she'd been with the company. So many crises, heart-
stopping stock plunges, rushed sales, frantic buyouts. She
had moved from that tiny corner office to a larger one
on the next floor, with a new desk and a secretary. Now
she was to split her time between London and San
Francisco. Yes, so much had happened. And nothing at
all.

Megan told Alex her life was exciting. Clementine said

it must be great to have all she'd always wanted. But as Alex stared at the paperwork stacked in front of her and felt the strange burning in her chest she always felt when she realized this was all there was, this continual flow of papers to read and sign, she didn't feel her life was all that exciting or successful. Was there some twisted dimension inherent in success, so that it could never be seen from the inside? Yes, she might have loved being in London if Megan were with her, so the two of them could sightsee. Jackson would love Devon and the old fishermen. And Clementine would adore Buckingham Palace.

But no one was there. Alex had not yet developed any close friendships with the employees at Rock Solid's London branch. And Brent was in San Francisco.

Her heart skipped a beat as she thought of him. Four and a half years, and nothing had changed. He still intrigued her, challenged her, made her mind and body come alive. He was still married.

Two weeks before she'd left for London, she'd taken a report to his office after the rest of the staff had gone home. He'd been standing by the window, staring at the bay.

"The Andersen report," she'd said, walking up to him.

He took the file from her and, as he did so, grazed her fingers with his. She looked into his eyes, and it was as if there were nothing else in the world but the two of them.

"Alex," he said. Her body literally ached to press against him. He touched her shoulder lightly, just enough to send shivers up her spine. He stepped toward her, and she was ready to kiss him, but then some treacherous, moral part of her pulled away.

"Don't," she said.

He sighed and moved back. "Don't be such a pillar of honor, Alex. It doesn't become you. You know I've always wanted you."

Her legs wobbled as she walked back to the door. She had to get away from him and hide the blush she knew was creeping into her cheeks. More than anything, she wanted to turn around and throw herself into his arms.

She was so tired of pretending that loneliness didn't affect her. She had the feeling that this was her only chance, that women like her were given one opportunity for a man like this and if they didn't grab it, it never came again. But Alex couldn't grab it.

"You may not think that highly of me," she said, "but I have more respect for myself than that."

He set the file down on his desk, then walked over to her.

"There's so much more to life than work and honor, Alex," he said, running his finger along her cheek. "I want to show you things you've never dreamed of."

Now, alone in her London flat, Alex could picture every inch of him, the squareness of his jaw, the stubble that appeared, like clockwork, after six P.M. It was ridiculous, she knew, that a man she had never made love with could invade her body and soul more deeply than all the men she had slept with and discarded. But when Brent looked at her with eyes that said he wanted her, sanity, morality, right and wrong flew out the window. It was absolutely thrilling to be desired by him. She didn't think even consummating that need would match it. Wondering what his lips tasted like fueled her fantasies more than any kiss ever would.

She stared again at the paperwork in front of her. Brent was flying in on Monday to go over the London files, and she had planned to have everything ready by then. Yet it was already Sunday morning, and she'd done no more than glance at the figures since she'd gotten home from the office Friday night. She was too wound up to concentrate. One more day, and he would be there. His wife would be across the Atlantic, thousands of miles away. And Alex was lonely. God, she was lonely.

She walked back into the living room and sat on the chintz sofa she'd bought secondhand from Kate Bradshaw, her neighbor down the hall and one of the few friends she'd made since she'd arrived in London four months earlier. She didn't want to admit it—in fact, she wouldn't even say it out loud—but life had not turned out as she had expected it to.

She felt cut off somehow, away from the places and

faces she knew, the cord to her world severed. The people who worked for her kept their distance, were afraid of her. Her peers, like Maxine, saw her as a threat. Her friends were too far away, only voices now who worried about long-distance phone bills and had time for just the facts, what she did, when she did it.

When she was in San Francisco, she met Jackson once a week for coffee and called Megan and Clementine every couple of weeks just to check in, but things were no longer the same. She didn't know when they had changed. Perhaps when Megan got married, or when she and Clementine took off at full speed toward their goals. The truth was, they were all so different now, like ambassadors from different lands trying to explain their cultures in stilted English. Perhaps they had been different all along, but when they were young, differences were a challenge, not a detriment to friendship.

Clementine and Megan had managed to stay close, living together, and Alex envied them. When the rain came down, someone was there to open an umbrella. Alex was in her own world—a world she'd chosen, but she was nevertheless alone in it. Money, she thought, did not make up for everything. Megan had told her that when they were young, but she hadn't listened.

From her isolated cocoon, she'd watched Clementine's life unfold. On the outside, life had never been better for Clem. Her second film, *Loving Again*, was due out next spring. It had been almost two years since the premiere of *Guilty Verdict*, too long a hiatus for most actors, but just the right amount of time for Clementine to find another great script. This picture was about a woman learning to love and trust again after the senseless killing of her young husband. Despite her time away from the camera, Clementine was still popular, still in demand, and Alex knew this film would only make her more so.

On the inside, though, Clementine was still struggling. Even now, when something reminded her of that long-ago night in New York, her voice broke. She rarely talked about it straight out with Alex, but it was always there. Late one night on the phone a couple of months ago,

Clementine had been talking about a new man who was interested in her.

"I told him I just want to be friends," she said.

"Is he nice?" Alex asked.

"Incredibly nice, and gorgeous too. But . . . you know. He's just not right for me."

"Maybe you should talk to someone, Clem," Alex said. "A counselor. Someone with more knowledge than me or Megan. Someone who understands about rape."

Clementine was quiet. Alex had crossed a forbidden boundary, said the word "rape," and that wasn't allowed. But someone had to say it. Clementine couldn't make the past go away by ignoring it.

"I didn't say it was still bothering me," she said finally.

"You didn't have to say it. You won't date. You keep every man at arm's length. What happened is still such a part of you, and you need to find a way to let it go."

Clementine changed the subject quickly, and Alex did not pursue it. She couldn't be certain that Clementine had heard her at all.

In some ways, Alex thought, she and Clementine were identical. Full-steam-ahead careers, plenty of money, and lackluster personal lives. They had chosen vastly different tracks, but they suffered from the same consequences. Their all-consuming professions seemed to exclude a happy love life. Not that it was impossible, but it sure as hell wasn't easy. Men who could handle making less money than a woman, having less power or fame, were hard to come by, and even harder to hold. Clementine never let on that it bothered her, but Alex wondered if she was as lonely in the limelight of California as Alex was in the fog of England.

Clementine had moved three times in the last year, always taking Megan with her. They went from the rented house in Hollywood Hills to another rental in Santa Monica, to another in Malibu, until Clementine finally gave in a month ago and bought a beach house in the Malibu Colony. She had sent Alex a picture of it. It was Mediterranean style and small, with high ceilings and white walls, only fifty yards from the ocean. Alex smiled when she thought of Megan cautioning Clementine about floods and high tides.

Megan, of course, had her own completely bewildering story, which Alex couldn't understand. She was still working at the boutique, practically running the place, from what Clementine said. But she didn't have any desire to move up, maybe buy out the owner with her trust fund money or start a chain of her own. She rarely talked about Jackson anymore, but she still held back with Joey. They were steadfast friends, seeing each other twice a week, going to the movies or out to dinner. And Megan attended all of Joey's concerts. It amazed Alex that everyone around them could see how right they were for each other, yet Joey and Megan couldn't see it for themselves.

Alex looked at the stack of papers on the kitchen table once more before disregarding them completely and hurrying out the front door. For the rest of the day she'd be Scarlett. She'd think about work and Brent and dying friendships and all the rest of her problems tomorrow. She was going crazy being cooped up; she had much too much time to think. She raced down the stairs and out into the gloom. Looking up at the thick gray clouds, she was certain heaven had gotten the raw end of the deal.

• • •

Alex and Brent stood on the small wrought-iron enclosed balcony of her flat. Surprisingly, the fog was gone and the night was clear, speckled white with stars. They were silent; the air around them was thick and tense. The work was done, and Brent had no more excuses to be there. Alex pulled her white cable sweater close around her. She felt unaccustomedly young, much younger than her twenty-eight years.

Brent was dressed in tweed pants, a white shirt, and gray cardigan. He looked more youthful than his fifty-eight years. And incredibly handsome. He smiled at her.

"You've done well here," he said. "This place was dying before you moved in. I wouldn't have chosen anyone else for the job."

She smiled, pleased, but nevertheless wishing that he'd complimented her on her hair or her eyes, something other than her work for once. They grew silent again, and she picked at imaginary lint on her sleeve.

"Do you want me to go?" he asked finally.

She looked at him before she could stop herself. His gray eyes were intense, hungry, but she knew he wouldn't push her. He wanted her to come to him; he had wanted her to make the first move for over four years. She had told herself that what she felt for him was only infatuation, that it would pass, that some day, other men would affect her the way he did. But none of that was true. Brent had penetrated her core and wouldn't leave. She knew with undeniable certainty she would never get him out of her system. Married or not, he was the man for her. And suddenly, his wife, his son, all the rules, vanished. She took a step closer.

"No," she said. "I want you to stay."

He reached out, and she thought his hand was shaking, though that was ridiculous. He brushed her hair back from her face slowly, so she would remember his movements forever.

"You make me feel young again," he said.

Then he bent down and kissed her. Every touch from that moment on was magnified a hundred times. Alex was aware of everything, the wind through her hair, the smell of him, the way they leaned to each other and molded together. The firsts were so important, and she didn't want to miss anything.

His lips were firm and warm and tasted of the wine they'd drunk earlier. Alex sighed when his arms slipped around her waist. His tongue tickled hers, and in that moment she knew what she had been missing all these years. What Megan had wanted more than anything with Jackson. What Clementine refused to see. Alex knew this was the most exquisite pleasure the world had to offer. This skin on skin, this giving up and giving in, this letting someone into your soul and trusting him not to steal it.

He led her into the bedroom and turned on the light.

"I want to see you," he said.

Alex looked around the room, suddenly nervous. She had been with enough men to know about sex, but this was different. Her pleasure wasn't what mattered now.

"You're shaking," he said. He gathered her in his rms, and she could hear his heartbeat. "Don't be frightned, Alex. I would never hurt you."

She kissed his neck, his cheek, his beautiful patrician ose. At some point, though she couldn't recall when, leir clothes fell away, and they lay down side by side on le bed.

He was a wonderful lover, as she'd known he would e. His fingers were both feather-light and strong, stroking all the right places. She came quickly, then he made ove to her again, taking his time. Every move, every senation, was ecstasy, perfection. She felt like clay in his ands, wet and pliable, and he made her into the most reathtaking sculpture, spending hours getting every urve exactly as it should be.

After, she made coffee and brought two cups to the ed. Brent was sitting up, smoking, smiling.

"You were wonderful," he said.

She crawled in beside him and shared his cigarette, hough she didn't smoke. She wanted to share everything.

"It's never been like that before," she said.

"Like what?"

"Like losing myself. With other men, I'm always aware f the clock or the rain or what I have to do in an hour. can always see myself moving, playing at it. All my novements seem rehearsed and forced."

Brent stubbed out the cigarette and sipped his coffee. So there have been a lot of others?"

He said it straightforwardly, without jealousy, and she hrugged.

"Yes. But no one of any consequence. Not until you."

He stared out the window, and Alex abruptly came ack to the world, to their situation, to what she had let lerself do. She jumped out of bed and searched for her lothes.

"I didn't mean anything by that," she said too quickly. he found her underwear and slipped it on, but her weater and slacks had disappeared. "I just meant you nake me laugh and we get along and . . ."

He was suddenly beside her, holding her, and Alex was

amazed to find herself crying in his arms. What had he done to her? She didn't want to be like this. She had lived her whole life doing everything she could not to end up like this, crying like a schoolgirl in a man's arms, her emotions too close to the surface, every word magnified so greatly.

"It's all right," he said. "I know."

But he didn't know. He was Brent Gibbons, millionaire. He was married. He was a man. He hadn't given up anything to make love with her. Alex felt as if she had given up everything.

"I'm sorry," she said when her tears finally subsided. She pulled away and finally found her clothes. She put them on, taking the time to compose herself. "I'm not usually like that."

"Don't you think I know that?" He put on his clothes too, and they walked into the kitchen, where everything seemed less intense.

Alex poured herself more coffee. "I didn't plan on that happening. I didn't want that to happen."

"Why not?"

She stared at him. "Because you're married."

He shrugged. "I told you before, Carlotta is very understanding. Our marriage has been platonic for years now."

Alex couldn't believe it. How could Carlotta live with a man like this, a lover like this, and not want to be with him?

"Why stay then?" she asked.

He smiled at her. "Very simply, because of Peter. I love him more than anyone, and I've denied him so much over the years. I won't hurt him again."

He took her coffee cup out of her hands and kissed her hard. It was as if he sucked the world away in those few moments, stopping her lips from uttering, *What if the right woman came along? Would you leave Carlotta then?*

"I'm going to extend my trip," he said when he finally pulled away. "Two weeks. I want to be with you."

He kissed her again, and Alex stopped caring about anything but his arms around her. Nothing mattered as long as he never let her go.

• • •

They toured the countryside, saw castles and farmland, pubs and churches. During the day, Alex worked, or rather, tried to work. For the first time in her life, work felt like drudgery. The clock dragged, and she wished time away. Meetings and contracts were only pointless inconveniences that took her away from Brent.

At night and on weekends, Brent was more than she ever dared to hope for. He was sophisticated, cultured, intellectual. They sat in restaurants for hours, discussing politics and Hemingway and the state of the world. He loved to talk, a rare quality in a man, and he had solid ideas, unbudgeable stances on everything. They didn't agree on many things, like the death penalty (he was for it, she was against), or abortion (she was definitely for it, he was definitely against), but Alex thought that was wonderful. He made her debate things, back up her point of view with hard evidence. He made her think.

He seemed to know everyone, made friends everywhere. She noticed that he never moved out of the way for people in a crowded street; others always moved for him. He commanded respect wherever he went, and beside him, she commanded it too.

Alex lived a lifetime in fourteen days. She cherished each second, stored up every happiness, every kiss, to make up for all the lost time. Just holding Brent's hand gave her pleasure. They could be walking through Westminster Abbey, and the grandeur meant nothing compared to the feel of his fingers intertwined with hers like an Indian basket, woven with precision and grace.

She longed to call Megan and Clementine, but she didn't want to spare the time with Brent to do it. When he left, she would tell them everything. They would be like teenagers again, giggling over what he said, how he kissed.

At night, with candles burning everywhere, he made love to her like a man trained for just that purpose. Time flew by in those moments, speeding from nine o'clock to midnight in what seemed like seconds. It wasn't fair. Alex thought of all the miserable couples with hour after tedious hour together, while she and Brent grasped at precious minutes. It wasn't fair.

After that first night together, he never mentioned Carlotta or Peter again. Alex was too afraid of what he would say to bring them up herself. Instead, she reveled completely in the moment. She thought he was feeling what she was feeling, a magnificent burst of love that had sprung from left field. If their situations were reversed, she knew she couldn't go back to a husband she didn't love. She would move heaven and earth to stay with Brent. But their situations were not reversed, and he was frustratingly silent on the subject.

They spent their last day together in her flat, making love, laughing, pretending they didn't have to say goodbye. Alex had not thought about what the next two months would be like, with her still in London and him back in the States. She couldn't think about it.

At three, Brent glanced at the clock and started getting dressed. Alex knew this was the time to say something, to state her feelings firmly, proudly, but no words came to mind. When they were both fully clothed and Brent was packed and ready, he sat on the edge of the bed.

"You'll keep me up to date on the Weston deal, won't you?" he asked.

She nodded. She didn't trust her voice.

"Come now, Alex. Don't be sad. We had a good time, didn't we?"

She walked to the window. "Yes. We did."

He came up behind her and slipped his arms around her waist.

"You knew the situation from the start," he said quietly. "I told you about Peter. I know it's difficult to understand when you don't have a child of your own, but you have to realize he is everything to me. I won't leave Carlotta and hurt him."

Alex jerked away and stared at him.

"I know what you said." Her voice was even and smooth, just the way she wanted it, despite the churning in her stomach. "I thought perhaps these last two weeks had changed your mind."

He took a step toward her, then abruptly turned around. He walked into the living room and organized the papers in his briefcase. She followed him and stood in the doorway.

"This time together has been perfect, Alex," he said. "I wish I could stay here and pretend that the rest of the world doesn't exist, but unfortunately, it does."

She leaned against the door frame, hardly breathing. She felt barely alive and incredibly stupid. The tender part of her that he had reached, touched, made love to, hardened instantly. She felt bitter and deceived, tricked into loving a man who only wanted her heart as a souvenir. He had no idea how much she'd given of herself. Or perhaps he did know, and he was giving it back.

"Of course," she said. "What we had was a fling. I never expected you to leave your wife for me."

They stared at each other, both trying to see past the other one's words and bravado, but neither succeeding. Alex's mind was screaming, *I did expect it! You have to leave her. What will all this mean, what will happen to me, if you don't?* The words were so loud, in her ears, she was amazed that none of them escaped her lips. Finally, Brent snapped shut his briefcase and walked to the door.

"Would you believe me," he asked, "if I said I love you?"

She felt her knees weaken and gripped the door. God, she was good at pretending. Tears stung her eyes, but she held them back. She wanted to let go, wanted to scream and cry and beg, but she was Alexandra Holmes, and that still meant something. Yet all the bravado in the world didn't stop the pain in her chest. It burned in her lungs, then spread to her stomach, her arms, her legs. She had never hated anyone as much as she hated Brent for loving her, for making her love him back.

"No," she said.

He sighed and put his hand on the knob. "I guess this is it then."

Alex took one more deep breath. If he walked out that door, she would cease to be. Yet if he kept standing there, gazing at her with his regretful but cool eyes, he would kill every last bit of love inside her.

"Yes," she said. "I guess it is."

He opened his mouth to say something more, but only nodded and left.

Alex remained in the doorway. She couldn't be sure how long she stood there, staring at the place where Brent had been standing. She could see him even when he was gone. She could feel him, even though he had stopped touching her. She kept waiting for him to come back, to take her in his arms and tell her he'd changed his mind, but he never came. When Alex finally shifted her gaze, the bright sunlight had been replaced with shadows.

She walked to the couch. It was all so unreal. The perfection of the past two weeks and the brutally quick way it had ended. She had never even had a solid hold on him before he'd slipped through her fingers. She wasn't even given a chance to get accustomed to what he felt like.

She looked at her hands and legs; everything was still intact. How strange that her body didn't just dissolve, the way her heart had. Then the pain hit her like a blow to the stomach. She gripped her arms around her knees and pulled them tightly to her chest. The tears came hard and strong and didn't stop for hours.

•   •   •

Jackson was waiting at San Francisco International when Alex arrived back in town two months later. He had appointed himself her honorary chauffeur.

She spotted him quickly as she walked into the terminal. He was easily the most handsome man there, holding a bouquet of purple helium balloons with her name printed on them in bright red letters.

She hugged him tightly when she reached him. Actually, she wanted to cry again, the way she did only at night, after work, when she was sure nobody could hear her, but that wasn't the Alex he remembered. The sad part was, she didn't think any traces of the old Alex remained.

"You're looking great," she said, meaning it. She took the balloons from him as they walked toward the baggage area.

"I wish I could say the same for you."

Alex had spent fifteen minutes in the airplane bathroom, fixing her makeup and trying to hide the dark circles under her eyes. She covered up her surprise at his observation with anger.

"Oh, thanks, Jack. Just what I need. Insults."

He stopped walking, oblivious to the passengers who had to maneuver their way around them, and held on to her arm.

"What's wrong?"

"You insulted me."

"Besides that."

She pulled her arm away and started walking. Jackson caught up to her and kept up with her quick pace.

"You're not going to tell me?" he asked.

"No. There's nothing to tell."

They were silent as they reached the baggage area, and remained that way for ten minutes until Alex spotted her three bags. She carried one and Jackson the other two as they walked to the parking lot. When the luggage was packed in the trunk and they were inside his car, Jackson turned to her.

"I've poured my heart out to you over the years," he said. "About Megan, about painting, about everything. Don't you think it's time you returned the favor?"

She felt a dam burst inside her. One minute she was strong, emotions held back, and the next her control was flooded by surging tears. Jackson held her tightly while she cried.

"It's okay," he said over and over, running his hand through her hair. Holding her, Jackson was reminded of how surprisingly small she was. Standing in her office in a suit, with a pencil behind her ear and her hair gelled into a spinsterish bun, she appeared tall and powerful and impervious to hurt. In his arms, though, she felt almost like a child, small-boned, petite—though she screamed at anyone with the guts to call her that—and fragile. He held her until she quieted.

"God, what an idiot," she said at last.

"You or me?"

"Me. I hate that. Crying is so pointless."

"Maybe if you'd cried more in the past, you wouldn't be feeling whatever it is you're feeling now."

"Don't get Freudian on me."

He smiled and pulled away. "I'd say some old-fashioned American hamburgers and french fries are in order. To McDonald's?"

She smiled through her tears and nodded. "That sounds heavenly."

•   •   •

Jackson was tempted to stick a french fry up each nostril to lighten Alex's mood, but he decided against it. He'd never seen her like this. Sure, she'd been depressed before, angry, frustrated, and even sad now and then. But never lost, almost devastated.

They found an empty corner in McDonald's and sat down with their food. Alex swiveled her bright yellow chair back and forth, picking out the pickles in her Big Mac. Jackson waited patiently for her to speak.

"I am the world's biggest fool," she said finally.

"Nothing new there," he teased.

"Jack, I'm serious. I made the biggest mistake of my life."

"Which is?"

She looked out the window. "I lost myself. I fell in love."

Jackson sat back, stunned. Alex in love? It didn't seem possible. Not that she wasn't lovable, but she had never seemed particularly interested in returning anyone's affections. She had never come close to giving her heart; she was too afraid of losing the hard edge she'd gained over the years.

"Who is it?" he asked.

She shook her head. "It doesn't matter. The point is that I did all the things I swore I'd never do. I rearranged my schedule for him. I let work slide. I let him know me, the way no one's ever known me. And the worst part is, I liked it. I loved it."

"What's so bad about that?"

She drew a deep breath. "It was like uncorking my soul," she said softly. "I never knew I could feel these things. Megan was the emotional one. I was just ... I don't know. Stoic. Armor-plated. Above it all."

Jackson laid his hand over hers. "No one's above falling in love. It happens to the best of us."

"But I wasn't ready. No one told me it would be so intense. No one prepared me for the exhilaration of being with him or the desperation I'd feel when he disappeared around a corner. No one said that even if I loved him more than anything, he still might decide to leave me."

Jackson squeezed her hand. "Did he leave?"

Alex closed her eyes. She saw Brent again, at the door, her will trying to tie him to her and his will taking him back home, to his wife.

"Yes."

They were both quiet. Alex waited for Jackson to give her some remedy. There had to be something she could do to make the pain stop. She'd never encountered any problem she couldn't get around before.

"There are a million clichés I could use right now," he said finally. "But the only one that comes to mind is 'Love stinks.' It hurts. It rips you apart. There's no getting around that."

"I feel like I'm walking around in darkness," she whispered.

He reached over and wiped a single tear away, then stroked her cheek.

"That's how you're supposed to feel. You're supposed to feel lousy, like you want to curl up and die. It's supposed to hurt like hell. Life is like that, Alex. You can't live in the clouds forever, the way you want to, the way you have been. Sometimes you have to come down to earth, walk in the mud, get a little bruised and dirty."

"I liked living in the clouds," she said. "I was perfectly happy with my career before he came along and made me see all that I was missing."

"Were you really happy?"

She tapped her fingers on the table. "Oh, I don't know. I'm twenty-eight years old now. I know that's a long way from over the hill, but it's too old to change who I am. This just proves I'm not cut out for love. I treat it the way I treat my work, and that's too intense. I go overboard, put everything I have into it, the way I would a market analysis report. And then I expect the same kind of results. Total success."

"We all go overboard in the beginning. Nothing is as intense as those first few days of romance."

"That's not true," she said. "Power is as intense. Closing a deal, making money, besting a competitor. That can be like sex."

"It sounds lonely."

"So what if it is? It's safe. I'm good at it. And I won't ever have to go through this again."

She pushed her hamburger away. Jackson was quiet for a long time before he finally said, "I can't live your life for you. You have to make your own choices. I've always thought that was the hardest part, the choices we have to make. The high road or the low. Everything's a choice. And don't let anyone tell you you can have it all, because you can't. There are trade-offs in everything. Sure, we try to pick the best path, but there's always the possibility that the road we left behind was really the right one."

"Do you feel that way?"

"Hell, yes. Look, I chose to marry Megan. At the time, I knew the alternatives. A life as a husband and father, working regular hours, or a life as an artist, usually poor, creatively eccentric, and free. I chose Megan."

"But you changed your mind."

"Yes, but not without incredible heartache. The harder the choice, the greater the repercussions when you realize it was a mistake."

"And how does this Hollywell theory of life apply to me?"

"I'd say your choices are similar to mine. One part of you has always strived for a high-power career. The other wants what everyone wants. Love, maybe marriage and kids, a place to call your own. With you, though, the career part has always been dominant. You never even gave love a chance."

"Until now." She looked at him. "Jackson, tell me.

When does the love stop? When do I get back to normal?"

He smiled. "This is normal. We've all got that lost love we're pining for, or bitter memories of some relationship that ended before we were ready to say good-bye. And I can't say that the love will ever stop. Do you really want it to?"

"Yes. Oh God, yes."

"Alex, look." He stopped for a moment, mulling over his words as he toyed with his napkin.

"Life's not easy," he said finally. "And love's the most complicated thing of all. If you decide that love's not for you, then I guess you make that choice and live with it. No one said life is fair or even very pleasant. We just have to make the best of what we have and try to forget what we're missing."

They finished their food and cleaned up the table. As they walked out the door, they passed the McDonald's playground, where a dozen children were racing up the steps of the slide and laughing all the way down. They stopped to watch them for a minute, then Alex put her head on Jackson's shoulder and they walked to his car. No matter what Jackson said, she knew she could never forget what she was missing. Every couple holding hands would remind her. Every laughing child, blushing bride, and lovesick teenager would practically shout at her, *Look what you don't have. Look what you gave up.* The memories of Brent were everywhere, in everything, and she would have to stare at them every second of every day for the rest of her life.

# CHAPTER

## 19

*JACKSON TOOK A DEEP BREATH AND PUSHED* open the door to the gallery. He gripped his heavy portfolios tightly under each arm and walked into the cool, dimly lit room. His appointment with the curator, Donald Lithgow, was for two-thirty. It was two-twenty-nine and twenty seconds.

The gallery was empty, and he set his portfolios down on a brass-and-glass table. He looked around, his skin prickling as he surveyed the paintings. A few traditional landscapes and seascapes, Indian portraits, abstracts. The majority of the room was filled with the work of a young artist, Claudette Harsins, who lived up in Mendocino. Jackson had been reading about her for months. Her paintings were modern and abstract, done in bright colors and bold strokes—so different from the popular pastel, subtle trends that her pieces couldn't help but stand out. Jackson looked at her work with a critical eye, finding it striking, innovative, and worthy of the attention she'd received.

The burning in his stomach returned, like acid eating the lining away, as it did every time he entered a gallery and felt so strongly the urge to have his paintings displayed, it became a physical pain. The Lithgow Gallery, more than any other he'd seen, paralleled his own style. His work was perfect for this place. Now, if only he could make Mr. Lithgow feel the same way. Jo's recommendation had gotten him in the door. The rest was up to him.

Donald Lithgow, an austere, completely unartistic man, walked out of the back room. He was dressed in a rigidly formal dark brown suit, his gray hair parted at the side and hair sprayed to perfection. He was a mannequin man, painted and unemotional, completely out of place in individualistic, off-center San Francisco. He wasn't smiling.

"Mr. Hollywell, I presume?" he said. His voice held the lingering hints of a British accent.

"Yes, sir. It's a pleasure to meet you."

"I'm sure. Well, let's get to it. I've got another appointment at three-fifteen."

Jackson hurried back to his portfolios and tried to steady the nerves leaping like frogs in his stomach. He'd been through this same ordeal a dozen times already. Most gallery owners were friendlier than this, but they all ended up at the same conclusion. Your work is good, they'd say, but not for us. We like more modern, more traditional, more anything-other-than-what-you-have. Ironically, Jackson had just decided to take a break from the sales circuit when Jo suggested the Lithgow Gallery. She had seemed so sure that Lithgow would be interested, but now Jackson wondered about her judgment.

Lithgow had a young female assistant bring out a dozen easels, and Jackson carefully arranged his paintings. He'd changed the order at the last minute. Usually, he went from the more subdued landscapes to the bolder abstracts, trying to gain attention along the way. Since that philosophy hadn't worked yet, he'd decided to start with an abstract, then switch back to a landscape, alternating the brighter work with the pastels. He liked the effect. He stood back and waited.

Donald Lithgow studied each painting for exactly three minutes. He was completely silent. No "ah-has," or "hmmms." Jackson leaned against the brass entry railing, watching this man view his life as if it were a boring golf match.

When Lithgow had finished perusing each painting, he went back to the third one, Jackson's favorite. It was an abstract portrait of Clementine, done in pink and white oils and taken from memory. Drawing her had been easy, but then he'd taken it a step further and blurred the contours, merging her hair with the light behind her, softening her face so that the viewer first thought it was a woman, but after closer observation, was not so sure. The only feature he'd kept clear and straightforward were her eyes, her mesmerizing, see-through eyes.

As of yet, he hadn't shown the portrait to anyone. For a long time, he'd thought he would save it for himself. The more he looked at it, though, the more he wanted to share her beauty with the world. He'd made up his mind at the last minute and brought it along. This one had come from the heart. If it couldn't sell him as an artist, nothing could.

"This one," Lithgow said, standing back and tilting his head to see it from a different angle, "this one is quite . . . extraordinary."

Jackson's heart leapt. "Yes," he said. "It's very special."

Lithgow paced in front of the canvases again, and Jackson wondered how much longer he'd be able to stand there without screaming for an answer or breaking down in tears. It shouldn't be like this. If you had the energy to be an artist, the will to live on little sleep, working irregular hours as the muse drove you, spending money on paints that should go for food instead, you should be given an opening, no questions asked. If no one was interested after that, you could give up knowing you'd given it your best shot.

"Well," Lithgow said at last, turning away from Jackson's work and glancing down at his watch. "I think I've seen enough."

The young assistant started taking down the canvases.

"Careful with those," Lithgow said. He turned back to Jackson. "Tell me, Mr. Hollywell, how long have you been painting?"

"All my life really," Jackson said, trying to figure out where this was leading, trying to keep his rising expectations down so he wouldn't be disappointed. "I started on the walls of my mother's kitchen." He laughed, but Lithgow didn't smile.

"I meant professionally," Lithgow said.

Jackson wiped the smile off his face. "Since the beginning of college. About twelve years, I guess."

"And is this the extent of your work?"

"No, sir. I've got about two dozen other pieces at home." He thought back to Megan's demolition rampage and clenched his fists.

"But these are your best?"

"I'd say so. Although the others are done in similar styles and textures, these are the ones I find most fascinating."

Lithgow nodded and watched the assistant as she exited the room with half of the easels.

"The last opening I sponsored," Lithgow said, "was Claudette Harsins, as I'm sure you know. It was a smashing success. I've sold three quarters of her work already, and I've only held on to the others to push up the price. She's working like mad now. Eight clients commissioned work within a one-month period. They don't even care what it is, as long as it's a Harsins."

Jackson nodded. God, this man was evasive. Either he wanted Jackson's work or he didn't.

"My point," Lithgow went on, and Jackson squelched his desire to breathe a sigh of relief, "is that I do not gamble. I choose my artists carefully. I know the public. I know the level of brilliance they expect from work shown in my gallery."

Jackson watched as Lithgow walked to the table and lifted the portrait of Clementine. He stared at it as Jackson often did, intensely, then he laid it down.

"I'd like to schedule an opening for your work at the end of March," he said.

Jackson was speechless, his blood frozen. He'd been hoping, praying throughout Lithgow's monologue, but he hadn't let himself actually believe it could happen. Twelve years. Twelve years, and finally he would have an opening. It sank into his brain slowly until finally it reached his consciousness and he smiled.

"Any time you say, I'll be there," he said, rushing to

Lithgow's side and shaking his hand. "You won't regret this."

Lithgow smiled slightly—apparently the best he could do—and released his hand from Jackson's strong grip.

"I'm sure I won't. I'd like you to bring in the rest of your work tomorrow, and we'll go through it. I'm not sure we'll show everything. Leave that up to me. I'll start on the details and give you a copy of the guest list when I have it. I usually allow the artist to invite fifteen friends. Is that sufficient?"

Jackson's head was in the clouds. Anything at all would have been sufficient.

"Definitely," he said, grinning like an idiot and not caring.

"I'm glad you're pleased, Jackson." He catalogued the paintings and wrote out a receipt. "I'll see you tomorrow then."

Jackson realized he'd been dismissed when Lithgow picked up his paintings one by one and carried them to the back room. He would miss the portrait of Clementine. He'd seen it every night for the past two years. He'd painted it in three days, barely sleeping, right after he'd left Los Angeles when his memories of his time with Clementine at the beach were still fresh.

Jackson turned around and walked out. The air was fresh and surprisingly warm, the December sun burning away the fog. Jackson caught the bus home and went immediately to his phone. There were so many people to tell, but first, first ...

"Clementine," he said, thanking God it was she who answered the phone and not Megan.

Clementine's body went rigid. Only his voice could do that, capture her mind and body from hundreds of miles away and hold it captive until he severed the connection. She leaned against her bedroom wall.

"Hello, Jackson. Did you want to talk to Megan?" Her well-modulated voice was a tribute to her acting abilities.

"No, I wanted to talk to you. I wanted you to be the first to know that I'm going to have my work shown at the Lithgow Gallery in March."

Her tension evaporated, and she sat down on the bed.

"Oh, Jack, that's wonderful. I'm so happy for you. Really."

Jackson smiled. He didn't know which was better. Showing his work or knowing that she cared about his happiness.

"Thank you," he said. "That means a lot. I'm calling because I came to your opening, and now I want you to come to mine."

The tension was back. Talking with him was like riding a seesaw, she thought. Up, loose, and happy one minute, down, tense, and miserable the next.

"I don't know, Jack. I'd love to be there, of course. I've never seen your work. But . . ."

"But Megan, right?"

"Right," she whispered.

"Dammit, Clementine. I've had it with that excuse. It's been three years since the divorce. Can't I have a life? You can't tell me that she still cares about me."

"Yes, I can," Clementine said, her voice growing quieter as his grew louder.

"Well, then, that's her problem. Look, I'm not trying to be cruel. I'm trying to be happy. Don't I have a right to that too?"

Clementine went out with friends, sometimes even with men friends, but always on a completely platonic basis. Well-meaning coworkers and friends, who couldn't understand why there was no man in her life, had tried to set her up on dates. For the most part, she wriggled out of them with excuses. A few months earlier, however, when there was no way out, she'd suffered through an evening with a man who looked about as harmless as a favorite brother. He'd made no demands, had not touched her. But in the back of her mind, she'd been thinking, *This is a date. Be careful.*

She'd spent the evening trying to breathe normally, to keep her smile steady, as black images of Him flashed through her mind. The man never asked her out again.

It was getting so draining, always playing the victim and running scared from even the slightest breath of life. Jackson was offering her a chance to break out a little, take a step in the right direction. There was no harm in it. She'd see him, see his work, and come home. Maybe that would help her get him out of her system.

"You're right," she said. "I'm being ridiculous. This is your day, and I want it to be perfect. I'd love to go to the opening."

"Fabulous!" he said.

She laughed at his enthusiasm and marveled at the warm glow that spread through her from knowing he cared so much. Every other man had to move mountains to make her happy, but Jackson had only to talk or smile and she melted.

"Let me know the exact date," she said, "and I'll be sure to get the time off."

"Alex tells me you have another film due out in the spring."

"Yes. *Loving Again.* I'm really proud of it. It's been a long time since *Guilty Verdict*, and I think I've come a long way."

"You're enjoying yourself then?"

"Yes, I guess so. It's a job. I always thought it would be more glamorous, but making a movie isn't anything special. I just stand around most of the time, say a few lines, then stand around again."

"It sounds like being a star isn't all it's cracked up to be."

"It's not that. It's just that the excitement of the early days has worn off. The truth is, the fame that I loved in the beginning is rather tiring now. Almost every day, I have to deal with reporters and people tugging on my sleeve and whispering about me as if I can't hear them. Even the little bit of notoriety I have is too much."

The moment she stopped talking, Clementine wondered where her words had come from. Her mild unhappiness with acting had been only a vague thought, and most likely the unconscious force behind her decision to take such a long break between films. Yet she had spilled everything to Jackson as if she'd been talking about it for months.

"I'm sorry," he said. "I wish I could make it better."

She smiled. "Have you ever thought of running for Charmer of the Year?" she asked.

"Mmmm. Good idea. Oh, one more thing. I want you to be my date for the opening. With the way our lives tend to go, I might never get another chance to be with you."

Clementine thought of every reason why she should say no and tossed each one aside. It would be a good step for her, to accept a date willingly, to have—she hoped—a good time without fear. And Megan didn't have to know she would be his date. It meant nothing really; there was no need to hurt her. Besides, it was only for one day, not for a lifetime. What harm could there be in that?

"I'd love to be your date, Jackson. I'll talk to you later."

She hung up the phone, then sat motionless on the bed. She was afraid that the tiniest movement would break the spell of happiness that had engulfed her. She was concentrating so hard on remembering every word he'd said, every nuance, that she didn't hear Megan creep down the hallway into her bedroom. Later that night, she assumed the redness in Megan's eyes was only the beginning of a cold.

•   •   •

Surprisingly, the road was the same. Clementine thought things would have changed by now. She drove slowly up the winding asphalt road she used to walk every day to and from school, looking down Megan's old street to her parents' house at the end. It was as perfectly groomed and painted and lifeless as always. She had already driven by Alex's old house. The Holmeses had changed the trim from red to dark green and added a concoction of pink, blue, and yellow daisies to the garden. Now, there was a family who knew how to leave its mark.

She felt odd returning here, as if time had swooped down like a vulture, speared her with its claws, and carried her backward. As her mother's house, still rickety and in need of paint, came into view, Clementine's iron will melted around the edges and her hard-earned sophistication disintegrated. She was her mother's child again.

She parked along the curb and stepped out of the

rented Buick, then stared at the house for a long time.
More than ten years ago, she had hated the sight of the
overgrown hedges and ripped shingles. Perhaps time had
softened the house's ugliness, or age had given her the
wisdom not to judge everything by standards of perfection, for now Clementine found the house charming.
The imperfections gave it character and individuality.
Even if her mother and stepfather didn't live there, she
would take a second look at this house and imagine people inside working, playing, cleaning. When she looked
at her house in Malibu, with its uncracked stucco, tinted
windows, and color-coordinated flowers tended by the
gardener who came three times a week, she saw four
walls. Period.

She strode up the walk and opened the front door
without knocking.

"Mom, it's me. Clemmie."

Angel walked out of the kitchen, an apron tied
around her thick waist and a smile wide across her face.
She hugged Clementine tightly.

"I'm so glad you're here. You don't know how much
I've missed you."

Clementine pulled back and looked at her mother.
The gray was taking over now, covering her dirty blond
hair like weeds. Her wrinkles were more pronounced,
and the arms that clutched Clementine were looser with
rough skin. But Clementine thought she looked wonderful, the way a mother should look.

"I've missed you too, Mom," she said, meaning it. The
aroma of roast beef wafted in from the kitchen.

"You are staying for dinner, aren't you?" Angel asked.
"John would really like to see you."

Clementine doubted that, but she accepted the invitation anyway. She wanted so much to talk to someone who
was objective enough to listen. Megan, of course, would
be hurt and jealous. Alex would be critical. That morning, when she'd stared at the phone and known she
could call neither of them, she'd realized for the first
time that their friendship had limits. That discovery had
both surprised and hurt her. She'd thought they were
different somehow, immune to the boundaries most

friends faced. It was disappointing to realize the three of them were only human, governed by human jealousies and emotions.

She had thought then that there was no one else she could turn to, until suddenly, gratefully, she remembered she had a mother.

She had never confided in Angel, daughter to mother, when she was growing up, but their recent years apart had put them on more equal ground, woman to woman. Clementine had delayed her flight back to Los Angeles for a day and asked Angel if she could stop by.

They sat down at the kitchen table. It was the same table, with a deep scratch down the center and one leg that was too short. There were new flowery seat cushions on the chairs, though.

Angel poured them each a cup of coffee and stared at her daughter.

"I can't tell you how proud I am of you," she said. "I must have seen *Guilty Verdict* ten times. The whole neighborhood was buzzing after it came out. I've never had so many people stop by. They all wanted to know how you'd done it, where you got your start, everything. They all said they'd known all along that you'd make it, but that's a crock of bull."

Clementine laughed and ran her hand along the table scratch. It felt good to her, familiar. She could close her eyes and find the gouge, know exactly where it stopped and started. It felt good being in this house. Despite the bad memories, the last battle with John, the ease with which she'd left, this place was home. And with the balm of time, all was forgotten.

"Mom, I need to talk to you."

"I know. I heard it in your voice earlier."

"You did?"

"Of course. It's been a long time since we've talked, but I'm still your mother."

Clementine stood and walked to the kitchen window. Out back, the small yard was lush with weeds and flowers and bushes. A black cat darted beneath a shrub.

"His name is Jackson," she said, closing her eyes.

At eight o'clock the previous evening, Jackson picked

her up at the Hyatt Regency for his opening. He knocked on the door of her room and walked in dressed in a white tuxedo, outperforming every fantasy she'd had about him in the time they were apart. His dark hair was longer than she remembered, the tips touching his shoulders in loose curls. His eyes were greener, like turquoise, and more penetrating. When he smiled, so happy to see her, it seemed impossible she'd ever resisted him.

"Hello," he said softly, not moving from the doorway as he stared at her. She was wearing a tight-fitting black sequined dress that flared up the side of one leg and draped in three layers to the floor.

"Hello," she said, and was afraid to say anything else. He took a step toward her, and her heart beat loud in her ears.

"God, it's good to see you." His voice was barely a whisper, but it had the power to lock her in place. She had to do something, move, lighten the air, make a joke. But she stood still. He took one more step toward her, so that he was standing only inches away.

Their gazes locked, as they always did, as if it were impossible for each to look at anything else when the other was in the room. Clementine wondered if he would kiss her, or touch her, or tell her to forget about Megan. At that moment, she would have done any of those things easily, without fear. His presence made her powerless. But he only smiled.

"Shall we go?" he asked, holding out his arm. "I don't want to be late. I am the star attraction at this opening."

She hid her disappointment behind a smile. What had she been thinking? One look at Jackson, and she was ready to throw away her armor and risk stirring up memories of Him. She lifted her chin and called up her reserves of caution. This was only one night, after all, then she'd be back in her house with Megan, and life would go on as planned.

"Clemmie?"

Clementine turned at the sound of her mother's voice, then walked back to the table and sat down. Angel held out her hand, and Clementine squeezed it.

"Are you in love with him?" Angel asked.

Clementine lowered her head. A few tears rolled down her cheeks, but she didn't wipe them away.

"It's more complicated than that," she said.

"What could be more complicated than love?"

"Me. Too much has happened. All the years of being alone have made me scared. It's like I've forgotten how to act. I don't think I'd be able to . . . be with him."

Angel looked at her daughter a long time before speaking. Then she said, "Well, there's obviously still a chance, or you wouldn't be so upset."

Clementine closed her eyes, thinking back to that night in the alley. Sometimes it seemed so long ago, not even of consequence anymore, then His face was suddenly right in front of her, as terrifying as ever. Was she normal? Shouldn't she be over it by now? Perhaps if she had forced the issue in the beginning, gone to counseling, been with a man, any man, the fear wouldn't have solidified into a tangible part of her, the way it was now. But she had done none of those things. No one had bothered to make her do any of that.

"Even if I were different," she said finally, "it wouldn't work. He's Megan's ex-husband."

Angel stood up and opened the oven door. She maneuvered the vegetables around her roast and spooned the juices over the meat before sitting down again.

"So?" she asked.

"So!" Clementine was amazed that everyone did not immediately see the problem. "So, Megan still loves him. She doesn't talk about him anymore, but she won't move on to someone new. It would kill her if he and I got together."

"I doubt it would kill her, Clemmie."

"All right. I'm exaggerating. But it would hurt her. She's my best friend."

Angel sipped her coffee. "Why don't you tell me what happened?"

Clementine sighed. "I came into town to go to his art opening," she began, forcing the quiver out of her voice. She quickly described the elegance of the evening—the champagne, highbrow conversation, and exotic hors d'oeuvres. The men were all in tuxedos, the women in evening dresses. It was as tasteful and luxurious a party as Clementine had ever been to, yet she hardly noticed. For as soon as they arrived at the gallery, Jackson offered his arm to escort her inside. She took it hesitantly, waiting for the memories to overwhelm her, or the ants to crawl out on her skin, but nothing happened. She clutched him tighter, and still nothing happened. She smiled at him widely. This was his day, but now it was hers too. They each had their own triumphs.

"It was like a dream," she said, more to herself than to her mother. "Like a fairy tale where the most handsome prince in the land takes the lovely maiden to the king's ball."

She closed her eyes and could almost feel the touch of his skin on hers again, the way his eyes softened when he looked at her, the unfair speed of the clock, which whizzed from eight o'clock to midnight as if it had a date and was determined to hurry things along.

The opening was a stunning success. The art critics raved, deals were made quickly, Jackson was cornered continually by wealthy art connoisseurs who wanted to know how fast he worked and what else he had available. Clementine had been prepared to be impressed. She'd known all along that Jackson was talented. The sensitivity of his hands, the intensity in his eyes. It wasn't possible that he wouldn't be. But when she walked into the gallery, she was spellbound by the depth and beauty of his work. His soul was poured out on canvas. The abstracts portrayed his wild side—crazy, unconventional, bold—while the landscapes captured his gentleness—his quest for love, security, and romance.

She went from painting to painting, staring at them in awe and wondering how Megan could have dismissed his art as inconsequential. She particularly loved the landscapes. There were more countrysides than seascapes, a preference Clementine felt, as well. He captured the serenity of first light through the trees and the melancholy of twilight. He trapped the feelings of the moment and transferred them to canvas.

Though the softer pieces were more to her liking, she was impressed by all of them. Jackson was so thrilled with her reaction, she felt like a mother who had just posted her child's first-grade artwork on the refrigerator.

It was the final piece, though, set off from all the others, that stole her heart.

It was obviously a woman. Or at least, she thought it was at first. She was shaded in pinks and whites, blurred to make her appear almost one with the air. Her hair appeared light, but Clementine wasn't certain. Then she looked at the eyes. They stared back at her with a clarity so familiar, she felt a jolt of recognition. She turned to Jackson, who was watching her.

"You like it?" he asked.

She looked from him to the portrait and back again. She had been praised for her beauty, her acting, her modeling techniques. But this man had taken her essence, the heart of her, and with his gentle, loving strokes, made her last forever. She touched his cheek with the palm of her hand. It was so easy, so good, to touch him.

"When?" she asked. "When did you do this?"

He covered her hand with his own. "Right after our night together. I thought painting you would get you out of my system. I was wrong."

She shook her head, blinking back tears. A group of women appeared beside them and looked at the picture, then at Clementine.

"Well, my dear," one of them said, "it looks as if you were the inspiration." They all looked at her then, agreeing.

"Yes, indeed," another said. "How wonderful it must be for you to know he loves you that much. It's really his best work."

Clementine looked back at Jackson, ready to explain that they were just friends, but he was staring at her so intensely, she said nothing.

She extricated herself only once from Jackson, and only to find Donald Lithgow and make sure no one else bought that painting.

"I have to have it," she said firmly.

Lithgow looked at her curiously, then smiled. "Ah. I can see why."

She nodded, amazed and proud of the effect Jackson

had achieved, of making the painting so mysterious, so unrecognizable. Until she was seen and then, of course, everyone had known it was her all along.

"Please, Mr. Lithgow, I can't bear to see it in someone else's hands. You must understand."

"I do. I do. Getting Jackson to part with it was quite an ordeal, as well, let me tell you. But unfortunately, I didn't realize there was a model for it. I've already sold it."

"Well, then, buy it back," she said loudly. "Look, I'll give you double what he paid for it."

Lithgow's nose twitched, the way it always did when money was the topic. "It went for quite a pretty penny," he said.

"I don't care. I can afford it."

"The man paid twelve thousand. Can you afford twenty-four?"

She sucked in her breath and stood up straight. The money didn't matter. If she couldn't have Jackson, she would damn well have that painting.

"Yes."

"I knew that piece would be a hit, but I never knew it would do this well. It's a deal. But let me tell you first that I'm keeping all of the work here for a month, to draw more interest until Jackson can produce more. Is that acceptable?"

"Fine. I'll bring a check by in the morning."

She walked off, certain for the first time since she'd begun making what her friends called "the big bucks," that she was spending her money on something important. She linked up with Jackson again, her arm sliding under his as naturally as if she'd been touching him for years. They laughed and talked and ate and drank, and then, like Cinderella's ball, the evening was over almost as soon as it had begun.

Jackson took her back to her hotel and parked along the curb. When they stood outside in the lamplight, he asked to come up.

"I don't think so, Jackson."

"Well, if you won't let me in, when will I see you again?" Jackson was trying to be calm, but his voice broke just the same.

She stepped closer in response. "Please don't be angry," she said. "I had a wonderful time. I've never seen more brilliant work. I mean that."

He smiled. "Really?"

"God, yes. I always knew you were talented, but never like that. I wish I'd known sooner. I could have helped. I have friends in the art world. I could have arranged a showing, done something."

He grabbed her hand and brought it to his lips. He had her in his range now, close enough that she could smell him, feel the warmth of his body.

"Don't you know what's happening?" he asked.

She shook her head. "I don't want to know. I can't."

"Why not?"

Tears of frustration slid down her cheeks. "Too many reasons. But mostly, I would lose Megan."

He stared at her, as if to make sure that what she said was true, then he stepped back, letting her go. She felt an empty ache where he had been.

"So, let me see if I have this straight," he said. "If you stop pretending that you don't need anyone and let me into your life, you'll lose Megan. And if you stay friends with good old, wonderful, fragile-as-china Megan, you'll lose me. Is that right?"

She nodded, the tears running down her cheeks, onto her dress.

He rushed forward again and grabbed her chin roughly in his hand. He tilted her head back until they were eye to eye.

"And you choose Megan?"

She closed her eyes, unwilling to see the bitterness in his. He shook her until she opened them again.

"Yes," she whispered. "I choose Megan."

He squeezed her chin, his fingers wet now from her tears. "Well, then, damn you," he said, pushing her away. Turning, he jumped into his car without another word. He pulled quickly away from the curb and was gone before she could catch her breath.

Angel was standing behind her, her arms wrapped around her daughter's chest, her head resting on top of hers as Clementine cried.

"I was trying to do the right thing," Clementine said. "All my life I only cared about me, about getting to the top. I want to do the right thing now."

Angel handed her a paper towel, and Clementine blew her nose. When she had stopped crying, Angel sat down opposite her again.

"Just how long is Megan supposed to mourn losing him?"

"I don't know. I just know that she's not over him yet."

"So until she is, you're going to sacrifice your happiness?"

"Mom, I can't hurt her. She's been through so much already."

"We've all been through a lot," Angel said, an edge to her voice.

Clementine watched the lines multiply on her mother's face, as if just thinking about the trials of her life made her age and shrivel.

"Tell me," Clementine said, "how long after the divorce was it before you fell in love again?"

Angel stiffened, and Clementine thought she saw something close to fear in her eyes, as if Clementine was probing too close to the truth. Angel stood up abruptly and walked to the refrigerator, where she took a head of lettuce out of the crisper. She kept her back to Clementine as she spoke.

"That's different," she said.

"Why?"

"Because Duke was different."

Clementine stood up and leaned her chin on her mother's shoulder.

"I know that, Mom. It's not wrong to always love him, at least a little bit."

Angel turned around. "You're right. I do love Duke a little bit. I always will. But I love John more. He is my husband, and I'm happy. And Megan will be happy, too, whether you and Jackson are together or not. It's ridiculous that you should stop your life until Megan gets on with hers. Don't be an idiot."

Clementine turned away. "I'm trying not to be."

# CHAPTER
## 20

*CLEMENTINE WAS READING A NEW SCRIPT* in her living room when the doorbell rang. She heard a whistle, familiar but at the moment unplaceable, and without giving it much thought, she opened the door.

She felt dizzy at first and gripped the edge of the solid oak door to steady herself. Duke stood before her, smiling his white smile, dressed in corduroys and a T-shirt, with only the white streaks in his hair telling her that years had passed since she last saw him.

"Surprised to see me, aren't you?" he said. It was the same voice, always with a chuckle behind it, as if everything he said was part of a joke only he knew the punchline to.

"Yes, a little," she said, forcing herself to stand up straight. Every kind of emotion was churning through her, joy to see him, shock that he'd come, anger that he'd waited so long. "How did you get past the guard?"

"Just told her I was your dad. Lucky for me it was a pretty little blond thing working today. Charmed the socks off her."

Duke brushed past her, and Clementine closed the door. She was steadier now, but still felt like she was walking on unstable ground. Since his letters had stopped, she'd done her best to put him out of her mind. Most of the time, except perhaps in her dreams, she was unsuccessful. She had resigned herself to the fact that he would never come to her on his own. Yet here he was, almost mocking her resolutions to forget him. Why was life like that? Why did she have to reach the point of no return, of complete defeat, before she was given what she wanted?

"Can I get you something to drink?" she asked. Duke was walking around the living room, ogling the furniture and tapestries.

"A beer would be nice."

"Sorry, I don't have beer. Would wine do?"

"I guess so. Quite a place you got here, Clem." He opened the French doors and walked to the edge of the patio. The waves rolled in fifty yards away. Clementine brought him a glass of wine and leaned against the railing beside him.

"It's okay," she said.

"You must be raking it in. What does a place like this cost? A million?"

"A lot," she said brusquely, then sat down at the umbrella-shaded patio table. Looking at him, she didn't feel as nervous or overwhelmed by him as she thought she would. She'd gotten over the initial shock and was simply curious. Why, after all this time, was he here?

"I saw *Guilty Verdict*," he said, glancing at her. "Carol just loved it. Laughed and cried like an idiot."

"Carol?"

Duke laughed and sat down at the table beside her. "That's right. You never met her. We got together about a year ago. She's pretty good for me. Keeps me sane, if you know what I mean."

Clementine nodded. She was feeling stranger every second. She had dreamed about this reunion for so long, pictured him sitting right where he was, yet she had not gotten anything right. He was handsome, but not nearly as breathtaking as in her fantasies. He slumped too much. He guzzled the wine. He wasn't saying any of the things he was supposed to, like "Clementine, I'm so sorry for not getting in touch sooner. I wanted to, but I was afraid you'd be angry." Or "Please forgive me. I want to get to know you again." Instead, he just leered at a girl jogging down the beach and remained silent.

"What are you doing here?" Clementine asked finally.

"Come right to the point, I see." He laughed again and gulped down the wine. "Piss water. That's what wine is. A woman's drink. I'm a beer man. Always have been, always will be. You obviously don't have a man around the house. No real man could stand not having at least a six-pack in the icebox."

"The point?"

"Jeez. You'd think you'd be happier to see me, Clem. I haven't seen you since that day in the bar, and we didn't get much time then."

"That was your choice, not mine."

"Come on. Don't be angry. I want to make it up to you now. Why are you rushing me?"

"I'm not rushing you," she said, feeling guilty. He seemed to be trying to say the right things. Maybe he did only want to spend time with her. He was getting older now. Perhaps he simply wanted to get to know his daughter, finally, while he still had the chance.

"I'm sorry," she went on. "I was just surprised to see you, that's all."

He nodded, appeased. "I flew in from Phoenix this morning. Been living there for the last year or so. Carol's a secretary, supports me when I'm in one of my off times."

"Is this an off time?" Clementine asked, clenching her fists as she saw where this was heading.

"Afraid so. I was doing some construction there for a while, but let's face it, I'm not twenty-one anymore. Then I tried to get into real estate. Phoenix is booming now. God only knows why. Hottest goddamn place on the planet. In the summer, it cools off to eighty at night, if you can call that cool."

"So, did you find a job?"

"Nah. Real estate ain't my field. Too aggressive. So, I've been looking around. But then poor Carol, she got laid off. Company went under. We've been trying to make a go of it. She's looking for work. I'm looking. But in the meantime, we've got bills to pay. We've got to eat."

"So here you are," Clementine whispered, standing up and walking to the railing again. A man and his dog strolled along the water's edge.

"What's that?"

"I said, so here you are. You need money, so here you are."

"Hey, it's not like that. It's just that you're doing so good, and I am your father, and I thought . . ."

She whirled around. "How dare you use your father-hood to try to get money out of me again! I gave you thousands of dollars before, and you didn't even have the decency to say thank you. When you had enough, you cut out, as always. Why should I go through that again? You've never been a father to me."

"Come on. Don't be like this. I did my best. You know that. I just wasn't cut out for the family scene. I couldn't settle down."

"I never asked you to. I only asked you to keep me in your life. How much effort does it take to write a letter?"

"You know I never was much of a writer."

"You were when you wanted money. I understand that you didn't want a family, you needed to live your own life. I can accept that. But what I don't understand is how you could exclude me so completely. You left me and Mom without saying good-bye. You only called when your conscience caught up with you or you needed some-thing. It's like you didn't care at all. You still don't. You only pretend to when you need money."

He looked away, giving himself time to plan his next attack, she was sure. She wasn't angry at him anymore. Being mad at him was like yelling at a brick wall; it frus-trated the hell out of her that she got no response. Now she felt only hurt and disappointed and humiliated that she still hadn't learned to stop throwing herself at a man who didn't want her.

All these years, she'd kept hoping to recapture what she thought she was missing. But now she knew that wasn't possible. Duke could never be the father she wanted. Probably no man could. She wanted a man who would shield her from harm, love her more than anything, be proud of her every accomplishment. She wanted someone she could admire and respect, so that she could stop associating all men with that man in the alley. She wanted to be held and cuddled and treasured and adored. But as she looked at Duke, just an ordinary man, perhaps too self-centered and lazy, but certainly not anything awful, she knew what she wanted was plausible only for babies, whose smallest achievement was considered a miracle by their parents, whose every feature was perfect in their eyes.

"Clementine," Duke said, standing up. He put his hand out, but she stepped away.

"No more money," she said firmly. "I'm sorry if you're having a hard time, but you'll have to deal with it yourself. So if money's all you want from me, you can leave."

He opened his mouth, then closed it again. When he turned around, she felt her stomach fall, as if she were on the highest crest of a roller coaster ready to go down. *Please want something else,* she pleaded silently. *Want me.*

He walked away, and her hopes shattered. It shouldn't hurt this much anymore, she thought. She'd always believed that once she became an adult, fears and sadness would diminish, or at least she would be better able to deal with them. That wasn't true. If anything, she felt that she was becoming more fragile and vulnerable with age.

He paused and glanced back at her. "You've got all this and more money coming in every day, and you can't spare me a dime?" he said bitterly.

"No. I can't."

"You're a selfish bitch, aren't you?"

She jerked back as if he'd slapped her. He started to walk inside, but stopped again.

"By the way, how's your mother?" he asked.

Surprised at his change in tone, Clementine looked at him warily. "Fine. Happily remarried."

He raised his eyebrows, then laughed. "So that's what she told you. Figures. Angel never could stomach a scandal. Even a little one. We even had to move out of town after you were born so nobody would know. But I guess I always thought she'd tell you the truth some day."

"What are you talking about?" She crossed her arms over her stomach, chilled by the ocean breeze.

"I would have protected Angel's secret forever if you'd given me the money. But since you're Miss High and Mighty now and don't want anything more to do with me, I don't see why I shouldn't tell you."

"Tell me what?" she asked, impatient with his stalling tactics. For almost twenty years, she had ached to have him back in her life, and in less than ten minutes after getting her wish, she wanted him gone.

"Did you really think I married Angel?" he said. "Come on. Me getting married at all is farfetched enough, but marrying that mouse? Be serious. So I guess that makes you a bastard. Hell, I know that doesn't matter much today, and especially not out here in crazy Hollywood, but it still gives me the last laugh, don't you think?"

She whirled away from him and stared at the waves until her breathing slowed and her hands and arms stopped shaking. When she finally turned around again, Duke was gone.

•   •   •

Megan dug her feet into the cool sand, watching as Joey splashed out of a wave and shook his wet hair the way teenage surfers and dogs did. He ran out of the ocean smiling, his white shorts clinging to his skin.

"That was great," he said, grabbing his towel and drying his face. "I haven't body-surfed for years."

"You looked like a kid out there," she said. "All this time you've been pretending not to be a risk taker."

She was smiling, but there was a tightness to her voice. Joey dried his arms and sat down beside her.

"I haven't been pretending to be anything, Meg."

She nodded, knowing what he said was true, then glanced over her shoulder at the house. It still looked empty. Clementine had been vague about where she was going that day. She had been acting strangely for the last few days in fact, nervous and jittery. Megan had waited for Clementine to confide in her about what was going on, but she hadn't. Since she'd snuck away to Jackson's gallery opening six months ago, it seemed as though she and Megan didn't confide about anything anymore, as if they were friends on the surface only and empty underneath.

She reached over and took Joey's hand. It was cold and wet and gritty with sand.

"Come on. Let's go inside," she said.

They walked back to the house and entered through the patio French doors. The living room, temperature-controlled at seventy degrees, was pleasant as always.

"You can change upstairs, and I'll make some coffee," Megan said. When she was alone, she tried her usual trick of squeezing her eyes shut as hard as she could. She wanted to blot out everything—thoughts, feelings, and images—but still her mind raced forward, laughing at her. Jackson's face lurked behind every corner. And although she tried to hide behind trees and bushes, Clementine's was there too.

Joey came downstairs a few minutes later, dressed in jeans and a sweater. She smiled at him, pleased by his attractiveness the way she would be about a pretty baby. In the past year, he'd grown completely into himself. He no longer looked awkward in a suit, although his job at the high school and the private music lessons he gave rarely required one. He'd let his straight hair grow longer, until it brushed his neck in the back and fell in a heap over his forehead. His clothes were usually slightly wrinkled, as if he'd taken them out of the dryer too soon, and his eyes were always soft, sensitive, focused on her when she needed his attention, and turned away when she needed to be alone. He was completely Joey now. And she wondered again why she didn't love him.

"The coffee's ready," she said. He followed her as she carried a tray with the coffeepot and mugs on it into the living room. She poured them each a cup, then sat on the oversize, modern white chair opposite him.

Joey looked out the window, as everyone who came to the house did. The ocean glittered blue and white, and near the horizon, a whale-watching boat headed north to Santa Barbara.

"Do you want to talk about anything?" he asked, still not looking at her.

She sipped her coffee and, finding it too hot, set it down on the table beside her. Looking around the room, she focused for a moment or two on each Mexican tapestry, on the white brick fireplace, the modern Mediterranean furniture, then finally settled on Joey's profile again. He was the only thing in the whole house that she felt comfortable with.

"It's the same thing," she said.

He nodded and looked at her. "Ah, yes. Let me see. You're still hurting over Jackson, and you're damn mad that Clementine went to his opening without telling you and you had to find out from the photo in the newspaper. Alex calls every week to brag about how fabulous her career is going. Clementine just got another starring role. People treat her like some kind of goddess, screaming when they see her and clamoring for her autograph. And then here you are, still plain little old Megan. Does that about cover it?"

She smiled, touched by his ability to make the problems she considered overwhelming seem funny, not even worthy of her time.

"Yes, that covers it."

He sipped his coffee and sat back in the plush couch. "Did I ever tell you how I felt about Alex when I was little?"

She shook her head. "Not as much as I'd like to hear."

"I used to hate her sometimes," he said, staring at a place just over Megan's head. "I hated her for her beauty and laughter. Her nerve. I was scared to death of failing, of hurting myself or going too far, and then Alex sped past me, her eyes closed, not looking where she was going and not giving a damn where she ended up."

"Alex is incredible," Megan whispered.

Joey held out his hand, and she moved to join him on the couch.

"You lived in her shadow too," he said. "And then along came Clementine. So strong and resilient and breathtaking, and it was like they were hitting you from all sides, taking away the last pieces of yourself that you thought were special."

"But they're my best friends," she said. "I love them. I hate myself for wishing them unhappiness."

"Of course. I love Alex. I love her with all my heart. But I knew that I had to find my own specialness, the part of me that stood out, so that I could live with myself and be proud of my accomplishments. I'm a world away from Alex, but I needed the spotlight, too, if only for a minute or two."

"And you found music," Megan said.

"Yes. I found music. And suddenly, it didn't matter so much anymore that Alex was smarter, or had more friends, or made everybody laugh. Because when people looked at me, they said, 'Oh, yes, Joey Holmes. He's the one who plays the piano.' I had something."

"That's wonderful, Joey," Megan said. She leaned back into the thick cushions, so consuming, they felt like they would swallow her up. "But I don't see where that will help me."

"You need to concentrate on what makes you special, instead of living behind Alex's sparkling career or Clementine's beauty and fame."

She stood up and walked to the fireplace, then whirled around. "And just what do I have? I live in this mausoleum because Clementine bought it and I'm too afraid to live by myself. I have a job in a boutique, which, by the way, I love, but everybody thinks I should do more—try to overthrow my boss or open my own store or something. No one even stops to think for a moment that I might be happy doing what I'm doing. No one ever thinks that maybe there's something different that I want."

After a moment of silence, Joey sat forward. "What do you want?"

She looked down at her hands, clenched into fists. She loosened them and leaned against the cool walls. "I know I don't want this," she said, waving her hand around the room. "I don't want a dustfree house on the beach. I can't even walk down the street here without worrying about the tear in my sweatpants or the tweak in my hair."

He laughed, and she returned to the couch. "I don' want a fast-pace career like Alex has. No matter what she says, I know she's not always happy. She's got eyes. She sees the empty pillow at night. She isn't all that crazy about going to movies by herself and cooking for one. And I don't want fame, like Clementine. She's got every thing money can buy, and yet I hear her at night, crying just like I do, as alone as I am."

She leaned her head on Joey's shoulder; the familiar ity of his bones and smell and soft wool sweater soothed her. She closed her eyes.

"I just want a happy life, I guess. I want to be married again. I want a husband who loves me first, above every thing else. I want kids. I want PTA meetings and bag lunches and station wagons. I want camping trips and lemonade and Boy Scouts. None of those things are go ing to make me very special."

He put his arm around her and held her closely. "That's where you're wrong, Meg," he whispered. "That makes you very special. When people talk about Alex, they'll say 'the financial whiz.' And for Clementine, they'll say 'the famous one.' But when people talk about you, they'll say 'Megan, the woman who knows what's re ally important.' "

She smiled and looked up at him. His eyes were warm, and she could feel his breath on her cheek. She'd never been this close to him before, or if she had, it was only briefly, when she moved in and out for a chaste kiss. But now he was here, so close, and she felt not even a quiver of fear. There wasn't the wildly racing heartbeat she'd had with Tony and Jackson, either, but she doubted that she ever wanted to experience that again.

She lifted her hand to his cheek. "Please kiss me, Joey."

He smiled before his lips touched hers, then every thing else except his tenderness stitching the broken seams of her heart back together disappeared.

·   ·   ·

At that same time, Clementine sat in the back of a small room, behind a group of women, a scarf over her head and dark glasses disguising her face. She kept her arms around her stomach to fight the nausea. She was shivering badly as she listened to the women speak.

"It was the process afterward that was the worst," a woman named Margie said. "The policemen had no clue what I was feeling. One of them even made a comment about my clothes, like what I was wearing had anything to do with it."

"They rape you again," Sandy, a teenage girl, said. "They stick their instruments inside of you to make sure you're telling the truth. They ask you all those questions, trying to trip you up, like you were the one committing the crime."

"It's not always like that," Dr. Levinson said. She was the group counselor and the woman Clementine had called three days earlier. Clementine had not given her real name, for fear that it would be leaked to the press. She had not told Megan, either. It wasn't that she didn't think Megan would understand, but more that Clementine was ashamed that she was still reeling from the rape after so many years.

She'd been crying when she called. It was late at night, as it always was when the memories came on strong. They trapped her back in that alley, and she thought if she suffered through one more second of it, she would go insane. It was like being haunted by her own mind every night.

She had seen a number on the television one night during an ad for the Los Angeles chapter of the Rape Victims' Center. She'd felt silly writing it down; she was certain she would never call it. But she did. She had finally had too much. She thought it might have to do with Duke's last visit, when he finally shattered her stubborn hope that her father was the man in her childhood fantasies, a man who would kill her demons for her. She asked Dr. Levinson what the center could do to help her, and the doctor suggested she try one of these group support sessions.

"Our rape victims' group is making some headway,"

the doctor told the group. "We're helping the police to
understand the trauma. What *we* have to understand is
that men are coming from a different point of view. Most
of them can't even imagine rape. They have no concept
of it. They still think it has something to do with sex, so
it can't be all bad."

Walking into the center was one of the hardest things
Clementine had ever done. When the first woman stood
up and told her story, she had wanted to turn and flee.
It did not feel good or comforting to know rape was such
an epidemic. She didn't want to be part of this group.
She wanted to be on the outside, normal, without any demons in her past.

She stayed, though. She pulled the scarf tighter
around her head and listened. No one bothered her. No
one asked her to stand up. They all seemed to understand her need for anonymity.

Another woman stood up.

"My name is Karen," she said. "I was raped by my husband."

Clementine started crying. She did it silently, so that
the woman could finish her story. She cried for herself,
and she cried for all of these women. She cried for the
years of touching and making love that she had lost. She
cried for the innocence that none of them would ever regain.

Karen finished her story, but did not sit down. She
walked through the group to Clementine. Sitting down
in the chair beside her, she took Clementine's hand.

"You can talk," she said. "You can say anything here."

Clementine cried harder. She had told Megan and
Alex and Arthur about what happened. But none of
those revelations had eased her guilt and horror. The
rape was still her private scandal. It still ate her up inside.

She looked around the room. The glasses distorted
her vision, but she could make out the kind eyes of this
woman and the others who didn't look at her head-on,
in a show of respect for her privacy.

"I don't think I can," she said.

"That's all right too," Dr. Levinson said, coming to

her other side. "You do whatever feels right. There's no pressure."

But there was pressure. Clementine could feel it inside her head, pounding, begging her to release it. She wanted so badly to speak, to spit out this awful legacy He had left inside her and be rid of it, finally.

She stood up. Her legs shook, and Karen stood up beside her. She held Clementine's hand and guided her to the front of the group. Then she let go, and Clementine was standing alone.

She looked at their faces. They were all mirror images of hers, beautiful but tragic, scarred on the inside. She opened her mouth, but nothing came out. The tears still slid down her cheeks.

Dr. Levinson came and stood beside her. Then, as if they could read her mind, feel the sense of isolation that had haunted her since Him, all of the women stood up and came to her, touching her with soft, safe hands. They moved in close, forming a shield around her. She could hear them crying too.

"It was so long ago," she said. "It shouldn't matter."

"It matters," Dr. Levinson said. "It matters more than anything."

"Oh, God." Clementine felt as if she couldn't breathe, as if all of the air had been sucked out of the room. But arms rose tight around her, and it was as if they were carrying oxygen. She gulped at it.

In her mind, she turned and saw His face. She could even smell Him. She tried to run, but she was frozen. He touched her, stabbed her, violated her, and she couldn't move. She cried out. It was like living it again. Her memories were so strong, it was like being raped not once, but thousands of times.

"He raped me," she said. She looked up through her tears. The women were all there, with moist eyes that *knew*. They were there with her, in the alley. Not even Megan and Alex could offer her that.

"He raped me," she said again. And again. "He raped me. He raped me."

She felt His hands on her, those cold, sick hands. She could feel the dampness of the ground beneath her back, the jabbing pain in her head as she slammed it against the concrete, and His penis ramming inside her.

"He took my life away," she said. "He took away all of my courage. He made me so weak, so small."

She was sobbing, and the women held her.

"It was in New York. I walked down the stairs of an old building, and He was there." She told her story, not leaving out any details for fear they would turn away. No one turned away. She still felt His hands until the very end, when gradually they loosened their grip and were replaced by female hands, soothing her.

She raised her head. "I was raped."

Dr. Levinson moved in front of her, took her chin in her hand.

"Yes, you were raped. He did this to you. You were the victim. You didn't do anything wrong."

Clementine dropped her head on the doctor's shoulder. She felt exhausted and empty. The doctor walked her back to a chair and sat her down. The women were still there, wrapping her in warmth.

"Mine was in an alley too," one woman said.

"I was stabbed, just like you," another one said.

"I didn't go to the police, either," another said. "I knew they'd never find him."

Clementine looked at them. Her cheeks were still wet with tears, but she smiled. For the first time in a long time, she really smiled.

• • •

Alex tried alphabetization, color-coordinated folders, and occasionally even ESP as possible filing systems. None of them worked. Here she was, a college graduate with a master's degree in business, heading up two offices of brokers in London and San Francisco, and she couldn't even handle the simple task of finding the file she needed when she needed it. Wasn't it true that geniuses like Einstein and Edison were helpless and incompetent when it came to everyday problems? It was a comforting thought.

She shoved the paperwork aside and called in her secretary to handle the mess. She had enough to do to get ready for her annual visit to the dreary city the following week without worrying about paper organization, as well. Actually, now that the nightmare with Brent was over and she'd managed to pull herself at least partly back together, her time in England had vastly improved. In the past couple of years, she'd made close to a dozen good friends and grown more accustomed to living in London half the year.

She owed most of her recent ease with the city to Kate Bradshaw. Kate was warm and witty, and the two of them were able to talk about anything. Alex had told her more about Brent than she'd let on even to Megan and Clementine. Kate was just one of those people who knew how to listen, but not advise; sympathize, but not pity.

Every weekend, Kate guided her through parts of the city only the locals knew about, and out through the still unspoiled countryside. It took time, but eventually Alex developed a taste for the idiosyncrasies of England: the London pomp and tradition, the unassuming warmth of the sailors in Devon, the history attached to almost every place and landmark—so unlike the unhaunted, lookalike minimarkets and tract homes in California. This year, she even had seats for Wimbledon.

Mostly, though, London was enjoyable because Alex felt a rush of adrenaline every day she went to the office. She had started with nothing; no clients of her own, no office rapport with the staff, who were barely keeping their heads above water, and she had made a name for herself and the company. *She* had done it. Brent had given her the ball, and she'd run with it. She'd worked with the advertisers to produce a new sure-shot logo and slogan. She'd chosen the new offices—in a Victorian building downtown with surprisingly modern equipment—and had overseen the decorator's use of neutral paints and fabrics and rich cherrywood furniture. She'd retrained each and every broker zealously, until she was certain they were all calling her a slave driver behind her back. And she'd pulled and prodded and cajoled all of Rock Solid's clients, wining and dining them until the firm's reputation for friendly service and sound, profitable investments grew and word of mouth took over for her.

Yes, she had done it. She was at the pinnacle of her career. It had been two and a half years since Brent had walked in and out of her life. It seemed like forever ago, yet the memory was as fresh as today's news. She fought the heartache the only way she knew how, with work. She came in early and went home late. She filled her weekends with paperwork. She would have liked to say that she was always either too busy or too exhausted to think about him, but that wasn't true. Whenever she had a spare moment, he still crept into her mind.

Peace had not come yet. Not completely. Oh, she could laugh again, enjoy herself now and then. But there was always a darkness around the edges, a melancholy tinge to her smile. Even when she woke up and didn't think of Brent right off, when she found other men again, the kind who thrilled her body but never penetrated her mind, even then she was not the same. She'd had a glimpse of what love could be, and the vision haunted her. She tried to seal off the pain the way she used to, in an airtight compartment she had no access to, but the memory of Brent was stronger than that.

Still, she went on, focusing on what she was good at: work. She could at least push Brent out of her mind during the day. Dick Collins, the current vice president, was due to retire soon, and despite their history, Alex thought Brent would give her the job. She had earned it. And Brent wasn't the type to let his personal life interfere with business.

Her secretary returned, carrying the employee guideline changes Brent wanted to make and portions of the latest inch-thick stock analysis. Alex thanked her and immediately took out the European stock figures. Mencol Pharmaceuticals was still inching up, just as she had predicted. Her clients would be pleased. Bradbury and Sons was down another point, but she was sure that was only part of a temporary slide that would end when Eurotech's takeover bid was leaked.

The intercom buzzed, and Alex picked up the phone.

"Miss Waterdell here to see you."

Alex rolled her eyes. Not again.

"Fine. Send her in."

A moment later, Maxine, dressed to the hilt in a slim navy skirt and tight-fitting white sweater, swished in. Her nails were red, as usual, ten little daggers, and the dark kohl lining her eyes reminded Alex of Cleopatra, or a raccoon.

"Yes, Maxine. What can I do for you?"

Maxine sat in the chair opposite her, taking her time to cross her legs and straighten the sleeves of her sweater before speaking.

"I hear you're going to London again," she said at last. Her husky voice belonged in an old movie, Alex thought, not in a committee boardroom. Again, she wondered what Brent was thinking by keeping her on staff, no matter what her business talents.

"I always go to London this time of year, Maxine. You should know that by now."

Maxine pushed a straight lock of hair behind her ear. "Of course. Of course. And is Brent . . . I mean, Mr. Gibbons joining you?"

"No. I don't think so. Why?"

"No reason. Just curious." Maxine leaned toward the desk and toyed with Alex's crystal paperweight. Did she never tire of drawing these encounters out? Alex wondered. It was like something from a heroic comic strip, overdrawn, overplayed, with the villainess taunting her prey and then storming out on a great exit line that left the reader salivating for the conclusion tomorrow. The only problem was, Alex refused to be taunted. And that drove Maxine crazy.

"Is that all?" Alex asked. "I have a lot of work to do."

"Just one more thing," Maxine said, standing up. "I thought you should know that Dick Collins announced his retirement today. He'll be stepping down in six months. And I have it on the strictest confidence that I'm as good as sitting in his chair."

"You can't be serious," Alex said, forgetting her vows of nonchalance and jumping out of her chair. "Brent would never give you the VP's job. I'm the only one who could take over for Dick."

Maxine threw her head back and laughed, enjoying the game much more when Alex was a full-bodied player.

"My goodness, we are a little jealous, aren't we? As a matter of fact, *Alexandra*, while you've been off on your little sojourns to England, I've been gathering the largest portfolio in this company. I've been here longer than you, worked harder, and come further. You really do overestimate your own abilities."

Alex walked to the window and tried to calm herself. Losing control would do no good. Besides, Maxine was only bluffing. She turned around.

"We'll just wait and see what Brent decides."

"Yes. I guess we will. But isn't it too bad that you're going to be all the way in London while I'm here, with Brent, every day."

Maxine drew the words out slowly, taunting her.

"Look, Maxine, you can use your feminine wiles on Brent all you want. That's not going to get you the job. He never lets his personal life affect the business. And I know for a fact that he's not going to leave his wife for you or anyone else."

Maxine's eyes widened, then she laughed again. "Can it be you haven't heard? For some reason, I thought you and Brent were closer than that. He told me first thing."

"Told you what?"

"That he and Carlotta are separated, of course. They filed for divorce ages ago. It should be final in three months."

Alex stood still and breathless. She felt nothing, not surprise nor horror nor anger. Just pure emptiness. Then, as if her life had become the script for a nighttime soap, the door opened and Brent walked in. It had been ages since he'd come to her office. He avoided her just as she avoided him, giving her messages through secretaries and memos, reminding her of the childish fights she and Megan used to have.

As she looked at him now, she saw that the lines around his eyes and mouth were more pronounced than she remembered, but otherwise he was tan and healthy-looking. Just as they had after he'd left her in her London flat, the emotions rushed into her stomach like an unexpected flood. She still loved him. How could she, after all this time, still love him? What an unbelievably idiotic thing to feel. Her head spun like a record on high speed. He and Carlotta were separated. Separated. Separated . . .

"Here you are," he said, talking not to her but to Maxine. He smiled at her the way he once smiled at Alex, and her blood went cold. *No. Please no.*

"Ready for lunch?" he asked.

"Of course, Brent," Maxine said. "I've just been wishing Alex a safe trip."

"That's right," Brent said. "I'd almost forgotten. But then again, Alex is so efficient, I hardly have to worry about anything when she's around."

He smiled at her for only a moment, without a hint of intimacy, then the two of them started for the door.

"Brent," Alex said. She had to stop him, had to say something. He turned around, and their eyes met. She knew instantly that the hunger he'd once felt for her was gone; his eyes were calm and cool, and they devastated her more than any insult could. For so long, she'd fooled herself into thinking she was over him. Now, in less than five minutes, he'd pulled her back to the starting blocks.

"Yes?"

She found her courage. "Maxine tells me you and Carlotta are getting a divorce. I wanted to say how sorry I am."

She wasn't sure, but she thought the air went out of him for a moment, that his shoulders sagged. When he spoke, though, he was the same as always.

"Thank you. It hasn't been easy."

"Especially not for Peter, I imagine."

Maxine tugged on his arm, but Brent continued looking at Alex. It was clear to her then how many unspoken words were left between them. They had so much unfinished business, and she doubted if they would ever resolve it all. It was so unfair that life was like that, that there weren't solid endings with all the loose ends tied up, like in the movies. Life had too many frayed edges.

She thought he might get angry at her for prying where she no longer had any right to pry, but instead he spoke softly.

"I realized not too long ago that I can't live my life for

my son. He's twenty now, in college. Even though I know this upsets him, it will not ruin his life. I think it would have ruined mine to stay with a woman I didn't love."

"Well, I'm starving," Maxine said, opening the door and breaking the spell. Brent nodded and followed her out. He turned around once more, however, when Maxine was out of earshot.

"I couldn't leave back then," he said, his eyes searching Alex's. "I thought I owed it to Peter. I . . ."

She shook her head, struggling to control her shivering. She hated him and loved him so powerfully, for a moment those two emotions were the same thing.

"You don't have to explain it to me," she said, her voice breaking. "It's not me you're leaving her for."

With every last bit of willpower she had, she turned her back on him. A moment later, the door clicked closed. Alex hunched forward, wrapping her arms around her stomach as if Brent had just taken his best shot in her gut. When she had been with him in London, she'd felt young and inexperienced. Now she felt incredibly old. She walked to the window and looked out. She couldn't cry anymore. She'd gotten out all the tears in those months after he'd left. This was worse, though, this emptiness, this lack of all hope. Everything she did mattered so little. She couldn't make him love her again. She couldn't turn back time. And she couldn't love someone new; Brent had spoiled her by being everything she wanted.

A few minutes later, she saw his car speed out of the underground parking lot, its two occupants seated much too close together to be considered only business associates.

In a flash, as if someone had flipped the switch to her emotions, Alex whirled around. She grabbed the nearest thing she could find, the crystal paperweight Maxine's slimy hands had touched, and threw it across the room. It shattered beautifully.

# CHAPTER
## 21

*TWO WEEKS AFTER HIS DIVORCE WAS FINAL,* Brent asked Maxine to marry him. Still in London at the time, Alex received the wedding invitation in the mail. She was surprised by the tears that stung her eyes when she picked up the cream-color envelope. It was not her sadness that shocked her, but the fact that she could cry again. She seemed to have everything backward, acting stoic and untouched when she should be devastated, and crying when the pain should be long gone.

She stared at the envelope for a long time before opening it. This would seal things somehow, take Brent away from her completely once she read the words. Hating herself for her weakness, she tore it open.

Brent Gibbons and Maxine Waterdell request the honor of your presence at their wedding on . . .

She would go. Of that much she was certain. She would take Jackson. She would dance and drink and show everyone, including herself, that she could handle this. She would be Alexandra Holmes again, strong and steady. And if it hurt, well, then, it would hurt. As Jackson had said, sometimes you have to come out of the clouds and get dirty.

The ceremony was to be held October 18 at the Fairmont Hotel in San Francisco. Two days after Alex returned from London. One week before the vice president's position opened. Maxine had planned well, the snake.

Alex resisted the urge to tear the invitation into a dozen pieces and instead taped it to the refrigerator door as she was supposed to.

"Oh, Brent," she said softly, wiping away the last of her tears. "You never really gave me a chance, did you?"

Kate Bradshaw knocked on the door then, and Alex let her in.

"Ready to go, love?" Kate asked, a picnic basket in her hand. They had planned another day in the country, this time along the coast in Norfolk County or Essex; Kate hadn't decided which yet. The sight of Kate, wearing a rain slicker and a smile, brightened Alex's gloom. She hadn't had such a good woman friend since Megan and Clementine. Kate was someone she could confide in, do in men with, laugh and carry on with. She almost filled the void created since Megan and Clementine had drifted away. Almost.

Alex grabbed her raincoat, and they headed for the door. "Brent is getting remarried," she said.

Kate looked at her for a moment, then squeezed her shoulder. "You told me a few weeks ago you thought it was possible."

"Yes. But I hoped I was wrong."

Alex locked her apartment door, and they headed down the hallway.

"You know I'm here for you," Kate said.

Alex smiled. She did know that. Despite her lack of success with men, she had been inordinately lucky with her women friends. She could only hope that some day, some day soon, that would be enough to make her happy again.

"Do you think life is fair?" she asked Kate.

Kate tilted her head to the side, looking at her quizzically. "Well, I don't think I've ever really thought about it before."

"I think about it all the time." It was raining hard when they got outside, and they ran to Kate's car and got in quickly. Once they were settled, Alex said, "I wonder if there's a scorecard and everything evens out in the end. It has to, don't you think?"

Kate brushed out her wet hair and put the key in the ignition.

"No, it doesn't have to. You've got this crazy sense of right and wrong and cosmic justice that just isn't plausible. What about starving children in Ethiopia? Men forced to fight wars they don't believe in in the Middle East? How do you explain the fairness of being dealt a life like that?"

Alex shook her head. "I don't."

"We all have to make do with what we're given," Kate said. "Nothing's fair."

"But I hate that!" Alex said as Kate started the car. They drifted out into the London Saturday traffic. "I want so much. A career, a man to love, friends, a home. I want everything."

"Oh, Alex." Kate laughed. "Even you can't have everything, and you know it. Why not let Brent go, and appreciate what you do have?"

"How do I just let go? I don't understand how that happens."

"You wish Brent and his new wife well. You spend more time with me instead of holing up in your apartment when you're depressed. You go on. It's time, you know."

Alex was silent. She knew Kate was right, but her heartache over Brent was the only part of him she had left. Letting go of it meant letting go of him. Her greatest fear was that she would never love again, never be inspired to feel as much as he had made her feel, both good and bad.

"Look, you like what you do, don't you?" Kate asked.

"Yes."

"And you've got good friends and family?"

"Yes."

"You make plenty of money, right?"

"Right."

"And you don't intentionally try to hurt people?"

"No."

"Well, then, stop all of this damn philosophizing and start being happy. Life is too short to worry about choices and fairness and love that got away. You're wasting your time thinking about life when you could be happily living it instead. Just remember that you're better off than most and enjoy what you do have."

Alex stared at the other people sitting in traffic, their faces grim and determined. She wondered what they had, and what they didn't have. It was a curse, she decided, this human ability to think and analyze. She watched a pigeon sail over the cars, heading for the park, for the old men who fed it. Oh, to be that bird, she thought. To fly and eat and sleep and never know there was anything more.

Kate squeezed her hand as they finally left the confines of London and headed out to the country.

"Do the best you can, Alex," she said. "That's all any of us can do."

Alex nodded and tried not to think anymore.

•    •    •

Jackson and Alex sat on the groom's side of the aisle. Brent stood before the altar, not smiling. He looked stern, as he always did, but the tightness around his jaw was gone. Although very few people would know it, Alex could tell he was happy. For some unknown, strange-as-hell reason, Maxine made him happy.

The hotel garden was lovely. Yellow roses and white orchids lined the aisle and adorned the tables. The tent above the dance floor and dining tables was soft yellow, as were the tablecloths and napkins. Very classy. Definitely Brent's doing.

Maxine walked in to "The Wedding March" wearing a yellow tea-length chiffon dress. The only touches of her overdone personality were her darkly lined eyes and the thick gold bracelets jangling on her arm. Alex could hear them, like bells on a cow's neck, as she walked.

The ceremony was brief and efficient, the kiss perfunctory. Alex did not falter as she watched them. She did not cry or scream or cling to Jackson for support. She watched Brent smile at his new wife, and she said a silent good-bye to him. He had made his choice, and Alex had made hers. She would try to be happy. She would work and date and see her friends and make that enough for her. And if another man came along who interested her, she wouldn't be afraid to try.

She held her head up and felt, for the moment, remarkably good and strong, as in the old days. Then the couple turned around, their vows completed, and Maxine's eyes were triumphant. Whether she was thinking about Brent or snaring the vice presidency, Alex didn't know, but she couldn't meet Maxine's gaze.

Later, while the wedding party had their pictures taken, Jackson and Alex sat at a corner table drinking champagne.

"Does it hurt?" Jackson asked softly.

Alex started, and Jackson smiled. "Of course it was Brent you fell for. It couldn't have been anybody ordinary, and besides, you can't hide your eyes."

She reached out and loosed his hair from beneath his collar. He'd kept it shoulder-length for over a year, and the curls at his nape were irresistible.

"I loved him," she said. Jackson nodded, and she sipped her champagne. "Losing him has been the hardest thing I've ever had to deal with. I can still feel him sometimes, even now." She paused for a moment. "It's hard to think that what we had meant nothing to him, that he would leave Carlotta for Maxine and not for me."

"Maybe you meant more to him than you think."

"No. He married Maxine, after all."

"Men marry for all sorts of reasons, Alex, some of which haven't the slightest thing to do with love."

Alex hesitated a moment, then smiled at him. "I'll be all right," she said. "I really think I will. I mean, watching him marry another woman is the worst it can get, right? It's got to be downhill from here."

They laughed, and Alex kept her gaze on his face.

"What are you thinking?" she asked. "You've been quiet all day."

He scratched the stubble of his beard. He'd worn a beard for two months, shaved it off, and now was trying to grow it back again. It seemed he didn't know what to do with himself.

"I'm thinking lots of things," he said. "I'm thinking about growing older, marriage, wedding vows that disintegrate before your eyes."

"I shouldn't have asked you to come with me."

"Nonsense," he said, holding her hand. "I always love being your date."

She smiled. "Megan's doing much better now. She and Joey see each other most every day, I hear."

"I'm glad. I've always wanted her to be happy."

"Joey even called me in London once, to ask what he should get her for her birthday. He didn't think she was quite ready for an engagement ring yet, but he wanted something special. He really loves her."

Jackson drank some champagne and sat back. "She's thirty-one years old now. God. I'll always remember her as twenty-one. Young and full of dreams."

"She's still full of dreams," Alex said. "Just different ones."

After they'd sat there glumly for half an hour, their minds in the past instead of the present, dwelling on endings instead of beginnings, Jackson hoisted Alex out of her seat and they danced through a complete set. They held each other close on the slow songs, with the tenderness of a friendship undaunted through years and crises, and they cleared a wide path around them on the fast dances, forgetting temporarily their heartaches and aching feet and sore backs and the fact that they could never be kids again. They sat down exhausted when the band took a break.

"I haven't danced like that for years," Alex said. Her bun had unfastened, and she swished her hair around her head.

"Me, either. I can't breathe."

She laughed and fetched them each more champagne. When she returned, they were both breathing easier.

"Tell me," Jackson said, "have you talked to Clementine lately?"

Alex shook her head. "Why did I know you'd ask me that?"

"I don't know," he said, not looking at her.

"Well, I do. It's because every time I talk to Clementine, she asks about you. And every time I talk to you, you ask about her. What is it with you two?"

"She asks about me?" Jackson said, forgetting once again his daily decision to forget her, the decision that failed miserably every night when he went to bed alone.

"Look at you," Alex said, laughing. "If only Clem knew you're putty in her hands."

"She does know. She's afraid of hurting Megan."

"It seems to me that Megan's doing fine on her own now. She's even talking about getting her own place."

"Then why doesn't Clementine make a move?" Jackson asked, sitting forward.

"Maybe she's waiting for you to do it."

"I've already done it. Over and over again, I've let her know how I feel about her."

Alex looked around until she saw Brent. Maxine was by his side, basking in the glow of his love. Alex closed her eyes.

When she opened them again, Jackson was watching her. Her loyalties were split; she wanted happiness for both Megan and Clementine, with a minimum of pain. But the truth was, love was a rare commodity, hard to find and harder to keep. One of them should be lucky enough to have it.

"Life is short, Jack," she said. She downed the rest of her champagne, then pulled him to his feet. "Too short not to go after what you want. Clementine is a busy woman. She probably doesn't have time to get in touch with you."

"Maybe."

"Oh, come on. Stop keeping count of how many moves you've made. Don't you understand how precious love is? Haven't you paid attention to my life at all? Don't be a fool and throw your shot away. If you want to be with her, make another move. And if that fails, make another one. Keep making them until she's in your arms, and then never let her go. Make love enough for all of us."

He smiled, the smile that took women's breath away, and she laughed.

"It's a good thing I've built up an immunity to you, Mr. Hollywell. Otherwise, you'd have three best friends in love with you. And then what would you do?"

He shook his head. "Good God. A choice between the three of you. I think I'd rather die first."

She tugged him onto the dance floor as the band began playing again. "Or one of us would kill you," she said, and smiled.

• • •

Alex stood at the back of the committee room, nodding to the top-level management suits, as she called them, as they entered. They took their seats one by one, ten men and two women, all stiff as cardboard. Alex glanced down at herself and was jolted to find she looked just like them. It was her secret that inside she was still Alex, the crazy, loud-mouthed girl from Sausalito. She wondered if they had secrets too.

She had thrown up twice that morning, but it had done no good. She still felt queasy. A little voice inside of her kept saying, *If I don't get the vice presidency, I can't go on.* But, of course, that wasn't true. She'd have to go on. What alternative did she have?

Maxine and Brent entered together, last. Even from the back of the room, Alex could see Maxine's ring glimmering in the light. A four-carat diamond. Her red nails reflected in it nicely.

"Thank you all for coming," Brent said, standing at the head of the long, narrow table while Maxine took the seat to his right. Alex usually sat there, and Maxine knew it. Maxine smirked when Alex sat down at the opposite end.

"As you undoubtedly know," Brent went on, "Maxine and I were married last week."

Congratulations were issued all around. Brent beamed, and Alex saw again how happy he was. That was what she wanted for him, she realized. Her bitterness was slowly being replaced by the admiration and respect she'd felt for him in the beginning.

"Thank you very much," he said. "It's been a whirlwind courtship, and I'm afraid I've let some of the business slide, but I'm ready to change that now."

Alex looked away from him and stared straight ahead, but she didn't see the boardroom. She saw instead her bedroom in her parents' house in Sausalito, and she was sitting on the bed with a math book in her hands. Megan was reading a novel by the window, and Clementine was digging through Alex's albums. It was a warm Saturday afternoon, that magical time between school days, when homework was done and parents were busy and the hours until Monday morning stretched out deliciously like saltwater taffy. No responsibilities, no boyfriends yet, no businesses to run. Just three girls deciding how to spend an afternoon.

"Let's go swimming," Clementine said.

"No, too cold," Alex said. "How about bowling?"

Megan shook her head. "I hate bowling."

They stared at one another, then Clementine smiled wickedly.

"Let's steal toilet paper from the diner and decorate Johnny Piedmont's house with it."

They all agreed instantly that it was a perfect idea. As they walked out of the bedroom, Alex glanced back at her math book, at the formulas she had to learn, but she didn't care. She had yet to find anything better than being with her friends, getting into trouble and sharing secrets and laughing until their stomachs hurt. No boyfriend or perfect test grade had ever matched it.

She'd understood more then, Alex thought, about priorities and the meaning of life than she did now. She'd always assumed she was getting smarter as time went by, but now she wondered if she'd had it all figured out early on, then had forgotten the most important parts, like an old woman losing her memory.

She remembered how Clementine and Megan had pulled her out of her bedroom, linking their arms with hers, their sweet voices drifting around her. She'd known then that she was the luckiest girl alive. She'd known their friendship would last forever, and that was all she needed.

Alex focused on Brent again and thrust her chin out. Part of that girl was still inside of her, thank God. She hadn't forgotten everything. She didn't need Brent or this promotion. She was older and more cynical than she had been on that day so many years ago, but there were still good friends and Saturday afternoons in her life. Other things still made her happy. This didn't mean everything. It didn't mean . . .

"First of all," Brent went on, "as you all know, Dick Collins retired last week. That leaves open the position of vice president. It's a hell of a job, as Dick will tell you, but for some reason, most of you want it, anyway."

The room was silent, the pencil scratches suddenly stopped, and faces went red with embarrassment. Brent looked at each of them, and his expression did not change when he got to Alex.

"I'm aware of the rumors going around. I know about the back-stabbing tactics you've all used to try to outdo each other. I'm not saying it's wrong. Precisely the opposite. A stockbrokerage has to be devious and cutthroat to a fault. I just want you to understand that I am not an outsider here."

He paused to look around the room again. "My decision is based on many factors," he said. "Experience, time at the company, track record, management skills. I have known all of you for years, watched all of you in action. I'm sure none of you will question my decision or my ability to do what's best for this company."

He stared directly at Alex then, and she knew. She leaned back in her chair and tried to breathe.

"Maxine Gibbons is your new vice president," he said.

A murmur ran down the table. Alex watched Maxine jump up and throw her arms around her husband. A few of the suits looked at Alex sympathetically, but she didn't see them. One by one, they all congratulated Maxine, commended Brent on his judgment, as if they could do anything else, and left the room to gossip, no doubt, about how the boss had let his penis rule his mind.

Maxine hugged Brent again, then turned to Alex, still

sitting in her chair. Alex knew she was supposed to take this gracefully, but her legs wouldn't move, her mouth could form no smile.

"Oh, Alex," Maxine said. "I'm sorry. I really am. But I am more qualified." She laughed and kissed her husband. "Can I go see my new office?" she asked him.

"Of course. I'll be along in a minute."

Maxine practically danced out of the room. Brent walked the length of the table and sat down beside Alex. This close, she could smell his familiar cologne.

"I don't deny," he said, "that part of my decision was made because she is my wife."

Alex forced herself to look at him. "At least you admit that."

"I have to go home with her every night, Alex. You know Maxie. She'd make my life a living hell if I didn't give her this. Besides, she can handle the job. She's a good worker."

Alex looked away. "You love her, don't you?"

"Yes. I love her. She's softer than she appears, more vulnerable. I loved you once too. Unfortunately, at the wrong time in my life."

Alex shook her head. "I always thought of you as the greatest businessman alive. You put the company above everything. You were my hero."

Brent smiled. He reached for her hand, but she pulled away.

"I still put the company first," he said. "You may not believe this because you're hurt now, but the VP job is shit work. Paper pushing, hassles, phone calls. You sit at that desk twelve, thirteen hours a day getting an ulcer and clogged arteries. Yes, it's more money. More prestige. But it would stifle you, Alex. I need you here and in London, working. You have too much talent to waste."

"And Maxine doesn't?"

"Let's just say I'd like her close to home."

"I never thought you'd mix your personal life with your professional one. I was so sure of it."

He shrugged. "Sometimes the two should be mixed. There is room for both. And whether you believe it or not, this is the best decision for the company."

"Maybe," Alex said. "But certainly not the best decision for me."

"Come on, Alex. You've got to know by now, after all these years in this business, that there's more to success than your name on the door and a big desk."

She stood up. The anger rumbled in her stomach and head, and she walked quickly to the door. She was almost out before the bitterness exploded. Pulling back her arm, she threw her fist against the wall as hard as she could. She cried out when the bones in her knuckles split, and pain shot up her arm like a cannonball.

"My God! What the hell are you doing?" Brent said, hurrying to her side.

She glared at him. "Taking it like a man."

# CHAPTER
## 22

J ACKSON SAT LOW IN HIS CAR WITH A NEWS-
paper in his hands, ready to cover his face if need be.
He'd been sitting there for two hours, while the sun set
behind him, waiting for his chance. He'd seen Joey arrive an hour earlier, and by the look of his suit and tie,
Jackson had assumed he was taking Megan out. Dammit,
he wished he'd do it already.

Driving down to Los Angeles was the most spontaneous thing he'd done in years. One minute he was sitting
in his studio, a paintbrush in his hand, trying without
success to start a new painting, and the next he was in his
car, heading down Highway 101, Alex's words of "Life is
short" and "Make love enough for all of us" ringing in
his ears.

He didn't have a plan in mind at first. He figured he'd
just knock on her door and sweep Clementine off her
feet. As he got closer to Malibu, though, the doubts re-
surfaced. What if she didn't want to be swept off her
feet? What if she didn't want him at all? What if Megan
was there?

Despite all the questions, he kept driving south. During the past eight months, since he'd gone to Brent and
Maxine's wedding with Alex, he'd thought of little else

but Clementine. She was a cancer growing in him, multiplying, feeding on itself, and sapping his energy and strength. Finally, he couldn't take it anymore. Alex was right. He had to stop counting moves and give it another shot. Clementine was worth it.

Finally arriving on the beach at six o'clock, Jackson had convinced the guard to let him into the exclusive community. Now here he was, hiding in his car like a fugitive, praying that Joey and Megan would leave, praying that if they did, he'd have the guts to knock on the door.

Fifteen minutes later, the front door to Clementine's house opened, and Megan and Joey walked out. Jackson covered his face with the newspaper, but peeked over the top. In the glow of the red and blue garden lights, Megan looked lovely. She was wearing a gray skirt and sweater and was laughing at something Joey had said. Jackson was struck by how different she looked now than when they were married. She moved easily, comfortably; her smile was not forced. She had tried harder than anything to be happy with him, just as he had with her, but it had always been an effort, whether she wanted to admit it or not.

They stepped into Joey's car, and Jackson slunk down farther when they drove by. He waited until they had vanished down the street before he sat up. The coast was clear. The house stood a hundred feet away. Clementine's car was in the driveway. The only thing that stood between him and the woman he wanted more than anything was his nerve.

He opened the car door and threw the newspaper down on the seat. He'd come all this way for a reason, and he wasn't going to back out now. He'd make one final move, and if Clementine didn't follow his lead, then he'd give up for good.

He walked toward the house, glancing down twice at his jeans and flannel shirt to make sure he looked the best he could after half a day on the road. As he strode up the concrete walkway to the door, he studied the perfectly tended planters of wildflowers and ice plants on either side, trying not to think. Finally, he reached the front door, took a deep breath, and knocked.

Clementine heard the knocking from where she sat outside on the patio. She hoped it wasn't a neighbor wanting an evening of wine and talking. She wasn't up to it. She'd gone to another group counseling session that day. It was exhausting, all the talking and crying. In the end, though, she always walked out feeling lighter than she had in years. Every time another woman spoke of feeling dirty or guilty about being raped, she thought, Thank God someone else feels that way. Every time she left a session, she thought, I'm getting better. I'm healing.

The counseling sessions had gotten her thinking. So many years ago, in the Saks Fifth Avenue modeling contest, she had vowed to change women's lives. Maybe she could. At least, some women's lives. Some day, when she was stronger and ready to go public, she could use her celebrity status to help get more funding for rape victims. She could help teach policemen and doctors and attorneys to treat rape victims with more respect and understanding. It was just an idea, but it gave her something to work toward. She had to get well enough to help other women, to do something important.

The knock came again at her front door. She walked to the entry, pausing to glance at herself in the mirror. She was wearing a white terry cloth robe and no makeup. Far from glamorous, but it would have to do. She opened the door.

They stared at each other for a long time. Clementine had imagined him standing on her doorstep so often, just as he was, handsome and perfect, she wondered if this was a dream. Once Megan and Joey had started dating seriously, she'd wanted to call him, but her fingers never completed his number. What if she got hurt again? What if he was with someone else? What if he'd already given up on her? What if they got together and she couldn't make love with him, couldn't even let him touch her? What would he do then?

Yet here he was. Standing before her as gorgeous and intoxicating as ever. She clutched the collar of her robe closer to her chest.

"I wasn't expecting anyone," she said.

"May I come in?" he asked.

She nodded and stepped aside. Jackson looked around as he walked into the living room. His gaze was drawn by the French doors at the far end, framing the fluorescent waves of the ocean like a perfect picture.

"This is some place," he said, running his fingers along the back of a hand-carved oak chair.

"It's an investment," Clementine said. Usually, she let people think that she loved the house, but with Jackson, it was important to let him know she wasn't comfortable with the opulence and expense. "My agent kept telling me to settle somewhere, get a tax write-off, and he found me this place."

Jackson walked to the patio doors and stared at the ocean. The roar of the surf was louder than he expected. He wondered how Clementine slept at night.

He turned around and found her leaning against the doorway to the kitchen, watching him.

"Why didn't you call me when Megan and Joey started dating seriously?" he asked abruptly. "I thought that was the reason we couldn't be together."

She walked to the couch and sat down, fidgeting with her robe. "I don't know. I was scared, I guess."

He sat down in the chair across from her. "Of what?"

She forced her fingers to stop their nervous fiddling, forced herself to look at him. "Of being hurt again. I thought I was in love with Connor, and then the whole relationship fell apart before my eyes. And then—then New York changed me. It made me see the bad side of things, the darkness. I couldn't get involved with anyone. I made a pact with myself to be independent and to keep my guard up. But with you, it always seems to fall back down again."

They were quiet for a long time, the silence broken only by the surf pounding in and out.

"I can't get you out of my mind, Clementine," he said at last, staring at her so intensely, she felt a red-hot heat traveling up her body. "I never could. Not from the first moment I saw you."

"Me too," she whispered, almost as if her strength were gone and she could no longer fight her words. "But that doesn't matter. I don't want this. Can't you see that? It's more than just Megan. There are things you don't know." She looked out to the ocean and toyed again with the frayed edges of her robe.

"Tell me," he said. His voice was urgent, his eyes fixed on her as if they were locked in place. For a moment, she thought she could tell him, but the moment passed.

"It's just me," she said. "I don't want to be hurt. Maybe fate put Megan between us. Maybe it's our destiny never to be together. You have your art and your friends and your home in San Francisco. I'm only a conquest to you, the one woman you haven't been able to get yet. Once I give in, it will be over."

Jackson stood up and paced the floor quickly. It wasn't fair, he thought. Didn't she know this was different? He wasn't like the other men in her life, just as she wasn't simply any woman to him. They both were special. Yet here he was, so close to her, all he had to do was reach out to touch her, and still she kept moving a step away. He whirled around.

"Don't talk to me about fate. We make our own destiny. If we weren't meant to be together, we wouldn't have stayed interested for this long. We each would be with someone else."

"Maybe that would be for the best," she said.

"Don't give me that!" he shouted. "You can't judge me by what Connor or any other man did. You have to give me a chance on my own. What do you want to do? Spend your whole life running because you're too scared to take a risk? That doesn't sound like the Clementine I know."

She looked away. Jackson confused her, jumbled her thoughts and feelings until she felt like only a mass of inert gas with no substance or strength. She wanted him to leave; he was cutting too close to her. More than anything, though, she wanted him to stay.

"I can't take any more risks," she said softly.

Quickly, before she had a chance to move away, he was beside her. He grabbed both of her hands and held them to his lips.

"Look at me, Clementine."

When she kept her eyes averted, he jerked her hands. "Look at me."

She raised her gaze slowly. She didn't want to. With him this close, his breath on her fingertips, his thigh against hers, she knew she wouldn't be able to resist him. His green eyes were intent, fixed on hers.

"I swear to you," he said, "I will never hurt you. I love you. I don't know when it started or how, but I love you. I want to give you the stars and the moon and the Alps and a tropical island all your own. I want to learn every joke so I can make you laugh every day. I want to take care of you, protect you, support you in your career, and be there for you whenever you need me. I want to be everything to you."

Clementine was crying. She pulled her hands from his grasp and held them against his cheeks, stubbly with dark whiskers. Her eyes closed, she ran her fingers along his cheekbones and nose and lips.

"I can't be with you," she said.

"For God's sake, why not?"

She opened her eyes when she felt his tears wet her fingers. She was so tired, so immensely tired. It didn't seem to matter what she said now. She dropped her hands from his face and told him.

"When I was in New York, I had a photo shoot in this old apartment building. We didn't get done until late at night, and I was the last to leave. A man ..." She faltered, and Jackson held her hand. This was like confessing for the first time all over again, like coming clean. She held her head up and continued.

"A man was waiting for me. I think he only intended to rob me, but then that wasn't enough. He pulled me out to the alley. He had a knife. He raped me."

There, she'd said it. Her tears had stopped. She wasn't sad or angry. If anything, she felt light, relieved. The secret was out.

Jackson squeezed her hand tightly, and she looked at his face. He was staring out at the ocean, tears thick on his cheeks. She reached up and wiped them away.

"It doesn't seem so bad now," she said. "Isn't that crazy? This thing has ruled my life for years, and now I tell you and it doesn't seem so terrible. Just this bad thing that happened to me years ago."

He turned to her and cupped her face in his hands. His eyes were crystal clear and mesmerizing. Clementine couldn't have looked away even if she'd wanted to.

"You are the most incredible woman I've ever known," he said.

She shook her head. "I'm not. Most rape victims deal with it and get over it. It took me years just to work up my courage enough to tell other victims I was raped. I don't think I could . . . we could make love. It's been so long, and even the thought of it now makes me uneasy."

His expression became even more tender, more loving. "Do you think I care whether we make love or not? I want to more than anything, but that's not what's important. I want to be with you. That's all I've ever wanted. I want to make sure nothing like that ever happens to you again."

At his words, she felt the past crumble, like ancient, brittle bricks. With Jackson this close, protecting her, she could no longer remember that man's long-ago face. He was just a man, after all, human, too, with strong hands and a weak mind, and he couldn't touch her. Not here.

"I love you," she whispered.

Jackson felt the final part of him click into place. He was complete and whole for the first time, as his mother always said he would be when he found the right woman, his soulmate. She had known much more than he ever gave her credit for. He stared at Clementine, soaking in the beauty of her. Her skin was flawless, like tanned butter, her cheekbones high and refined, her lips a soft swirl of pink. The woman men everywhere longed for. And she was with him.

He leaned forward and kissed her cheek, so softly, it felt like butterfly wings brushing her skin. He kissed her forehead, her eyelids, her nose and chin. Clementine closed her eyes, afraid to open them and break the spell.

Finally, his lips touched hers, and it was just as she'd known it would be. His lips were warm and sweet, and his tongue danced in rhythm with hers. If she let herself, she could drown in him.

She pulled away. "Will you wait? Until I'm ready. I'm afraid to try. Afraid to ruin what we have."

He buried his face in her hair. "I would wait for you forever."

"Don't let go," she said, wrapping her arms around his neck.

"Never." Jackson kissed her face again, reveling in the softness of her skin that he'd only dreamed about. He'd be damned if he'd ever let her go again.

Clementine pulled back only enough to see his face clearly. She still had doubts, about him and definitely about herself, but with him here at last, loving her, how could she resist him? If she didn't try now, wouldn't there always be a space between them, a hesitancy and tension? Wouldn't Jackson always wonder if she'd ever be able to make love with him?

She ran her hand along his arm, feeling the muscles beneath his shirt. He watched her without moving, without even blinking, as if he was afraid that any action would scare her off. She touched his chest, his neck, his ear. He was so perfect.

He reached out slowly and traced her collarbone. His fingers slipped beneath her robe to the warm skin above her breasts, then down around her nipple. He squeezed gently, then harder . . .

"Stop," she said, pulling away. Her skin felt prickly, balancing precariously on the border between pleasure and disgust. She moved to the edge of the couch, hating herself.

"I'm sorry," he said.

She shook her head. The tears came again. She had never in her life cried as much as she had that day.

"It's not you. I just can't. Your fingers felt hard and . . . I can't explain it. You should just go."

He slipped to the floor at her feet and stared up at her, holding her hands tightly.

"Listen to me. I'm never going. Not even if you beg me to. I'm going to stay here and love you and make you forget. And if we never make love, then we never make love. There is no pressure."

"How can you be so good?" she murmured.

He smiled. "Born that way, I guess."

"I'm not easy to get along with," she said. "There's more than just this. I don't cook, I hate television, and I need maximum closet space."

He laughed. "I smell like turpentine, and I like coffee at three in the morning, and I never, ever, wear pajamas to bed."

They both laughed, and Clementine looked down at their fingers, perfectly intertwined.

"I like you, Jackson Hollywell," she said.

"Great. So you want to go steady?"

She laughed again. For the very first time, she knew what it was like to feel true, honest happiness. It wasn't perfect. She still had a long way to go. But one thing she knew for certain, she would never let anything come between them again.

•   •   •

By the time Megan and Joey returned home that night from the Los Angeles Philharmonic concert, Clementine was long gone. She had left a note taped to the refrigerator door.

Needed to get away for a week or two. Just to relax a little. I'll see you when I get home. Don't worry.

Love,
Clem

"That's very strange," Megan said while she made a pot of coffee. "She was so tired today. She said she was going to read over a few scripts and get a tan. I wonder what changed her mind."

"Maybe she got tired of the same old thing," Joey said, loosening his tie. "I suppose making millions for memorizing a few lines can get pretty tedious."

Megan laughed. "I'm going upstairs to change. Help yourself to something in the kitchen if you're hungry."

After she left, Joey wandered around the sterile kitchen. He had always felt especially uncomfortable in this room, with its pictureless walls, impersonal bare counters, and softly humming fluorescent lighting. The cupboards and drawers were stocked with dozens of shiny never-used gadgets, courtesy of Clementine's agent, Will, as a housewarming gift. Come to think of it, Joey thought, Megan and Clementine were rarely in the kitchen at all, except to make coffee or pour a glass of wine. They had the number of every take-out restaurant in town.

After finding the last piece of a store-bought lemon cake in the refrigerator and pouring two cups of coffee, he sat down on the couch. Megan came downstairs a minute later, her skirt and sweater replaced by a loose blue sweat suit. She'd washed off her makeup, and her blond hair was loose around her face. She looked like Megan again; natural, artless, and pure. The woman he loved.

"I hope she's all right," she said, sitting beside him. She blew on the hot coffee before sipping it.

"I'm sure she's fine. Clementine can take care of herself. Besides, there're more important things to think about."

Megan pulled her legs up beneath her. "Such as?"

"Such as us. Such as . . ." He reached into his pants pocket and pulled out a dark blue velvet box. "This."

Megan took the box from him, not sure if her heart was racing from terror, joy, or guilt. She loved Joey. It had taken a long time, much longer than he should have waited, but she was certain she loved him. Yet it wasn't what she'd always imagined. With Jackson, she'd been on center stage, caught in a magical, make-believe world where she drowned in the applause. With Joey, however, she was only in the wings, in the real world of sweat and sets and cue lines. She kept waiting for the sparks when he smiled at her, the gut-wrenching emptiness when he left the room. It didn't seem right somehow, always knowing that Joey would come back.

"What is this?" she whispered.

"Open it."

Joey tried to hide his disappointment behind a smile. He'd been silly to think he could sweep Megan off her feet. He wasn't romantic enough, strong enough, enough like Jackson. Yet this had seemed like the perfect moment. The past few weeks had been wonderful.

Megan's eyes had been focused on him instead of locked in their usual faraway gaze that could only mean she was thinking about Jackson. She'd said she loved him dozens of times, and he finally believed her. He'd picked up five new students for his private music lessons, and his last month's raise at the high school gave him more than enough money to support them. Not on the beach in Malibu of course, but either in his current place or in the home of Megan's choosing. Fate's pieces had fallen into place. He only wished she could see that too.

Megan opened the box slowly. Inside was a small, perfect flower-shape diamond in a simple gold band. It was exactly what she would have chosen if she'd been given the option. And Joey was exactly the person she imagined when she thought of the perfect man to marry. The two of them thought alike, felt alike, laughed alike, even looked alike.

"It's beautiful, Joey," she said.

He smiled, his whole face lighting up like a child's, and some of her doubts faded away.

"May I put it on you?" he asked.

She nodded, not trusting her voice. Tears filled her eyes, tears of joy and sorrow. He lifted her left hand and slid the ring on her third finger.

Still looking down at the ring, he asked, "Megan Hollywell, will you marry me?"

Megan closed her eyes, remembering another proposal, the intensity of her feelings then, the sense of desperation that had accompanied every aspect of her life with Jackson. When she opened her eyes, Joey was staring at the wall, his body stiff while he waited for her answer. She looked down at the ring, a perfect fit on her finger.

"Yes," she said.

He turned to her suddenly, his mouth dropping open as if he'd expected a much different response.

"Say it again."

She laughed. "Yes, I'll marry you."

He hugged her tightly, so happy, and she knew that behind the veil of bittersweet memories and melancholy, she was happy too. A different happy. A contented acceptance. Grown-up and realistic. No fireworks or heart aches. Simply happy about having a man who loved her and would take care of her forever.

"What about eloping?" he asked.

"What?"

"I've got two weeks of vacation coming. We can get our licenses and blood tests secretly, elope, then run off to England for our honeymoon. I've got enough savings to cover it. You've always wanted to go there, and so have I. Think how romantic it would be."

She stared at him, amazed once more at his ability to see through her to her thoughts and needs. Jackson had brought out in her her most intense love and hatred. Joey had always just made her happy. It was crazy that she would ever choose a life with Jackson over one with Joey.

"That sounds heavenly," she said. Joey jumped up and grabbed his jacket off the counter.

"I'm going to start making plans right away. I've been gathering some brochures, just in case you said yes. Not that I was sure you would, of course, but a man can hope, can't he? I'll call a travel agent in the morning and make an appointment for blood tests."

She walked him to the door, his enthusiasm beginning to rub off on her. "You're really going to take me to England?"

He held her face in his hands. "I'd take you around the world if it would make you happy."

"Being with you makes me happy," she said, meaning it.

He smiled again and opened the door. Turning, he picked up her hand and kissed the engagement ring.

"You won't tell anyone, will you? I think we should just call people from Europe and say, 'Oh, by the way, we're married.' "

"Fine with me."

He kissed her again and ran to his car. "I love you Megan," he shouted when he reached it. She laughed and waved. She waited until he had driven off before she closed the door. Picking up her coffee cup, she turned off the lights and walked upstairs.

When she reached her bedroom, she immediately

opened her jewelry case. There on top, as it had been
for the past seven years, was her wedding ring and another engagement ring. The diamond in it was still shiny,
more opulent than the one on her finger, more unlike
her. She rubbed it against her cheek before tucking it
and the wedding ring under the bottom flap, out of
sight.

"Good-bye, Jackson," she whispered. She looked down
at her new ring and thought of Joey and England and
dreams that can magically, like roses beneath winter's
snow, spring back to life.

• • •

Jackson was sitting in a chair at the edge of a sand
dune, facing the light blue ocean. In the past week his
skin had darkened to a deep coffee brown. It had been
Clementine's idea that they run away to Mexico in the
middle of the night, leave the world behind and get to
know each other. He also knew, although she didn't say
it in so many words, that she was scared to death of a
confrontation with Megan.

He dipped his brush into the yellow paint and carefully applied it to the canvas. He had developed a tech-
nique over the last couple of years of working with a
mixture of precision and free-reining creativity. But he
was certain he could have painted this particular piece
blindfolded. He knew exactly what he wanted, every contour and fold. Although the vision had been in him for
years, it had taken Clementine's love to release it.

He heard rustling in the sand behind him, and he
stiffened. The painting was harmless, a testament to old
love, but perhaps Clementine wouldn't understand. Perhaps . . .

Clementine stopped abruptly two feet behind him.
She stared at the picture, still formative but clearly recognizable. The jealous sting lasted for a second, then she
smiled.

"Megan," she said.

He stood up and put his arm around her waist. "Yes,
it's Megan. Please understand. She'll always be a part of
me, through love and guilt. I've wanted to do this for so
long, I needed to, but it was stuck inside of me. And

then, when you finally came to me, I felt free for the first time."

Clementine nodded and inched closer to the painting. It really was beautiful, she thought. With her own portrait, Jackson had captured her mystery. With Alex, he'd shown strength and vitality. But with Megan, he used earth tones, yellows, and golds to bring out her warmth. She turned to him and smiled.

"I think you're the most wonderful man I've ever met." She kissed his lips tenderly, tasting the salt the ocean air had left there.

He ran his fingers through her hair, streaked lighter than ever in the hot sun.

"Do you know how much I love you?" he asked. "Do you have any idea how good it feels to finally be with you? I feel like a soldier coming home from war with the guarantee that he'll never have to leave again."

She looked out at the ocean, paler and more inviting than her own beach at home. The past week had been wonderful, almost perfect. During the day, they walked, combed the beaches, explored cliffs and tide pools. At night, she lay content in Jackson's arms. He hadn't approached her about making love again, and she knew she should be grateful. But so often, listening to his heartbeat, feeling his warm fingers stroke her arm, she had wanted to kiss him passionately, feel his hands on her, make him burn the memories out of her. His last touch on her breasts had been so close to pleasure. Perhaps all she needed was one more push. But always, at the last second, she pulled back, the hesitancy and fear she'd accumulated and honed to unbreakable perfection over the years still more powerful than anything. He'd said he would wait forever. She wondered if that was true.

Still, she was happy. She would be happy anywhere as long as she was with Jackson, but she wished they had chosen somewhere inland, maybe in the country. She missed the shadow of trees, the soothing smell of dirt, wearing sweaters in the evening.

"I'm afraid all of this will end," she whispered.

He stood behind her and laid his chin on her shoulder. "I won't let it."

She smiled and tilted her head back, pressing her cheek against his. "My hero."

"Always."

Two days later, when Jackson had finished Megan's portrait, Clementine stood staring at it in the living room of their rented cottage.

"What are you going to do with it?" she asked.

"I'm not sure." He sat down on the couch. "On the one hand, I'd love to get all three of your portraits together and start a gallery of my own. 'The Women I've Loved,' I'd call it."

"What an ego."

He laughed. "But I'd also like Megan to have it. I'm just afraid she'd take it the wrong way."

"What way?"

"I don't know. Maybe as a sign that there's still a chance with us. I don't want to hurt her again."

"She seems happy with Joey."

"Maybe you're right," Jackson said. "I'll play it by ear. I'm just glad to finally have it out of my system and on canvas. Now, enough of that. Come here, wench," he said, opening his arms.

"I'm a wench now, am I?" She fell into his arms on the couch, laughing. She thought briefly of how strange life was, how a little bit of love overshadowed a lifetime of pain, how nothing but this moment with this man was real to her.

•   •   •

Clementine and Jackson spent two full weeks in Mexico, laughing, drinking margaritas, dancing to the music of mariachi bands, and waking up to watch the dawn. He told her everything about himself, even things he hadn't thought of until then, like how much he missed having his family close and how the void created inside him by his father's death had never been filled, not even by his stepfather. Clementine told him about Duke, about her unquestioning love that had turned sour during their last visit, and about her newly discovered illegitimacy that hurt like a raw wound left open to infections.

"This time together has been perfect," Jackson said on their last day. "To tell you the truth, I'm surprised a man and a woman can have such a good time without having sex."

They were sitting on the sand outside their cottage. A warm breeze blew Clementine's hair, and she looked away.

"I'm sorry."

"Clementine, don't be. I'm glad we haven't made love. It proved what I've known all along, that what we have isn't based on physical attraction only, but on something deeper. I just love being with you, sharing life with you."

She rested her head on his shoulder. "The funny thing is, I'm not afraid of the physical part anymore," she said. "I'm afraid of what I'll think, what I'll remember. It's all in my mind."

"Your mind is part of your body. It's all connected. I wouldn't want you to turn off your thoughts just so I can have your body. We'll wait until we can have it all."

During the drive home, Clementine planned exactly what she would say to Megan. She would be firm but understanding, prepared for anger or tears, whatever Megan would throw her way. When they reached her beach house, though, Clementine found her rehearsals were for nothing. Megan had left a note in the same place Clementine had left hers.

I'll be gone for the next three weeks. It's a surprise.
Don't worry about me, either.

                                                    Love,
                                                    Megan

Whatever the surprise was, it was a blessing. A three-week reprieve.

Jackson was still unloading their bags from the car when the phone rang. It was Alex, loud and blunt as always.

"Where have you been?" she asked Clementine immediately. "Don't you think your friends at least deserve to know where you are so they won't worry?"

"I was in Mexico with Jackson," Clementine said calmly.

Alex paused for only a second. "Well, that explains why I couldn't get in touch with him, either. I should have realized."

"Don't be mad," Clementine said.

"I'm not mad. I'm happy for you. If you're happy, that is."

"I've never been happier, Alex. I don't know how I ever lived without him before."

"Don't get mushy on me. I can hardly stand it. Everyone else's love life is wine and roses, and mine is dog food."

"Oh, come on. Enjoy what you've got."

"You sound like another friend of mine. Anyway, Megan wanted me to give you the news."

Jackson walked in the door at that moment and kissed Clementine's neck, sending delightful shivers down her spine. She never wanted to go more than a day without feeling them again.

Alex paused for effect, then said, "Megan and Joey were married two days ago. They're in England for their honeymoon."

Clementine closed her eyes and whispered a prayer of thanks. Finally. She was glad for herself, but also for Megan. Her friend deserved happiness. Of everyone she knew, Clementine thought Megan deserved happiness most of all.

"Megan and Joey got married," she said to Jackson, smiling. "They're on their honeymoon."

Jackson let out a huge breath of relief, and Clementine wondered if he'd been holding it in for seven years, since the divorce. He kissed her. "You see? Everything has a way of working out for the best."

She nodded and returned to the phone. "That's wonderful, Alex. Why were they so secretive?"

"I don't know. Romance, I guess. I didn't get the call until yesterday. They sounded like kids, giggling so much."

"I'm really glad for them."

Alex hesitated again before speaking. "Why don't you just say what you mean? You're glad for you, right?"

"I'm glad for both of us. You said you weren't mad."

"I'm not. I want you both to be happy. But sneaking off to Mexico with Jackson wasn't what I had in mind. Just because things worked out in your favor doesn't mean you have to gloat."

"I'm not gloating."

"You are. And you could have been more up-front with Megan. Just because she's married now doesn't mean she won't feel betrayed when you tell her you were off on a secret romantic getaway with Jackson."

"Maybe I shouldn't tell her."

"God, don't you have any morals?"

"Why should I hurt her if I don't have to? I can just tell her that we've started seeing each other. She'll understand."

"I give up. You'll do what you want no matter what I say, anyway."

"Alex, don't be angry."

"Who the hell is angry? Just because I'm the only one who cares about Megan's feelings and you treat her like dirt."

Clementine jerked back from the loud click of the receiver as Alex hung up. Jackson watched her as she set the phone back on the hook.

"I take it Alex wasn't too thrilled with our little vacation," he said.

"No." Clementine opened the French doors and stepped out on the patio.

Jackson came up behind her and wrapped his arms around her waist.

"Don't let her get to you," he said. "Alex is wonderful, but she can be a little self-righteous at times. If nothing's going on in her own life, she loves to get into the thick of everyone else's."

Clementine nodded and leaned back against him. It was amazing how comforting the feel of his body was.

"I don't care," she said, turning around and looking into his eyes. "I don't care about anything as long as I'm with you."

"Yes, you do," he said softly, rubbing his fingers across her cheek. "When Megan comes back, you'll care about not hurting her. And you care about Alex, no matter how much your two egos beat heads. And you care about your career. You're certainly not going to stop acting just because we're together."

"What am I going to do without you?" she asked, thinking of the miles that would separate them when he returned to San Francisco in two days.

"You're going to go on being Clementine Montgomery, superstar actress. But inside, you'll hold the secret of our love, and you'll know that soon, when the time is right and we're both ready, we'll be together."

She took a deep breath. "I'm ready now, Jackson."

He took a step back. "What are you saying?"

"You know what I'm saying. I'm ready to make love with you."

"Are you sure? I mean, I thought you'd want more time. These last two weeks, we haven't even come close."

She turned away. "You didn't try."

"I thought you didn't want me to. I thought we'd have to work up to it. You know, take a little time kissing and then touching and then . . ."

"If you give me any more time, I'll never be able to be with you. Unless that's what you want."

He ran his fingers through his hair. "Of course that's not what I want. You've got to know that."

"I don't know anything except that the longer we put it off, the more scared I get that I'll never be able to. I want you to make love to me, Jackson. I want you to burn Him out of me."

He looked at her, and she thought, *Do something. Hurry. I'm running out of courage.*

Then, all at once, Jackson had her in his arms and was kissing her. She was surprised for a moment, hesitant, then she remembered it was Jackson, the man she loved, and her doubts disappeared. She wrapped her arms around his neck and held him tightly.

He unbuttoned her blouse, still kissing her. The sea breeze was cool, the beach empty, but none of that mattered. Her blouse fell away, then her pants, then his clothes, and they were lying naked on the patio, with the roar of the waves around them.

"I've always wanted you," Jackson whispered. "From the first day I saw you, I've wanted you more than anything I've ever wanted in my life. But I'm so afraid of hurting you, of making it worse."

"I'm not afraid anymore," she said. "When you're this close to me, I can't remember anything but you."

She lifted his hand and placed it on her breast. He sighed, and she closed her eyes as he traced patterns over her skin.

His hands seemed to be everywhere, making her tingle, exciting her. The wind brushed against her, too, so that she didn't know what was what. She trailed her fingers along Jackson's thigh, his stomach, the hair that ran down below his belly button. His body was beautiful to her, not dirty or frightening in any way. She loved the solidness of him, the exotic muscles and hair. There were no memories while she touched him, no hauntings. She was only sorry it had taken her so long to reach this point.

"Are you sure?" he asked.

She opened her eyes and looked at him. He was here with her, loving her. How on earth had she gotten so lucky?

"Positive."

He slid his hands down between her legs, touching her softly until she relaxed. He kissed her neck and each breast, drawing her up and out, stroking away her fears. Everything he did felt so good, perfect.

He placed his hand on her cheek and stared at her as he slid inside her. Clementine almost laughed in pleasure. Oh, it felt good. It was so different, so far from that violent scene in the alley that she knew one had nothing to do with the other. She raised up to meet him and kept her arms wrapped tightly around his back. If she could, she would hold him inside her forever.

Later, after he'd masterfully built her pleasure until it exploded from the core of her, racing out to her fingers and toes; after he'd cried out her name when he let himself go, filling her; after they came back down to earth, to the sound of a child playing in the waves down the beach and a fine layer of sand on their skin, Clementine laughed.

"Oh, so I was funny, was I?" he said.

She squeezed him, feeling so good, so complete.

"You were wonderful."

"No memories?" He propped himself up on his elbow.

"None. Only you."

"You know you'll have to fight me off now," he said. "I've got a lot of stored-up energy to spend on you."

"I don't think that will be a problem."

The sun was falling fast, tinging the sky with orange. Jackson helped her up, and they got dressed. They walked inside arm in arm, and Clementine imagined she was in a dream. Her body felt sweet, sensual, totally feminine. She was clean again.

# CHAPTER

## 23

*MEGAN STEPPED OUT OF HER CAR, WEARING* a new white dress and a turquoise silk scarf. There was something noticeably different about her, Clementine thought, as she watched from the kitchen window. Her hair was the same, her makeup understated as always. The change was the bright look in her eyes and the high thrust of her chin. Megan was finally at home in herself, relaxed. She met the gaze of a man walking his dog down the street before she entered the front door.

"Clementine, I'm home. Are you here?"

Clementine walked out of the kitchen, willing her heartbeat to slow. She hugged Megan tightly.

"Well, Mrs. Holmes, thanks a lot for inviting me to your wedding."

Megan laughed. "Oh, Clem, it was so romantic. Really. Just like one of my novels."

Megan took her hand and led her to the patio. They sat down at the glass-and-wrought-iron table, facing the ocean.

"We got our blood tests and found a minister to marry us on a hill overlooking the ocean. And then we were off to England. You wouldn't believe how beautiful it is. I felt like I belonged there, among the rolling green hills and flowers. Like I'd finally come home. Joey and I are even talking about moving there if we can arrange it."

"It sounds wonderful," Clementine said.

"It was. You know, I wasn't quite sure about getting married again. Isn't that crazy? With Jackson, I plunged right in, sure it was meant to be, and look what happened. But with Joey, I said yes and went through with it, all along thinking, Am I doing the right thing?"

"Were you?"

"Yes. Definitely. Once Joey and I got to England and were completely alone, I realized there had never been anything more right in my life. We walked through the countryside for hours, talking about everything. He's a part of me. He knows what I'm thinking and feeling, sometimes even before I do."

"I'm happy for you."

"It's not the same as it was with Jackson," Megan said, staring at the ocean. She hesitated, watching a group of young men push their kayaks out past the waves and hop in. "That was bothering me for a long time. I felt like it had to be the same. But while we were in England, it suddenly dawned on me that I wasn't happy with Jackson. I loved him. God, I loved him. And I kept trying to be happy. But always, deep inside, I knew things weren't right between us. With Joey, I can just be me and know that will always be good enough."

Clementine stood up abruptly and walked to the edge of the patio. The wind whipped her hair around her face.

"There's something I have to tell you," she said, not turning around.

"I'm sorry," Megan said. "I've been doing all the talking, and you want to talk about your vacation. Where did you go? Did you relax?"

Clemetine turned and stared at Megan. Megan looked better than ever, more confident, happier, full of life and hope. Surely, the fact that Clementine had gone away with Jackson would mean nothing to her. She'd probably laugh it off.

"I didn't go alone," she said.

Megan's eyes widened. "I don't believe you. You've got some man stashed in the wings and you didn't even tell me. How mysterious. Who is he? I'm dying to know."

Clementine turned back to the sea, afraid to look at her. "Jackson," she whispered.

Megan felt the blood drain from her face and an unsteady wave wash through her head. She leaned back in the chair, gripping the arms.

"It isn't like it's been going on for a long time," Clementine continued quickly, facing her again. "He came the night you and Joey went to the concert. We'd been, well, interested for a long time, but we never acted on it. I didn't want to hurt you. And then, even though you seemed happy with Joey, I was still scared of telling you, so I suggested we go to Mexico for a while until I could work up the nerve."

"Mexico," Megan repeated.

"We needed time to be together, just like you and Joey. I'm sorry, Meg. I know how much you loved him. But I love him too. He's everything to me."

There, she'd said it. And Megan wasn't crying. She wasn't yelling. She wasn't doing much of anything. Her face was pale and drawn, but she didn't look angry.

"All you all right?" Clementine asked.

Megan wondered where the warmth from her body had gone. One minute it had been coursing through her, making everything sunny and hopeful, and the next she was chilled to the bone. She'd known this was coming, of course. She would have to have been stupid not to. She'd known about the gallery opening. She'd seen the picture in the paper of Clementine holding Jackson's arm in front of one of his landscapes as if he belonged to her. She knew he had painted the portrait of Clementine that hung over her bed. Five years of marriage, and not once had Jackson taken the time to paint her. But one look at Clementine, and a masterpiece was born.

All that was only circumstantial evidence, though, and since Clementine had never said anything about it, Megan had chosen to believe her silence. She had thought, however naively, that Clementine would never lie to her. Strangely, the hurt didn't come from knowing

she and Jackson were together. What hurt was having
been duped. Maybe they had never acted on it before,
but they'd both felt the attraction. Why hadn't they told
her? Why had they treated her as if she were a chipped
piece of crystal ready to shatter? Sure, it would have hurt.
It would have hurt like hell. But she would have been angry, and then, eventually, the pain would have gone away.
Instead, whenever she saw them together now or even
thought of them, she would feel like an idiot. A trusting,
stupid idiot. Poor little Megan had been taken in again.

She looked up and saw that Clementine was watching
her with the usual condescending concern in her eyes.
So, Clementine loved Jackson and wanted Megan's blessing. How ironic that only Megan could keep Jackson and
her from having the perfect storybook romance they
longed for.

"I came to pack the rest of my things," she said, standing up. "We'll be living in Joey's house until we can find
another. I want something with three bedrooms. A music
room for Joey and a nursery. I'm going to start trying to
get pregnant right away."

"That's wonderful, Meg, but—"

"I won't need your help, thanks. I've got some boxes
up in my room, and whatever I can't fit, I'll send Joey
over for on the weekend."

She turned around and walked back in the house.
Clementine took a step forward before changing her
mind. She should have known it would be like this. No
anger. No tears. Not even an acknowledgment of what
had happened. Megan knew she had no right to be angry, so she had turned to the next weapon she had. Her
kindness. She would kill Clementine with kindness.

• • •

For the next year and a half, Clementine worked non-
stop. She filmed two movies, playing leading, meaty roles
in both. In the first, she played a wealthy socialite with a
penchant for murder. In the second, she landed the role
of a schizophrenic, shipped off by her family to a mental
institution, where she fell in love with a fellow patient.
Though she worked every day, she occasionally still went
to counseling sessions, and gathered ideas for some day

getting more funding for rape victims. She did everything she could think of to fill the lonely hours when she
was in Los Angeles and Jackson was in San Francisco.

The film about the schizophrenic, *Love in All the Wrong
Places*, meant the most to her, not because of the character she played but because the movie sewed up a part of
her life with neat, long-overdue stitches. The role of
Benny, the mental patient she fell in love with, was given
to a relative newcomer, an actor who had been slowly
working his way up the ladder, starring in two soaps and
a few television movies. Clementine had followed his rise
as closely as anyone, and after he'd read for the part,
she'd used her influence with the producers to help him
win the role.

That first day on the set was the hardest. They stood
in front of each other, awkward, until Clementine spoke
first.

"Connor," she said.

He smiled and held her, and the memories of those
first intense nights of lovemaking came back full force.
Aside from Jackson, he was the only man she had ever
given herself to freely, and that would always make him
special in her life.

"I told you you'd make it," she said. He laughed and
called to his very pregnant wife, Angela, to join them. He
slipped his arm around her waist, and Clementine knew
he'd found someone who gave him all that he needed,
something she never would have been able to do. She
was happy for him.

She worked from dawn to long after dusk, then
crawled home to fall into an exhausted sleep, devoid of
dreams. Makeup artists transformed her every day into
someone different, someone who didn't have to worry
about what the man she loved was doing hundreds of
miles away, or about her best friend who never returned
her phone calls and treated her like an acquaintance she
no longer had any use for. Those worries came only on
the weekends, when Clementine was alone in her big,
lonely house on the beach.

When the dust settled after that whirlwind eighteen
months, after the films were over and Clementine had a

three-month hiatus until work began on the next project, the loneliness and doubts came back strong. She was bombarded daily with thoughts of Jackson. She tried to control her feelings, temper them with reason and realism, but her heart had other ideas. Her love for him fed on itself and grew stronger every day. If he had done one thing wrong, angered her in some way, it would have been easier. Instead, whenever she was down and lonely, he drove seven hours just to sit with her and hold her hand. He made her laugh with tales of the colorful art world personalities he met. He painted her landscapes that took her breath away.

For the first time in her life, she understood why people got married. They wanted to be together not just for the big moments, the film openings or art exhibits, but for the little things. For coffee in the morning and the Sunday paper. She wanted to close her eyes at night, secure that he was lying beside her and would still be there in the morning. She wanted permanence. She wanted to introduce him to her friends as "my husband, Jackson." She wanted to share his name, sit beside him, hear his confidences every single day and night.

But Jackson had made it clear how he felt about marriage. Or, at least, marriage to her. One night, when they were lying in bed together, she worked up her nerve and broached the subject.

"I hate introducing you as my boyfriend," she said. "It sounds so juvenile."

He laughed. "There really isn't a good word for what we are. 'Lovers' sounds too illicit. 'Companions' or 'friends' doesn't say enough. We're stuck with 'boyfriend' and 'girlfriend,' I guess."

"Certainly not 'husband' and 'wife,' " she said.

He pulled away so he could look at her. "Is that what you want?"

She steadied her breathing and forced herself to smile at him. "I'm in no hurry." She didn't even blink as she said it. Alex would be so proud of her. Clementine had the look of nonchalance down pat.

"I'm glad," Jackson said, pulling her close again. "You know I want to marry you some day. But I've got to devote myself to my painting right now. I never did before, with Megan. I have so much time to make up."

Clementine didn't trust her voice, so she just nodded. She knew she shouldn't be sad. Jackson loved her. If she was patient, he would come to her eventually. But this love she had for him was not patient. It had expectations and a force of its own.

"If we got married now," he went on, "I'd only be Clementine Montgomery's husband. I've got to find my own success first. I need to be an equal partner. You understand that, don't you?"

She kissed his cheek. "Of course," she said.

She lay back in his arms, pretending to him and to herself that it didn't matter, that marriage was only a piece of paper, anyway, so what was the big deal?

One April afternoon, Clementine walked up the patio steps to her house after her daily jog on the sand. She had just taken off her shoes when the doorbell rang. She hurried inside to answer it.

Alex stood on the front porch in her crisp business suit, her hair stuck to the sides of her head like glue. Clementine laughed.

"It's illegal to wear a suit in Malibu, you know," she said.

"Oh, shut up," Alex replied. She walked past her and sighed contentedly at the air-conditioned interior. Unfastening the top button of her blouse, she sat down on the couch. "I flew in this morning, had a breakfast meeting, then a lunch date with Megan, and now I'm here to relax and have dinner with you. I didn't have a chance to change into my bikini yet."

Clementine sat down beside her. "You saw Megan?"

Alex nodded and kicked off her shoes. "Of course."

"How is she?"

Alex shrugged. "She was kind of sick, actually. She didn't eat much. If I'd known she was feeling so bad, I wouldn't have taken her to Spago. For twenty-five bucks, she ate three lettuce leaves and one bite of veal. You wouldn't believe the prices they charge now that the place is so trendy. Outrageous."

"Did she ask about me at all?"

Alex sat forward to slide off her jacket, then pulled the pins from her bun and let her hair fall down to her shoulders. "Are you two still not talking?"

"We talk. I call her twice a week, and when she answers the phone, she talks to me. Or rather, she answers my questions in monosyllables. But she never calls. She never returns the messages I leave with Joey. Poor Joey. He apologizes to me all the time, says to give it time and all that."

Alex walked into the kitchen and poured herself a glass of tap water. She drank it, thinking about the rarity of her visits to L.A. now that she was spending so much time in London. Her life had started to come together. Finally. She had reached that day when seeing Brent didn't twist her heart. She had truly settled in in London, with Kate and her other friends to keep her company. Even though she didn't have the vice presidency, her work was challenging. There were men, too, though so far no one special, yet that was all right. *Alex* was all right.

Still, she missed the closeness she'd had with Clementine and Megan. She wondered if Clementine felt the loss of it as profoundly as she did.

"Megan's just hurt," she said.

"Alex, Jackson and I have been seeing each other for more than a year now. She's a happily married woman. Why can't I be happy too?"

Alex stood at the kitchen counter, sipping her water. "Have you really talked to her about it?"

"I told you. I call her twice—"

"No, have you really tried to talk to her about how you feel? None of us talk anymore. You ask how my job is, and I say fine, even though at that very moment it's probably frustrating the hell out of me. I ask about your movies, and you say they're great, even though I know they don't fulfill you the way you thought they would. When did we stop talking? When did we stop telling the truth?"

Clementine stared at her, and Alex slammed the glass back down on the counter. Part of her was embarrassed for her outburst, but the other side was glad she'd said what she had. For years now, the three of them had been like wealthy women at a country club, smiling and glossing over rotten marriages and criminal kids, afraid of shattering the illusion of perfection. Alex had always thought their friendship was better than that.

Clementine stood up and walked over to her. Alex prepared herself for the worst, for the possibility that Clementine didn't need her anymore, that the friendship that meant so much to her had run its course for Clementine. But Clementine only put her arms around her and held on as tightly as she could. Alex let out her breath and stopped fighting the tears that pressed against her eyes. They held each other and breathed in the fragrances they remembered. Alex was amazed that Clementine felt no different now than she had when they were teenagers. Age didn't change things nearly as much as she once thought it would.

"Tell me everything," Clementine said when she pulled away.

Alex shrugged. "I love London now, but that doesn't mean there aren't days that nearly kill me. I'm at work from seven in the morning until ten at night. The men that come and go don't mean much, and it's debatable if that will ever change. Nessy, the retriever I got, is better company than any of them. And I miss you and Megan more than I can say."

Clementine shook her head. "Megan hates me, and that's like hating myself. I keep making these damn movies, and I don't know why. They don't make me happy. Jackson has this crazy notion that he has to make as much money as me before we can get married, and it's beginning to drive me crazy. I'm frustrated as hell. I went so long without sex, and now that I can have it, Jackson's up in San Francisco most of the time, painting his brains out. I'm beginning to feel like an eighteen-year-old boy with a hard-on and no privacy."

They stared at each other, then laughed.

"That's better," Alex said. "Now I know we're both pathetic excuses for women."

They walked back to the couch and sat down. Alex still held on to her hand.

"You need to talk to Megan too," she said.

"Yes, I know."

"You need to stop beating around the bush. Tell her you love her, you're sorry you hurt her, but you love Jackson and that's that. She can take the truth."

Clementine was silent for a moment before standing up again and grabbing her purse from the table.

"You're right. Come on."

"Now?"

"Yes, now."

"I just got here. And I need to change. And if I drive on another L.A. freeway, I'll go insane."

"Go change, and I'll drive. But we're going. This has gone on long enough."

• • •

Megan stepped back in surprise when Alex appeared on her doorstep for the second time that day. The surprise turned to wariness when she saw Clementine standing behind her.

She moved aside to let them in. "I wasn't expecting you two."

"You know us," Alex said, walking through Megan's ceramic tile entry to the family room. A black grand piano stood majestically by the sliding glass door. "We always did love surprises."

Megan offered them a seat on the couch before sitting down herself in her rocking chair.

"How are you feeling?" Alex asked.

"I've thrown up twice in the last hour," she said, stopping the rocking when her stomach knotted up again.

"Do you think you might be pregnant?" Clementine asked.

Megan cringed at the sight of the two of them sitting there, both regal and as self-possessed as always. Her best friends. A wealthy stockbroker and a movie star. Both of them made up beautifully, dotted with expensive perfume, and dressed in the exact clothes and accessories sophisticated fashion magazines tell you to wear.

"I don't know," she said quietly, not quite meeting Clementine's eyes. "I've never been regular, and I've only been sick for a couple of days. I made an appointment for Wednesday, but I don't want to get my hopes up."

"That would be wonderful for you, though," Clementine said.

Megan looked at her then, wondering if Clementine realized how deeply it hurt to have her there. This was Megan's home. She had picked it out, checked the closets for storage space and the foundation for settling problems. She'd chosen the pictures on the walls and instructed Joey where to hang them. It was her sofa, her rocking chair. By being there, Clementine had managed to violate the only space she could call completely her own. Every spot on her carpet and crumb on her table stood out like neon beside Clementine's perfection.

"Yes," she whispered.

They were quiet then, Megan again rocking her chair, Clementine running her fingers along the sofa arm, and Alex looking from one to the other, waiting for either of them to begin.

"This is the most ridiculous thing I've ever seen," Alex finally said. "Just look at you two. Friends for over twenty years, and now you can't even look at each other. And why? Because of one man, that's why. Look, I love Jackson too. Hell, we all love Jackson. But we were here first. We had each other first." She looked at Clementine, still not taking the initiative, and then at Megan, who had stopped rocking.

"It's not about Jackson," Megan said.

"Well, then, what the hell is it about?" Alex asked.

Megan felt as if there were a bubble inside her stomach, blowing larger and larger, pressing everything else to the sides, sucking out the air. She stood up and walked to the piano, keeping her back to Alex and Clementine.

"It's about my whole life," she said, gulping at the air so she'd have enough breath to speak. "It's about being best friends with Alex the brain and Clementine the model. And here I am, just Megan. I've always been just Megan, and neither of you has any idea how much that hurts."

"That's not true," Clementine said, standing up. She

walked toward Megan, but Megan drew away to the window.

"Oh, no?" she asked. "Then tell me, what's special about me?"

Clementine opened her mouth, but nothing emerged.

"Oh, that's wonderful," Megan said. "You can't even think of anything."

"Well, I can," Alex said, standing up. "You're kind and loving and giving and—"

"Stop it, stop it, stop it!" Megan held her hands up over her ears. "Do you think that helps me? Do you think that's enough? Would being nice be enough for you?"

Alex looked away, and Megan took her hands down. She gazed at them both, and the feelings of her whole life urged her on, making her, for the first time, careless with her words.

"All my life," she said, "I've taken a backseat to you two. First, there was Alex. Funny, smart, popular Alex. I rode on your coattails, holding on with all my might. I was petrified that you would run too fast or suddenly realize that it was me tagging along behind you."

"Meg, I—"

"Let me finish!" she shouted. She paced the floor, her stomachache forgotten, the words tumbling out of her mouth before she could stop them.

"And then Clementine came along. So beautiful, I could hardly stand it. I used to watch the way you moved, the way you spoke. I tried so hard to be like you so the boys would look at me the way they looked at you."

Clementine stared at her, seeing, for a moment, life through Megan's eyes.

"I was so young then," Megan went on more quietly. "I didn't mind being the plain and stupid one as long as I could be with you two. But now I'm older and wiser, and being the gawky third wheel isn't good enough anymore."

She walked to the rocking chair, ready to sit down, but she changed her mind and whirled around, facing them. "Do you realize I've never had one thing in my life that was totally mine?"

Alex opened her mouth, but Megan held up her hand. "You dated Tony before I met him, and everything he did to me was because of you." She glanced at Clementine. "Jackson left me for you, even though both of you were too scared and stupid to come together for years. Even Joey is Alex's brother. What the hell is mine? Just mine?"

"Jackson loved you," Clementine whispered.

"Don't you dare tell me how Jackson felt!" Megan yelled, stalking over to Clementine, stopping only inches from her. "You didn't even give me the courtesy of telling me your feelings. You treated me like I was an idiot, a child, like I wasn't even capable of handling my own anger or sadness. Dammit, Clementine, I don't give a damn what you do with him. Marry him for all I care. But couldn't you at least have treated me like an equal for once? Like somebody you respected? Like you would have treated Alex?"

"I was only trying to do what was right. I'm sorry," Clementine said, a tear spilling down onto her cheek.

Alex reached over and grabbed her hand. "I think you're going too far, Megan."

Megan stepped back and looked at her. "Too far," she repeated. "Tell me, how far would you go if you were me, Alex? What if you were the one living in shadows all your life? Taking the leftover praise, the leftover love. What if you were second class, with no career success to back you up? The one men used to get back at someone else, the one men left so they could be with the woman they really loved?"

"Our lives are not perfect, either," Alex said. "You don't know what it's like, always being alone, pretending that ten business suits in the closet make up for all the lonely nights."

"Maybe I don't know," Megan said, "but that was the choice you made. I didn't even get the choice. And Clementine has never had anything but success. Except for the rape—"

Clementine whirled away, wrapping her arms around her stomach.

"Stop it, Megan," Alex said.

"I won't! Except for the rape, Clementine has gotten everything she ever wanted. All my life, I've been your best friend, and what has it gotten me? Kicked in the face. I thought what the three of us had was special, a once-in-a-lifetime kind of friendship, and that's what kept me beside you all these years, swallowing my pride. But now I see I was the only one who felt that."

She spun around and stomped to the front door, flinging it open wide.

"You want to know something," she said, walking out onto the front porch. "I feel great! I've never felt this good in all my life. And do you know why? Because I don't need you two anymore. I used to think having you as friends was the only thing that made me special. But now I've got Joey and my dreams and maybe even a baby growing inside of me. You can have your damn shadows back. Get some other fool to stand around in them. I've got my own life to lead."

Clementine and Alex stood there, silent, staring at Megan as she leaned against the porch wall.

"Now, I want you out of my house."

Clementine moved first, rushing past Megan and out to the car. Alex walked more slowly. She stopped when she reached Megan.

"No matter what you choose to think," she said, "I have always thought of you as my equal, my best friend. The only person who ever thought you were any less than that was you."

She walked to the car and got in. Megan watched Clementine's head drop and the tears trickle down her cheeks. Alex hugged her once before they drove away.

Megan knew she would regret all she'd said. Later, she would cry and hate herself for her cruelty, for giving up the two people she had loved most. But for now, she smiled. She held her head up and walked back into the house. For now, for once, she was the strong one. And it felt damn good.

# CHAPTER
## 24

$N$O GOOD EVER COMES OF A CALL AT TWO o'clock in the morning. The jarring ringing is an immediate code red alert. Unless, of course, the sound incorporates itself into a dream, as it did in Clementine's, transforming into bells in a distant city while she and Jackson picked flowers in the countryside. Clementine fought to stay there, where the world was exactly what she made it, but Jackson's unrelenting voice eventually broke through her barriers.

"Wake up, Clem. It's your phone."

She sat up quickly, still groggy but with her heart thumping fast, and grabbed the receiver.

"Clementine Montgomery?" a woman's voice said. The line was marred by static, the words difficult to hear.

"Yes. Who's this?"

"This is Carol Shornburg."

"I'm afraid I don't know any Carol—"

"I'm a friend of your father's."

Clementine grabbed Jackson's hand, soothed to find it there beside her, warm and strong. He had come down often in the two months since that awful episode at Megan's house, as if trying to fill the gap left by Megan's absence. This time he was here for a couple of days, and since the moment he'd arrived, Clementine had been watching the clock tick away their seconds together. When he was gone, when there was only a pillow to cuddle with, time seemed to stand still.

"Yes," she said, trying not to assume the worst. This could be about anything. Even something good. A job, perhaps? Marriage? "What can I do for you?"

"I'm afraid I have bad news," Carol said.

Clementine gripped the receiver tighter, until the blood left her hand and her skin turned white.

"There's no easy way to say this except to just come right out with it," Carol went on. "I'm afraid Duke died a few hours ago. A massive coronary. He . . ." Carol started crying then, uncontrollably, pausing only when she had to gasp for air. Clementine took the receiver away from her ear and set it on her lap. Staring at a point on the far wall, the bottom left corner of Jackson's painting of a white schoolhouse in the country, she didn't move or blink or breathe.

"What is it?" Jackson asked. He could hear the sobbing coming out of the receiver. "Tell me."

Slowly, calmly, the way Brittany, the psychopathic murderer she played in *Out of Control* would have done it, Clementine turned her head toward him and shrugged. "My father is dead."

Jackson stared at her a moment, at the strange smile and glazed eyes, before taking the phone out of her hand. When the woman at the other end calmed down, he asked for the details.

Clementine heard him talking from far away, in a tunnel, separate from her. She had only to reach out and touch him, and she would be there too. But, of course, she didn't want that. She would just stay here, in a safe place, and focus on the corner of the picture until her eyes blurred and she fell asleep.

She heard the click of the receiver and felt Jackson's fingers on her shoulder.

"Clementine, I'm so—"

"Ssssh," she said, still staring, but having to work hard now to keep herself separate from him, from the phone call, from life. She was being pulled back. "Duke died . . .

Duke died . . . Duke died . . ." The words echoed in her head, and Duke's face swam before her—not the face she had seen last, but the one she'd known as a child, happy and perfect. She thought she had stopped loving him, or at least gotten him out of her system. But now he was dead, and hatred was a wasted commodity when there was no one to turn it on.

"I want to go to sleep now," she said. She pulled the covers up to her chin and slipped onto her side, away from Jackson. The ocean still roared, the clock ticked, a car sped by outside. The world went on, and Duke was dead.

Jackson pressed the full length of his body against hers and wrapped his arm around her stomach.

"I love you," he whispered.

Clementine shivered once and, with masterful control of her body, forced herself to go to sleep.

In the morning, Jackson awoke to an empty bedroom. He hurried downstairs and out to the patio, where he found Clementine sitting quietly, her eyes bloodshot, a blanket wrapped around her as she stared out to sea.

"I feel so alone now," she said. He sat down beside her and took her hand. "Having a father, even a bad one, meant I was still somebody's little girl. There was still someone to be proud of me."

"You've got your mother to be proud," Jackson said. "And me."

"I woke up this morning and for just a moment thought everything was fine. Then I remembered." She shivered and wrapped the blanket tighter around her. "I felt like there was this huge hole in my stomach, a whole piece of my life ripped away. He was a free spirit, lazy, devious, but irresistible. I can't believe I'll never see him again."

"I know," Jackson said.

"There're so many things I should have told him. I let it end so bitterly between us. I always thought that some day, when we were both older and wiser, we'd get together again and tell each other all is forgiven. I assumed I had plenty of time."

"We all think we've got time enough to say the things

we have to say. So we put off the reconciliations and for-
giveness day after day, always saying, 'Tomorrow, I'll call.
Tomorrow, I'll say I'm sorry.' "

They were quiet for a long time, watching the morning sun toy with the edge of the horizon, coloring the
purple sky with a thin streak of yellow.

"When my father died," Jackson said quietly, "I
thought it was my fault. He used to ask me to come into
his den every night before going to sleep and kiss him
good night. On the night before he was shot, I was having such a good time playing football with my friends in
the street that by the time I got in bed, I'd completely
forgotten about him."

"Oh, Jackson," She leaned her head against his.

"I thought if I'd only kissed him good night or ould I
loved him like he always wanted me to, he'd still be
around. It would have taken so little to make him happy,
but I was too caught up in my own life to make the effort."

"You were just a kid."

"I know. But I still feel guilty about all the things left
unsaid."

"So, that's it then. This is how it ends."

Jackson stood up. "You make peace the best way you
know how. You've got to hope that he knew how you felt
even when you didn't tell him. And, who knows, maybe
he's here somewhere, watching over you."

He kissed the top of her head and walked inside the
house. The wind brushed over Clementine's face, and
for a moment, she thought it felt like a breath, drying
her tears.

• • •

Clementine flew into Phoenix on the following Saturday for the funeral. The service was brief, the mourners
few, with only Carol and her family and friends and
Clementine in attendance. Afterward, they drove from
the funeral home to the cemetery and, when the minister finished his last words, stood watching as the casket
was lowered into the ground. Clementine threw a red
rose down onto the coffin before stepping back beside
Carol.

"He missed you, you know," Carol said.

Clementine wiped away her tears and smiled at Carol, who was so different from what she had expected. She'd always pictured Duke with skinny, young blond bombshells, the kind of scatterbrained women he'd long ago left her mother for. But Carol was middle-aged, dark-haired, slightly overweight, and surprisingly plain. Her greatest assets were her warmth and humor, attributes Clementine had thought Duke held little stock in. There were obviously a lot of things about him she would never understand.

"You don't have to say that," she said to Carol. "I know how much I infringed on the kind of life-style he wanted, and I can live with that. I loved him, anyway."

"Just because you don't want someone in your life doesn't mean you can stop yourself from loving them."

Clementine smiled. She was glad that when Duke went, Carol had been at his side.

"Do you know what he used to do?" Carol asked.

Clementine shook her head.

"Every time one of your pictures came out, he'd haul me down to the movie theater three or four times. And as soon as your name rolled across the screen on the opening credits, he'd stand up and yell, 'That's my daughter!' "

"No," Clementine said, laughing.

"Totally true. Of course, nobody believed him. He was so gruff and poor, and you were a beautiful star. But he didn't care. He was proud of you, Clementine. Even if he couldn't admit it to himself, I know deep down when he looked at you he thought, My God, that beautiful creature is *my* daughter. And that made him happy."

Clementine squeezed Carol's hand and walked back to the edge of the grave, covered with dirt now. She knelt down beside it.

"I'm still your little girl," she whispered. She picked up a handful of dirt and put it in her pocket.

•    •    •

The world was black. Clementine tugged at the corners of the handkerchief covering her eyes, but Jackson swatted her hands away.

"Stop it," he said. "I told you, no peeking."

"I'm so disoriented," she said, and sniffed the air to try to get some sense of where they were headed. They had picked up a rental car at JFK hours ago, and as soon as they were in it, Jackson had blindfolded her. For a while, she'd slept. But the rougher road they were traveling on now had woken her.

"How long have we been driving?" she asked.

"Anywhere between one and five hours."

"That's not fair."

"Life's not fair."

"Come on, Jackson, I have no idea where we are."

"That's the plan," he said, smiling. He was surprised at his own excitement. He'd planned this for so long—fifteen months, in fact—that he had expected his initial enthusiasm to dim. Yet now that he was there, he felt like a kid on his first trip to Disneyland. He glanced at Clementine, sniffing and twisting and turning, and he almost burst at the seams with joy. Nothing in the world gave him more pleasure than making her happy.

Bringing this day to reality had taken almost herculean efforts. First, the proceeds from two of his most recent paintings had to come through, then the deal with the Mossier Gallery in Manhattan, which had agreed to be the exclusive East Coast dealer for his work, had to be sealed, and the all-important guest list for the New York opening had to be ironed out. And then, once all the deals had been settled and the property bought, Clementine had been too busy wrapping up her latest film to leave Los Angeles.

Finally, though, everything was settled. There would be no more waiting. He had found his niche, generated some success. When people asked him what he did for a living, he could proudly say, "I paint." Clementine still made more money—would probably always make more money—but he was not threatened by that. He could come to her as an equal partner now.

He drove on through the New Hampshire woods, the thick groves of poplars and birches on the verge of their autumn fire. The afternoon breeze was crisp, flicking crumpled leaves against the windshield. In all his life,

Jackson had never seen a more beautiful place. He could do without the beach and big cities and tropical islands. Give him New England in autumn, and he'd be happy.

He had turned off the main highway ten miles back and onto a secondary gravel road. Now, he made a quick right onto a private dirt drive. Clementine jerked her head up, feeling the change again. He laughed.

At the end of the path, he stopped. Before him stood twenty-five acres of dense trees, rolling hills, even a stream at the edge of the property. And it all belonged to him. He'd flown out four times to see the land, to confer with an architect about the laws on how many trees could be removed, any limits on maximum structure size or exterior design, and the best site for the house. They'd finally decided to clear out three thousand square feet at the crest of a hill, leaving trees on all sides for privacy, yet retaining a magnificent view of the valley beyond. When Jackson had walked with the architect to the edge of the hill where some day he vowed to carry Clementine over the threshold, he knew he had finally come home.

"We're here," he said.

"Where's here?"

He laughed again and hurried around to her side of the car. He opened the door and helped her out.

"It smells good," she said.

He guided her slowly through the trees and up the hill to where the house would stand. After looking around once more to make sure he couldn't find a better angle, he unknotted her blindfold. Clementine blinked once and stared.

She took a couple steps away from him and ran her hand along the trunk of a birch tree. Fallen leaves crunched beneath her feet.

"I don't understand," she said.

He put his arms around her. "This is home, Clem," he whispered. "All this land is ours. I want to build our house here."

For as far as Clementine could see, there were only trees, some green, some yellow, a few tinged with red. She could hear the trickling of water in the distance and the vibrant songs of birds up above.

"Is there water here?" she asked.

"A stream. Come on. I'll show you."

He took her hand and led her through the woods, down a hill that grew steeper as it slid toward the river.

"We can put a path in here if you want," he said, winding his way in and out of the trees.

"No. I like it just like this."

At last they reached the bottom of the hill, where a stream, still skimpy from summer's dryness, trickled over smoothed rocks green with algae. They sat down on the bank, sinking into the cushion of leaves.

Clementine closed her eyes and let the water's soothing rustle clear out the cobwebs and frustrations and worries that were such a part of her day-to-day life in Los Angeles. Jackson tilted his head up to the sun, which filtered in dusty beams through the branches.

They were silent for half an hour, with only the water and birds and wind to break the stillness. Eventually, Clementine opened her eyes and leaned her head against Jackson's shoulder.

"This is the most beautiful place I've ever seen," she said.

He kissed her forehead. "I hoped you'd feel that way. I've always had a love affair with the woods. The beach is wonderful, but there's something so basic about a place like this, so pure."

"I could lose myself here," she said, tossing a leaf into the stream and watching it drift downward.

"As long as I can come along."

She smiled. "Anywhere I go, I want you with me."

Later, they walked back up the hill to the house site. Jackson led her through his version of it.

"Here I'd like the kitchen, looking out over the valley. And over here a breakfast nook. It will get the morning sun that way. And what do you think about a big stone fireplace here?" He pointed to the area he imagined as the living room.

Clementine stared at him. He was making plans for a future she wasn't sure they had.

"Are you saying you want me to move out here and live with you?" she asked.

He held her hand. "Not just live with me. I want to marry you, Clementine."

She stood perfectly still. She had heard those words so often in her mind, she couldn't be sure they were real now. She looked down at their hands linked together and then up at his face, and she knew it was true.

"Say it again," she said.

He laughed and put his hand over his heart. "Clementine, will you marry me? I promise to be a good husband. To work hard as an artist. It may not be the most secure career, but I'll do my best to make a good living at it. And I promise to love you more than any man has ever loved any woman. And—"

"And tell me I'm beautiful every day," she said.

"Yes."

"And bring me breakfast in bed and rub my back and make love to me every night as exquisitely as you always do."

"I can live with that. Anything else?"

She gripped his hands. "Never leave me," she whispered.

He pulled her tightly to him. "We'll build our house together. It will be our haven against the big, bad world. Then once it's finished, we'll have a beautiful wedding and start the rest of our lives together. You'll make movies if you want or start working on the rape victims' funding. I'll set up a studio here so I won't ever have to be away from you. I promise you, you'll never have to be alone again."

She rested her head in the hollow of his neck and closed her eyes.

"I think once I'm here," she said after a long silence, "I could go public about the rape. It wouldn't be so bad, if I knew I had you to come home to."

"Then that's what you'll do. You know I'm behind you all the way."

"I know."

"So that means yes?" he asked. "You'll marry a loser like me?"

She laughed. "Oh, I suppose so. I haven't got anything better to do."

He hugged her. Just as when Arthur had first called her and asked her to come to New York, Clementine did not feel joy exactly, although that was part of it. What she really felt was relief. Pure relief that the waiting and wondering were over. She didn't think she was particularly special or beautiful because Jackson loved her. She felt simply lucky, as if her guardian angel had taken a liking to her and given her a priceless gift.

Jackson pulled her down to the ground and slowly took off her clothes. His gaze never left her face as he touched her. She was mesmerized by him, as she had been from the very first day she saw him.

They made love in the place that would be their kitchen. And when it was over, the joy broke through to Clementine. She wrapped her arms around him, holding on tight.

"You want to marry me," she said, still not quite sure it was true.

"You want to marry *me*," he echoed. He lifted himself up on one elbow, looking like a woodland god with leaves and branches clinging to his hair and skin.

"I love you," he said. "But it's getting cold as hell out here, and we'd better get dressed."

They laughed as they put their clothes back on, then Jackson pointed out where the rest of the rooms would be.

"I thought on the wall in the library, if you'd like, we could hang yours and Alex's and Megan's portraits side by side."

"That sounds good," she said.

"Do you think Alex will part with hers? Seeing herself on her wall every day feeds her ego."

Clementine smiled. "I think she'd like the idea of the three of us together in one place, even if we can't seem to manage that in real life." Her voice grew softer at the end, as she thought of her friends.

"I hope so," Jackson said. "Since I never did find the right time to give Megan hers, at least here it could hang proudly instead of gathering dust in a closet. And this way, no matter what happens between you and Megan, you'll always have a piece of her."

Clementine hugged him again. She wanted to run to the nearest phone and call her friends. What good was happiness, an engagement, if you had no one to tell? Megan and Alex had made all of her successes doubly good over the years. It was like living the glory over again when their eyes lit up and they told her how proud and happy they were for her.

But it was different now. They were different. Too much had happened, and they could never go back. Alex would be happy for her, but she wouldn't want to blatantly take sides against Megan, either. And, of course, Clementine couldn't call Megan. She hadn't talked to her in five months, not since that day at Megan's house. She had wanted to. She had dialed six of the seven numbers hundreds of times, but she never finished the call. What could she say? "Sorry" didn't cover it. Megan had a lifetime of resentments built up, and Clementine could not fight that.

The funny thing was, Megan didn't even know that Clementine was hurting too. Jackson couldn't be everything to her; he couldn't take Megan's place. Alex was still there, but it was not the same. It took the three of them to form that perfect circle.

Clementine tried to resign herself to hearing only tidbits of Megan's life from Alex—her plans to move with Joey to the English countryside, Berkshire County, to be exact; her ecstasy over her pregnancy, confirmed soon after the last time Clementine had seen her, then her despair when she miscarried a month later. Clementine had wanted to call her, give her her sympathy, but it was obvious her sympathy meant nothing to Megan anymore. All that had made their friendship so special over the years had turned sour.

So, instead, Clementine stayed within Jackson's arms, listening to his heartbeat, hoping to content herself with his love, his proposal, their secret place away from the rest of the world. She squeezed him tight, trying unsuccessfully to convince herself that he could fill the hole that Megan had left in her life.

# CHAPTER
## 25

$A$LEX KNOCKED ON THE BEDROOM DOOR.
She had plowed through this same door hundreds of
times as a child, never stopping for anything as senseless
as knocking. Things were different now. She and Megan
saw each other rarely and approached each other with a
certain timidity. Alex could find no way around it. Besides, she was an adult now, thirty-five years old, and as
she told herself over and over again, she'd better start
acting like one.

"Meg, are you awake?" she called.

"Yes, come on in."

Megan was sitting up in bed, her stomach pushing up
the covers, an open novel in her lap.

"Oh, God," Alex said in mock horror. "Three months
to go, and at a rate of five romance novels a week, I'd say
you and Joey will be divorced by the time the baby
comes."

"Don't say that," Megan said.

"Why not? No man can live up to the Brandons and
Ashleys and whatever else they call the heroes in those
books. No man is gorgeous and heroic and strong, yet
gentle and sensitive, too."

"Joey is," Megan said softly.

Alex smiled and sat down on the edge of the bed. "How does it feel to be under your parents' roof again? I think I'd rather kill myself than move back in with mine."

"Oh, it's not that bad. Since Dad passed away, Mom spends all of her time with charity events. It takes her mind off the loneliness of this huge house. The servants take care of me, mostly."

"Do you miss Joey?"

"More than you can imagine. But it's working out best this way. I haven't been much fun since the miscarriage last year."

"Don't be silly. Joey loves you."

"I know that. But he was upset when I got pregnant without talking to a doctor first. Of course, he was right. Everyone told me the miscarriage was God's way of saying I was rushing things, but that doesn't make losing another baby any easier. This time, though, it's going to be all right." She confidently patted her six-months-pregnant stomach.

"I think so too. You see the doctor every week, don't you?"

"Yes."

"And I know Joey has always understood how much you want a child."

"Yes, he knows," Megan whispered, staring past Alex to the image of Joey she held in her mind while he was away. The distance had made her see him more clearly, as the only man she had ever loved for exactly who he was, faults and attributes, good points and bad. She had no illusions about him, and that was wonderfully comforting. Just thinking about him made her smile.

"He always understood better than anyone else," she said. "I was devastated after the miscarriage. After that last visit with you and Clem, when I went to the doctor, I couldn't believe I was actually pregnant. And then, by the time I got used to it, I'd lost the baby."

"You seem stronger this time," Alex said.

"I feel stronger. I did exactly what the doctor said, waited three months after the miscarriage before getting pregnant again. And complete bed rest helps. If Joey were here, he'd only worry about me. This way, he can plan our move to England."

"I still can't believe you're really going to do that."

"Why not? I have goals, too, you know. They're just different from yours."

Alex stood up and walked to the window, framed by the same lace curtains that had been there during their school days. It seemed that everything she said now was a springboard for Megan's anger. Being with Megan was like walking through a mine field.

"I didn't mean it that way. It's just a big step."

Megan folded the page down in her book and set it aside, then looked at Alex.

"Never mind," she said. "Tell me about you. How's your job?"

Alex opened her mouth to give the usual response: "Fine. No problem." Then she changed her mind. She walked back to the bed and sat down.

"It's good now, like it used to be, but it was hell for a while. When Brent gave the vice presidency to Maxine, I thought I would quit. That job was all I ever wanted."

"I know," Megan said.

"You don't," Alex said. "I never told you. I never thought you were interested. You were the one with the feelings. I was the one with the ambition."

"I always knew you had feelings."

"I did. I do. I fell in love once."

Megan sat forward. "Why didn't you tell me?"

Alex shrugged. "I don't know. It was over so fast, and then I didn't want you to see me hurting. I didn't want you to think I'd lost my mind or gone back on all my promises."

They were quiet for a long time. Then Megan moved to the edge of the bed.

"Help me out," she said.

"I thought . . ."

"Just for a minute. Help me."

Alex pulled her out of bed, and Megan walked into the bathroom. She came back a moment later with a pair of manicure scissors.

"Remember?" she asked, smiling.

Alex laughed as Megan sat down beside her. Alex held out her finger, and Megan pricked it first, then her own.

"Now," she said as they pressed their fingers and blood together, "no more secrets."

Alex looked at her. "You're my best friend."

"Oh, Alex," Megan said, holding her. "Tell me you're happy. Tell me you're going to be all right."

"I am happy," Alex said as she helped Megan back into bed. "It's not your kind of happy or Clementine's, but it works for me. I really was made to be a business-woman. It's what I'm best at. At home, Nessy keeps me company, and my friend Kate helps me raise a ruckus. And I've got you and Clementine again. There's no special man now, but I'm not without hope. And if it doesn't happen, that's all right, too."

"You could change," Megan said. "Maybe if you quit and got an easier job, you'd find someone."

Alex shook her head. "I might, but the point is that work is the most important thing to me. I am who I am. I accept that. And despite everything, I love my life. I know now that Brent was right when he didn't give me the vice presidency and told me I'd be happier in the trenches. Maxine is going crazy sitting behind that desk all day, doing nothing. I'm out there working, living. Kate told me to stop thinking about life and start living it. That's what I've been trying to do."

"And what about the man you loved? Is there any chance for the two of you?"

"No. But it hardly hurts at all anymore. That's the honest truth. Time minimizes everything. And there is happiness without a man, believe it or not. It's different, quieter, but no less real. Good friends can make up for almost anything."

They sat together, holding hands, reveling in the com-panionable silence they had once taken for granted. Eventually, they went back to the subject of Megan's move to England.

"When will you go?" Alex asked.

"A few months after the baby's born. Probably early next year. Joey's going to fly there next month, try to set up a few contacts in London at the universities and schools. But even if he doesn't get a job right away, we'll have enough money from my trust fund and what we'll get for the house to make it for a while."

"You're sure you want to leave everything behind and just go?"

Megan smiled. "I've never been more sure of anything. I need a place that's totally mine. I know that's hard for you to understand, but . . ."

"I understand," Alex said. "But I'll miss you."

"You'll probably see us more than anyone, with all the time you spend in London. Besides, you've got to come and watch over your goddaughter."

"You still think it will be girl?"

"I'm sure of it. And I am absolutely positive that nothing bad is going to happen this time. I won't let it. She's strong."

"So's her mom." Alex took a deep breath and decided she should just tell Megan the news. Megan could handle it now, and besides, they had just outlawed secrets.

"Megan, I have to tell you something. Clem—"

"Clementine and Jackson are getting married," Megan finished for her.

"How did you know?"

Megan shrugged. "It was just a hunch I've had for the last few months, since you act like a nervous wreck whenever I bring them up."

"And?"

"And what? Do you want me to tell you I'm happy for them? I'm not. I'm not jealous. I don't give a damn what Jackson does anymore. I just don't care."

"Bullshit."

"You can say what you want, Alex. They're both out of my life now. I'm sorry if that hurts you, but I can't help how I feel. Clementine never tried to work out our problems, either, you know. It's been ages since we had that split, and she hasn't tried to get in touch with me once. She just went off and made movies and spent all her time with Jackson. I don't see her crying over what we've lost."

"You're hurting."

"I am not," Megan said loudly. She turned her head away and pulled the covers up to her chin. "And even if

I am, it doesn't matter. Clementine is a star, and she doesn't give one hoot about anyone who doesn't idolize her. She's got you and Jackson, and that's all she needs. I'm not crawling back to her."

"I'm not asking you to. But if you'd stop feeling sorry for yourself for a second, you'd see that she doesn't want to intrude on your life. She's not as rich and famous as you make her out to be. Sometimes I think she's the loneliest one of us all, even if she is with Jackson. She's just . . . Clementine. One of your best friends. She thinks you don't want her around anymore. That's why she hasn't made a move."

"I *don't* want her around anymore. And I don't want to talk about it, either. All anyone can ever talk about is Clementine. *I'm* going to have a baby. *I'm* moving to England. That's exciting too, isn't it?"

Alex sighed. "Of course it is. I'm always interested in your life."

"Then shut up about her. I don't want to hear it. Let them get married. And if it makes you feel any better, I hope they're happy together. But that's the end of it. I'm going to have my baby and start a new life with my family. And, once and for all, Clementine will be out of my life."

•   •   •

Megan was bending over her rosebush, clipping a perfect ivory bud, when she heard the laughter. She straightened and turned, catching sight of her daughter's body floating in the air, then being caught in the strong arms of her father.

Megan followed the cobblestone path to the back kitchen door and set the rose in a slim vase of water. Looking around the kitchen, she was pleased again with the work she'd done on it—the pink rose wallpaper, the copper pots hanging from the ceiling, the dried flowers above the sink, the fingerpaint handprints of year-old Anne on the refrigerator door. She was home here.

Outside the door stretched miles of lush hills, drenched by dew and raindrops. She had a rose garden to cultivate, a daughter to raise, good friends half a mile down the road, and a husband who simply gave her everything. Megan bent her head to the rose and inhaled the fragrance. Despite the pain she'd suffered over the years and all the heartache, she would go through every second of her life again if only to reach this moment.

She walked outside. Anne was gurgling happily in Joey's arms, staring up at him with total adoration.

"I think she's got a crush on you," Megan said.

"I can live with that."

They walked together to the love seat swing they'd put in at the edge of the yard. Joey handed Anne to Megan, who cradled her in her arms as they rocked up and back.

"What time is your first lesson tomorrow?" Megan asked, speaking softly as she watched Anne's eyes flutter closed.

"Ten. And then I've got a new student at twelve. Terrance Darby. How's that for a good English name?"

Megan laughed, holding out her free hand for him to hold. "Are you happy here, Joey?"

He squeezed her hand and slid closer to her. "Remember when you were little and you used to dream about what your life would be like? Well, honest to God, I used to dream of this. Of a cottage in the country, my music, a beautiful wife, and a child. As I got older and those things weren't happening, I just assumed they would always be a dream, tucked away in the back of my mind for only me to know. But now, here I am. Sometimes, I wake up in the night, sure it will all be over. I'll be back in L.A., the smog blowing in my window, with no one beside me. Then I hear the crickets and your gentle breathing, and I thank God for everything I have."

Megan leaned against him. The spring fog was drifting in through their valley, two hours outside London. Once, in her teens if she remembered right, she had vowed to live in sunshine all year long. Funny that she should end up here, with rain and fog as much a part of the landscape as it had been in Sausalito. Everyone had warned her about the dampness and gloom of England. Strangely, she welcomed the clouds and drizzle. It was as if the fog were a protective shield around her own perfect world. The weather suited her life, the ethereality of it, the feeling of being suspended in a dream too good to be true and terrified of waking up.

"How about you?" Joey asked. "Happy?"

"More than I ever could have imagined."

"Do you miss Alex?"

"Yes. But I'll get to see her in the fall, when she flies in for business."

"After Jackson and Clementine's wedding."

Megan stopped the swing with her feet. Just the sound of their names could overturn her life, like ghosts screaming through the midnight silence. She turned away.

"Does it still hurt you that much?" Joey asked.

She looked back at him and sighed. "It's not their marriage. Really it isn't. They've postponed it for so long, waiting for a lull in Clementine's filmmaking and for their house to be finished, that I'm glad they're finally going ahead with it. What bothers me is Clementine. I keep thinking that the hard feelings I have toward her will dim with time, but instead, they just get stronger."

"Maybe if you confronted her . . ."

"And said what? 'Oh, by the way, I hate you for being beautiful. For having fame and love and success when I had nothing.' Right."

Joey stood up and walked to the back of the swing. He pushed it forward gently, then moved to the side.

"She worked hard for the things she has," he said.

"Did she?" Megan asked, looking over her shoulder at him. She tucked Anne's silky blond hair beneath her cap and rubbed her cheek. "She won a modeling contest, moved to New York, became a model, moved to L.A., got great roles in great films, and bought a house on the beach. Does that sound like a tough life?"

Joey drew in a deep breath and spoke without looking at her.

"When I look in Clementine's eyes, I always see this incredible sadness there, like she has scars on the inside."

Megan was quiet, thinking of the rape.

"Her father abandoned her," Joey went on, "used her love to get her money, and then died, leaving a whole chapter of her life unfinished. Her mother was too busy trying to make her second marriage work to pay much attention to her. She lost love, too, and I don't think she and Jackson came together easily. And even though she finally achieved fame, I doubt it was as good as she'd always dreamed."

He pushed the swing again.

"At least, you always knew who you were and what you wanted," he went on. "You had a basic set of beliefs and values to fall back on, even during the worst times. Clementine had to build everything on her own. She was always searching for herself."

"Oh, come on," Megan said. Her loud voice woke Anne, and she rocked her until she closed her eyes again. "I don't buy all this searching-and-struggling-for-the-meaning-of-life stuff. She knew what she wanted. Fame. Success. She got it. And after she had that, she wanted Jackson. And she got him. What more is there?"

Joey walked around to the front of the swing and took Anne out of Megan's arms.

"Friendship," he said, rubbing his sleeping daughter's back. "The kind that starts when we're children and bonds us forever. Childhood friends are special, Megan. You and Alex and Clementine are special. You were there when Clementine was just a kid, like everybody else. You've seen her cry and laugh and succeed and fail. And Clementine was there for you. She knows your secrets, what hurts you most. She knows *you*, the child inside of you. Does it matter how much fame she has, or how much money? Does it really matter that the man she loves, the way we love each other, is Jackson? She's getting married in a few months. When you were kids, isn't that what you talked about, what you longed for? Deep inside, isn't that what you want for her?"

Megan stopped the swing and sat still, watching Joey walk back toward the house.

Just before he reached the kitchen, she called his name and he turned.

"Have I told you recently that I love you?" she asked.

"Not recently."

"I love you, Joey."

He smiled. "I know."

# EPILOGUE

*CLEMENTINE STOOD RIGID AS STEEL, HER* eyes cast downward, and Jackson felt a familiar sickly dread gnaw at his gut. She was thinking about her father again. About Connor and the rape and fear and doubt and Megan. About pain and chances she wasn't prepared to take, not even with him. She had changed her mind, and this time, there would be no second chances for him.

Alex stood to her left, though, and their friendship, at least, was solid. Clementine squared her shoulders. When the minister asked her to repeat her vows, she raised her head. Her eyes met Jackson's, and he felt a warm flood of relief wash over him. Her eyes, so clear and beautiful, were sure and strong and loving. She spoke her promises firmly, confidently, with the smooth voice he'd come to love as he loved no other. And when they sealed their marriage with a kiss, her lips were soft and trusting, and he could sense the smile that tugged at their corners like a playful child.

After the ceremony, they ran out of the chapel laughing, eager to get on with the day, the dancing, the drinking and celebrating, and, not soon enough, the honeymoon. She stood beside him in the receiving line, his wife, with the satin sleeve of her dress brushing against his arm. Her expression was as bright as the September day's sunshine as she greeted their guests. He put his arm around her waist and marveled again at the way her body conformed to his so perfectly, filling in every crevice.

The guests filtered past, a blur of puckered lips and embracing arms. Jackson paid little attention. How could he when he had the woman of his dreams beside him? She brought him so much happiness, blanketed every aspect of his life with the gauze of perfection, that he often found the past forgotten, left behind like a child's blanket no longer needed for comfort. Clementine gave him everything.

He was thinking of that, of the laughter that grew more frequent between them every day, of the house in New Hampshire, finally completed and filled with rustic furniture, that awaited them like a mother's outstretched arms, when he felt her squeeze his hand. Turning quickly, he saw the color drain from her face. He followed her desperate gaze and held himself steady against a wave of dizziness when he saw what she was looking at.

"She's here," Clementine said needlessly, her silky voice marred by an uncharacteristic tremor. "I can't believe she's here." Her eyes were wide as they focused on Megan, leaving Joey and what must be their daughter behind as she approached them alone in the receiving line. Neither of them had seen her during the ceremony, sitting in the back row, but then again, they really had seen only each other.

Alex squeezed Clementine's other hand in encouragement, and Jackson pulled her close to him, trying to steady her trembling body with his strength. He pressed his lips to her ear.

"I love you," he whispered.

She stood motionless for a moment, then he watched her transform. She pulled her scared, hunched body up straight again and smiled the smile that haunted men the world over. Her eyes met his, and he saw the tears filling them.

"And I you," she said, running her fingers along his cheek.

He returned his attention to the guests and watched, out of the corner of his eye, as Megan approached. He couldn't help being surprised by her beauty. It had been two and a half years since either of them had seen her, since she'd thrown Clementine completely out of her life. In that time, she seemed to have grown softer, more feminine, more fragile. Yet in her eyes he saw a new strength, a sense of belonging, a confidence that made her look straight at people instead of shrinking away in fear.

Jackson looked at the back of the line at the little girl, fair-haired like her parents, giggling in Joey's arms. The child she had always wanted. From the bottom of his soul, whether she would believe him or not, he was happy for her.

She was next in line to greet them, and the guilty pangs, from hurting her, from leaving her, long banished to the unnoticed, unwanted recesses of Jackson's mind, returned with violent intensity.

Finally, she stood before them, her chin up, her fists clenched. Jackson, Clementine, and Alex were silent as they faced her, Megan, Clementine's best friend. She had imposed a punishment of bitter silence on Clementine, a penalty worse than any fight or harsh words. Night after night, Clementine cried into her pillow, frustrated at not being able to fix things, to take away the pain she was sure she had caused, to have her oldest and dearest friend back.

Megan took a deep breath and let it out before she spoke. She looked first at Jackson, then at Alex, then finally at Clementine.

"Congratulations," she said. "I know how much you've wanted this."

Clementine nodded, and Jackson could feel her trembling.

"There's someone I'd like you to meet," Megan went on, and waved to Joey. When he reached her side, Megan took Anne out of his arms and handed her to Clementine. Clementine hesitated, then as she gathered the child in her arms, Megan's hand lingered on hers and they looked at each other. Through each other's eyes, they remembered junior high school science projects and cigarettes and ice-cream sundaes and hushed secrets and heartbreaks and first loves and proms and soap operas and scripts and tears and laughter. A whole lifetime of friendship, the special kind that always finds a way to forgive mistakes, even to forget them. A bond that, no matter what, could never be broken.

Alex stepped close to them and slipped one arm around each of their waists.

They leaned inward, together, a perfect circle, holding each other up.

"Clementine," Megan said, "say hello to your god-daughter, Anne."

# ABOUT
# THE AUTHOR

CHRISTY COHEN WAS BORN IN SOUTHERN California and graduated with a degree in Psychology from California State University at Northridge. She began her writing career as an editorial assistant at an entertainment magazine in Los Angeles, and then went on to free-lance work, placing short stories, articles, and poems in a number of national publications. She lives with her husband and Labrador retriever in Boise, Idaho.